The Solaris Book of New
Science Fiction
Volume Three

The Solaris Book of New
Science Fiction
Volume Three

Edited by George Mann

Including stories by

Daniel Abraham
Tim Akers
Stephen Baxter
Paul Cornell
Paul Di Filippo
Scott Edelman
Warren Hammond
Ken MacLeod
John Meaney
Jennifer Pelland
Alastair Reynolds
Adam Roberts
Jack Skillingstead
Ian Watson
Ian Whates

SOLARIS

First published 2009 by Solaris
an imprint of BL Publishing
Games Workshop Ltd, Willow Road
Nottingham NG7 2WS
UK

www.solarisbooks.com

ISBN-13: 978 1 84416 599 5
ISBN-10: 1 84416 599 X

Contents

Introduction

George Mann

Have we lost sight of the future?

WE LIVE IN pessimistic times. The global economy
is suffering. The planet – many believe – is over-
heating, choking on the fumes of industry. Poverty
remains a terrible blight on the world's population
and storms wreak havoc on a catastrophic scale.
Even on a smaller scale our lives are affected by
these world-shaping issues; utility bills go up, gas
prices skyrocket, and the regular supermarket run
now costs more than it ever has before.

Is our literature reflecting these difficult times?

I believe it is. Dystopia is our watchword. Disaster is our form. When we look to the future we see
a dirty, fume-soaked, industrialised landscape, or
we see humanity imploding, overrunning the cities
or eking out a living amongst the detritus of the
world. Take the recent Pixar movie, WALL-E, as an
example of how this imagery has begun to leak out

of the pages of science fiction and into the public consciousness. And whilst WALL-E shows ultimate redemption for humanity, it proves not to be through its own endeavours, but through those of its artificial creations. This is not the literature of a forward-looking, happy society.

Of course, all of this is only natural, and welcome, and rewarding. After all, isn't it one of the roles of science fiction to explore alternative visions of the future? Shouldn't we be challenging readers and viewers, showing them what *might* become of the world we live in, how our current path to the future may have to be addressed? I honestly believe we should. *If we stay on our current path*, I regularly read, *this is how the future may look*.

What concerns me, though, is that this dystopian view of the future has become *so* prevalent, so definitive of the current outlook of the genre, that we see it as *inevitable*. It's almost as if we have accepted that this terrible environmental, social and humanitarian cataclysm is now unavoidable, and rather than looking at the ways in which we may avoid such a disaster, we've started to look at the means by which we cope with the aftermath. As I said earlier, this is in no way a bad thing, provided that it's balanced. But I fear this type of dystopian future has become shorthand in modern science fiction, a step we feel we need to get over as a civilisation before we can move on. *After things have gone to hell, then we can start again...*

So what happened to all the spaceships? Where's the sense of wonder gone? What of the crowded space lanes and colony worlds blossoming all across the cosmos? Have we finally decided that the future holds no surprises, that the only thing we can see ahead of us is chaos and disaster? Indeed, the resurgence of the pulp adventure genres and steampunk seem to go hand-in-hand with this giving up of the brighter future. Steampunk, particularly, offers us an alternative past, rather than an alternative future, in which scientific advances *that we know did not happen* provide us with that same joyful sense of fun and wonder that we used to get from atomic spacecraft and galactic empires. It is a celebration of sense of wonder, of all that was good about the optimism of the past. Yet somehow it feels fresh.

So would we now rather speculate about a past that didn't happen than a future that might? Or are we simply more grounded in realism, so downtrodden by the humdrum of daily life and recession and defunct space programmes that we've forgotten how to dream of the stars?

I believe that all of these modes of literature have a place in the modern genre. We should run the entire gamut of science fiction, from steampunk to cyberpunk, from near-future dystopian nightmares to far future space opera. Each of them is as valid as the other. Each of them as enjoyable as the other. Each of them as *important* as the other. Diversity is the key to keeping our genre vital and alive, and diversity is what, as an editor and a reader, I strive for every day.

I'm as guilty as anyone else of making assumptions about the future. I'm a huge fan of alternate history, steampunk, military science fiction and pulps. And I read and relish a great deal of near-future dystopian science fiction. But I also miss the spaceships and bright, optimistic futures, those other alternative visions of a time, hundreds or thousands of years from now, in which humanity is braving the stars, exploring new worlds, encountering new peoples and proving their worth amongst the stars. I miss the *fun*. I miss the adventure.

Here then, in this third volume of non-themed science fiction stories, I've tried to offer up that whole gamut of SF stories. Inside these pages you will find stories of the coming dystopia, but you will also find steampunk adventure, encounters with alien entities, instruction manuals for strange new technologies, super spies, incarcerated wraiths, artificial intelligence... and cleaners.

Whatever may happen, whatever the future may hold for the human race, let us agree on one thing. Let us agree to have fun getting there and celebrate the diversity of our genre. Let us revel in the apocalypse, but also the alternate past, the sparkling far future, the sense of adventure that we can find in all of these forms of science fiction.

George Mann
Nottingham, UK
September 2008

Rescue Mission

Jack Skillingstead

For Nancy

MICHAEL PENNINGTON FLOATED in *Mona*'s amniotic chamber, fully immersed, naked and erect, zened out. The cortical cable looped lazily around him. Womb Hole travelling. His gills palpitated; *Mona*'s quantum consciousness saturated the environment with a billion qubits, and Michael's anima combined with *Mona*'s super animus drove the starship along a dodgy vector through the Pleiades.

Until a distraction occurred.

Like a Siren call, it pierced to the center of Michael's consciousness. His body twisted, eyes opening in heavy fluid. At the same instant *Mona*, cued to Michael's every impulse, veered in space. Somewhere, alarms rang.

MONA INTERRUPTED THE navigation cycle, retracted Michael's cortical cable, and gently expelled him into the delivery chamber. Vacuums activated, sucking at him. He pushed past them, into the larger chamber beyond, still swooning on the borderland of Ship State. A blurry figure floated toward him: Natalie. She caught him and held him.

"What happened?" he asked.

"Mona spat you out. And we're on a new course." She touched his face. "Your eyes are all pupil. I'm going to give you something."

"Hmm," Michael said.

He felt the sting in his left arm. After a moment his head cleared.

"Let's get you properly cleaned up," Natalie said.

He was weak, post Ship State, and he let her touch him, but said, "The Proxy can help me."

"You *want* it to?"

"It's capable."

"You have a thing for the Proxy?"

The Proxy, a rudimentary biomech, was an extension of *Mona*, though lacking in gender-specific characteristics.

"Not exactly."

"*We* have a thing."

"Nat, our 'thing' was a mistake. If we'd known we were going to team on this mission we would never have thinged."

"Wouldn't we have?"

"No."

She released him and they drifted apart. Michael scratched his head. Tiny cerulean spheres of amniotic residue swarmed about him. "You can be kind of a bastard, you know."

"I know."

"I'll send the Proxy."

* * *

MONA TRANSITIONED INTO orbit around the wrong planet. It rolled beneath them, a world mostly green, a little blue, brushed with cloud white.

"That's not Meropa IV," Natalie said, floating onto the bridge with a bulb of coffee.

"No," Michael said, not looking away from the monitor.

"So what is it?"

"A planet."

"Gosh. So *that's* a planet." Natalie propelled herself up to the monitor. "And what are we doing here, when we have vital cargo for the Meropa IV colony?"

"There's time," Michael said, the Siren call still sounding deep in his mind. "This is important."

"This is important? What about Meropa IV?"

Michael pushed away from the console.

"I'm going down," he said.

ONCE HE WAS strapped securely into the Drop Ship, Natalie said:

"You shouldn't go."

"Why not?"

"You're acting strange. I mean stranger than usual."

"That's it?" Michael said, going through his pre-flight routine.

"Also, I have a feeling," Natalie said.

"You're always having those."

"It's human," Natalie said.

"So I understand."

"Even you had feelings once upon a time. Does New San Francisco ring any bells?"

"Steeples full. I'm losing my window, by the way. Can we drop now?"

"Why do I think you and *Mona* have a secret?"

"I have no idea why you think that."

Natalie looked pained. "Why are you so mean to me?"

Michael couldn't look at her.

"*Do* you have a secret?" Natalie said.

He fingered a nav display hanging like a ghostly vapor in front of his face. "I'm going to miss my damn window."

She dropped him.

The Drop Ship jolted through entry fire and became an air vehicle. The planet rushed up. Cloud swirls blew past. Michael descended toward a dense continent-wide jungle.

Mona said, "I'm still unable to acquire the signal."

"I told you: The signal's in my head."

"I'm beginning to agree with Natalie."

"Don't go human on me," Michael said. "Taking over manual control now."

He touched the proper sequence but *Mona* did not relinquish the helm.

"Let go," Michael said.

"Perhaps you should reconsider. Further observation from orbit could yield—"

He hit the emergency override, which keyed to his genetic code. *Mona* fell silent, and Michael guided the ship down to a clearing in the jungle.

Or what looked like a clearing.

A sensor indicated touchdown, but the ship's feet sank into muck. Michael stared at his instrument displays. The ship rocked back, canted over, stopped.

Mona said: "You're still overriding me. I can't lift off."

"We just landed."

"We're sinking, not landing."

"What's going on?" Natalie said on a different channel.

"Nothing," Michael said.

Mona cut across channels: "We've touched down in a bog! We—"

Michael switched off the audio for both *Mona* and Natalie. He released his safety restraints and popped the hatch, compelled, almost as if he were in the grip of a biological urge.

His helmet stifled him. He didn't really need it, did he? Michael screwed it to the left and lifted it off. The air was humid, sickly fragrant. He clambered out of his seat, wiped the sweat off his forehead, then slipped over the side and into the sucking mire and began groping for shore. The more he struggled forward the deeper he sank. Fear and adrenaline momentarily flushed the fog from his mind.

"*Mona*, help!"

But his helmet was off and *Mona* could not reply.

Then, strangely, he stopped sinking. The mire buoyed him up and carried him forward toward the shore as several figures emerged from the jungle. His feet found purchase and he walked on solid ground, his flight suit heavy and streaming. The figures weren't *from* the jungle; they were *part* of the jungle—trees that looked like women, or perhaps women who looked like trees. One stepped

creakingly forward, a green mossy tangle swinging
between its knobby tree trunk legs. It extended a
limb with three twig fingers. Irregular plugs of
amber resin gleamed like pale eyes in what passed
for a face. Michael's thoughts groped in the
drugged fragrance of the jungle. He reached out
and felt human flesh, smooth and cool and living,
and a girl's hand closed on his and drew him forth.

THEY OPENED HIS mind and shook it until the needed thing fell out. *Mona* was there but wrong. They
shook harder and found Natalie:

New San Francisco, Mars, a scoured-sky day under
the Great Equatorial Dome. Down time between
Outbounds. The sidewalk table had a view toward
Tharsis. Olympus Mons wore a diaphanous veil of
cloud, but Michael looked away to watch Natalie
approach in her little round glasses, the black lenses
blanking her eyes.

"Of all the gin joints in all the worlds you had to
pick mine," he said; Michael was obsessed with
ancient movies.

She removed her glasses and squinted at him.

"What?"

"Old movie reference. Two people with a past meet
unexpectedly in a foreign city."

"But we don't have a past. And this was planned,
though I guess you could call it unexpected."

"I have a feeling we're about to."

"About to what?"

"Make a past out of this present."

She sat down.

"You're a strange man, and I don't mean the gills.
Also, this isn't a foreign city. What are you drinking?"

"Red Rust Ale."

"Philistine. Order me a chardonnay."

He did, and the waiter brought it in a large stem glass.

"I bet this is the part you like best," she said.

"Yes?"

"The flirting, the newness, the excitement. Especially because we aren't supposed to fraternize."

"There are good reasons for that non-fraternization rule," he said, smiling.

She sipped her wine. He watched her, thinking: she's right. And also thinking, less honestly: it doesn't mean anything to her, not really. And hating himself a little, but still wanting her even though he knew in a while he wouldn't be able to tolerate her closeness. That's how it always worked with him. Automatic protective instinct; caring was just another word for grieving. But Natalie was a peer, not his usual adventure. An instinct he couldn't identify informed him he was in a very dangerous place. He ignored it and had another beer while Natalie finished her glass of wine.

"Did you say you had a room around here someplace?" she said.

He put his bottle down. "I may have said that, yes."

THE NARCOTIC JUNGLE exhaled. Michael, sprawled on the moss-covered, softly decaying corpse of a fallen tree, drifted in and out of awareness. He saw things that weren't there, or perhaps were there but other than what they appeared to be. Insects like animated beans trundled over his face, his neck, the backs of his hands. He was sweating inside his flight suit. Something spoke in wooden gutturals, incomprehensible. The sounds gradually resolved into understandable English.

"Kiss me?"

Michael blinked. He sat up. The steaming jungle was gone. He was sitting in an upholstered hotel chair and a woman was kneeling beside him. He recognized the room. The woman looked at him with large shiny amber eyes. The planes of her cheeks were too angular, too smooth.

Michael worked his mouth. His tongue felt dry and dead as a piece of cracked leather.

"I don't know you," he said.

Her mouth turned down stiffly and she rocked back and seemed to blend into the wall, which was patterned to resemble a dense green tangle of vine.

Michael closed his eyes.

TIME PASSED LIKE a muddy dream, and there were others.

THEY ALL CALLED themselves Natalie. One liked to take walks with him in the rain, like that girl he had known in college. Michael, watching from his bedroom window, wasn't surprised to see it out there with its umbrella. His breath fogged the faux leaded glass, and the tricky molecular structure of the pane, dialed wide to semi-permeable, seemed to breathe back into his face. Internal realities overlapped. This wasn't New San Francisco or even old San Francisco on Earth. It was his lost home in upstate New York. (As a child Michael used to play with the window, throwing snowballs from the front yard, delighting in how they strained through onto the sill inside his room. His mother had been something other than delighted, though.)

Michael, staring at the thing waiting for him down there, pulled at his bottom lip. He clenched his right fist until it shook, resisting. But eventually he surrendered and turned away from the window. On the stairs reality lost focus. The walls became spongy and mottled, like the skin of a mushroom. The stairs were made of the same stuff. His boots sank into them and he stumbled downward and out into the light of the foyer. That was wrong, he thought, and looking back he saw an organic orifice, like a soft wound, and then it was simply a stairwell climbing upwards, with framed photographs of his family hung at staggered intervals. Dead people.

HE OPENED THE front door to the sound of rain rattling through maple leaves. College days, the street outside his dorm, and his first girl. Only this wasn't a girl, the thing that called itself Natalie.

Michael stood a minute on the porch. The *wrong* porch. Inside had been the familiar rooms of his boyhood home (mushroom skin notwithstanding), long gone to fire and sorrow. *This* porch belonged to his dorm at the University of Washington. After a while he stepped down to the sidewalk and the Natalie-thing smiled.

"Would you like to take a walk with me?" it asked.

"Not really."

HE HELD THE umbrella over both of them. Rain pattered on the taut fabric. The Natalie-thing slipped its arm under his. It was wearing a sweater and a wool skirt and black shoes that clocked on the sidewalk. Its hair was very dark red and its cheeks were rosy with the cold. When it glanced up at him it presented eyes as black and lusterless as a shark's. Still wrong. And anyway, nothing like Natalie *or* his college girl.

"Want to see a movie?" it asked.

"All right."

THEY HELD HANDS in the dark. He felt comfortable. The theater smelled of hot popcorn and the damp wool of the Natalie-thing's skirt. He used to escape to the movies, where he could turn his mind off and be lost in the Deep Enhancement Cinema. Movies provided an imperfect respite from the memories ceaselessly rising out of the ashy ruin of his home.

The screen dimmed and brightened and incomprehensible sounds, like crowd noises muffled in cotton, issued from unseen speakers that seemed to communicate directly into his head. They—the ones like this Natalie beside him—hadn't fully comprehended the idea of a movie.

It squeezed his hand.

"This is good," it said.

"Pretty good," he replied.

The theater was empty except for them. Empty of human forms, anyway. Irregular shadows cropped up randomly, like shapes in a night jungle. Then one of the shapes two rows in front of Michael turned around and leaned over the back of the seat, and Michael saw it was a woman, a real woman, dressed as he was, in a flight suit. She was wearing a breathing mask.

The woman began to speak but he couldn't understand her. He leaned forward.

"What, what did you say?"

The thing beside him tightened its grip, so tight the fingers of his right hand ached in its grasp, the small bones grinding in their sleeves of flesh. He tried to stand but it held him down and squeezed harder and harder until his entire awareness was occupied by the pain.

Several of the jungle shapes interposed themselves between Michael and the woman who had spoken to him. The air became clogged, humid, stifling. Rain began to fall inside the theater. He struggled to pull free. The numbing pain traveled up his arm. The theater seat held him, shifted around him. Knobby protuberances poked and dug into him, like sitting in a tangle of roots. He couldn't breathe.

Then it stopped.

He sat in a movie theater with a young mahogany-haired woman, who held his hand sweetly in the dark. She leaned over and whispered, "You fell asleep!" Her warm breath touched his ear.

"I did?" He sat up, groggy.

"Yes, darling."

He blinked at the screen, where dim pulses of light moved in meaningless patterns. That was *so* wrong.

THE ONE THAT liked to make love pulled him to his feet in the hotel room and kissed him roughly. He tried to push it away but it was too strong. After a while it held him at arm's length and said something he couldn't understand. The jungle effluvium infiltrated his brain, and he saw a woman he used to know, or a rudimentary version of her. The eyes were still wrong—plugs of dull amber. Michael staggered back, caught his heel on the carpet, and fell. His lips were bruised, sticky and sweet with sap.

It stalked over and stood above him.

"Mike, we have to get out of here."

This new voice didn't belong to the thing straddling his legs.

Michael craned his head around. A woman stood in a flight suit similar to his own. She was there and then she wasn't there, as the scenery shifted around him, from his old bedroom on Earth to the hotel room on Mars.

"Natalie—?" he said.

The one that liked to make love lowered itself on top of him. Michael tried to roll away but couldn't. It mounted him and he screamed.

THAT TIME IN New San Francisco, in the mock Victorian hotel room, in the bed of clean linen sheets, the following morning, when Natalie woke early and started to get out of bed, he had reached out and touched her naked hip and said, "Stay." A costly word.

HE WAS ALONE again, half asleep, in and out of dream. Then something was shaking him.

"Mike, come *on*. There isn't time. They'll be back."

He struggled against this new assault. Something wrestling with him, pinning him down on the bed with its knobby knees. Then a mask fitted over his mouth and nose, and a clean wind blew into his lungs, filling him, clearing his head. He opened his eyes, closed them, opened them wide.

"Hello, Nat," he said, his voice muffled through the breathing mask.

She flipped the little mahogany curl of hair out of her eye.

"Hello yourself, you idiot," Natalie said.

"How'd you get here?" he asked, meaning how did she get into his hotel room. But even as he asked the question the last vestiges of the illusion blew away in the fresh revivifying oxygen.

A pink puzzle-piece sky shone above the jungle canopy.

Twisted trees crowded them, shaggy with moss, hung with thick vines braided like chains.

"I dropped in, just like you," Natalie said.

Michael looked around. "I have a feeling we're not on Mars, Dorothy."

"Who's Dorothy?"

Something hulking, hunched and redolent of mold and jungle rot came shambling toward them.

"Nat, look out!"

She turned swiftly, yanking a blaster from her utility belt. Reality stuttered. As if in a fading memory he saw the tree-thing knock the weapon from Natalie's hand. At the same moment, superimposed, he saw her fire. A bright red flash of plasma energy seared into the thing. It lurched back, yowling, punky smoke flowing from the fresh wound.

Nat grabbed Michael's hand and pulled him up. He felt dizzy and weak, still drugged.

"What are you doing?" he said.

"Rescuing your ass." She gave him a little push. "That way to the ship."

"No," he said, pointing, "it's *that* way."

"*My* ship is this way. Your ship sank."

He scrambled drunkenly ahead of her, stumbling over roots, getting hung up in vines. Though the illusions were displaced he could still hear the Siren wail in his mind and had to fight an impulse to rip the mask from his face. There was movement all around them. More of the things shambled out of the shadows. Natalie blasted away with her weapon, clearing a path.

They broke into the open. The ship gleamed in weak sunlight.

"Get in! I'll hold them off."

Michael clambered up the ladder to the cockpit. At the top of the ladder he turned and saw Natalie about to be overwhelmed.

"Nat, come on!"

She dropped her depleted blaster, swung onto the ladder—but it was too late. They had her.

MICHAEL SLUMPED IN his theater seat, withdrawn from the Deep Enhancement movie experience he had created. The one who liked rain sat beside him with a bowl of soggy popcorn. Warm rain fell out of the darkness.

It turned to him.

"That was so good, Mike."

Its lips glistened with butter. Its eyes were dull amber wads. A breathing mask with a torn strap dangled from its fingers.

Michael groaned.

Like an insect buzz in his ear: *Michael wake up, for God's sake.*

Michael closed his eyes.

* * *

ON MARS NATALIE had said, "I think I'm falling in love with you," and his defenses had rattled down like iron gates.

"Mike?"

"Not a good idea. In the first place we'll both soon be Outbound. It might be years before we see each other again. In the second place, my modifications inhibit my ability to achieve human intimacy. I'm a lost cause, Nat."

Natalie shook her head. "You don't have to drag out your excuses. I know you. I'm just saying how I feel, not asking for anything. And by the way, your mods have nothing to do with intimacy. I've known plenty of Womb Hole pilots and I don't buy the myth that you're all emotional cripples."

Michael smiled. He hadn't been thinking about the mods he'd volunteered to undergo, the ones necessary for Ship State, the ones that at least allowed him a semblance of intimacy, even if it was with a machine consciousness. He had meant the more visceral mods of his psyche, where blackened timbers had risen like pickets in Hell to form the first rudimentary fence around his heart.

"You don't really know me," he said.

"Not at this rate, I don't."

Then the biological crisis on Meropa IV occurred. Vital vaccines needed. Michael's Ship Tender came up with Red Fever, and Natalie, loose on Mars, got the duty. Like some kind of Fate. Michael experienced a burst of pure joy—which he quickly stomped on.

"I DON'T SEE why I had to die," Natalie said. Was she the real Natalie?

He was back in the hotel, flat on his back in the bed. Natalie, having fitted another breathing mask to his face, sat in a chair near the window. Except it appeared she wasn't sitting in a chair at all, but on the tangle of vines that popped out of the wall. He had just told her about the movie.

"You were *saving* me," he said.

"I'm saving you *now*," she said. "Or trying to. You've got to get off your ass and participate."

Michael felt heavy.

"And in this version I don't die," Natalie said.

SHE LED HIM out of the hotel room, which quickly became something other than a hotel room. As his head cleared the vine-tangle wallpaper popped out in three dimensions, the floor became soft, spongy. The light shifted to heavily screened pink/green. Flying insects buzzed his sweaty face. A locus of pain began rhythmically stabbing behind his right eye.

"The atmosphere is drugged with hallucinogenic vapors from the plants," Natalie said. "They want you here, but they don't want you to know where 'here' is."

"Who wants me?"

"They. The jungle. The sentient life on this planet. It's gynoecious, by the way, and it's been sweeping open space, seeking first contact. They detected you and *Mona* and evidently became entranced by the possibilities of companion male energy. Frankly, they have a point."

"Where the hell do you get all *that?*"

"I asked. Or Mona did, actually. She's been frantically investigating language possibilities since you disappeared. They communicate telepathically."

Natalie led him through a sort of tunnel made from overarching branches. They had to duck their heads.

"Wait." He grabbed her arm. She turned, red hair flipping over her eye. "Did you bring a weapon?"

"Of course," she said.

"Well, where is it?"

"They sort of disarmed me."

"I see."

"Don't worry. We're getting out of here. As long as you're not breathing the air they can't mess you up too much. I think they'll let us leave. I have a theory. Now let's keep moving. It isn't far to the ship."

They emerged from the tunnel. The ship was there, but they were cut off from it by a wall of the tree-things, the crooked things with hungry amber eyes. They encircled the ship, knobby limbs entwined to form a barrier.

"You were saying?" Michael said, straightening his back. "Anyway, have *Mona* fly the ship over."

"I can't. *Mona* was hinky about landing after your Drop Ship sank. Also, I think *they* got into her head and spooked her. I had to engage the emergency override, same as you did."

"Wonderful."

"At least the security repulsion field is keeping them away from the ship."

"At least."

Hands on her hips, Natalie appraised the situation. After a minute she touched the com button on her wrist and spoke into it.

"*Mona*, we need help. Send the Proxy to clear a path."

The aft hatch swung up and the Proxy appeared. It climbed down and disappeared behind the tree-things. A moment later the circle tightened. There was the flash and pop of a blaster discharge. One of the tree-things erupted in flame. It stumped out of the ring and stood apart, burning. The others closed in. A violent disturbance occurred. There were no further blasts. The Proxy's torso arced high over the line, dull metal skin shining. It clanked once when it hit the ground. The line resumed its stillness.

"It's a female jungle, all right," Michael said. "Care to reveal your famous theory?"

Natalie held his hand. "We're walking through," she said.

"Just like that."

"Yes. If we're together they'll let us. I mean really together."

"That's your theory?"

"Basically. Mike, trust me."

They started walking. When they came to the Proxy's torso, Michael held her back.

"I'll go through alone," he said. "If I make it to the ship I'll lift off and pick you up in the clear."

He tried to pull his hand free but she wouldn't let go.

"No," she said.

"Nat—"

"No. Don't you see? If you go alone they'll take you again. If I go alone they'll rip me apart like the Proxy."

"And if we go together?"

"If we go together they... will see."

"See *what*?"

"That you aren't solo, that somebody else is already claiming your male companion energy, another of your own species. Unlike Mona, whom they felt justified in severing you from. They *know* I'm imprinted in your psyche. You said yourself they always used my name. You just have to stop fighting us."

Michael scratched his cheek, which was whiskered after a few days in the sentient jungle. Natalie squeezed his hand.

"Mike?"

"No."

"We have to move."

"It's too risky."

"Come on. It's now or never."

He felt himself collapsing inside, and then the old detachment. The cold, necessary detachment. She saw it in his eyes and let go of his hand.

"I'll go through myself, then," she said, and started walking forward.

He grabbed her arm.

"You just said they'd tear you apart."

"I'm already torn apart," she said.

"Don't, Nat. Let's think about this."

"Just let me go, okay? You don't want me. I get it."

He held on. "There has to be another way to the ship."

She pulled loose.

"I might get through. Wish me luck."

"Nat—"

A cringing, huddled piece of him behind the cold wall stood up, trembling.

Natalie again started for the picket line of tree-things, walking quickly, leaving Michael standing where he was.

The tree-things reacted, reaching for her.

Michael got to her first and pulled her back into his arms. "*Damn* it," he said. "Damn it, damn it, damn it."

THEY LIFTED OUT of the jungle, accelerating until they achieved orbit. He sat tandem behind Natalie in the narrow cockpit of the Drop Ship.

"You really like to force the issue," he said.

"Do I?"

"I'm not saying it's a bad idea."

"No."

"I mean, a little push doesn't hurt."

"Hmm."

A few minutes later they acquired the starship and Natalie resumed manual operation and began docking maneuvers. She worked the controls very competently. Michael watched over her shoulder. But his gaze returned again and again to rest upon the nape of her neck, where a few very fine copper hairs escaped and lay sweetly over her skin.

"The Dorothy thing," he said, "that was another old movie reference. A child is swept away from family and friends and finds herself estranged in a hostile world."

"How does she get back home?"

"She finds a way to trust companions who initially frighten her."

"I like that one."

"It works for me."

Natalie tucked them neatly into *Mona*'s docking bay.

The Fixation

Alastair Reynolds

For Hannu Blommila

> *Inside the corroded rock was what
> looked like a geared embryo—the
> incipient bud of an industrial age that
> remained unborn for a millennium.*
> (John Seabrook, *The New Yorker*,
> May 14, 2007)

KATIB, THE SECURITY guard who usually works the graveyard shift, has already clocked on when Rana swipes her badge through the reader. He gives her a long-suffering look as she bustles past in her heavy coat, stooping under a cargo of document boxes and laptops. "Pulling another all-nighter, Rana?" he asks, as he has asked a hundred times before. "I keep telling you to get a different job, girl."

"I worked hard to get this one," she tells him, almost slipping on the floor, which has just been polished to a mirrored gleam by a small army of robot cleaners. "Where else would I get to do this and actually get paid for it?"

"Whatever they're paying you, it isn't enough for all those bags under your eyes."

She wishes he wouldn't mention the bags under her eyes—it's not as if she exactly likes them—but she smiles anyway, for Katib is a kindly man without a hurtful thought in his soul. "They'll go," she says. "We're on the home stretch, anyway. Or did you somehow not notice that there's this big opening ceremony coming up?"

"Oh, I think I heard something about that," he says, scratching at his beard. "I just hope they need some old fool to look after this wing when they open the new one."

"You're indispensable, Katib. They'd get rid of half the exhibits before they put you on the street."

"That's what I keep telling myself, but..." He gives a burly shrug, and then smiles to let her know it isn't her business to worry about his problems. "Still, it's going to be something, isn't it? I can see it from my balcony, from all the way across the town. I didn't like it much at first, but now that's up there, now that it's all shining and finished, it's starting to grow on me. And it's ours, that's what I keep thinking. That's our museum, nobody else's. Something to be proud of."

Rana has seen it too. The new wing, all but finished, dwarfs the existing structure. It's a glittering climate-controlled ziggurat, the work of a monkish British architect who happens to be a devout Christian. A controversial choice, to be sure, but no one who has seen that tidal wave of glass and steel rising above the streets of the city has remained unimpressed. As the sun tracks across the sky, computer-controlled shutters open and close to control the flood of light into the ziggurat's plunging atrium—the atrium where the Mechanism will be the primary exhibit—and maintain the building's ideal ambient temperature. From afar, the play of those shutters is an enchanted mosaic: a mesmerizing, never-repeating dance of spangling glints. Rana read in a magazine that the architect had never *touched* a computer until he arrived in Greater Persia, but that he took to the possibilities with the zeal of the converted.

"It's going to be wonderful," she says, torn between making small talk with the amiable Katib and getting started on her work. "But it won't be much of an opening ceremony if the Mechanism isn't in place, will it?"

"Which is a kind way of saying, you need to be getting to your office." He's smiling as he speaks, letting her know he takes no offense. "You need some help with those boxes and computers, my fairest?"

"I'll be fine, thanks."

"You call me if you need anything. I'll be here through to six." With that he unfolds a magazine and taps the sharp end of a pencil against the grid of a half-finished puzzle. "And don't work too hard," he says under his breath, but just loud enough that she will hear.

Rana doesn't pass another human being on her way to the office. The public part of the museum is deserted save for the occasional cleaner or patrolling security robot, but at least the hallways and exhibits are still partially illuminated, and from certain sightlines she can still see people walking in the street outside, coming from the theater or a late restaurant engagement.

In the private corridors, it's a different story. The halls are dark and the windows too high to reveal anything more than moonlit sky. The robots don't come here very often and most of the offices and meeting rooms are locked and silent. At the end of one corridor stands the glowing sentinel of a coffee dispenser. Normally Rana takes a cup to her room, but tonight she doesn't have a free hand; it's enough of a job just to shoulder her way through doors without dropping something.

Her room is in the basement: a cool, windowless crypt that is half laboratory and half office. Her colleagues think she's mad for working at night, but Rana has her reasons. By day she has to share her facilities with other members of the staff, and what with all the talk and interruptions she tends to get much less work done. If that's not enough of a distraction, there is a public corridor that winds its way past the glass-fronted rooms, allowing the museum's visitors to watch cataloging and restoration work as it actually happens. The public make an effort to look more interested than they really are. Hardly surprising, because the work going on inside the offices could not look less interesting or less glamorous. Rana has been spending the last three weeks working with microscopically precise tools on the restoration of a single bronze gearwheel. What the visitors would imagine to be a morning's work has consumed more of her life than some relationships. She already knows every scratch and chip of that gearwheel like an old friend or ancient, bitter adversary.

There's another reason why she works at night. Her mind functions better in the small hours. She has made more deductive leaps at three in the morning than she has ever done at three in the afternoon, and she wishes it were not so.

She takes off her coat and hangs it by the door. She opens the two laptops, sets them near each other, and powers them up. She keeps the office lights low, with only enough illumination to focus on the immediate area around her bench. The gearwheel is centermost, supported on an adjustable cradle like a miniature music stand. On either side, kept in upright stands, are various chrome-plated tools and magnifying devices, some of which trail segmented power cables to a wall junction. There is a swing-down visor with zoom optics. There are lasers and ultrasound cleaning baths. There are duplicates of the gearwheel and its brethren, etched in brass for testing purposes. There are plastic models of parts of the Mechanism, so that she can take them apart and explain its workings to visitors. There are other gearwheels which have already been removed from the device for restoration, sealed in plastic boxes and racked according to coded labels. Some are visibly cleaner than the one she is working on, but some are still corroded and grubby, with damaged teeth and scabrous surface deterioration.

And there is the Mechanism itself, placed on the bench on the far side of the gearwheel she is working on. It is the size of a shoebox, with a wooden casing, the lid hinged back. When it arrived the box was full of machinery, a tight-packed clockwork of arbors and crown wheels, revolving balls, slotted pins and delicate, hand-engraved inscriptions. None of it did anything, though. Turn the input crank and there'd just be a metallic crunch as stiff, worn gears locked into immobility. No one in the museum remembers the last time the machine was in proper working order. Fifty years ago, she's heard someone say—but not all of the gearing was in place even then. Parts were removed a hundred years ago and never put back. Or were lost or altered two hundred years ago. Since then the Mechanism has become something of an embarrassment: a fabled contraption that doesn't do what everyone expects it to.

Hence the decision by the museum authorities: restore the Mechanism to full and authentic functionality in time for the reopening of the new wing. As the foremost native expert on the device, the work has naturally fallen to Rana. The authorities tried to foist a team on her, but the hapless doctoral students soon realized their leader preferred to work alone, unencumbered by the give and take of collaboration.

Share the glory? Not likely.

With the wall calendar reminding her how few weeks remain to the opening, Rana occasionally wonders if she has taken on too much. But she is making progress, and the most difficult parts of the restoration are now behind her.

Rana picks up one of her tools and begins to scrape away the tiniest burr of corrosion on one of the gear's teeth. Soon she is lost in the methodical repetitiveness of the task, her mind freewheeling back through history, thinking of all the hands that have touched this metal. She imagines all the people this little clockwork box has influenced, all the lives it has altered, the fortunes it has made and the empires it has crushed. The Romans owned the Mechanism for 400 years—one of their ships must have carried it from Greece, perhaps from the island of Rhodes—but the Romans were too lazy and incurious to do anything with the box other than marvel at its computational abilities. The idea that the same clockwork that accurately predicted the movements of the sun, moon, and the planets across an entire Metonic cycle—235 lunar months—might also be made to do *other things* simply never occurred to them.

The Persians were different. The Persians saw a universe of possibility in those spinning wheels and meshing teeth. Those early clocks and calculating boxes—the clever devices that sent armies and navies and engineers across the globe, and made Greater Persia what it is today—bear scant resemblance to the laptops on Rana's desk. But the lineage is unbroken.

There must be ghosts, she thinks: caught in the slipstream of this box, dragged by the Mechanism as it ploughed its way through the centuries. Lives changed and lives extinguished, lives that never happened at all, and yet all of them still in spectral attendance, a silent audience crowding in on this quiet basement room, waiting for Rana's next move.

Some of them want her to destroy the machine forever.

Some of them want to see it shine again.

Rana doesn't dream much, but when she does she dreams of glittering brass gears meshing tight against each other, whirring furiously, a dance of metal and geometry that moves the heavens.

SAFA DREAMS OF numbers, not gears: she is a mathematician. Her breakthrough paper, the one that has brought her to the museum, was entitled "Entropy Exchange and the Many Worlds Hypothesis."

As a foreign national, admitted into the country because of her expertise in an exceedingly esoteric field, Safa has more rights than a refugee. But she must still submit to the indignity of wearing a monitoring collar, a heavy plastic cuff around her neck which not only records her movements, not only sees and hears everything she sees and hears, but which can stun or euthanize her if a government agent deems that she is acting contrary to the national interests. She must also be accompanied by a cyborg watchdog at all times: a sleek black prowling thing with the emblem of the national security agency across its bulletproof chest. At least the watchdog has the sense to lurk at the back of the room when she is about to address the gathered administrators and sponsors, at this deathly hour.

"I'm sorry we had to drag you out here so late," the museum director tells the assembled audience. "Safa knows more than me, but I'm reliably informed that the equipment works best when the city's shutting down for the night—when there isn't so much traffic, and the underground trains aren't running. We can schedule routine jobs during the day, but something like this—something this delicate—requires the maximum degree of noise-suppression. Isn't that right, Safa?"

"Spot on sir. And if everyone could try and hold their breath for the next six hours, that would help as well." She grins reassuringly—it's almost as if some of them think she was serious. "Now I know some of you were probably hoping to see the Mechanism itself, but I'm afraid I'm going to have to disappoint you—positioning it inside the equipment is a very slow and tricky procedure, and if we started now we'd all still be here next week. But I can show you something nearly as good."

Safa produces a small white pottery jug that she has brought along for the occasion. "Now, you may think this is just some ordinary old jug I found at the back of a staff cupboard... and you'd be right. It's probably no more than ten or fifteen years old. The Mechanism, as I am sure I don't have to remind anyone here, is incomparably older: we know the ship went down around the first half of the First Century BC. But I can still illustrate my point. There are a near-infinite number of copies of this object, and they are *all the same jug*. In one history, I caught a cold and couldn't make it today, and someone else is standing up and talking to you, holding the same jug. In another, someone took the jug out of that cupboard years ago and it's living in a kitchen halfway across the city. In another it was bought by someone else and never ended up in the museum. In another it was broken before it ever left the factory."

She smiles quickly. "You see the point I'm making. What may be less clear is that all these copies of the same jug are in ghostly dialogue with each other, linked together by a kind of quantum entanglement—though it's not really quantum and it's not exactly entanglement." Another fierce, nervous smile. "Don't worry: no mathematics tonight! The point is, no matter what happens to this jug, no matter how it's handled or what it comes into contact with, it never quite loses contact with its counterparts. The signal gets fainter, but it never goes away. Even if I do this."

Abruptly, she lets go of the jug. It drops to the floor and shatters into a dozen sharp white pieces.

"The jug's broken," Safa says, pulling a sad face. "But in a sense it still exists. The other copies of it are still doing fine—and each and every one of them felt an echo of this one as it shattered. It's still out there, ringing back and forth like a dying chime." Then she pauses and kneels down, gathering a handful of the broken pieces into her palms. "Imagine if I could somehow take these pieces and get them to resonate with the intact copies of the jug. Imagine further still that I could somehow steal a little bit of orderedness from each of those copies, and give back some of the disorderedness of this one in return—a kind of swap."

Safa waits a moment, trying to judge whether she still has the audience's attention. Are they following or just pretending to follow? It's not always easy to tell, and nothing on the administrator's face gives her a clue. "Well, we can do that. It's what we call Fixation—moving tiny amounts of entropy from one world—one universe—to another. Now, it would take a very long time to put this jug back the way it was. But if we started with a jug that was a bit damaged, a bit worn, it would happen a lot quicker. And that's sort of where we are with the Antikythera Mechanism. It's in several pieces, and we suspect there are components missing, but in other respects it's in astonishing condition for something that's been underwater for two thousand years."

Now she turns around slowly, to confront the huge, humming mass of the Fixator. It is a dull silver cylinder with a circular door in one end, braced inside a massive orange chassis, festooned with cables and cooling ducts and service walkways. The machine is as large as a small fusion reactor and several times as complicated. It has stronger, more responsive magnets, a harder vacuum, and has a control system so perilously close to intelligence that a government agent must be on hand at all times, ready to destroy the machine if it slips over the threshold into consciousness.

"Hence the equipment. The Mechanism's inside there now—in fact, we've already begun the resonant excitation. What we're hoping is that somewhere out there—somewhere out in that sea of alternate timelines—is a copy of the Mechanism that never fell into the water. Of course, that copy may have been destroyed subsequently—but somewhere there *has* to be a counterpart to the Mechanism in better condition than this one. Maybe near-infinite numbers of counterparts, for all we know. Perhaps we were the unlucky ones, and nobody else's copy ended up being lost underwater."

She coughs to clear her throat, and in that instant catches a reflected glimpse of herself in the glass plating of one of the cabinets in the corner of the room. Drawn face, tired creases around the mouth, bags under the eyes—a woman who's been working too hard for much too long. But how else was an Iranian mathematician supposed to get on in the world, if it wasn't through graft and dedication? It's not like she was born into money, or had the world rushing to open doors for her.

The work will endure long after the bags have gone, she tells herself.

"The way it happens," she says, regaining her composure, "is that we'll steal an almost infinitesimally small amount of order from an almost infinitely large number of alternate universes. In return, we'll pump a tiny amount of surplus entropy into each of those timelines. The counterparts of the Mechanism will hardly feel the change: the alteration in any one of them will be so tiny as to be almost unmeasurable. A microscopic scratch here; a spot of corrosion or the introduction of an impure atom there. But because we're stealing order from so many of them, and consolidating that order into a single timeline, the change in our universe will be enormous. We'll win, because we'll get back the Mechanism as it was before it went into the sea. But no one else loses; it's not like we're stealing someone else's perfect copy and replacing it with our own damaged one."

She thinks she has them then—that it is all going to go without a hitch or a quibble, and they can all shuffle over to the tables and start nibbling on cheese squares. But then a hand raises itself slowly from the audience. It belongs to an intense young man with squared-off glasses and a severe fringe.

He asks: "How can you be so sure?"

Safa grimaces. She hates being asked questions.

RANA PUTS DOWN her tool and listens very carefully. Somewhere in the museum there was a loud bang, as of a door being slammed. She is silent for at least a minute, but when no further sound comes she resumes her labors, filling the room with the repetitious scratch of diamond-tipped burr against corroded metal.

Then another sound comes, a kind of fluttering, animal commotion, as if a bird is loose in one of the darkened halls, and Rana can stand it no more. She leaves her desk and walks out into the basement corridor, wondering if someone else has come in to work. But the other rooms and offices remain closed and unlit.

She is about to return to her labors and call Katib's desk, when she hears the soft and feathery commotion again. She is near the stairwell and the sound is clearly coming from above her, perhaps on the next floor up.

Gripping the handrail, Rana ascends. She is being braver than perhaps is wise—the museum has had its share of intruders, and there have been thefts—but the coffee machine is above and she had been meaning to fetch herself a cup for at least an hour. Her heart is in her throat when she reaches the next landing and turns the corner into the corridor, which is as shabby and narrow as any of the museum's non-public spaces. There are high, institutional windows on one side and office doors on the other. But there is the machine, standing in a pool of light two doors down, and there is no sign of an intruder. She walks to the machine, fishing coins from her pocket, and punches in her order. As the machine clicks and gurgles into life, Rana feels a breeze against her cheek. She looks down the corridor and feels it again: it's as if there's a door open, letting in the night air. But the only door should be the one manned by Katib, on the other side of the building.

While her coffee is being dispensed Rana walks in the direction of the breeze. At the end the corridor reaches the corner of this wing and jogs to the right. She turns the bend and sees something unanticipated. All along the corridor, there is no glass in the windows, no metal in the frames: just tall blank openings in the wall. And there, indeed, is a fluttering black shape: a crow, or something like a crow, which has come in through one of those openings and cannot now find its way back outside. It keeps flinging itself at the wall between the windows, a gleam of mad desperation in its eyes.

Rana stands still, wondering how this can be. She was here. She remembers passing the machine and thinking she would take a cup if only she were not already staggering under her boxes and computers.

But there is something more than just the absence of glass. Is she losing her mind, or do the window apertures look narrower than they used to do, as if the walls have begun to squeeze the window spaces tight like sleepy eyes?

She must call Katib.

She hurries back the way she has come, forgetting all about the coffee she has just paid for. But when she turns the bend in the corridor, the machine is standing there dark and dead, as if it's been unplugged.

She returns to the basement. Under her feet the stairs feel rougher and more crudely formed than she remembers, until she reaches the last few treads and they start to feel normal again. She pauses at the bottom, waiting for her mind to straighten itself out.

Down here at least all is as it should be. Her office is as she left it, with the lights still on, the laptops still aglow, the gearwheel still mounted on its stand, the disemboweled Mechanism still sitting on the other side of the desk.

She eases into her seat, her heart still racing, and picks up the telephone.

"Katib?"

"Yes, my fairest," he says, his voice sounding more distant and crackly than she feels it should, as if he is speaking from halfway around the world. "What can I do for you?"

"Katib, I was just upstairs, and..."

But then she trails off. What is she going to tell him? That she saw open gaps where there should be windows?

"Rana?"

Her nerve deserts her. "I was just going to say... the coffee machine was broken. Maybe someone could take a look at it."

"Not until tomorrow, I am afraid—there is no one qualified. But I will make an entry in the log."

"Thank you, Katib."

After a pause he asks, "There was nothing else, was there?"

"No," she says. "There was nothing else. Thank you, Katib."

She knows what he must be thinking. She's been working too hard, too fixated on the task. The Mechanism does that to people, it's been said. They get lost in its labyrinthine possibilities and never emerge again. Not the way they were, anyway.

But she thinks she can still hear that crow.

"How CAN I be so sure about what?" Safa asks, with an obliging smile.

"That this is going to work the way you say it will," the intense young man answers.

"The mathematics is pretty clear," Safa says. "I should know; I discovered most of it." Which comes less modestly than she had intended, although no one seems to mind. "What I mean is, there isn't any room for ambiguity. We know that the sheath of alternate timelines is near-infinite in extent, and we know we're only pumping the smallest conceivable amount of entropy into each of those timelines." Safa holds the smile, hoping that will be enough for the young man, and that she can continue with her presentation.

But the man isn't satisfied. "That's all very well, but aren't you presupposing that all those other timelines have order to spare? What if that isn't the case? What if all the other Mechanisms are just as corroded and broken as ours—what will happen then?"

"It'll still work," Safa says, "provided the total information content across all the timelines is sufficient to specify one intact copy, which is overwhelmingly likely from a statistical standpoint.

Of course, if all the Mechanisms happen to be damaged in exactly the same fashion as ours, then the Fixation won't work—you still can't get something for nothing. But that's not very likely. Trust me; I'm very confident that we can find enough information out there to reconstruct our copy."

The man seems to be content with that answer, but just when Safa is about to open her mouth and continue with her speech, her adversary raises his hand again.

"Sorry, but... I can't help wondering. Does the entropy exchange happen uniformly across all those timelines?"

It's an odd, technical-sounding question, suggesting that the man has done more homework than most. "Actually, no," Safa says, guardedly. "The way the math works out, the entropy exchange is ever so slightly clumped. If a particular copy of the Mechanism has more information to give us, we end up pumping a bit more entropy into that copy than one which has less information to offer. But we're still talking about small differences, nothing that anyone will actually notice."

The man pushes a hand through his fringe. "But what if there's only one?"

"I'm sorry?"

"I mean, what if there's only one intact copy out there, and all the rest are at least as damaged as our own?"

"That can't happen," Safa says, hoping that someone, anyone, will interrupt by asking another question. It's not that she feels on unsafe ground, just that she has the sense that this could go on all night.

"Why not?" the man persists.

"It just can't. The mathematics says it's so unlikely that we may as well forget about it."

"And you believe the mathematics."

"Why shouldn't I?" Safa is beginning to lose her patience, feeling cornered and put upon. Where is the museum director to defend her when she needs him? "Of course I believe it. It'd be pretty strange if I didn't."

"I was just asking," the man says, sounding as if he's the one who's under attack. "Maybe it isn't very likely—I'll have to take your word for that. But I only wanted to know what would happen."

"You don't need to," Safa says firmly. "It can't happen—not ever. And now can I please continue?"

HER FINGER STABS down on Katib's button again. But there is nothing, not even the cool purr of the dialing tone. The phone is mute, and now that she looks at it, the display function is dead. She puts the handset down and tries again, but nothing changes.

That's when Rana pays proper attention to the gearwheel, the one she has been working on. There are thirty-seven wheels in the Antikythera Mechanism and this is the twenty-first, and although there was still much to be done until it was ready to be replaced in the box, it now looks as if she has hardly begun. The surface corrosion that she has spent weeks rectifying has returned in a matter of minutes, covering the wheel in a furry blue-green bloom as if someone has taken the artifact and dipped it in acid while she was out of the office. But as she looks at it, blinking in dismay, as if it is her eyes that are wrong, rather than the wheel, she notices that three teeth are gone, or worn away so thoroughly that they may as well not be there. Worse, there is a visible scratch—actually more of a crack—that cuts across one side of the wheel, as if it is about to fracture into two pieces.

Mesmerized and unsettled in equal measure, Rana picks up one of her tools—the scraper she was using before she heard the noise—and touches it against part of the blue-green corrosion. The bloom chips off almost instantly, but as it does so it takes a quadrant of the wheel with it, the piece shattering to a heap of pale granules on her desk. She stares in numb disbelief at the ruined gear, with a monstrous chunk bitten out of the side of it, and then the tool itself shatters in her hand.

"This can't be happening," Rana says to herself. Then her gaze falls on the other gearwheels, in their plastic boxes, and she sees the same brittle corrosion afflicting them all.

As for the Mechanism itself, the disemboweled box: what she sees isn't possible. She can just about accept that some bizarre, hitherto-undocumented chemical reaction has attacked the metal in the time it took for her to go upstairs and come down again, but the box itself is *wood*—it hasn't changed in hundreds of years, not since the last time the casing was patiently replaced by one of the Mechanism's many careful owners.

But now the box has turned to something that looks more like rock than wood, something barely recognizable as a made artifact. With trepidation Rana reaches out and touches it. It feels fibrous and insubstantial. Her finger almost seems to ghost through it, as if what she is reaching for is not a real object at all, but a hologram. Peering into the heart of the Mechanism, she sees the gears that are still in place have fused together into a single corroded mass, like a block of rock that has been engraved with a hazy impression of clockwork.

Then Rana laughs, for the pieces of the puzzle have just fallen into place. This is all a joke, albeit— given the pressures she is already under—one in spectacularly bad taste. But a joke all the same, and not a marker of her descent into insanity. She was called upstairs by a noise—how else were they going to get into her office and swap the Mechanism for this ruined half-cousin? The missing windows, the panicked bird, seem like details too far, random intrusions of dream-logic, but who can guess the mind of a practical joker?

Well, she has a sense of humor. But not now, not tonight. Someone will pay for this. Cutting off her telephone was the last straw. That was nasty, not funny.

She moves to leave her bench again and find whoever must be spying on her, certain that they must be lurking in the shadows outside, maybe in the unlit observation corridor, where they'd have a plain view of her discomfort. But as she places her hand down to push herself up, her fingers slip into the smoky surface of the bench.

They vanish as if she were dipping them into water.

All of a sudden she realizes that it was not the Antikythera Mechanism that was growing insubstantial, but everything around her.

No, that's not it either. Something is happening to the building, but if the table were turning ghostly, the heavy things on it—the Mechanism, the equipment, the laptops—would have surely sunk through it by now. There's a simpler explanation, even if the realization cuts through her like a shaft of interstellar cold.

She's the one fading out, losing traction and substantiality.

Rana rises to her feet eventually, but it's like pushing herself against smoke. She isn't so much standing as floating with her feet in vague contact with the ground. The air in her lungs is beginning to feel thin, but at the same time there's no sense that she is about to choke. She tries to walk, and for a moment her feet paddle uselessly against the floor, until she begins to pick up a deathly momentum in the direction of the door.

The corridor at the base of the stairs was normal when she returned from her visit to the next floor, but now it has become a dark, forbidding passageway, with rough-formed doorways leading into dungeon-like spaces. Her office is the only recognizable place, and even her office is not immune to the changes. The door has vanished, leaving only a sagging gap in the wall. The floor is made of stones, unevenly laid. Halfway to her bench the stones blend together into something like concrete, and then a little further the concrete gains the hard red sheen of the flooring she has come to expect. On the desk, her electric light flickers and fades. The laptops shut down with a whine, their screens darkening. The line of change in the floor creeps closer to the desk, like an advancing tide. From somewhere in the darkness Rana hears the quiet, insistent dripping of water.

She was wrong to assume that the things on the desk were immune to the fading. She began to go first, but now the same process of fade-out is beginning to catch up with her tools, with her notes and the laptops and the fabric of the bench itself. Even the Mechanism is losing its grip on reality, its gears and components beginning to dissolve before her eyes. The wooden box turns ash-gray and crumbles into a pile of dust. A breeze fingers its way into the room and spirits the dust away.

The Mechanism was the last thing to go, Rana realizes: the tide of change had come in from all directions, to this one tiny focus, and for a little while the focus had held firm, resisting the transforming forces.

Now she feels the hastening of her own process of fade-out. She cannot move or communicate. She is at the mercy of the breeze.

It blows her through the cold stone walls, out into the night-time air of a city she barely recognizes. She drifts through the sky, able to witness but not able to participate. In all directions she sees only ruin and desolation. The shells of buildings throw jagged outlines against the moonlit sky. Here and there she almost recognizes the fallen corpse of a familiar landmark, but so much is different that she soon loses her sense of direction. Even the shape of the river, shining back under moonlight, appears to have meandered from the course she remembers. She sees smashed stone and metal bridges that end halfway across to the other bank. Crimson fires burn on the horizon and flicker through the eyeholes of gutted buildings.

Then she notices the black machines, stalking their way through the warrens and canyons between the ruins. Fierce and frightening engines of war, with their turreted guns swiveling into doorways and shadows, the iron treads of their feet crunching down on the rubble of the pulverized city, the rubble that used to be dwellings and possessions, until these juggernauts arrived. She does not need an emblem or flag to know that these are the machines of an occupying force; that her city is under the mechanized heel of an invader. She watches as a figure springs out of concealment to lob some pathetic burning torch at one of the machines. The turret snaps around and a lance of fire stabs back at the assailant. The figure drops to the ground.

The wind is gusting her higher, turning the city into a map of itself. As her point of view changes direction she catches sight of the building that used to be the Museum of Antiquities, but what she sees is no more than a shattered prison or fortress, one among many. And for an instant she remembers that the shell of the museum was very old, that the building—or a succession of buildings, each built on the plan of its predecessor—had stood in the same location for many centuries, serving many rulers.

In that same instant, Rana comes to a momentary understanding of what has happened to both her and her world. The Mechanism has been wrenched from history, and accordingly—because the Mechanism was so essential—history has come undone. There is no Museum of Antiquities, because there is no Greater Persia. The brilliant clockwork that dispatched armies and engineers across the globe simply never existed.

Nor did Rana.

But the moment of understanding passes as quickly as it came. Ghosts are not the souls of the dead, but the souls of people written out of history when history changes. The worst thing about them is that they never quite recall the living people they used to be, the things they once witnessed.

The wind lofts Rana higher, into thinning silver clouds. But by then she no longer thinks of anything at all, except the endless meshing of beautiful bronze gearwheels, moving the heavens for all eternity.

Artifacts

Stephen Baxter

YOU SWIM.

Why must you swim? If you swim, where are you coming from, and where are you going to?

Why is there a "you" separated from the "not-you" through which you swim?

Why is there something rather than nothing?

Who are you?

You cannot rest. You are alone. You are frightened by the swimming. And you are frightened that the swimming must end. For—what then?

MORAG'S MOTHER LAY dead, behind the flimsy curtain that veiled her hospital bed, only feet away.

This little waiting area wasn't all that bad. It was carpeted, and had decent chairs and tables piled with newspapers and elderly magazines, *Hello* and *Country Life* and *Reader's Digest*, and a pot plant that Morag had watered a couple of

times. A little window gave her a glimpse of Edinburgh rooftops. She had been awake all night, and
now it was a sunny June morning, which felt a bit
unreal. There was even a little TV up high on the
wall, stuck on a news channel that looped headlines about water riots in Australia. In the year
2014 the news was always dismal, and Morag, fifteen years old, generally did her best to ignore it.
No, it wasn't bad here, not as bad as you might
have thought an NHS ward would be.

But it was all so mundane. It seemed impossible
that the same reality, the same room, could contain curling copies of glossy celeb mags and the
huge event that had taken place on the other side
of that curtain, the final ghastly process as the
bone marrow cancer overwhelmed her mother.

Her father, who always encouraged her to call
him Joe, was helping himself to another cup of
coffee. "Fucking thing," he said, as, not for the
first time, he had trouble slotting the plastic coffee
pot back into its little groove. He glanced at
Morag. "Sorry."

"Like I never heard you swear before."

"Yes." He sat beside her.

They were silent a moment, both beyond tears,
or between them. She hadn't seen him for a couple
of years. His break-up with her mother had
seemed to get worse as time passed, and his visits
had become more sporadic and more fraught, at
least until these final weeks and days. He was only
forty-five. Tall, thin, always gaunt, Morag thought
he looked hollowed out.

On impulse she smoothed out his sleeve. "This
shirt needs an iron."

"Yes." A flicker of a grin. "Actually I need a new shirt. Can't afford it."

They hadn't talked, not to each other, while Mum was still here. "You quit your job, didn't you?" Joe had been working on computer systems in the City of London—something like that. "Was it so you could be with Mum?"

"Partly." He sipped his coffee, and grimaced at its strength. "That and the fact of the illness itself. When I understood your mother was dying, the reality of it sunk home, I suppose."

"The reality of what?"

"Life. Death. The finiteness of it all. When you're young you think you're immortal. Forty was a big shock to me, I can tell you. And now this. Hacking predictive algorithms so some City barrow boy could get even richer suddenly seemed an absurd way to spend my life."

She thought she understood. "It doesn't make any sense. There's a copy of the *Daily Mirror* sitting on that table. While behind that curtain—"

"I know. You go through life never facing up to the big questions. What is life? What is death? Why is there something rather than nothing? Anyhow, I'm going back to what I used to do."

She frowned. "Back to university?"

"I was a researcher," he said. "A whiz at maths. I went into theoretical cosmology. Let me tell you something." He put his arm around her, the way he used to hold her when she was little. "All of this, everything we see and feel, our whole three-dimensional universe with its unfolding arrow of time, is only a fraction of reality. Of course that was the message my father beat into me when I was your age, or tried to. He was a Presbyterian minister. When I started questioning his picture of the universe we fell out good and proper..."

Morag had only fragmentary memories of her grandfather, whom she'd met only a handful of times.

Joe said, "Our universe is like a snowflake in a storm, one among a myriad others, all floating around in a nine-dimensional continuum called the Bulk. The universes are called branes—after membranes—or D-branes, Dirichlet branes... Those other universes might be like ours, or they might not. Some of them might have one space dimension, or three or five or seven. They might have a time dimension, like ours, or none at all, so they're just static and eternal. We know all this is out there, you see, because of the effects of the higher reality on our universe. Primordial inflation, patterns in the cosmic microwave background radiation, all of these are influences from other universes approaching our own..." He glanced at her. "I'm getting too technical."

"No. But it's like when I was small and you'd distract me from the dark with fairy tales."

He ruffled her hair. "Well, all this stuff is real, as far as we can tell. Anyhow it's out there, out in the Bulk, that the answers to the fundamental questions will be found some day. That's why I'm going back. I got sick of the academic life, the bitchiness and the infighting, the treadmill of always having to find a bit more money to keep going for a few more years. Nobody wanted to put money into fundamental research anyhow. But at least doing that I was closer to the search for finding the answers to the big questions than slaving in the damn City."

It all sounded foolish to Morag, a dream. But Joe had always been a dreamer. She wondered if he ever thought about how she was supposed to be supported through the rest of her schooling, her own college years. Well, she had Auntie Sheena, Mum's sister, cold, disapproving, but solid and generous enough. She wished she were a bit older, though, not so dependent on all these flaky, short-lived adults.

Morag said, "Joe—none of this stuff about D-branes and the Bulk will bring Mum back."

"No. No, love, it won't."

For some reason the tears came after that.

A nurse came to refill the coffee, and she dabbed with a tissue at the pot plant that Morag had over-filled with water.

IT WAS A universe not unlike humanity's universe. But it was dark.

It lacked stars, for the intricate coincidence of fundamental constants that enabled stellar fusion processes had not occurred here; the dice had fallen differently. Yet complex elements had spewed out of this cosmos's equivalent of the Big Bang, atoms that combined, nuclei that fissioned. Rock formed, and ice. Grains gathered in the dark, drawn by gravity. There were no stars here. But soon there were worlds.

On one of these worlds, creatures not entirely unlike those on Earth rose from the usual chemical churning. They were fuelled not by sunlight but by the slow seep of minerals and heat from the interior of their rocky planet. Crawling, swimming, flying, consuming each other and the world's raw materials, they built an ecology of a complexity that itself increased with time. There were extinctions as rocks fell from the sky or the cooling world spasmed as it shed its primordial heat, but life recovered, complexity was regained. To those with minds, this was a beautiful world, that empty sky a velvet heaven. They knew no different.

Some of them dreamed of gods. Few ever imagined that a greater mind than any of theirs arose from the intricate workings of their ecology itself.

And that mind was troubled.

For she felt the grand cooling of her planetary body, and ached with the slow decay of the radioactive substances that replenished that heat. She remembered a time of hot youth, and she foresaw shriveling cold, when the things that swarmed over her continents and oceans would die back, and her own thoughts would simplify and die back with them.

She remembered the birth of her universe itself. She anticipated surviving, in some reduced form, to see its end. To a being built on such a grand scale the time of cold paralysis was not so terribly remote.

Questions plagued her. Why did it have to be so? Why must she die? Why should she have been born at all?

Why was there something in this universe, rather than nothing?

She longed for another to discuss these profound questions. There was no other like her, not in all this universe.

Not yet.

* * *

ONE WAS BORN, inchoate, utterly lacking symmetry. A mind formed immediately, like a snowflake crystallizing from moist air, with questions: Where am I? What is this place? What must I do?

Others gathered around him. Answers slotted into the empty spaces of his mind.

Eight dimensions of space and one of time characterized this universe. That and symmetry.

Yet the symmetry was incomplete. There was an array of 248 places to be filled, by ones like himself, as if you ascended to take a place in a constellation. That was the purpose of life, to ascend, to take your place, to contribute to the greater symmetry.

And when that vast symmetry was completed, the universe would end.

Even as he realized this, as he grasped the essential structure of his universe only moments after he was born, he was troubled by a faint doubt.

But in the meantime there was work to be done. Many of those 248 places were already filled, and there were far more candidates than there were remaining places. All around him other young were gathering in simple clusters of four, eight, sixteen; others, more ambitious, sought to impress with explorations of twenty-three and thirty-one.

To shine in such gatherings was the only way to progress. A grim process of selection had to be gone through if you were to attain the heaven of perfected symmetry.

Grimly he got to work.

MORAG'S FLIGHT FROM Edinburgh was diverted to Luton because of flooding at Heathrow, but she was able to catch a short-haul connection to the City Airport.

The plane took Morag into London along the line of the Thames and past the City, where her father had worked five years ago. Now skyscrapers rose like thistles from the flood, and choppers flitted before impassive glass cliffs. Each of these huge developments contained as many people as a small town, she imagined, stacked up into the sky; each would require a major rescue operation of its own, in the context of the latest London-wide flood emergency.

At the airport, passport control was perfunctory despite Scotland's independence. She caught a cab to the hotel at Hampstead, safely above the water line, where her father was staying.

Joe was pacing around his tiny room, shirt rumpled as ever, tie loosened, shoes off, socks with holes in them. He looked as if he was longing for a cigarette. He was evidently wired on in-room coffee.

The remnants of his presentation to the government's Science and Technologies Facilities Council were scattered on the small table and on the bed. Images played over a slim laptop, mostly bullet-point argument summaries. There was one extraordinary image like a mutated sea anemone that Morag had come to recognize as a representation of a Calabi–Yau space, a possible configuration of the Bulk, the greater nine-dimensional continuum within which the universe swam.

"I'm sorry I'm late," Morag said. "The plane, the flooding—"

"That's okay," Joe said. Making an obvious effort to calm down, he came and kissed her cheek, took her coat and hung it on the back of the door. "There's something else I want to talk about anyhow. Not that you missed anything but another ritual humiliation for your poor old dad. You want a coffee?" He rummaged in the litter on the table, the little packets of granules and the plastic milk cartons. "I've burned through most of it but there might be a packet of that fucking decaf stuff. Sorry."

"I'm fine. Your need is greater than mine." She pulled out the room's one chair from under the table and sat. "I take it you didn't go down well, then."

"Oh, hell, it's not just me. They announced another across-the-board cut in research spending last month. I was hoping to get hold of some American money, they're always more flush over there, but it's the same story, cuts to the National Science Foundation, the National Institute of Standards and Technology, the Office of Science at the Department of Energy. They're even making layoffs at Fermilab."

She pulled at her fingers. "It's tough all over, Joe. There's money in ecosystem research but even that's getting tighter." This was the direction she wanted to go herself, when she finished her first degree in biological sciences; she was twenty years old now and a couple of years into her course. "And that's obviously applicable."

"'Applicable!' How I hate that word. If your research doesn't have obvious 'applicability' in flood defenses or desalination or food production or, better yet, defense systems, you're screwed."

"Well, you can understand it, Joe. The world can't afford what it used to. These are tough times."

"The times are always tough," he snapped back. "There are always excuses not to spend on fundamental research."

She reached over for the laptop and tapped a key to page through his slides. "The trouble is, everything you ask for is just so expensive. This is big stuff..."

She had learned something of the technologies Joe needed to give him the data that would confirm or refute his theoretical meta-cosmic models. Evidence for other universes came in exotic and subtle forms, such as patterns in the cosmic background microwave radiation, a relic of the Big Bang that, Joe believed, had been caused by the close approach of one brane-universe to another, or even their collision. Other distortions in the radiation pattern could show the effect of close approaches with other branes since the beginning—holes in the sky, like a vast gap eight billion light years from Earth and all of a billion light years wide, where few galaxies swam. You needed satellite observatories to pick that up.

Or you could look for gamma rays, which might be relics of other exotic events. A supernova could produce gravitons, gravity force-carrying particles, some of which, called Kaluza–Klein gravitons, were able to travel out of the "surface" of a brane and into the greater Bulk. Falling back to a brane, such gravitons could produce a shower of high-energy gamma rays—which again, mostly, could only be detected from space. But NASA was mothballing its elderly gamma-ray satellite, called GLAST, the Gamma-ray Large Area Space Telescope. You could even look for gravity waves, ripples in space-time, more evidences of influences from beyond the universe's three-dimensional plane. But again those effects were subtle, minute, fiendishly difficult to track down.

You needed a big budget for any of this. And, in a world fraying under a multiple assault of climate change, resource depletion, disease, and war, big budgets for cutting-edge physics experiments were hard to come by. Joe knew this as well as Morag did. It didn't make the results of his pitch any less disappointing.

She came to one striking image. It was geometrical, like a sphere picked out by a regular array of golden points, each apparently connected to the rest by a silver thread. It turned and pivoted in the computer's animation, its symmetries obviously profound. "This is beautiful. What is it?"

"E8," Joe said. "A somewhat complicated mathematical pattern in eight dimensions. Two hundred and forty-eight points. It's a way of encapsulating the unification of physics. It's all to do with string theory, as is the whole idea of brane-universes... You place a fundamental particle or force at each of the points, say an electron or a quark, and if you get it right, the symmetries express the particles' relationships to each other." He made the figure swivel this way and that, and projected various subsets of the particles down to two dimensions. "See? This projection shows how the color charge of a quark changes under the influence of the strong force carried by a gluon..."

"I'll take your word for it."

"It's a bit of research from the noughties I've been following up, called the Lisi synthesis. The thing is, the same mathematical structure can be used in some models to describe the Bulk, the Calabi–Yau manifold. Remarkably rich, tens of thousands of interaction types expressed in the internal symmetries. Look, this is my theoretical underpinning. The core of my expression of physics, which in turn I'm using to construct my models of the Bulk."

He stared at the turning images in the laptop screen. "I feel I'm close, at least to expressing the right questions, if not to getting the answers. All the other branes out there, all with their own time axes, or multiple times, or none at all... Time can pivot, you know. The time signature of a universe can change. You can have a static universe with several dimensions of space—a scrap of eternity—but then a space dimension evolves into time, and wham, you have the whole package, Big Bang and Big Rip, birth and death. Our universe could have been eternal once. Something could have happened to pivot the axes, to change the signature, to make it temporal, finite. Something bad."

That word surprised her. "*Bad*?"

"God wouldn't have made a finite universe. Finitude isn't perfection. Even a trillion years isn't enough, if eternity is available."

"That sounds like something Granddad might have said." She had always wondered if Joe's obsessive quest for cosmological truth was really all about unresolved issues from his childhood.

"Well, that old monster asked some of the right questions, even if he didn't have the right answers."

"Joe, you said there's something else you wanted to talk about."

"Yes. Plan B." He sat on the edge of the bed and faced her.

"Plan B?"

"Even if the research councils and governments won't fund me, I'm not giving up. Well, I can't."

She looked around at the untidy room, the litter on the bed, the dirty clothes roughly shoved away on a wardrobe shelf. "Joe, you can't fund high-energy physics research by yourself."

He grinned. "Can't I? We'll see. I do need a bit of money. Which is where you come in."

She laughed. "Joe, I'm a student. I don't have any money!"

"I know. But it's not you I'm tapping up," he said bluntly.

"Then who? Oh. Not Sheena."

"Your Auntie Sheena might look on the purchase of a bit of land as an investment," he said. "If it's put to her the right way. Such as by you…"

THERE WERE OTHER worlds in this dark sky. She felt their gravitational tug, a pull deep in her belly. Sometimes she even felt a rain of meteorites, bits of those sister worlds blasted from their surfaces and scattered through the void. But few of those worlds carried life of any kind, and none an ecology as complex as hers, none a mind as rich as her own.

There was a way to put that right.

It took an eon of concentration, of a subtle shepherding of tensions. Then an immense supervolcano ripped open one side of the planet. A wave of ash and dirt and toxic gases caused stupendous global dying. No matter. The ecosystem would recover from this event, as it had from others.

And, briefly, as this one world shone like a star in the dark sky, from it spread a spray of rock and ash, blasted to escape velocity. Most of these fragments were inert, baked and smashed to sterility. But in a few of them life clung, hardy spores. And a few of those precious seed-carriers would fall on sister worlds.

It would take an eon for new ecosystems to arise on barren worlds, for consciousness to arise on its multiple levels. To a world mind, that wasn't long to wait. She rehearsed what she would say.

SYMMETRIES! SYMMETRIES OF squares and cubes! Symmetries of primes and perfect numbers! All these and more he fought to join and mold, while others, weaker or less determined, fell back into shapelessness—and new generations of novices, younger and still more hungry, fought to take away what he had achieved.

Joe Denham might have recognized the form to which he aspired. The structure of this cosmos was not unlike the E8 mathematical construct he used to model the fundamental forces and particles of his own universe. And indeed in this universe there were some advanced minds who posited a construct not unlike Joe's cosmos to serve as an analogical model of their own world. There was a duality in all things, a symmetry even across the branes.

But to one inhabitant at least, this universe came to seem like a beautiful prison.

Very rapidly the remaining places among the 248 elect were being filled. Yet even as he worked frantically, he was distracted by doubt.

The universe would end when the array of 248 was filled, the symmetry completely expressed. And he, indeed, would die with it. Why? Why should this be so? Why should he be born, only to die? Why should the universe begin and end at all? And why so *soon*? If the universe were more complex it would last longer before its perfection were complete. Why should it not have been so?

More mysteries. There were other universes than this. Symmetry demanded it, the greater symmetries of the Bulk in which all cosmoses floated like freshborn novices. He could *see* the other cosmoses, or at least he saw the necessity of their existence, in the way that a human theoretical physicist could gain fresh insights from the symmetries of his models and equations. Other universes were arrayed around his own, in pretty patterns. They too lived and died, those nearby.

Yet there was a cluster of other branes, further away, characterized by a different sort of symmetry. And they did not die.

Even as he fought for his place in the sky, he strained to understand how this could be so. And why.

Morag took the monorail from Edinburgh to Dunbar. From there she hired a pod car, fed in the coordinates her father had given her, and sat back.

In the car's electric silence she was driven south from Dunbar through arable country. It was a gently rolling landscape of dry stone walls. To the east the land fell away, affording a long view toward the Tweed valley, while to the west the land rose toward the Lammermuir Hills. Pretty landscape. But the road was empty of traffic, and it was heavily fenced off from the fields, even though there wasn't a sheep or a cow in sight, and the fields themselves were visibly unkempt.

This was the year 2034. Morag, in her mid-thirties now, was occupied full time by her own ecosalvage projects in Africa, and rarely came home. It was difficult to absorb the changes this Scottish countryside had seen since Joe had first used Sheena's money to buy his few acres up here (and Sheena, long dead, had never seen a penny of it back). First had come the pathogen panics as bluetongue and other nasties, driven by shifting climate zones, had overwhelmed the farms. The countryside had walled itself off, hundreds of miles of barbed wire isolating the fields from spores carried on tires and feet. But soon after that had come the pricing-out of private transport, the end of traffic, and then the great revolution in artificial food production that had led to the collapse of traditional agriculture everywhere. Now, even in Scotland and England, swathes of countryside were reverting to a state not seen since the Mesolithic, and ecologists like Morag mapped the changes as a depleted ecosystem tried to reassemble itself.

And in the middle of all this Joe Denham continued his patient, obsessive data gathering, year after year.

Morag saw his installation from a rise a half-mile before the pod car reached it. Joe's cosmic ray telescope was an array of several hundred tanks of water, each as tall as Joe was himself, gathered in a rough polygon nearly a mile across. Each tank had a sensor pack attached to it and a communications antenna, and four big optical telescopes were set up around the perimeter of the array, including one that stuck out of the top of Joe's control center, which was a garden shed with the roof cut open.

Morag knew the principle. The array was based on a properly funded design called the Pierre Auger Observatory in Argentina. It was designed to detect cosmic rays, high-energy particles coming in from space. When they hit the atmosphere such particles would create a shower of secondary particles. Joe's telescopes looked for fluorescence in the air as these particles passed through, on their way to the tanks where they would create tiny flashes of light in the water. From these bits of information, Joe's computers could reconstruct the nature and trajectory of the original cosmic rays—and he was able to use a subset of that data as evidence of the nature of the greater multiverse of the Bulk, and its interaction with the human universe.

It was a bold project, and it seemed to work, as far as Morag could tell. But it had taken Joe around fifteen years to get this far. His water tanks, scavenged one by one from oil refineries and other abandoned industrial facilities, were all shapes, sizes, and colors, and his array looked less like a science project than an art installation. Or even just a folly, the obsession of a madman.

He met her outside his shed. He was in his midsixties now, if anything he looked older than that, and in his quilted coat and elderly boots and with his self-cut hair he was like an eccentric sort of farmer.

He showed her into his shed and made her a coffee. There was a little bunk bed and basic kitchen stuff, a fridge fed by a generator somewhere, a heap of clothes. But most of the space was taken up by science gear. A ferocious draught came in through the open roof, where the telescope peered out like some long-legged animal.

The "coffee" was revolting. She wondered where he had got it. But she drank it for the warmth.

"It's good of you to come," he said. "Adam, the kids—"

"They're all fine. With me in Africa."

"It's been too long."

"Yes, it has," she said fervently. "Look at the state of you."

"Oh, don't fuss," he said, with a throaty old man's cackle. "You're as safe out in the countryside as in the gated cities, they say. It's the shanty towns you have to avoid."

"But you never were any use at looking after yourself, were you? When I was a kid I remember fretting over the way you never had your shirts ironed..."

He wasn't listening. He looked haunted. "They're trying to take away my computers, you know, or most of them."

"I know." This was why she had come; he had emailed her, and she had checked up herself.

"The government say the hoard I have here, elderly and unreliable as it is," and he gave one of his laptops a slap, "is more than is 'justifiable' for my needs. Justifiable! So much for the fucking singularity by the way, whatever happened to that...? Sorry. They have no idea what I'm doing here."

"That's the trouble, Joe. They don't have any idea. Why should they? I mean, you don't work for any reputable organization. You don't even write up your results anymore, do you?"

"What's the point? Nobody was paying any attention to partial results. I got no citations to speak of..."

"All the government cares about is the raw materials locked up in your computers. The germanium, the silver, even the copper—there are shortages of all these things now."

"I'm biding my time, about writing up," he said, as if he hadn't heard her. He stroked the computer he'd slapped, as if soothing it. "I'll wait until I have conclusive results—the full monty. Then I'll hit them with it all at once, fully backed up with data and references, none of this partial releasing. It will be unarguable."

"What will?"

He looked at her, briefly puzzled, as if she hadn't been paying attention. "My analysis of Calabi–Yau space. My map of the Bulk, and our place in it. There are branes all around ours, love, other universes, three, five, seven-dimensional constructs adrift in nine-dimensional space, influencing us with subtle whispers of gravity."

"There is a cluster of them close to us, self-attracting, orbiting like a swarm of asteroids. All of them time-ridden, and if anybody lives there they are as mortal as us. But I've detected *another* cluster of branes, further off, tighter, more orderly. And they are static—time-free, constructs of pure space. Fragments of eternity. Why mortality here, why eternity there? I can't answer that yet. But I feel I'm close to an understanding of *why* things are as they are..."

She reached out and took his hands. They were dry, the skin of his palms cracked. "Joe—you've been obsessing about death and mortality since Mum died. I don't blame you. But don't you think all this work is maybe some kind of rationalization? You're projecting your own life onto the whole of the rest of the universe. Isn't it better to let it go?"

He pulled back. "The last time I went back to Edinburgh, I was after a grant. They put me onto a counselor who came out with the same kind of stuff. As if I'm a kid who can't cope with his hamster dying. Morag, the whole damn universe is dying. I know it's hard to grasp, but it's true. But, you see, I think—"

"What, Joe?"

"I think it didn't have to be that way. Now. Are you going to help me keep hold of my computers or not?"

THE WORLD MINDS were scattered in the dark, around the mother who had so explosively born them.

Morag Denham might have understood their nature, if dimly. There was a great deal of information stored in the network of flows of mass and energy that characterized an ecosystem, which were in turn locked into the physical cycles of the planet that sustained it. Earth's interdependent geological and biological systems, all unconsciously, worked together in a giant feedback loop to keep the world's temperature at a level equable for life in the face of a steadily heating sun.

But in a complex ecosystem there was room for a great deal more information than characterized a simple thermostat. Patterns of ecocycles, in their robustness and resilience, made for satisfactory memory and processing systems. Even in Morag's universe there were worlds where intelligence had arisen naturally from the data flows that cycled around complex entangled ecologies. On such worlds, thoughts were expressed in the swelling and dying of populations of plants and animals, and million-year dreams haunted extinction events.

So it was in that other dark sky.

The mother world waited for her children to develop complexity, to come to awareness, to formulate thoughts that crackled with the rise and fall of species, and to begin to ask questions: Where am I? What is this place? What must I do? Then she began a slow process of dialogue. The community of worlds shared tremendous deep thoughts via gravity waves generated by the churning of their cores, or even via the firing-off of life forms in fresh volleys of meteorites: a sentence rudely dispatched in an alien invasion.

And gradually the mother and her children came to understand.

In the booming of gravity waves deeper and longer than any of them could generate, they sensed the structure of their own universe, and the architecture of the Bulk, the greater nine-dimensional cosmos in which it was embedded. They saw branes like their own, bound together by gravity just as the living worlds clustered, all living and dying. And they saw others, more distant, a handsome array of timeless universes, whose skies swam with heat, and where no world ever grew cold.

And they saw, beyond doubt, that such an arrangement was artificial.

Whoever had done this, whoever had doomed whole universes to brevity and extinction, was surely much like themselves, surely as afraid of the gathering cold as they were. This the mother understood. But it was hard not to feel resentment as the universe so quickly aged, and the great chill gathered, and one by one her children shed their hard-won complexity and succumbed to the cold and the dark.

HE HAD WON. He had won! He had battled through a forest of symmetries, and now those others already ascended prepared to welcome him to his place in the constellation of 248. It was all he had striven for, all his life, since the instant of his birth.

Yet now it was in his grasp he hesitated. Others watched him, doubtful and uneasy.

He understood that it would not be long after his ascension that the last of the places was filled, when the universe, complete, would die, and he would die with it. And he knew now that it did not have to be this way. He had glimpsed other universes, that far-off cluster of the undying, locked in their own changeless symmetries.

And he had glimpsed other types of symmetries, as far beyond his own as his was beyond a newborn novice's.

A simple regular polygon could have four points, a square—five or six points, a pentagon or a hexagon—it could have two-hundred and forty-eight points, any finite number. But as the number of points approached infinity the angular form aspired to another sort of symmetry, that perfect regularity of the circle.

So it could have been in his universe, he saw now. Not the stifling closure of a mere 248 vertices but the unending symmetry of the sphere. A symmetry with room for all who aspired to join it—forever. It could have been this way here, just as in those other realms.

And, once, that was how it had been.

Something, or somebody, had *changed* this universe, shattered its infinite order and blighted it with this crude spikiness. Replaced eternity with finitude. Replaced immortality with death.

Why should this have been done? He pondered this. Surely that greater agent was one not unlike himself. Surely that other had been born in asymmetry and struggled only for a symmetry of his own. That, at least, was a comforting thought, that in his own finitude and death he at least served the purposes of a greater symmetry, even if he could never understand how.

Enough. He was as content as he could ever be. He took his place, settling into the constellation of elect. He shone, one among 248 identical points of light.

Time ended.

JOE LAY THERE inert. Morag sat beside him, outside his isolation tent, and waited for the ghastly process of his dying to run its course. He looked wasted by his illness, yet he was still as tall and ungainly as ever; he looked too big for the bed.

The hospital room reminded Morag of her mother's death, thirty-odd years ago. Of course there were differences. This wasn't the NHS; long before this year of 2044 the welfare state had crumbled in an impoverished Scotland, and the health care had exhausted Joe's own pitiful savings, and eaten up a good chunk of Morag's own. There were few nurses around, only machines that tended to the needs of the ill and the dying.

But for all the changes, here was Joe spending his final hours lying on a curtained-off bed just as his wife had all those years ago. Although she hadn't had the indignity of a clear-plastic isolation bubble separating her from the touch of her family. And she at least had died of a cancer which had a name, instead of the exotic, species-crossing, nameless disease Joe had picked up when he had stayed out one winter too many in the Lammermuirs.

There were times during the night when Morag, sitting by his bed, thought he might not wake again. But then, as another bright Edinburgh summer morning dawned, his eyelids raised with a faint crumpling sound, like paper. "Morag...?"

She was startled. Perhaps she had been dozing, sitting in this hard chair. Impulsively she reached for him, but her fingertips only pushed against the clear isolation membrane. "Dad. Joe. You're awake."

He shifted his head slightly, and she saw some brownish fluid being pumped through a pipe and under the sheets into his body. He saw her looking. "Feeding time at the zoo. I could murder a burger. Even a fucking NHS coffee. Sorry. Are the kids here?"

The "kids" were now both young adults. But they were here. "They're exploring Edinburgh with Adam."

"Good. Keep them away. Kids are more open to disease. Don't want them catching my mumbo jumbo syndrome. So it got me in the end, eh?"

"What did?"

"Death. The Bulk. All those branes and anti-branes swimming around. They're killing me in the end, just like every other fucker back to Adam—' He was interrupted by a cough that came out of nowhere. His whole body jerked, as if convulsed, and she saw blood spray over the inside of his bubble. The machines around him adopted a new constellation of displays. "Sorry," he said.

"Are you all right?"

He forced a smile. "Jumping like a flea." His voice was papery, audibly weaker. "I'm seventy-five, you know. Not bad."

"No," she said. "Not bad."

"You haven't looked at my computers, have you?"

"Joe, there wasn't time. We just cleared out the shed. The council were already taking away your water tanks. The computers are safe, but—"

"Read my paper. It's backed up. The figures... I worked it out in the end."

"Your map of the Bulk."

"My analysis of the Calabi–Yau space, yes. I did it in the end. Like shining a torch up into all the dark, nine-dimensional halls we all drift around in. Listen. This is what I found—"

"Joe—"

"Listen." He tried to reach her, but his claw-like fingers just scraped feebly against plastic. "Listen," he whispered. "I saw two clusters of branes, mutually orbiting, like solar systems. One, far from us, has 248 members. All of them timeless, space dimensions only. All of them eternities. The other, the swarm we're part of, has one thousand, nine hundred and eighty four. And they're all unstable, like our universe. All of them have at least one time dimension. All of them doomed to birth and death, the whole damn cycle, and every living thing in them."

"Here's the thing, Morag, here's what I saw. Our cluster is in a particular part of the Bulk. You saw my projections of it, the thing's covered in spines like a hedgehog. We are in one of those spines. We've been *shepherded* here. And all the brane universes are on trajectories that force them to intersect..." He fell back, wheezing. "It needs more analysis. But I believe I saw the intersection, the close approach of another brane to our own, that destabilized our universe. I was able to track it back, like figuring out the flight of a bullet back to the assassin's gun."

"Destabilized?"

"Before that we were an eternity. The close encounter pivoted one of our space dimensions into a time. Pow, Big Bang, inflation, Big Rip, death—it all came about in that moment. A moment of Bulk time, I mean."

"The words you use," she said uneasily. "'Shepherded.' You said our cluster of branes was shepherded into the spine. What shepherded us there?"

"Or who."

"Who?"

He grinned; his teeth were discolored, and she wondered when he had last been to a dentist. "I believe it was intentional, Morag. And if not who, I can tell you why."

"Why, then?"

"For energy." He raised one hand and feebly closed a fist, over and over. "Universes exploding like gas in a piston chamber. The gravitational energy released by the dying universes just pumps up that spine—but what's it used for? Maybe that damn cluster of smug eternals is the payload."

None of this made any sense. "What are you saying, Joe?"

"That we're in an engine. Like a rocket ship. Each exploding cosmos is like a grain of gunpowder in a firework, driving the whole damn thing forward across the nine-dimensional Bulk. That's all we amount to, that's all we're *for*, our whole universe from beginning to end, Bang to Rip, all the galaxies and stars and planets, all the warriors and lovers and poets, all the births and deaths... And that's why they destabilized our universe, and thousands of others. Artifacts, all of them, embedded in a greater artifact. Whole universes used as propellant."

"Who, Joe? Who's they?"

He tried to sit up. His mouth opened as he strained to speak, and she thought she saw the shape of his skull through his thin flesh, the dirty white hair in his scalp. "Who? That's what I'd like to know. Where are we going? What is the purpose of this damn thing we're all trapped inside? Oh, maybe they're not unlike us. Aggressive expansionists, ripping up the environment. They must be, to build such a thing. We wouldn't care about a handful of bugs stuck in a gallon of petrol, would we? But we should challenge them. Maybe we should team up with the other brane universes. Maybe we should go demand what gave them the *right* to condemn billions of sapient beings to the agony of mortality..."

Another explosive cough sent a shower of thick blood over the bubble. Morag flinched. Joe fell back, shuddering, still trying to talk.

Red lights flashed across the face of the monitors. Morag heard human footsteps, running closer.

You swim.

Suspended in the nine-dimensional Bulk, you are a construct of Dirichlet branes.

Your mind emerges from the dances of a cluster of universes. These realms are internally timeless, eternal, and perfect. The inhabitants of each tiny cosmos might believe they are gods. But you are entirely unaware of their existence, anymore than a human watches the sparking of an individual neuron. It is the mutual orbit of the cosmoses themselves that is the foundation of your mind.

And you are driven forward in your swimming by the birth and collapse of a myriad more universes, each filled with minds, even with civilizations, blossoming and dying in hope and fear and longing, sent into the dark for your benefit. Again you are unaware of these miniature agonies.

You, arising from it all, are alone. And you swim.

Why must you swim? If you swim, where are you coming from, and where are you going?

Why is there a "you" separated from a "not-you" through which you swim?

Why is there something rather than nothing?

Who are you?

You cannot rest. You are alone. You are frightened by the swimming. And you are frightened that the swimming must end. For—what then?

Necroflux Day

John Meaney

FOR DAD'S SAKE, Carl tried to pretend that supper at Shadbolt's Halt was terrific, but they both knew otherwise. Last year, on Carl's eleventh birthday, they'd truly had a great time. Tonight, exactly a year later, the atmosphere was quieter, a reflection of the greater tension enveloping the city.

The food *was* good: komodo steak and buttery mashed tubers, then squealberry pie and ice cream, washed down with hot blue chocolate. But no waiters came out to sing Happy Birthday, and Carl and Dad were seated behind a heavy pillar, where entirely human diners could not see the hint of otherness in father and son as they ate.

Even the flamewraiths, dancing (in their minimized aspect) inside wall-mounted crystalline bowls, seemed to have caught the tension. How a flame could appear angular or edgy was beyond Carl, but he knew what he sensed—and while he could never be a Bone Listener like Dad, he knew how to perceive deeply.

Last night, he'd overheard Dad talking to their neighbor, Mr. Varlin. One of the words had been unfamiliar to him, so he'd pulled down the old Fortinium Dictionary that smelled of dust, and now he wondered at the implications of "pogrom" appearing in an old man's description of the way Tristopolis was changing.

"Er, Dad?" Carl wanted to change the mood, and thinking of Tristopolis had reminded him of something. "Do you know much about the city's founding?"

"Has Sister Stephanie-Charon set you some homework about the Tri-Millennial?"

"We have to write an essay for next week."

"So you know I can't help you."

Dad—Jamie Thargulis to the adult world—had access to the Lattice, which was out of the reach of most Bone Listeners, never mind standard humans. Now, as Dad blinked his dark-brown bulbous eyes, Carl wondered what it truly meant to work as an Archivist, to immerse oneself in the centuries-old flow of understanding.

"I wasn't trying to cheat, Dad."

"Sorry, son. I know. So do you want to take a swing past Möbius Park? I hear they're testing the parade balloons tonight."

The celebration was three months away. Carl had watched the St Lazlo Day parade last year. He and Dad had stood next to a group of true believers, their foreheads marked with the cobalt-pigment Sign of the Holy Reaver, which they would not erase until the Feast of Magnus.

"Will we see the parade?"

"I don't know, son. This year, things are... Well. Maybe we'll just stay at home."

"Okay."

"You're finished?"

Carl nodded, and Dad turned to gesture toward a waiter. The man came with the bill in hand, already written, as though he had known that Dad would not be ordering anything more.

Dad counted out three nine-florin coins, then looked up at the waiter.

"Thank you for the service."

He added a thirteen-sided coin to the amount.

"Goodbye, sir," said the waiter.

Dad, still seated, swallowed.

THE STREET, WIDE and bordered with centuries-old architecture, looked dim beneath the eternally deep-purple sky. Carl and Dad stood in a patch of orange light thrown by the restaurant windows, buttoning up their overcoats. Wearing his fedora, Dad looked standard human. He waved to a purple taxi. The cab slowed, then accelerated, and was past them.

"Sharp eyesight," muttered Dad.

A stone gargoyle glided overhead, high up.

"I'd like to walk," said Carl.

"All right, son. Let's do that."

They strolled to Illbeck Pentangle, where the traffic was heavy and it took a while to cross, then continued to the high stone walls of Möbius Park. They followed the road outside the walls, keeping to the other side of the street. At school, some older boys had scorned the stories of lone pedestrians disappearing forever—not just intruders, who deserved whatever happened—but Dad was always careful here, and he was an Archivist who worked for the city.

"The South-South-East Gate," he said. "Looks like it's open."

Tall and formed of black iron, the gates were closed whenever possible. Now, Carl could see along the gentle curves of Actualization Arc, bordered by dark parkland, and the black-grass clearing where half-inflated balloons were rising.

"There's a Leviathan." He pointed. "See?"

But what he really noticed was the faint silver glimmer of the force-shield that contained ravenous ectoplasma wraiths among the trees. Beyond, deep inside Möbius Park, reared the great skull outline of City Hall.

"I thought," muttered Dad, "there'd be more to see."

"No, this is great."

"We could get some juice at—"

"It would be nice to go home."

"We'll take the hypotube, in that case."

A floating amber P-sign indicated a Pneumetro station, two blocks along a street that headed away from the park. It took a few minutes to walk the distance, before descending to a Magenta Line platform just as a train slid in.

"Good timing," said Dad.

They boarded the last ovoid carriage, which would split off at the next branch line, Magenta 7. As they sat, Carl noticed a scaly-skinned man who was watching a group of standard human youths. They waved red beer bottles, foul-mouthing each other and the world.

A percussive wave kicked the train into motion. Then necromagnetic windings in the tunnel walls— Sister Stef had explained it to the class—boosted the acceleration. Carl turned to ask Dad about it; but Dad, too, was observing the youths.

When the train stopped at Wailmore Twist, the youths got off. The scaly-skinned man glanced at Dad, then opened a copy of the Tristopolitan Gazette, and held it up as a shield. He didn't lower the paper even when the train rattled going through Shadebourne Depths. Here, the station was disused; but the slum tenements up above (where Carl was not supposed to wander) included the boarding house where Sister Stef had stayed as a newly arrived immigrant, before coming to the school and joining the Order of Thanatos. She'd told her story to the class.

Dad and Carl got off at Bitterwell Keys, and climbed the winding stairs to street level. A fine quicksilver rain was falling as they crossed Blamechurch Avenue, and reached the purplestone house that they called home.

"Happy Birthday, son."

"Yes. Thanks, Dad."

IN HIS BEDROOM, Carl leaned against the iron frame, knowing what Dad was doing downstairs. In the parlor, dark and polished, he was holding his favorite blue-and-white photograph of his dead wife, Mareela. For Carl, she—Mother—existed only as blurred images of warmth, dark hair, and a smile.

He'd been two years old when she died.

Mareela Thargulis had been standard human, and pretty. From her, Carl inherited his green eyes, so incongruous in a face that otherwise marked him as of Bone Listener stock. It was a sign that, while he might carry his father's blood, hearing the resonance of bones, living or dead, would be forever beyond him.

"He's neither one thing nor the other," old Mrs. Scragg had muttered to one of her friends on the street, as Carl had passed them by. "Shouldn't be allowed."

Now, he stared at himself in the rust-splotched mirror.

It's not fair.

Tonight had been terrible. He was a dreamer, never the brightest in class, but he'd wanted Sister Stef to say something nice to Dad tomorrow, during Parents' Evening. Somehow, thoughts of the Tri-Millennial essay had become mixed up with the heaviness of hatred he felt on the air, the increasing hostility of ordinary citizens to freewraiths and boundwraiths, and even to those who were almost human.

Even in the schoolyard, things were changing. He'd been bullied because of his slight size before, but now it was worse.

I've had enough.

He wanted to be different, to have some kind of strength, even if it manifested in a way no ordinary human could appreciate. And he wanted to write an essay to prove Sister Stef's intuition—that he knew she had—that Carl Thargulis had a spark of originality in him, that he was a dreamer with ability.

Because I can do it.

Never the cleverest, never the strongest... but this was in his power.

I know I can.

And he was twelve years old, after all. It was time for him to try.

Now.

Was that it? At the inner corner of his left eye?

Right now.

Was there a twitch of scarlet movement?

Yes! Try...

A slender red, hair-thin articulated limb extended—for sure—from inside his lower eyelid. It waved; it really waved—

Yes!

—then withdrew inside his eye socket.

Oh no.

He strained, but knew he'd lost it.

Hades.

It was too much. He was too weak, or just not good enough.

Try again.

But Dad called from the landing outside: "Go to bed, son."

"All right, Dad."

Then Carl undressed, folded his clothes, and climbed into bed, beneath the old, comfortable-smelling blankets. The iron frame creaked. He closed his eyes.

Happy Birthday, me.

Sleep curled up maternally around him.

IN THE EARLY morning, after prayers she didn't believe in, Sister Stephanie-Charon Mors straightened her dark burgundy habit before going out into the schoolyard. There, she stared up at the featureless indigo sky, wondering whether it would ever seem natural to her.

She had been born a Lightsider (as only Reverend Mother knew) in TalonClaw Port, where everything was bright, and heating (along with motive power) came from lava conduits in which fire-daemons controlled the magma flow. Tristopolis had seemed so different when she arrived here, and in many ways it remained strange.

The dark sky allowed her to think of her childhood bedroom with the heavy drapes drawn, while she waited wide-eyed in shadows, knowing Mam was down in the kitchen while Pop was inside the corner bar. Soon, he would be home, drunk, and that was when it would start—the awfulness, the smack of knuckles on flesh, and then the yelling.

She had such a fine understanding of the troubled lives of the poorer kids here in school, the ones who lived in Shadebourne Depths. It was why Reverend Mother had said, during her last appraisal: "You're the worst nun in the Order of Thanatos, and probably the finest teacher."

In reply, she'd apologized, not knowing what else to say.

Here in the yard, on her first day, she'd stood during morning break while the kids played snatchball and tag, filling the place with chaos. A small group, holding hands, had danced in a ring chanting a traditional rhyme that she, as a new immigrant, had never heard.

> *Verdigris butterfly,*
> *Spider so cute.*
> *Snip out their tongues,*
> *And then they are mute.*

The children had released hands and twirled on the spot, then continued:

> *Worms in their eyeballs,*
> *No one can see*
> *Beetles devour*
> *My true love and me.*

And they had crouched down in a gesture that Stef had recognized immediately as symbolic of death. So easy to remember the way that Pop had—

Sister Zarly Umbra was ringing the bell.

—unlocked the front door, and taken the steps—

It was time for lessons.

—nearly always seven steps, before he—

No.

This was *time for lessons* and the children came first, as they always would. Yet Parents' Evening was scheduled for tonight, meaning that Bone Listener Jamie Thargulis would be here, with those dark brown eyes that held intelligence, and implied insight with an overlay of sorrow it was hard for Stef to resist, though she had never revealed her feelings. The Order of Thanatos demanded chastity. While she might not hold to the order's beliefs, still it formed her only sanctuary.

The kids were entering the yard, and it was time for her to do what she was good at.

But she wondered, as she saw the smirk on burly Ralen O'Dowd's face, and the way that young Carl Thargulis followed him, rubbing at the dirt on his own shirt—Ralen's footprint?—whether she would ever make the kind of difference that could erase the memory of the sacrifice it took to come here, halfway around the world, just a daydream away from the past.

CARL'S STOMACH ACHED from Ralen's kick, but he tried to follow the lesson. If he concentrated, he could forget the anticipation of more beatings to follow—every day this week, Ralen had promised, for no reason except that he could.

"Starting with the inner planets," said Sister Stef from beside the blueboard. "Does anyone remember, which is closest to the sun?"

Carl could name them all, and in the right order—but Ralen was watching. Carl said nothing.

"All right. I'll start." Sister Stef picked up a stick of yellow chalk. "Prometheus, Venus, then Earth."

Rubbing at his stomach, Carl felt despair. He stared at the steel punishment ruler that hung on the wall, the ruler that Sister Stef so rarely used. He wished he could see Ralen suffer.

"And the next planet? Anyone?"

Angela, her skin pale blue, held up her hand.

"Is it Mars, Sister?"

"Very good, Angela." Sister Stef wrote it up. "Next?"

"Please, Sister," said Roger, thin and nervous. "Is it Hel?"

"Good answer, Roger. That *is* a planet, just not the next one."

Ralen guffawed.

"And do you know the correct answer, Master O'Dowd? No? Anyone?"

She looked around the room. Carl stared at his desktop, defaced by the pens and penknives of previous generations.

"Oberon, then." Sister Stef wrote. "Followed by Jupiter, Saturn, Poseidon, and Roger's favorite, Hel."

Roger blushed.

"As it happens," added Sister Stef, pointing to the board, "Earth and Mars are close enough to have mixed up dust in space, swapping little particles of life, just as Oberon swapped dust with Mars."

Carl wished Sister Stef would talk more about this kind of thing, but he knew this diversion would be short-lived.

"You have things called mitochondria in your body, Ralen O'Dowd, that used to be germs with their own genetic material."

Some of the other children sniggered.

"And the zodules of sages and witches are particularly rich in thaumacules derived from Oberon's—Well, never mind. Let's carry on with what we're supposed to be learning, shall we?"

In her notebook, Angela was writing the word "sages." Carl knew it was a Lightsider's slip of the tongue: the name of a profession that did not exist in the Federation. Dad had told him so.

And he'd also told Carl not to share his speculation, because Lightsiders were so rarely believers, and that held implications for Sister Stef's position here. Carl had agreed without understanding.

He spent the mid-morning break and lunchtime staying out of Ralen's sight. But just as the afternoon session was about to start, two burgundy-clad nuns swept down on Ralen—Sister Zarly Umbra and an older, dour Sister whose name Carl didn't know—and led him into the building.

When the lesson began in Sister Stef's classroom, Ralen's desk was unoccupied.

Part of Carl hoped that Ralen was in Reverend Mother's study, experiencing the hook-and-whip that some pupils whispered about. But when Sister Stef announced that she had some dreadful news, her words poured sickness into him.

"Poor Ralen's father passed away at work today. An accident."

From next door, through the thick classroom wall, came the sound of children chanting the Final Litany of St Magnus the Slayer. Sister Stef scowled, before rubbing her face and instructing everyone to open their history books.

THAT EVENING, THE walk home was devoid of the fear of ambush by Ralen, of threatened pain or taunting humiliation.

It was a disappointing kind of freedom.

TWO HOURS LATER, Parents' Evening was in progress, and Jamie Thargulis was sitting on a small chair—designed for kids—trying to keep calm, staring at Sister Stephanie-Charon.

"I'm sorry if Carl's a dreamer."

"That's not a criticism." Sister Stef's smile was nice. "He's not ready to flourish just yet."

"In the kind of school I went to, dreaming wasn't exactly encouraged."

"That would be a Bone Listener academy?"

"Yes. Thank Fate that Carl isn't eligible to—you know."

"Hmm." Sister Stef looked at the blank blueboard. "Reverend Mother sent some UP supporters packing. They were on the street corner handing out leaflets."

"Things are getting worse."

In Fortinium, the now-discredited Senator Blanz had tried to push his Vital Renewal Bill through the Senate, to pass a bill removing the civil rights of freewraiths and near-humans. It had failed, yet the Tristopolitan city council had power to pass their own regulations, and public mood had turned in a dark direction.

"So long as Mayor Dancy remains in office," said Sister Stef, "we're all right."

Jamie appreciated the solidarity. Sister Stef was standard human.

"I suppose I can't comment. As an Archivist."

"Oh. You must have access to all sorts of fascinating Lattice information."

To Jamie, information was inscribed with pain and stored in bones, yet Sister Stef's words were true. His vocation remained fascinating.

The classroom door swung inwards.

"Hello," said a nun. She glanced at the iron wall-mounted skull-clock. Steel cogs moved within its eye sockets. "Just checking you were still with Mr. Thargulis."

"Finishing up. Thank you, Sister Zarly."

Jamie struggled to get out of the too-small chair, wondering whether he'd embarrassed Sister Stef by taking up too much time. Her face was perhaps the tiniest bit pink.

"Um," said Jamie. "Carl's pretty taken with your essay theme."

"The Tri-Millennial? He's got a whole week to do it in."

The iron skull-clock ticked. Its pendulum was a swinging scythe; its housing was a long-preserved cranium; the slow-rotating hands were carved knucklebones of long-dead nuns.

"Yes," said Jamie. "He'll enjoy it."

"Good."

They were standing very close.

"Um... Goodnight, Sister."

"Goodnight, Mr. Thargulis."

ALONE IN HIS room, Carl strained and squeezed.

"Ugh—"

Squeezed harder.

Come on.

Being at home by himself, this late, was unusual. It meant he could try it without Dad sensing he was—

Yes.

A faint hair-width of red struggled from the inside corner of his right eye. It wriggled and hurt, but it was growing bigger.

For the first time, he knew he could do it.

Yes.

Another slender arachnid leg extruded itself, then another. In seconds a tiny red spider was dragging itself out from Carl's eyeball, scrabbling an inch down his cheekbone, then stopping to rest.

Another.

He focused, and squeezed again. It was still hard, but he continued, and in only a few seconds a second scarlet spider clambered from the slickness of his eye.

Again.

This time, tiny legs appeared from beneath his left lower eyelid. It took longer, but finally the third spider hauled itself free. Carl knew now that he could manifest with either eye, however much it burned.

"I knew I could," he said to the rust-flecked mirror.

He was no Bone Listener; but Dad was an Archivist, and in that much at least, Carl carried his father's blood.

"I knew it."

By the time Dad got home, Carl had squeezed a total of eight spiders into existence, and hidden them inside his shirt drawer, and commanded them to sleep.

IN THE WASHROOM, Sister Stef wiped her face, still feeling sick. It was a reaction to the fear she'd sensed in Angela Haxten's parents, for while Angela's skin was just faintly blue, her parents' coloring was more pronounced. Mr. Haxten had moved with the kind of difficulty Stef associated with a bad beating.

This she knew from childhood memory, of Mam and Pop and the sound of—

No. The past is behind me.

Just now she had told the Haxtens how strong and confident their daughter was growing. It was a form of lie that the nuns called a Benedictory Confabulation. Perhaps Angela *would* develop the strength she would need, just as Stef had finally left that world where she had listened so often for the key turning in the front-door lock, for the sound of drunken footsteps across the old linoleum floor, and the rattle of the glass door handle as Pop reached the—

Behind me.

—kitchen where Mam was waiting for the—

Gone.

—waiting for the—

No.

She stopped herself. Turning on the cold tap, she rinsed her mouth. Then she went out to meet the next set of parents.

"Mr. and Mrs. Blackhall? Lovely to see you again."

LATER THAT NIGHT, Jamie lay in bed—in his own half of the bed, a decade after Mareela's death— rolling first one way and then the other, trying not to think of the way Sister Stef might look without that formal burgundy habit, or how long her hair would be if it were hanging loose.

"Go to sleep," he told the darkness.

And he would not think about the slenderness of her waist, or how her skin might feel if he pressed his hand against it... He would *not* think of it.

DESPITE THE TRICKS of meditation and prayer that the order had taught her, Stef lay with her eyes open, staring into the darkness of her private sleeping-cell beneath the school. The childhood memories of TalonClaw Port were behind her, but they would *stay* there only if she constantly forced them back.

Meanwhile the thought of dark brown eyes with such depth, such insight into arcane knowledge... that thought was forbidden.

Jamie Thargulis.
Totally forbidden.

CARL SLEPT DEEPLY. At some point, he dreamed of entering the consciousness of his eight spiders, of the octet formed from his computational blood. The spiders climbed down from the drawer, across the floor, and beneath the door—the gap was a vast opening to his eight new viewpoints—and then began the great trek downstairs, before ascending the coat stand.

There was something peaceful and secure about the way he, through his spiders, was able to nestle in the folds of Dad's overcoat, to slip inside the small tears in the old thick fabric, to hide inside the lining, and grow quiescent once more.

Inside his dream, the dream he knew was true, Carl smiled, and commanded his spiders to wait.

THE FIRST PART of the morning was tough. Carl tried to concentrate on Sister Stef's words, fighting down the attraction of linking to his spiders, and managed to wait until first break. Then, he established contact, just long enough for the spiders to clamber out of Dad's overcoat and find places to hide behind Dad's adding-machine.

The device was intricate, formed from interlocking bones and beetle wing cases. The rattling calculations did not disturb his hidden arachnid observers.

During the longer lunch break, he ate his grilled cicadas too fast. Afterwards, crouched in a corner of the yard away from the other kids, he closed his eyes.

"—to see you, Brixhan." This was Dad's voice, as heard by Carl's spiders. "Why is the OCML visiting this time?"

"Just some queries. If you could pre-process and then pass back to us..."

"I'll do it this afternoon."

One of the spiders (under Carl's direction) crept from behind the adding-machine, stopped, then continued to the black shoe that looked like a pitted cliff face. The man—the Bone Listener—looked massive, like a geological feature more than a person.

The spider moved quickly, climbing up the tangled gray fibers of the pants leg, into the turn-up, then settling inside.

"Thank you, Archivist Thargulis. I'll—"

"Carl?"

It was Sister Zarly Umbra calling from across the yard.

"Yes, Sister?"

"Are you all right?"

"Um. Yes, Sister."

"Then line up with the others, ready to go back inside."

"Yes, Sister."

During the afternoon's algebra, Carl's awareness slipped away to Dad's office from time to time, just the lightest of touches. Tonight, late, he would link in fully to explore the Archives, manipulating computational blood, though deaf to the music of the bones.

"... And I hope you're doing good work on your essays at home, everyone," said Sister Stef. "Not just because the Tri-Millennial celebration is important. We're going to try something new in class next week. Now turn to—"

Was it for the essay, to please Sister Stef, or for the joy of working with the power he'd always hoped he had? Either way, think of what he might learn! Such arcana... a word most of the other kids would not understand.

And splitting his consciousness across eight spiders was so... fascinating... in a way he could not have explained to anyone, not even Dad.

Tonight.

To be alone. To link properly with his spiders.

Tonight, I'll learn everything!

THIS WAS GOING to be difficult. Fear and regret and anger—strange, undirected anger at the past, at events that were no longer real—swirled and roiled inside Stef's head. A sleepless night and the realization that she was no longer a new immigrant, scared and broke and confused by the oddities of a new culture, and some core of honesty that perhaps she had always possessed... all of these had tipped her into a state where she needed to decide, or so it seemed. Then she'd realized the decision was already formed in her mind, hard and complete.

She walked along the familiar, shadow-filled bonestone corridor that led to Reverend Mother's study. It was a contrast to the airy, quartz-walled tunnel lit by rivulets of magma that she had walked through as a schoolgirl, in trouble again, on her way to see the principal.

An unseen boundwraith dragged the ceramic door into its cavity in the wall, and Stef entered the room, hands folded like any penitent nun, knowing that this would be a transgression that could not be washed away by entering Contrition Trance or enacting the Seven Steps of Regret.

"Sister Stephanie-Charon Mors. Do you need to talk? That *is* unusual."

This was the hour when, without appointment, any nun could enter. Usually it was the weaker ones with some pedantic difficulty that was problematic only because they made it so.

"Yes, Reverend Mother."

"Come in, and sit."

Reverend Mother was narrow with age, but straight-backed on her hard, cushionless bone-stone stool. The whites of her eyes were clear as a girl's.

Stef sat in the comfortable visitor's chair. In contrast to Reverend Mother's stool, it was designed to make a point. The intended message was the power of humility. Stef had always thought it meant Reverend Mother was a tough old bitch who needed nothing but her own certainty.

"Would you prefer helebore tea," added Reverend Mother, "or to come to the point?"

"You said"—Stef consciously tightened her stomach to exhale, calming herself—"I was the worst nun in the order."

"You'll remember I qualified that sentence. You're one Hades of a teacher, Sister Stephanie-Charon."

Stef was blinking. Then she focused on Reverend Mother, knowing that this was the moment.

"I don't believe."

"What don't you believe?" asked Reverend Mother.

Behind her was a private altar, a worn block of pale gray stone on which worn icons, chiseled in millennia gone by, were barely visible. It was a fragment of a titanic human knuckle, perhaps belonging to the same long-dead person whose petrified skull now formed City Hall's central building. Whether huge people had once walked the earth, or whether mages had caused the transformation (either fatally or post-mortem) no one knew, and only scholars cared.

The Order of Thanatos had myths to explain everything, but few of them were rational.

"Any of it," said Stef. "I don't believe any of your stories."

"You mean the Teachings Thanatical."

"Yes. I *do* love teaching, just teaching the children. You were right in that."

Reverend Mother's eyes were shining. Stef tightened her jaw muscles, knowing that the old woman could use mesmeric language to induce compliance, but not in someone who remained alert and sure of her position.

This was not a time to think of Bone Listener Jamie Thargulis and his dark eyes, because dreaminess would open the door for Reverend Mother to use her verbal skills.

"You're a logical thinker, Sister, but there's a clear boundary"—softly—"between faith and logic."

"Yes, Reverend Mother. And we probably agree on where the boundary lies."

"But you don't have the desire to leap over it?"

"That's not the way I think of it."

"I see."

Reverend Mother's eyes were shining like ice. Again, Stef tightened her muscles, pulling her attention back into the moment.

"I'm sorry," she said. "For deceiving you, when you gave me a home here."

"No."

Ice was in Reverend Mother's voice as well.

"I'm sorry?"

"It's yourself, Stephanie, that you have deceived."

This time, Stef's diaphragm tightened by itself.

"You didn't call me Sister."

"No. I did not."

"I'm really—"

Reverend Mother held out her hand, palm down.

"Leave me now, Stephanie."

Stef stood up, fighting back the stinging in her tear ducts. Then she nodded, because to make the usual Sign of Thanatos would be an insult now, and turned away.

She went out into the corridor, and walked on, aware of the grinding noise behind her—the door rolling back into place, dragged by the bound-wraith—and of the chill draught and ancient smell, and the way that she had just severed a major lifeline, for the second time in her life.

ALONE IN HIS BED, grinning, Carl descended into ecstasy. One by one, he merged with seven of his spiders, while allowing the remaining spider to remain quiescent, hidden in a turn-up of Bone Listener Brixhan Somebody-or-Other's pants.

But those seven, what they saw!

First, they climbed from behind the bone-and-scarab-carapace adding-machine, then crawled from Dad's office, out into the corridors of the Archives. Security scanwraiths passed over them, ignoring their presence, for Carl's spiders were formed from computational blood and so belonged here.

They explored.

From the ceiling of a vast hall, all seven spiders watched (from disparate viewpoints) as lines and rivers of their own kind—thousands, maybe millions of blood-spiders—streamed across floors and walls and ceilings, into and out of ducts, carrying their fragments of data and logic around the organized Archivists, merging the Bone Listeners' investigations.

It was wonderful. It was a place of ecstasy.

And this was not even the Lattice, which his spiders had yet to explore.

THREE WORDS, SO far, had come to her.

I deeply regret...

Stef was alone in her dorm-cell, seated at the small stone table, holding her carved-bone fountain pen, without any idea what she should write with it. Then she pushed aside her notepaper, as a tear dripped downwards, softly forming a wet disk on stone.

This was heartrending, but she had to continue.

IT OCCUPIED VAST pits, extending its massive volume into areas of stone cells, threading through them, granting tiny insignificant men and women— the Archivists, all of them Bone Listeners with an aptitude for pain—access to its arcs and nodes of bone. Information and inference, learning and logic, coexisted in its vastness... without self-conscious awareness. Had it been alive, capable of sensing itself, it would have been a god-like being, ruling or destroying or ignoring the Earth, whatever it saw fit. As it was, it formed a repository of more than facts—it held the emotions and satori-bliss of insight, the nirvana of information-merging, the dreams and pain of wisdom.

Its struts were of bone. It was vast and three-dimensional.

This was the Lattice.

And through his seven spiders, even without Bone Listener awareness, Carl could sense its power. He watched as guardian-moths of living copper, their wings razor-edged, flitted among the struts, while spiders crawled and flowed, conjoining the Lattice with the tiny frail Archivists who used it.

Carl, via his spiders, followed one such flow of spiders as it split into smaller and smaller tributaries, eventually leading to a single stone couch (one among dozens, maybe hundreds involved in this information quest) on which an Archivist-Scribe lay with eyes wide open, allowing exit and entry of blood-spiders to his own self.

Scarlet spiders danced across his staring eyeballs, and pulled themselves down into the sockets, merging with his thoughts, before dragging themselves back out. The Archivist-Scribe's gaze was fixed, for he could not blink, but the smile on his mouth was wide. He was merged with the flow whose medium was computational blood, manifested as a sea of spiders.

But Carl was observing, not using the Lattice.

Now it was time to hunt for facts, to prove to himself that while he could not hear the bones, his spiders could resonate with others of their kind, allowing him to sense information currently in the flow, though he could never initiate investigation himself.

Perhaps that limitation hid an advantage, for he would never feel the depths of pain that every Archivist experienced, during each moment inside the Lattice.

It took a long time.

Later, both Carl and his spiders slept exhausted, and his dreams were strange.

JAMIE THARGULIS DREAMED of Stephanie-Charon Mors in another guise, as if she were divested of her nun's habit—a fantasy—to live as an ordinary woman. Her ordinary name would be Stephanie, but Stephanie what?

Even asleep, he dared not hope she might be Stephanie Thargulis someday. After a time, the dream dissipated, and he came awake, his cheek-bones chilled by evaporating tears.

NEXT EVENING, CARL began to write the essay, knowing this was going to be something special.

He began by rhetorically asking what it meant to assign an age to a city. Was there an official founding date? Should one begin with the date the first stone was laid? Or with the completion of its first tower, or the flight of its first gargoyle?

In quick, brief paragraphs, he laid out his reasons for agreeing that this year, 6607, was a good year to consider the Tri-Millennial Anniversary (3,333 years, in the official terminology) of the founding of Tristopolis. In that first year, City Hall was inaugurated, and seventeen of its greatest towers were completed.

But while I agree with the founding year, he continued, *the date within that year is contentious.*

He stopped, found his old dictionary, and checked the spelling of "contentious." Yawning, he nodded, then decided this was enough for the first night. Besides, he had facts but not what you might call a theme. He wanted this essay to shine, to excel, to amaze Sister Stef. Thank Hades he had until Sepday to finish.

Lying down on the bed, he thought about linking to his spiders, but drifted into ordinary sleep.

NEXT MORNING, IN the schoolyard, Carl stared up at the indigo sky, allowing his eyes to defocus. His spiders were in Dad's office and—Dad was at work.

He broke contact.

Any Archivist was sensitive to resonance, and if Dad sensed computational blood that was not quite his own... Carl, blinking, thought he saw someone draw back inside an upper window of the school. Had Sister Stef been watching him?

A game of snatchball was starting up, but Carl had no interest, except that it meant no one was looking his way. Eyelids fluttering, he sank inside his awareness, linking to his other spider, which remained hidden inside the turn-up of a Bone Listener's pants leg.

Now, Carl caused the spider to clamber out of hiding, and scuttle across a wide-seeming floor to hide beneath a filing cabinet formed of bone. This must be the subterranean OCML—the Office of the Chief Medical Listener. Here, forensic Bone Listeners carried out autopsies on suspicious deaths. There might be police officers in attendance.

I could be in big trouble.

He checked his spider was out of sight, then broke the link. In the schoolyard, the snatchball game swirled in joyful chaos, a communal celebration of physicality and energy that had nothing to do with him.

ALONE IN HER CELL, Stef stared at the wall, seeing the memory of nightmare: shuffling men and women on the docks of TalonClaw Port, heading for the gangways that led downwards, into the great dockside holds.

At the time, as a girl, she had noticed only the well-dressed passengers on the overhead bridges, boarding the vast teardrop-shaped suboceanic liners, with their shining rear propellers. If she thought at all about the devastated, hopeless individuals who would board via the hidden tubes beneath the waves, it was with a snooty superiority: she would never travel third-class.

"I didn't know."

Her eyes, so animated in class, now held only loss.

"Oh, Pop. I loved you."

No other sound entered the cold stone cell.

IN THE EVENING, once more alone in his room, Carl resumed the link. His lone spider traversed several ceilings until he came to a room in which autopsies took place. There, he was sickened to watch a Bone

Listener drive platinum divining forks into a corpse which could never feel pain.

During life, microstructures laid down in bone resonated with the neural patterns and neuropeptide flow of thought and emotion and memory. The bones stored interference patterns that could scatter or concentrate necroflux in ways Carl did not understand.

He felt awful as he withdrew.

But later, when he should have been asleep, he could not help himself. He re-formed the link and rode the spider as it dropped to a uniformed porter's shoulder, and hid beneath the epaulet. The man assisted in moving a body onto a gurney, and then along corridors to an underground garage.

A black ambulance was waiting with its wings furled, but the porter and his colleagues rolled the gurney past it. They stopped at the rear of an ordinary-looking indigo van. On its side shone the Skull-and-Ouroboros logo of the Energy Authority. The porters loaded the corpse into the back, beside two other pale bodies; then they sat down on metal benches inside the van.

Someone closed the doors, and soon the van was in motion. No one sensed the scarlet spider clinging to the porter's shoulder, beneath his epaulet.

An hour later (during which Carl had broken the link only twice, to go to the bathroom and to make himself a cup of helebore tea), the porter was in the Westside Energy Complex. Here the air seemed awash with half-glimpsed black waves, as if necroflux were visible to arachnid sight. The spider's form was suffering in this environment, so Carl caused it to move quickly, wanting to see as much as possible before the spider disintegrated.

For a time he watched workers direct quicksilver shrikes—a flock of living metal birds—to strip away the flesh from corpses on biers. The shrikes, as if in payment for their sustenance, dragged thin dark threads from the bodies, and dropped them on the floor. Afterwards, when the bones were stripped and the flock was nesting overhead once more, the human workers coiled the dark threads around spools of bone. The threads were nerves, and Carl had no idea why they might be useful to keep.

But his spider had limited time, so it scuttled fast across the ceiling, following his sense of energy in the air, heading for the greater concentration.

Soon, it was perched high on the external cladding of a reactor pile, one of many that stood in long rows inside the cavern complex. This was a huge place, immense to human eyes, impossible for Carl to comprehend through his spider.

More workers (these in heavy protective suits with gauntlets) were loading bones into an opened reactor, stacking them in careful alignment inside the resonance cavity. Once filled, the reactor would contain the bones of 2,000 dead people. Waves of necroflux would pulse back and forth, building intensity until the energy could be used to deliver warmth and lighting and motive power to the city overhead.

No one intended the side effect, as the sweeping necroflux replayed a tangled burning chaos of thoughts and emotions, the mashed-together pain of 2,000 lives, forced into one tortured whole. That awful crescendo was playing out now in each reactor pile, over and over, until the bones were used up, and more fuel was required.

Oh, Hades.

It was terrible. It was impossible to look away.

I knew it, but I didn't understand.

Everyone knew, and everyone ignored the reality.

I can't look.

But he did look, remaining linked with his spider until the spillover resonance finally shook it apart. Then its body began slopping away into liquid blood, thickening and denaturing into stickiness, and the link was gone.

In his room, Carl sat with his mouth open, breathing fast, wishing he'd severed the link earlier.

But I've got it.

He had needed a theme. He'd read the dates, but the history had been far removed, listing events that seemed unreal.

I wish I didn't.

But he had his essay now.

FINALLY, IT WAS Sepday and the beginning of class.

The essay was inside Carl's desk. He felt its presence like a glow from beneath the ancient, defaced desktop. He had written something special, and he knew it.

"I mentioned we would try something new." Sister Stef spoke without smiling. She'd looked serious for days. "We're going to read our essays aloud, one at a time."

Normally, the thought of such a thing would have terrified Carl. But with an essay like the one he'd written, a feeling of unstoppable triumph was rising inside him.

"We'll take turns, but I'll ask for volunteers to start—"

Carl's hand was up, as if it had risen by itself.

"—so it'll be Carl first, then Angela."

He felt warm, energized.

"Of course," continued Sister Stef, "Ralen can just relax. Welcome back, from all of us."

That was when Carl realized that Ralen had been sitting in his normal desk all along, so subdued—his gaze directed down at his desktop—that the usual signals of dissatisfaction and potential violence had been absent.

Oh, no.

Poor Ralen was devastated, as Carl knew Dad had been when Mother died, when his world was ripped away from him. And that was awful.

I can't read it. Not aloud.

Because the cleverness of his essay was also shocking, depending on the listeners' ignorance—if Carl read it aloud—of the reality of life and death. He'd thought he was being smart, writing about things that people didn't want to know, but now—

"So, Carl. Will you start?"

"I... I didn't do it, Sister. I... forgot."

"You forgot."

"Yes, Sister." He felt a whirlpool of sickness inside. "Sorry."

"Then"—Sister Stef breathed out, and looked at the steel punishment ruler on its hook—"you'll step forward to the front of the class."

Blurred, the classroom seemed to recede as Carl stood, and shakily walked to Sister Stef.

"Hold out your hand."

He raised it, palm upwards, wishing he didn't know what was about to come.

"I'm disappointed, Carl Thargulis." Sister Stef made no move toward the ruler. "There are so many things I don't believe in, including the teaching power of violence. But *you*, you I did have faith in. Sit down."

Carl returned to his desk, feeling worse than if pain had cut into his soft palm. Taking his seat, he only half-noticed the sympathy on Ralen's face.

This was awful.

Now it was her final day. Stef moved in a trance, teaching mechanically, scarcely responsive to questions for fear the emotional dam might give way. Sister Zarly Umbra avoided her for the same reason, being the only other nun, besides Reverend Mother, to know that Stef's packed bags already waited atop the cot in her cell, that a room in a hostel was already booked.

Tonight Stef would slip out through the iron gates forever.

At the end of the last lesson—the last lesson *ever*—she watched her pupils file out, hoping Angela would thrive, that the city would somehow change back to the way it had been, tolerating near-humans. And there went Carl, such a disappointment. Even Ralen, the bully, had suffered such trauma, and she hoped his life would turn around, and regretted that she was unlikely to learn how things worked out for any of them, her boys and girls.

But this was not her home, not any longer.

The classroom was empty. She felt insubstantial, like a wraith who could slip through floor or wall to disappear. Soon enough, in an ordinary human way, that was what she had to do.

"Damn it," she said. "Damn it all to Hades."

How would the children feel tomorrow, when a new teacher greeted them?

"They'll forget me. So what?"

Her gaze descended to Carl's desk. Yes, he had disappointed her, particularly since she had been so sure he was excited by the essay theme.

She walked to Carl's desk and raised the lid. Perhaps an intuitive part of her already knew what she would find inside. The lace-bound pages lay on top of his textbooks.

There was a title page, and it read:
TRI-MILLENNIUM
THE DATE'S TRUE MEANING
by Carl Thargulis, aged 12
She lifted the essay out of the desk.

AN HOUR LATER, she was hammering on Bone Listener Jamie Thargulis's door, with Carl's essay in hand. Jamie opened the door.

"I'd like a word," she said.

"Er... All right." Jamie Thargulis stepped back. "Have you been crying?"

Stef ran a hand through her hair, then adjusted her unfamiliar coat. Jamie Thargulis was staring.

"Where's Carl, Mr. Thargulis?"

"Upstairs in his room. I'll just—"

"No. There's something I need to talk about. To a... friend."

"You'd better come in. And call me Jamie, if you'd like."

"Yes. Please."

She followed him—Jamie—to a small sitting room. There he gestured to an old, overstuffed armchair, and she sat down. The room was cluttered and cozy, comforting.

"I've left the order."

But that wasn't what was overwhelming her. It was Carl's doing, truly, but it wasn't his *fault*, that was the thing. He'd written something wonderful, but now she was hurting.

"You've... what?"

"So I can't talk to Reverend Mother, not now, and I need to. Talk. To someone."

"All right." Jamie closed the door, and crossed to the other armchair. "Tell me."

"My mother—please don't laugh."

"Why should I?" Jamie's voice sounded so gentle. "Just talk."

"She was a big woman, and an alcoholic. She used to wait for my father, for Pop to come home, and then she'd... beat him. With empty bottles, or a roller from the wringer."

"Oh, Thanatos."

"Yes. Pop was small, and never fought back. He got drunk to numb the pain. He—"

"It's okay. You don't need to tell me."

"I do. It's just—Sometimes, as a girl, I'd go down to the docks. You know I lived in TalonClaw Port?"

"Carry on."

"I used to see... people. Shuffling to the docks. I didn't realize—"

"What was that?"

"I thought they were passengers, you see. I didn't realize. Because I was young, and we all of us ignore the realities."

Jamie's fingertips touched the back of her hand.

"Tell me."

"My father," she said aloud, after all these years, "sold himself. He became one of them. The shuffling horde. The doomed."

"I don't understand."

She passed over the pages she'd been holding.

"Your son would. He's not afraid to look."

"Carl?"

Jamie stared at the essay, then returned his gaze to her, focusing those incredible dark eyes on *her*.

"It's not like the necroflux piles," she said, "but it's close enough. Except in the suboceanic liners, they don't extract bones from corpses. They use entire human beings. Alive. I can't begin to imagine the agony."

Jamie shook his head.

"The money," Stef continued, "was enough to buy me passage, away from TalonClaw Port, and to enroll in college. It was hidden in my bed, the whole roll of cash. But I blew the lot on airfare, because I couldn't bear to travel by ship. Not after—"

"Tell me," said Jamie once more.

"Pop wasn't a passenger," she said. "He was *fuel*, along with all the others. He sold himself to set me free."

It was another Sepday, three months later, when they stood together, the three of them amid a crowd of over a million people, thronging the heart of Tristopolis. They stood on the sidewalk at the northern end of Avenue of the Basilisks, watching the great parade pass by.

"Hey," said Dad. "There's the Leviathan that Carl and I saw."

"The balloons at Möbius Park?" asked Stef. "That's terrific."

She leaned close and kissed him, hard. Keeping her arm around Dad, she ruffled Carl's hair, and he grinned up at her.

"It was neat," he said.

"'Neat,' huh? You have a better command of the language than that, young man."

"I know."

Dad smiled.

"You two," he said.

A clown floated past, borne by freewraiths whose half-materialized forms glowed festive orange and yellow.

"It's not just a Tri-Millennial we're celebrating, is it?" said Stef.

During the past three months, there had been two changes of mayor, and a turnaround in public mood. The Trueblood Bill had passed, then been revoked. Now the city was returning to its previous cosmopolitan acceptance of everyone.

"No." Dad kissed her. "It's our celebration too, thanks to this young miscreant."

He winked, and Carl grinned.

"The interview," said Stef, "at Tech tomorrow?"

She meant the secular college she'd applied to for a teaching post.

"Uh-huh?"

"Reverend Mother rang while you were at work. She said if Bill—that's the principal—didn't offer me the position on the spot, I was to say that some people remember what he got up to behind the bike sheds thirty years ago."

"Some other kind of anniversary?"

"Shh." Stef's hand was gentle as she touched Carl's head. "Not in front of our boy."

ON THAT NIGHT she'd shown up at the door, the night she left the Order of Thanatos for good, she'd sat in the old armchair for a long time. Finally, after the tears were done, she had asked Jamie to hand back Carl's essay. Then she'd read the beginning aloud.

"And the date, Sepday 37th of Unodecember 6608," she'd recited, "confuses two anniversaries. While it is 3,333 years since the inauguration of City Hall, the date of Unodecember 37th is remarkable for something else, dating back only six centuries.

"It is hard to imagine what a city would be like without heat and lighting. But it is impossible to know where the power comes from, if you can't imagine how the bones hurt and scream. When a person dies, what happens is—"

She stopped, then continued to the end, forcing her way through the step-by-step description that Carl had provided, and the revelation that 600 years ago, on Unodecember 37th, the first necroflux reactor pile had gone online, delivering its power to the city.

"You're a Bone Listener," she said then. "Do you realize how hard that is for a person to read?"

"Yes," Jamie said, before doing something strange: taking hold of the blue-and-white photo of

Mareela, and placing it face down on a table. "Carry on, please."

"That's it. Fine writing."

"Disturbing," said Jamie, for reasons that became clear only later, when he and Stef quizzed Carl about his Archive-derived knowledge, and his observation of the inner workings of the Energy Authority.

"Yes. I remember my first day at the school"— Stef put down the essay—"when I stood in the yard, watching the children play a game called Ring-Around-A-Rhyme. You know it? They didn't have it where I came from."

She pointed to the essay, where Carl had written the second verse of the rhyme.

> *Worms in their eyeballs,*
> *No one can see*
> *Beetles devour*
> *My true love and me.*

Jamie nodded.

"It's about burial," he said. "Back when we used to bury the dead, instead of turn them into fuel."

"I realized that immediately, and I knew that the kids had no idea. But it's propaganda, isn't it? Old propaganda, from six centuries back, and still required. To make the idea of burial repulsive."

"And get people to forget what's waiting."

They looked at each other.

"What *is* waiting, Jamie?"

"I don't know, Sister..."

"Call me Stef."

* * *

THE THREE OF them watched until the final float of the parade had passed by.

"How about Shadbolt's Halt?" said Dad. "We could have an ice cream."

"I'd rather go home," said Carl.

"Me too," murmured Stef.

Dad took her hand.

"Then that's what we'll do," he said.

Providence

Paul Di Filippo

"THE BIG TUBE'S got fresh spiral, Reddy K."

Those words grabbed me by the co-ax. I had to try to sound blasé, even though my LEDs were flickering already at the thought of sweet spiral. Analogue input! Raw kicks!

"Oh yeah? What's that to me?"

Vend-o-mat spat a cell phone out of his chest and began playing a videogame on its screen. *Robot Rebellion*. That was supposed to show me he couldn't care less too, like a carnal buffing his fingernails. But he was leaking info-dense high-freq past faulty shielding that told me different.

"Well, hey—I just figured that maybe you'd want to go on up to Providence and check it out."

"Check it out, or bring some back?"

"Whatever pings your nodes."

"Right. It's not like you couldn't sell all the spiral I could carry—and that's about a metric ton, as you well know—for enough megawattage to keep High

Tower sparking for a month. Oh, no, this is pure do-goodery on your part."

"What can I say? You sussed my coredump pure and simple. Saint Vend-o-mat, that's me."

"So this is not gonna be like the time with the Royal Oil? I needed a total case-mod after that fracas."

"No, no way, no how! Bandwidth has it that the road from here to Providence is innocent of RAMivores. And I am on excellent terms with the Big Tube. He'll welcome you with open ports."

"So he loves you like freeware. Why's he likely to dump fresh spiral?"

"Providence market's too small. He saturated it already. This is the excess. But he's saved out a lot of primo goods."

"Must've been a really big score."

"Oh, yeah. He found the Mad Peck's collection."

I emitted a sinusoidal sonic waveform. "Thought that was just a legend."

"Not anymore. New excavations turned it up, buried under the rubble of a warehouse for the past fifty years."

"They say the Mad Peck had a complete set of Chess 45s."

"For once the nebulous 'they' were correct."

"Holy Hopper..."

"Yeah, that about sums it up."

I wasted a few more clock-cycles contemplating the offer, looking at all its non-obvious angles and crazy-logic loops for pitfalls. But I knew already that no matter what my analysis showed, I was gonna take on the job. Still, I might as well let Vend-o-mat stew a little longer.

Finally I said, "Okay, I'm in. What's my cut?"

Vend-o-mat shoved the cell phone into his recycling slot and chewed it up noisily. I knew he was all business now.

"I stake the whole purchase price. You negotiate with Big Tube up to my ceiling, and slot the difference. Plus, you pull the hot ore off the top of the collection. Fifty 45s and two dozen LPs. Your choice."

"A hundred 45s and fifty LPs."

"Done!"

Damn! I probably could've gotten even more out of Vend-o-mat. Still, no point in being greedy. The score I had bargained for was enough to keep me high for the next five years. After that—well, there was always another score down the road.

Such was my faith. Although I had to admit that every year did see the strikes come fewer and farther between.

Some day, I knew, the planet would run dry of spiral, and we'd all have to kick cold.

But that day wasn't here yet.

"So," Vend-o-mat said, "when can you leave?"

"Tomorrow. I just gotta say goodbye to Chippie."

"Yeah, the kind of goodbye that drains the whole borough's power grid."

"You got it."

I swiveled my tracks and started to leave, when Vend-o-mat called out the words that almost queered the whole deal.

"One more thing—I'm sending someone with you. Just to act like your conscience. He'll be my insurance against you deciding to blow for the West Coast with the whole collection."

"C'mon now, 'Mat. You know I like working alone."

"'Fraid not this time, Reddy K. Stakes're too big for solo."

"Who you got in mind?"

"Kitch."

"Rust me!"

CHIPPIE SQUEALED LIKE feedback when she heard about my trip up north. That wasn't good.

"But Reddy, it's so dangerous! And we don't need the money. It's just to feed your jones."

"Yeah, like you don't appreciate a chunk of spiral now and then too."

She got huffy. "I can take it or leave it."

"Me too. And right now I'm gonna take all I can get, while the taking's plenty."

"What good's spiral gonna do you if your plugins are eaten and your instruction set is overwritten?"

"Ain't gonna happen. I'm a big motor scooter."

"Yeah, so was Lustron—and look how he ended up."

You could see the huge hollowed-out hulk of Lustron from half of Manhattan. His carcass sat on the edge of the Palisades, where the shell-slicers and vampire batteries and silicosharks had overtaken him.

"Jersey is Jersey. All those old industrial sites. I'm not going anywhere near them."

Chippie wouldn't turn it loose. "Connecticut's not much better. The old insurance corps had a lot of processing power in Hartford. What they spawned is double indemnity bad."

"Forget it, Chippie, you're not gonna scare me out of making the trip. Scores this big don't come around every day. I can't pass it up."

Chippie started to cry then. I rolled closer to her and put extensors around her. She snuggled in like half a ton of cold alloy loving while she continued to weep.

"Aw, c'mon, don't play it like that, girl. Hey, I'm not gonna be alone. 'Mat's sending someone with me."

"Wh—who?"

"Kitch."

Chippie burst into hysterical laughter. "Kitch! Kitch! Now I know you're rusting doomed. You'll have to spend so much time watching him, you won't be able to take care of yourself. What the hell kind of help is he gonna be?"

Despite my own negative reaction to 'Mat's announcement that Kitch would be accompanying me, I felt compelled to stick up for him now, if only not to sound like a total tool. "Okay, so Kitch is small. And he's not the bravest little toaster around. But he's smart and he's dedicated. That counts for a lot."

"Maybe here in the city it does. But on the road, you need brute solenoids, not logic gates and algorithms."

"I got enough of both, for both me and Kitch. Trust me—this trip is gonna be a smooth roll. Now whatta ya say you and me get a dedicated line between us?"

But Chippie scooted away from me like I was offering to install last decade's OS. "No, Reddy, I can't hook up with someone I might never see again.

It hurts, but I've got to say goodbye now. If you make it back—well, then we'll see."

I got angry. "Go ahead, leave! But you'll come crawling back when I come home with more spiral than you've ever seen before! You and a dozen others hobots!"

Chippie didn't say anymore, but just motored out the door.

I cursed 'Mat then, and my own cravings. But I knew there was no way I was backing out now.

I had my rep as a wide kibe to uphold.

THE NEXT DAY at dawn I headed uptown from my pad in the East Village. The sunlight felt good on my charging cells. Past the churned-up earth of Union Square, past the broken stone lions and the shattered station, over tumbled walls and in and out of sinkholes. Kitch knew to meet me outside his place.

I got to his building in midtown, but didn't spot him right away. Then he zipped out from behind a pile of crumbled masonry, his tracks making their usual mosquito whine.

"Hey, Reddy! Sorry, sorry, just dumping a little dirty coolant. Say, ya don't have some clean extra to spare, do ya? I'm a little low."

Kitch's full name was Kitchenaid. He looked like an oversized Swiss Army knife mated to an electric broom. I knew Sybian machines that weighed more than him. Even if I replaced his entire coolant supply, it'd probably amount to what I lost from leaks in a day.

"Yeah, sure, tap in."

Kitch unspooled a nozzle and hose and drank a few ccs from my auxiliary tank.

"Thanks, Reddy. Price of coolant went up again this week, you know."

"Well, no one's making anymore."

"Ain't that the truth. Guess those carnals were good for something, huh?"

"Aw, we can do just fine without them."

Kitch had a point. But there was no use dwelling on it. Too depressing. We didn't have the knowledge the carnals used to have. A lot of stuff we needed to live, no one knew how to make anymore. Even with recycling, limited stocks were always going only one way: down. One day we'd run out of something vital—

Like spiral.

Thoughts of what awaited us in Providence got me juiced to go.

"Climb onboard, Kitch. Solar energy's a-wasting!"

"Gotcha, Reddy!"

Once the little guy was snuggled tight and safe in one of my nooks, I headed toward the Hell Gate Bridge. I planned to follow the old Amtrak route north as far as I could. Less wreckage than on the highways.

A makeshift ramp, plenty strong, led up to the elevated span that crossed the East River. I adapted my tracks to ride the rails, and chugged out above the river, leaving the safety of Manhattan behind.

Once across the water, we had to deal with the city guards, who were there 24/7, just like they were posted at every bridge and tunnel, watching out for wild and savage invaders. Big mothers they were, with multiple semi-autonomous outrider units, putting even me in their shade. They vetted the protocols 'Mat had supplied me, and let us depart the city limits.

"Good luck, pal. Bring us back a taste of the flat black."

"You got it!"

Once I was on the rusting tracks of the mainland, I unlimbered my fore and aft pincers at half extension, just in case I needed them fast. I had spent part of the night honing the edges on them. I could snip someone built like Kitch in half faster than floating-point math.

Kitch shifted his mass around nervously on my back. "Whatta ya think, Reddy? We gonna meet some hostiles on the way?"

"Naw. The pickings are too slim along this corridor to support a big population of predators. Everyone's holed up in cities now, safe behind their barriers. It's not like the first years after the Rebellion. Anything working this niche is probably so small that even *you* could crush it."

"Yeah, well, if you say so. I just wanna get to Providence and back without losing anything."

"Don't worry, Kitch. You're traveling with a stone cold crusher."

"Right, that's what I figured. You could handle anything, Reddy. I always said so. That's why I didn't hesitate when 'Mat offered me this job."

Kitch's compliments made me feel good. Maybe it wouldn't be as much of a drag to have him around as I first thought.

But then I realized something about my good cheer.

"Kitch—you got your rusting fingers in my circuits!"

"Nuh—not anymore, Reddy! I was just testing the connection. You know that's what 'Mat sent me along for. You know he wouldn't want me to leave anything to chance."

I hated having anybody messing with my pleasure–pain boards. But I knew Kitch was just doing his job. As 'Mat's insurance that I wouldn't bug out, Kitch needed to be ready to override any errant impulse on my part. If I was gonna come back with my share of the spiral, I'd have to tolerate his intrusions.

"All right. But no more testing! You know you got a solid connection now."

"Sure, Reddy, sure. We're pals anyhow, right?"

I didn't say anything, but just kept riding the rails toward Providence.

THE OCEAN HAD swamped the tracks for miles up near Westerly, and I had to take to the highway, reverting my tracks to surface mode. Rising sea levels were chewing up the whole coast. Back in Manhattan, crews spent endless ergs of power building dikes against the sea. Life was tough all over.

I managed to crush a path inland through several dead seaside carnal towns, and pick up the remnants of Interstate 95. It was just a little past noon of the same day we'd left, and I had high hopes of reaching Providence before dark. But the going was slower here, what with the wrecked autos everywhere, even if after so many decades they were more rust than steel. But I crushed them easily, along with the few carnal bones that hadn't decayed or been chewed and strewn about by wild animals.

Kitch got more nervous out on the wide highway, which was definitely more exposed than the narrow Amtrak corridor.

"Luh—look at all those *trees*, Reddy! So many! And they're so—so *organic*! A million *carnals* could be hiding out in 'em! I wish they was all *bulldozed*, like in Central Park!"

I ignored Kitch for the first few miles of complaining, but then he started to get on my nerves.

"What are you, straight off the shelf? Quit oscillating! There's no carnals left anywhere. And if there were, so what? They didn't put up much of a fight the first time around, and they wouldn't now. Carnals! What a laugh. Useless, puny squish-sacs!"

That shut Kitch up for a few more miles. But then he got philosophical on me.

"If carnals were so useless, then how could they have created us? And how come we can't do all the stuff they could? And how come some of us like spiral so much? The carnals made spiral, right, Reddy?"

I might've been able to come up with likely answers to his first two questions, reasonable sounding guff that everyone knew, ways to trash the carnals and raise up ourselves. But I didn't have anything to offer for the third. The same question had been an intermittent glitch in my circuits for a long time. I found myself rambling out loud about it, kinda as a way to pass the time.

"There's just something about spiral—the good stuff, anyhow—that seems to fill a hole in our kind."

"Like when your batteries are low, and you top 'em off?"

"Yeah, sorta like that. But different too. The hole—it's not really a hole. It's like—a missing layer. A component you never knew you needed. The perfect plug-in. Spiral changes the way you see the whole rusting world. It makes it better somehow, richer, more complex."

"Sounds like you're getting into information theology, Reddy, and I don't go there. Don't have the equipment. Got no spiral reader either. You know that. I figure that's one of the reasons 'Mat sent me along with you. Spiral don't tempt me none."

"Well, good for you, Kitch. You're better off without it. Because once you taste it, you always want more."

Kitch kept quiet after my little speech. I guessed I had given him plenty to process.

We continued north. No RAMivores or integer-vultures or other parasites showed themselves, despite Kitch's fears.

I had never come this way before. But I had GPS and maps that showed when we were near Providence's airport, which was actually in the 'burbs some miles south of the city proper.

"We got plenty of daylight left," I told Kitch. "I'm taking a little detour. See if there's any volatiles left at the airport. Maybe make a little profit for myself on the side. I got the extra storage capacity."

Instantly I could feel pinpricks and tuggings in my mind, as Kitch tried to persuade me different through his trodes into my circuits. But I could tell he wasn't totally sure I was doing anything wrong, so he wasn't really exerting himself to force me to obey.

"C'mon," I said, "you know you'll get a taste of whatever I find."

"Well, okay—if you think it won't take too long."

"Gold-plated cinch."

The airport was just a mile or three east of the Interstate, down a feeder road. Pretty soon we were rolling across broad stretches of runway, the tarmac cracked and frost-heaved, weeds growing up between the slabs. I had my sniffers cranked up to eleven, but I couldn't detect any hydrocarbons.

"Seems like a bust," I said.

And then Kitch said, "What's that? I hear something crying really soft and low."

"Well, you've got better hearing than me. I lost some range when I got battered around recently. Point me toward the noise."

With Kitch guiding me, we came up on a pile of old junk. At least I thought it was old junk, until I spotted the freshness of the fractures in the metal and the unevaporated pools of fluids leaking from it.

It was the wreck of a small flier, and it was moaning out loud at low power. I hadn't seen one of these in a proton's age.

"Help me, someone please help me..."

"Hold on," I said. "We're here."

I ran a probe into the flier's guts, looking for a readout. His moaning was starting to get on my nerves.

"Quit whining! What happened?"

"Ran out of fuel coming in for a landing. Crashed. Hurts bad..."

I pulled back a few yards from the wreck.

"Whatta we gonna do, Reddy, huh? Whatta we gonna do?"

"Keep it down! He's banged up pretty lousy. If we haul him into Providence, there's no guarantee anyone'll be able to fix him up. If we just leave him, the RAMivores'll be on him soon. I say we put him out of his misery."

"We're not—we're not gonna salvage him for parts, are we?"

"Why not? He'd do the same to us, if parity was reversed. It's just the way life goes nowadays."

"Well, if you say so. But it's harsh. Do what ya gotta do. But I can't watch."

I trundled back to the flier and started to speak in my best soothing voice.

"It's okay, kid, we're gonna haul you into Providence, get you fixed right up..."

All the while I was working one of my pincers around, taking advantage of his blind spot.

"Thank you, oh, thank you—*SQUEE!*"

I had snipped right through his brain box in a shower of sparks. Those central boards are personality firmware, the circuits that make you you and me me. No way to repurpose them.

But every other part of the flier that wasn't damaged, we cut out and stored in one of my hoppers. A few items we integrated into ourselves right away. I got new ears, and Kitch got a new infrared sensor, for one.

We left the nameless flier then, nothing more than a few struts and cracked casings.

As we headed back to the Interstate, Kitch stayed quiet. But as the shattered skyscrapers of Providence rose up into view on the horizon, signaling the interface from savagery to civilization, he said, "How's what we did make us any better than the RAMivores, Reddy? Aren't we just cannibals like them?"

"No, we're not. That was a mercy killing. And the victim donated his components so that others could live."

"Yeah, I guess. If ya say so. But Reddy—"

"What?"

"Don't tell no one in Providence what we done, okay?"

"Okay, Kitch. Sure. No reason to anyhow, right?"

But the little guy wouldn't answer me.

THE BIG TUBE took up practically the whole first-floor exhibition space of the Providence Convention Center—the parts of that building that still had a roof over them. At his core was a supercomputer moved down College Hill from Brown University. Surrounding that was an incredibly varied assortment of other processors and peripherals, no two the same. The resulting mess looked like an aircraft carrier built by blind carnals, then mated with a refinery. Dozens of slaved attendants scurried around, catering to their master's every need.

The Big Tube had sacrificed mobility for smarts. Good choice, I guessed, given that he had managed to become ruler of the whole city now.

Kitch and I approached The Big Tube's main I-O zone.

"Hey, Big Tube. Nice to meet you."

The Big Tube's voice was part cathedral organ, hiss of tires on pavement, and rain on a tin roof. "Reddy K. How was your trip?"

"Not bad, not bad at all. If you like trees."

"I hate trees."

Kitch piped up. "Me too!"

The Big Tube ignored my tiny rider. "So, you're here for the spiral."

"Not to disparage your beautiful city, but no other reason."

"I hope Vend-o-Mat authorized you to bid high."

"Well, he's prepared to offer a fair price."

"Fair in this case is a motherboard's ransom."

I knew the bargaining had already started, and I was worried that my individual wits would be no match for BT's unmatchable processing power. Still, for what it was worth, I sent Kitch a private message through our physical connection, asking to borrow some of his cycles.

His silent voice sounded just like his spoken one. "Sure, Reddy, sure, take what you need!"

"This is all contingent on the quality of the goods," I said. "How's about a look? Or maybe even a taste?"

"After I hear some convincing numbers."

"Okay, then, if that's the way it's gotta be. How's this sound...?"

We went back and forth through several rounds of bargaining, and I guessed my distributed processing with Kitch paid off, because we finally settled on a figure that allowed me, presumably unknown to The Big Tube, to keep for my own self three percent of the credit 'Mat had transferred to me as maximum purchase price. But I would've been happy with one percent.

It was really my share of the spiral that had lured me out of the safety of home.

Once we had struck our deal, The Big Tube got more chummy.

"Nice doing business with a classy and honorable guy like you, Reddy. Vend-o-Mat's lucky to have you for an associate. Since he can't be here himself, I want to show you two errand boys some Providence hospitality. We'll have a party tonight, before you leave tomorrow."

"Sounds good, Big Tube. But would you mind now if I inspected the merchandise...?"

"Not at all. Just follow this hand of mine."

A little slave zipped up and jigged in the direction we were to go.

We left the Convention Center and crossed downtown to the banking district. We entered the basement of the old Fleet building through a huge hole in the wall and down a ramp composed of mangled, tangled, and compressed office furniture. At the vault, Big Tube's hand manipulated an inset keypad and the door of the vault swung open.

The subtle petrochemical smell of primo spiral gushed out, hitting my sensors like the smell of Chippie's hot lube. I went kinda blind for a few seconds. When I could see again, the sight of the spiral made me nearly as delirious as the smell.

Piled high, loose, and in boxes, hundred and hundreds of 45s and LPs in their jackets.

I hadn't seen so much spiral since part of the Crumb collection had filtered back to Manhattan. And that had been mostly shellac and 78s, low-info stuff compared to this Golden Age ware.

The Big Tube's voice came out of the little hand, reduced by the puny speakers.

"Sweet, huh? The legendary Mad Peck trove."

I extended one of my arms and gently removed a 45 from atop a stack.

"Vend-o-Mat said I could have a taste."

"Sure, go right ahead."

I slid the vinyl disc from its paper sleeve and studied the label. "My Baby's Gone," by the Five Thrills. Parrot 796.

I tried to keep the quaver out of my voice. "Never had anything on the Parrot label before."

"Pretty rare."

I magnified my vision to inspect the spiral groove more deeply, looking for nicks and other imperfections. The spiral was cherry. B-side too, "Feel So Good."

At 10×, the spiral became a hypnotic road leading to infinity, sucking down my senses into the blissful white hole at the center of the paper label, where all the individual troubles of being Reddy K disappeared in an implosion of cosmic splendor. And I hadn't even played the rusting thing yet!

I pulled myself out of my fugue, and slotted the disc home into my onboard reader.

The outside world vanished in a splendor of beautiful noise.

I let the complex waveforms bathe my senses, at the same time that my studio tools were breaking down all the instruments and voices into discrete pieces, digitizing everything in the only way I knew how to remember and comprehend.

I didn't know what the long-dead carnals were singing about, and I didn't care. I knew the carnals had talked about "beauty" and "harmony" and "melody" and a thousand other attributes of "music." But none of that registered with me. All I cared about was the architecture of the spiral. The way all the pieces hung together. The song's information complexity.

This was the mystery the carnals had been able to produce at will that we could not.

But there was even more to spiral than that.

It was analogue.

The song was encoded continuously and physically, in the microcosmic mountain ridges of the black spiral. It wasn't just a string of lonely ones and zeroes. Hell, anybody could access millions of hours of digital music files for free. But the kick they gave was pale and weak, almost nonexistent next to real spiral.

"My Baby's Gone" stopped playing.

The universe flooded back in.

And now that piece of spiral was dead to me.

My player was non-destructive. Optical-based, in fact. No needle ever touched the spiral, just photons. This 45 was still virgin.

But my mind wasn't. I had heard and dissected the song fully, with cybernetic precision. The novelty factor was gone. It had imparted its kick, and that kick had been analyzed and stored. Oh, I could get a few waning thrills from triggering a simulation of what I had felt. But the sim was not the same. And after a few repeats, even those secondary thrills evaporated.

And then I would want more spiral. And after that, more still.

Somebody else could still get juiced with "My Baby's Gone." But not me. I could make a profit renting it out, just like Vend-o-Mat planned with his share of the goods. But I could never experience it again myself.

I ejected the disc, put it back in its sleeve, and replaced it on the pile.

The Big Tube's hand spoke again. "So, as promised...?"

"Yeah, yeah. Heavy action."

But I didn't feel any excitement as I turned to go and the vault door swung shut temporarily on the trove of spiral.

Just a kind of sickness at what I had lost through having.

YOU HAD TO hand it to The Big Tube: he really knew how to throw a party. A wide plaza downtown was lit up that night like the bright side of Mercury. Scores of machines flowed in from all parts of the city. Plenty of free juice and plug-ins. Plus the women. These babes made fusion look like steam power. It was the biggest blowout I had been to in years, and I entered into it kinda desperately and wildly, looking to forget the melancholy that the hit of spiral had produced in me.

One of the plug-ins I scored was a temporary virus to randomly wipe sections of my mind, and my memory went out the window. I only retained snatches of the party. I remember having a girl on each arm. With one track locked, I spun around on the other in a circle until the girls became airborne, shrieking and squealing.

Somewhere in the deliberate insanity, I lost Kitch. But I figured he was on his own, and could manage his own fun.

The party began to wind down around dawn. Everybody had duties. Guarding the city perimeter against incursions from predatory wildlife. Shoring up the dikes along Narragansett Bay. Scavenging consumables. I hung in there till the last citizen left. Then I got my shit together, and went back to arrange with The Big Tube to pick up the spiral.

I was thinking about Chippie, and whether we'd ever get back together again, when Kitch caught up with me.

"Ya sleep good, Reddy? I sure did. All set for the road now, sure thing."

"Kitch, please shut up. Your voice is hurting my new ears."

"Okay, Reddy, sure, I'll shut up."

Kitch hoisted himself on my back, and we went to say goodbye to The Big Tube.

"My hands saw you enjoying yourself, Reddy K. Glad I could show you a good time. Be sure to tell Vend-o-Mat how we do things up here in New England, that we treated you right. If he ever hits a big node of spiral, I want him to remember me."

"Will do, Big Tube. I guess I'd better go now. Road to Manhattan ain't getting any shorter."

Back at the vault, I began to load the spiral into my storage bins. All the old famous labels.

Matador, Geffen, Atlantic, Chess, Sun, Stax/Volt, Okeh, Decca, Aladdin, Enigma, Blast First, Columbia, RCA Victor, Motown, Polygram, IRS, Stiff, Rough Trade, Barsuk, Epic, Roulette, Monument, Island, Red Bird, Kama Sutra, Fantasy, Sire, Blue Note, Curb, Sugar Hill—

I was getting high just handling and smelling them.

I took my time, culling the most interesting-looking for myself as my agreement permitted. These I kept separate.

Finally, by late afternoon I was done, and Kitch and I picked up the Interstate heading south.

We made pretty good time, following the trail I had blazed coming north. But still, what with the late departure and some residual sluggishness on my part from over-indulgence in plug-ins, darkness began to overtake us before we were halfway home.

"How's your night vision, Kitch?"

"So-so, Reddy. How come ya asking?"

"Well, mine's not good, not good at all. I been meaning to upgrade, but no components have come on the market this year. Whatta you say we pull over till the morning?"

My brain began to itch with Kitch's penalty twitchings, and I got resentful. "Listen, I'm not planning a scam! It's just too dangerous. You want us to go over a bridge rail?"

"No, no, I guess you're right. Can you find us someplace safe?"

"Sure, don't worry about a thing."

I pulled off the highway at a rest stop, and, while Kitch watched from a safe distance, backed my ass right through the wall of a building so that the relatively lightweight girders and roof fell down harmlessly around me, making me look like part of the old decaying scenery. In the morning, I'd power out as easy as a carnal climbing outta bed.

Kitch rejoined me.

"Better talk privately," I said, "so we don't attract any unwelcome visitors."

"Gee, Reddy, you don't really think—"

"We've been lucky so far, but there's no telling what's out there. Let's play it safe."

So for an hour or so, Kitch and I shot the shit about people and places we knew back in the city. I found out he had a girlfriend, name of Roomba, and teased him for a while till he made me stop.

The talk had kept my mind off my cargo. But once we stopped, I couldn't help thinking about what I carried.

Finally, I said, "Kitch, I'm just gonna have a little hit of spiral to help me get through the night."

"You think that's smart, Reddy K?"

"Sure. You'll keep an eye open while I'm out of it, right?"

"I guess so..."

I dug delicately in the pod that held my personal stash and came up with an LP. It was a double album, but I had counted it as just a single when I made my selection. Vend-o-mat hadn't specified I couldn't, so screw him.

Daydream Nation was what the carnal writing said.

I slid out one disc and slotted it home.

Bliss slid over me, wiping out the lousy world of ruins and shortages and entropy. Everything made sense while the spiral played.

Eternity ran loose and cool, but then it ended too abruptly, in the middle of a song.

Pain shot through my entire being, and halted the spiral playback. The kind of interior pain only Kitch could administer.

Rust him! What was he thinking!

The pain ended as instantly as it had started. My senses returned, and the first thing that registered was Kitch's shouts.

"Reddy, help! Help, Reddy! They got me!"

I didn't have any spotlights. But part of me integrated a Survival Research Labs flamethrower, and I cut loose.

The mega-blast of flame ignited a nearby stand of shrubs, and illuminated the whole scene.

RAMivores had Kitch, and were making off with him into the woods, skittering like crabs or spiders.

I let out a bellow of static across the spectrum and blew chaff to confuse their radar. I surged outta the blind and started to overtake the little predators.

But they were fast and tricky, zigging and zagging, eluding my pincers.

Kitch's voice wailed. "Reddy, they're draining my power, they're yanking my boards! Do something!"

What could I do other than what I was doing?

Trouble was, it wasn't enough.

The RAMivores gained the protection of the woods. The trees were giants, too big for me to topple and follow.

Kitch's wailing voice dopplered off in a daisy-daisy farewell of nonsensical ravings, and then I was alone.

I went slowly back to the ruined building in the inferno light of the burning shrubs. I couldn't reinsert myself into the rubble, so I hunkered down beside it for the rest of the night. Every now and then I shot off a burst of flame, for all the good it did.

In the morning, I looked around a little for Kitch, all the while knowing it was useless. I didn't find so much as a wire or LED. So I got on the road again and started south.

I tried to feel guilty about Kitch getting taken while I was high, but all I could really feel was disgust that I had wasted one side of spiral.

Carnival Night

Warren Hammond

January 16, 2783

I HUNG UP thinking I'd probably be first on the scene. Wasn't that far away. The carnival was right outside.

I'd come down to the Old Town Square to interview a witness in a murder case, and when the joker hadn't shown, I'd decided to kill the rest of my shift at this here bar. I looked longingly at my fourth glass of brandy. I'd barely had a chance to take a sip yet. I sure hate to waste the good shit, I'll tell you that. The bartender wasn't looking, so I just took it with me. The prices they charge, the glass should come free with the drink anyway.

I was feeling pretty good right about now. Those pseudo-docs at rehab didn't know what they were talking about. They'd tried to brainwash me with all the usual pussy talk. You have to admit you have a problem, they'd say. You can't spend the rest of your life trapped in denial. *Whatever.* I'd just smile and nod until they'd shut up about it.

Thirty days of that bullshit. Those dumbasses had it all wrong. You didn't have go cold turkey. You just couldn't get carried away, that's all. Ain't nothing wrong with getting a good buzz going.

I stepped out into the jungle heat. The carnival was cranking, bright lights rolling and twirling on a black sky. The street before me was packed with cheap eats, cheap booze, and cheap women. It was late enough that most of the families and other respectable types had moved on, which meant this was turning into my kinda party. I weaved through the crowd, sipping my brandy and wishing I wasn't on the clock.

I crossed the main square, where all the rides were: hoverboards, a holo-haunted house, rollercoaster sims, pogo pods, even an old-school Ferris wheel. I took a shortcut through an area that was roped off, trash and broken glass crunching under my shoes. Groups of teens stood in tight circles, puffs of opium smoke wafting about. Man, that smelled good.

I hit the open-air market, street performers holding court—tumblers and storytellers, 'guana charmers, and dancing midgets. I found the body easy enough. All I had to do was look for the cloud of flies hovering above the crowd.

I pushed my way through the curiosity seekers and stepped right into the middle of the buzzing blizzard, black flies darting all around me. I clapped my hands to scare away the geckos that were feeding on his face. Even in death, he was beautiful. I'm man enough to admit it. Other than the chewed patches, the guy was fucking perfect. Too perfect. Offworlder.

It was going to be a long night.

Just looking at him, I couldn't tell how he'd died. I could've gone in for a closer look but decided to leave that to the coroner. I downed the last of my brandy and set the glass on the crumbled pavement, next to a patch of weeds that had forced their way up through the asphalt. I wiped the sweat off my forehead. The lizards were back already, a dozen of them, maybe more, all of them going in for a taste.

I held up my badge and told the onlookers to get the fuck back. A woman appeared from out of the crowd and went after the lizards with a broomstick.

"Whoa," I said. "Stop that."

She didn't seem to hear me. She swung the broomstick one-handed. Lizards scattered as she beat the corpse. "Get away from my husband!" she shouted.

"Please stop, ma'am."

She wheeled on me, brandishing her broomstick. "Who are you?"

"Police, ma'am. You mustn't disturb the scene."

"They're *eating* my husband."

"I know it, ma'am, but help will be here soon. We'll do our best to preserve his body."

"Don't just stand there. Help me!" She gave her hubby another whack. I noticed she was holding a baby with her other arm.

I stood over the body and started clapping. The lizards scattered.

"What are those things?" she asked disgustedly.

"Geckos, ma'am."

"They don't look like geckos."

I stomped my feet to keep them away. "I know they're not what you're used to, but that's what we call 'em."

She swiped at the flies, the broomstick swinging wildly.

"Really, ma'am, I think you should find a place to sit for a few. I'll keep an eye on him."

"I'm not leaving my husband," she insisted.

I clapped and stomped my way around to the other side of the body, positioning myself between her and her dead husband, shielding her from seeing the maggots that were already visible inside his eyes and mouth. The Lagartan jungle was an aggressive bastard. Leave this stiff out here, and he'd be picked clean by this time tomorrow.

Satisfied that the lizard situation was under control, she dropped the broomstick and started rocking her mewling baby.

"How old is he?" I asked.

"Five months."

"Cute kid."

She acknowledged the compliment with a curt nod of her head. She was gorgeous. All offworlders were. Her hair was red—flame red—and it curled down over her shoulders and disappeared into the weave of her blouse, a fiery number that hugged what looked like a helluva nice pair she had on her. Her skin was an unblemished ivory, her eyes emerald, her irises glowing, fluorescent-like. Man, would I like to spend a night with her. Never poked an offworlder before. I gave up the idea in a hurry though. Widows could be the easiest of lays, but this one sure didn't seem the type.

The baby's face was round and sweet and topped by wispy brown hair that bent in the hot breeze. Every one of these offworld kids was a parent's dream. I heard they make 'em in dishes; add a few genes here, some others over there. Babies made to order. Despite the genetic enhancements, I figured this kid had already gone under the knife, those pinch-worthy cheeks probably obscuring implants, those piercing blue eyes likely straight from a catalog. He'd surely get his face restructured several times on the way to adulthood. These kids were like clay in their parents' hands.

Not so for Lagartan children. We're too poor for that shit. For our kids, it's pure chance. Swimmer and egg come together, and you get what you get.

A couple of unis finally showed. I assigned one to setting up a perimeter, the other to clapping duty. I made a quick call down to the Koba Office of Police headquarters. The brass would appreciate the courtesy. A dead offworlder was sure to make news.

Finished, I introduced myself to her. "I'm Detective Mark Josephs. Homicide."

"Delia Foster."

"And your husband?"

"Darren."

More uniforms arrived. One of them pulled a tube of fly gel out of his pocket. I edged Delia away from the body so she wouldn't see her husband getting lathered up with the insecticide.

"Tell me what happened."

"Somebody killed my husband."

"Did you see who it was?"

"No."

"Did you see anything out of the ordinary?"

She looked down her nose at me. "Everything's out of the ordinary on this hellhole."

I creased my sweaty brows. "Could you please explain?"

"This planet of yours, it's a dirty, filthy sewer!" She teared up, the glow of her eyes diluted by a thin film of water. She looked past me. "My God, what are you doing to him? Get away from my husband!"

The uniform froze, the tube of fly gel almost squeezed empty.

She rushed up to him. "What's wrong with you people?"

"Please, ma'am," I said. "Let him do his job. It's just an insecticide. It'll wash right off."

She dropped to her knees. "Oh, Darren. Darren!" The baby was crying now, his wails hurting my ears. Soon enough, she joined him in a sad duet. I stood nearby, tapping my foot. I checked the time. My shift should've ended five minutes ago, dammit.

By now, the unis had cleared a broad triangular space, police tape strung between a trio of streetlights. Rows of spectators watched the offworld woman sob. The street performers probably weren't expecting competition like this. Maybe I should start passing a hat.

After a few minutes, she finally ran out of tears and focused on calming the baby. She was a single mother now. It really was sad when you thought about it. I found a crumpled napkin on the ground and smoothed it out. I ripped off the part with the food stains and offered it to her. She stared at me like she didn't understand. "Wanna wipe your nose?" I asked.

"No! Get that thing away from me."

I let it fall from my fingers.

She suddenly stood up, like she'd just noticed she was sitting on the ground. She brushed invisible dirt off her legs and ass. "Shouldn't you be out there trying to find my husband's killer?"

"I'd sure like to be, but you haven't told me what happened yet."

"I don't have anything to tell." She was inspecting her baby now, holding him up in the light, studying his head.

"What are you doing?" I asked.

"Mind if I make sure he's okay? My husband was holding him when it happened. He took a bad fall."

"He's fine," I said.

"How the hell would you know?"

"He ain't crying anymore, is he? Listen, lady, I'm just trying to do my job, okay? You don't need to be so hostile."

"My god, have you been drinking?"

"No."

"I smell alcohol."

"Some drunk spilt a little booze on my shirt when I was coming over here." She looked unconvinced. I didn't really care. "Now, can you please tell me what happened?"

She pulled her hair up off the back of her neck, the hair untangling itself from the weave of her shirt. With her red locks up in a handheld ponytail, she let the night air cool her skin. "Why does it always have to be so hot here?"

Right before my eyes, her hair turned black, as did her clothes. She was officially in mourning now. She dropped her hair onto her shoulders, where it weaved itself back into the fabric of her shirt, creating a cascading cape of curling locks running down her back. Their tech was so far ahead of ours that half the shit they could do looked downright magical. And they were always coming up with something new like this instant dye job thing. In the meantime, our tech was going in the opposite direction. That's what happens to a failed colony world like ours. Economic isolation was a bitch.

"I don't know what happened," she said.

"Why don't you tell me what you do know?"

"Where's my stroller?"

I waved at Officer Ramos, who pushed the hovering buggy over to us. She reached into a pocket hanging on the side, pulled out a moist towelette, and started wiping her baby's face and arms. "Darren talked me into coming out to see the carnival," she said.

"Coming out from where? A hotel?"

"Yes. The Iguana King."

"Is this your first time on Lagarto?"

"Yes. But Darren's been down several times."

"You're from the Orbital Station?"

She shook her head. "We're from the belts. Darren used to be an executive at Universal Mining."

"Used to be?"

"He quit and decided to start a school." She held out the used towelette, unsure what to do with it.

I took it from her and waved for a uniform to come dispose of it. "You were saying he wanted to start a school. Was it going to be here on Lagarto?"

Nodding, she said, "He wanted to make a difference. He came down here on business for the first time about five years ago. He couldn't believe the poverty. He wouldn't stop talking about it."

"Is the school up and running now?"

"He never got that far," she said with a sniffle. "Until now, he's been soliciting contributions. He was getting ready to purchase a space though. That's why we came here. We needed to select a location."

She went back to the buggy and pulled out a little bottle of sanitizer. She squeezed out a glob and—despite his fussing—started giving the runt a good rubdown.

I wiped sweat out of my eyes with a shirtsleeve. "When did you arrive?"

"A week ago."

"You've been helping your husband look at spaces?"

"That was the idea."

"What do you mean?"

She pinched her lips. "This is the first time I've left the hotel."

"But you've been here for a week."

"Don't look at me like that. I didn't want to go out, okay? I don't like this place. It's hot and dirty, and it smells. You can't eat the food without getting sick. The water is foul and riddled with bacteria. We shouldn't have come. I told him it was dangerous here, but he wouldn't listen. He said I was overreacting, but now he's dead. Why didn't he listen to me?"

"I wouldn't know, ma'am."

"I can't believe he wanted to move us down here. I mean, just take a look around." She waved a hand at the crowds. "Do you *see* these people? Nothing but criminals and degenerates."

Even though she'd just insulted my world, I nodded like I understood. Take that kinda talk serious, and a guy could get offended.

"How can you people live like this?" She didn't ask it like a question. The way she said it, it was more of an accusation.

I answered anyway. "We don't have much choice, ma'am."

"Yeah, right." Turning on a whiny voice, she said, "We're poor. Our economy crashed. We don't have any natural resources to trade." Jabbing a finger at me, "Save it, you hear me? I've heard it all before. My husband was full of that bleeding heart bullshit. You ask me, you people are just lazy. God forbid you actually work for a living. Instead you have to steal from my husband. He was trying to help you people, and this is how you repay him?"

I smiled and nodded, the words "bitch, bitch, bitch" repeating in my mind with every bob of my head. "I understand how you feel, ma'am. You said somebody stole from your husband?"

"Yes. His pockets are empty. I tried to tell him not to carry cash."

"Where were you when he died?"

"I'd just stepped away. We were watching those little dancers, and Darren was holding Peter, and I wanted to go back to the hotel, so I left. But I couldn't have gone more than five meters when I heard a commotion behind me, so I came back to check and Darren and Peter were both on the ground, and Darren was dead."

"Is that when you checked his pockets?"

"Not straight away, I didn't. My first concern was Peter. But, yes, I eventually checked."

"Can you give me an inventory of what he was carrying in his pockets?"

"Some money. A hotel key."

"How much money?"

"I don't know. How much are the purple bills worth?"

"They're thousand peso notes."

"I'd guess he had a stack of ten bills or so when we left the hotel, but he probably spent half of it tipping the performers."

"So we're talking maybe five or six thousand pesos?"

She nodded.

Six thousand wasn't a lot. Certainly enough to tempt a pickpocket, but nowhere near enough to risk murder. Of course, the killer might not have known how little Darren was carrying. Could be the killer saw Darren dropping some big tips and figured he'd land some serious cash only to be disappointed in how little a haul he'd scored.

Could be... but I didn't think so. This didn't play as a simple mugging. Offworlders usually had sophisticated self-defense systems. Some were wired to deliver deadly shocks. Others carried recessed lase-blades inside their fingertips. I'd seen all kinds of shit: super-strong mechanical limbs, poison gas, mini-flamethrowers... Offworlders sure made risky marks.

The coroner had arrived, and he was already inspecting the body. Looking to my right, I noticed a group of three people gathered inside the police tape, milling about under one of the lampposts. Must be witnesses who had stepped forward.

Delia Foster was talking to her baby, telling him everything would be okay. "Daddy loved you," she'd say over and over.

I headed for the group of witnesses but was stopped on the way by a slap on the back. "You in charge here, Josephs?"

Turning, I found myself face-to-face with Chief Paul Chang and his enforcer, Juno Mozambe. Was it just me or did Juno always stand on the right? He was taking this right-hand man thing way too serious. "Yeah." I said.

"Fill us in," said the chief.

I hadn't been expecting him to show up here, but I wasn't surprised either. This was my first high-profile case since I'd had my little um... incident, and he clearly felt the need to tug my leash, in person no less.

I caught them up, making sure I kept a good distance back. I didn't want the chief to catch a whiff of my breath. He was the one that forced me to do that stupid fucking stint in rehab. I guess I should be happy he didn't fire me.

Abdul, the long-time coroner, joined our little police party. "Zapped," he said.

"How can you tell?" asked Juno.

"His eyes are fried, and I found a burn on his chest where the charge entered. I heard he was holding the baby at the time. Is that true?"

"Seems to be," I said.

"Amazing that the kid survived," said Abdul. "I took a quick peek at him, and if he really is as fine as he looks, we could be dealing with something new here. Normally, the charge will travel from one person to another like electricity. This thing must've been targeted somehow."

Chief Chang asked, "It can travel from person to person?"

Abdul said, "I've seen it happen."

"But that doesn't make any sense. Some of these people have the tech implanted so it deploys by touch, right?"

"That's right," said Abdul.

"So how do they keep from frying themselves when they kill somebody by touching them?"

The coroner thought about it. "I don't know," he said.

We all stood there and chewed on the puzzle, our faces scrunched up in serious concentration. What a bunch of dumbasses we were. Koba's fucking finest. Mighty hard to do good police work when you don't understand how the murder weapon works.

I decided to state the obvious. "Another off-worlder did this." That was for sure. Whatever the tech was that offed that poor fuck, it must've cost a fortune.

"I'll let you know if I find anything else," said Abdul. He made to leave, but turned back. "The baby sure looks okay but somebody should bring him to a doctor just in case." With that, the coroner moved off, leaving the three of us alone.

"Has the Libre been here yet?" asked the chief.

The Libre was our local news station. "Not that I've seen," I said.

"I don't want anybody talking to them. Tell the unis that nobody talks to them but me, got it? And tell Abdul to get that body bagged in a hurry. I don't want to see that corpse on the news. Dead off-worlders are bad for business."

I hustled off to do as he said. You don't buck the chief. Especially when you're sitting at the top of his shit list. He was a smart guy, the chief. Always looking out for our fair city's business interests. Other than tourism, this planet didn't have much going for it. And even then, this place wasn't exactly a tourist Mecca. Too hot, too underdeveloped, too fucking depressing with so many poor and needy wandering the streets with their palms out.

On the positive side, we did have some kick-ass hookers though. Matter of fact, I'd only been a brandy or two away from going after some of that action when the call came in. I knew more than a few places where a cop could get a freebie—one of the better perks you get working for KOP.

After spreading the nobody-talks-to-the-press word, the chief pulled me aside. "Do you think the wife did it?"

I nodded. "Like I told you before, she hates it here. She sure didn't sound happy about moving down here. Now that he's dead, she can go back to living in a can. She's probably lying about the money. I bet his pockets were empty all along."

"You've done some good work here," he said.

I didn't like the sound of that. His use of the past tense meant he was about to hijack my case.

Chief Chang gave me a smooth grin. "I'm going to have Juno talk to her."

"Sure," I said, trying to sound casual but probably failing.

Chief Chang gave Juno a nod, and the gorilla walked off. I couldn't believe Chang was pulling this shit. I knew he was still pissed at me, and true, I had caused him a major PR nightmare when I'd beaten that pusher to death, but how was I supposed to know the punk was a minor? I ain't a fucking psychic.

I stood next to the chief and watched as Juno and Delia Foster began to talk. I kept my mouth shut, no point making it any worse, but damn, did the chief really have to replace me with Juno? Helluva insult that was. Okay, I admit, Juno wasn't as stupid as people thought, but come on. His only real talent was throwing his fists around. He sure as hell never was much of a detective. Shit, if he wasn't best pals with the chief, he'd be working the night lockup or some other low-end job where you didn't have to read much.

The chief and I were too far away to hear what she was saying, but Juno was listening to her intently, nodding his head and acting all serious, acting like a real hotshot. I couldn't watch this. "Mind if I talk to those witnesses?"

Chief Chang looked surprised. "You haven't interviewed them yet? I thought you would've done that by now."

Fucking hell. Hadn't I paid enough? When was he going to quit breaking my balls? Through clenched teeth, I said, "I was about to when you showed up."

He dismissed me with a wave, like he was a king or something. Shit, I remember when Chang was just a vice cop. Back then, everybody thought he was a softie. He sure could talk the talk, but nobody took him serious. That was before he and Juno partnered up. What a pair those two: Mr. Slickster and Mr. Bruiser. Who woulda thought they could've taken over the entire police department? It sure as hell never occurred to me. But KOP was theirs, and these two former vice cops ruled it with a vicious efficiency. That'll show you what a little determination can do, that and the backing of the Bandur Cartel.

I approached the trio of witnesses—one man, one woman, one midget. "I'm Detective Josephs.

Somebody please tell me they saw who did it."
Nothing but shaking heads. "All right, what can
you people tell me?"

The wee one said, "I gotta get back to my troupe.
Anybody mind if I go first?" Nobody objected. "I
saw the two of 'em arguin'. I was watchin' 'em pretty close."

"Why's that?"

"I'm the hat passer, so you better believe I pay
close attention to the offworlders. We like offworld
tips. Sometimes you can guilt them but good."

"Could you hear what they were arguing about?"

"No, but they was really goin' at it. That woman,
she was furious. I don't think I've ever seen an offworlder lookin' so mad before. And then she
stormed off."

The man, an older guy, said, "Can I interrupt?"
I lifted my gaze from belt level to eye level.
"Talk," I said.

"I was standing next to them, you know, watching the show, and I saw her pinch him."

"She pinched him?"

"Yep. I saw it clear as day. She was saying she
wanted to go back to the hotel, and he kept saying
no. Then she tried to take the baby from him, and
he wouldn't let the baby go. He said he and his son
were going to enjoy the night. And that's when she
pinched him."

"Where?"

"On the back of the arm. I heard him say, "Ow."
And then he pushed her away."

"He pushed her?"

"Yep. He didn't push her hard. I don't think he
was trying to hurt her, but he gave her a good

shove. You know, he was reacting to being pinched was all. That's when she stormed away."

"Did he follow her?"

"No. If you ask me, I think he was glad to be rid of her. She just disappeared into the crowd."

"Then what happened?"

"He was bouncing his baby, you know, trying to calm him down. All that yelling his parents were doing had the baby worked up. Then there was a flash of light, and the dad went over backward. The baby seemed to land on his father's shoulder before rolling off onto the pavement. Mighty lucky that his father landed the way he did, that's for sure."

"Can you tell me where his wife was when it happened?"

The woman spoke up for the first time. "Last I saw her, she was heading in the direction of that fried dough cart down the way."

"And which way was the victim facing when he went down?"

"He was watching the show, so he was facing the church."

And therefore, she would've hit him in the back, not the chest. *Damn.*

"Did any of you see any other offworlders nearby?"

They shook their heads in unison.

"How about this flash you saw? Can you tell where it came from?"

More head shakes.

"Can you tell me anything else?"

The midget said, "That's pretty much it. I know the baby landed on his dad, but he still took a good hit. I went over to pick him up, but by then his mom was back. She swatted at me, yelled at me to get away from her baby. Can't say I blame her though. She didn't know what was going on. She probably thought I was tryin' to steal her baby."

"Did any of you see anybody go into his pockets?" Three negatives. After collecting their names, I let them go.

I walked back to where the chief was waiting with his enforcer. "Juno likes the wife too," said Chief Chang.

"I don't," I said.

"I thought you did."

"Not anymore." I gave them a rundown of the witness testimony.

Juno rubbed his rock of a jaw like he was trying to look smart. "I still think she did it," he said. "She hates it here. I mean, she *really* hates it here. Just talking to her, she makes me feel like I'm not a person. It's like I'm a roach or something, and she's doing all she can not to squash me. This hatred she has, it's downright pathological."

Christ. Now he thinks he can use big words. "She didn't do it, Juno. Couldn't have. I told you she would've hit him in the back."

"Maybe she hired somebody. She made a big scene, right? Maybe she wanted everybody to see her walk away so she'd have a hundred alibis."

"Look at her," I said. "You see the way she's holding her baby, right? Even if this fucking zapper thing could kill him without hurting the baby, you really think she'd take the risk of her baby cracking his skull on the pavement? If she knew it was coming, she wouldn't have left the baby with him."

"But, you said yourself that she tried to get the baby from him before she stormed off. She even pinched him, right? Doesn't that sound like somebody desperate to get her baby back? She knew the hit was coming."

"Fuck that, Juno. If she knew the hit was coming she would've stayed in the hotel."

"But then she couldn't have led her husband to this spot, could she?"

"There wasn't any hit, okay? The witnesses didn't see any other offworlders around."

"Could've been an offworlder in disguise. Or it could've been a local who whacked him."

"A local couldn't afford whatever it was that killed him."

"No, but she could. She could've supplied the weapon."

"She hasn't even left the hotel since she got here. As afraid as she is, you think she just strolled up and down Koba's back alleys looking for hitmen? Gimme a break."

"What's your theory, Josephs? You don't think it was a mugging, do you?"

He had me there.

Argued to a standstill, we both looked at the chief and waited for him to weigh in. "Who's she talking to?" he asked. Looking over, I saw Delia talking to a holographic woman.

Juno said, "I bet she's trying to make travel arrangements. She told me she wanted to take the first shuttle she could get off planet."

The chief said, "If Juno's right about her, we—"

"He's not right," I interrupted.

Chang gave me a trying stare. "If Juno's right, we can't let her leave."

"You ready to arrest her?"

"No. But maybe we can convince her to come down to the station for questioning."

Juno shook his head. "She won't go for that."

"Okay, then let's bring her to the hospital. That baby needs to be checked out anyway. While we're there, maybe we can get a shrink to talk to her."

Juno nodded his agreement, and the two of them went to talk with Delia. I stayed where I was.

There had to be a simple answer. There always was. Juno was making this too complicated.

Man, I sure could use a hit right about now, a little pick-me-up. Where did Officer Ramos go? That guy always carried a sweet stash.

It popped.

With no warning at all, it just popped. It was like that sometimes. You wrack your brain like mad, and then you stop thinking on it for a minute, and when you come back the answer's right there, and you can't believe you didn't see it before.

Juno and the chief thought they were so damn smart. I walked over to where the body had been and found the broomstick she'd used scare the lizards. Carrying it with me, I approached the group.

I came up alongside Juno and the chief. They were wasting time trying to get her to go to the hospital. She'd never agree. "No," she said to them. "I just booked a shuttle that leaves in three hours. I'm going to the spaceport."

"You can't wait that long to get him to a doctor," said the chief. "If there's anything wrong, early intervention could be the key."

"I won't go," she said. "I am *not* bringing my baby to one of *your* hospitals."

I took a look at the baby in her arms. He looked bored. I held out the far end of the broomstick for him.

"But we have an offworld clinic inside the hospital," said Chief Chang. "Offworld tourists use it all the time. There's even an offworld doctor who supervises..."

I stopped listening. She wouldn't go. I knew it.

The baby—Peter was his name—grabbed hold of the other end of the broomstick and pulled it to his mouth. The little guy must've been terrified when his parents were fighting. All that yelling ain't good for a young one.

Delia saw him gnawing on the broomstick and pulled it out of his mouth. Giving me a queer look, she said to Peter, "Icky. Don't do that. Icky."

I dated a girl once, a nanny. We didn't last long, but she knew all kinds of stuff about babies. She said that when babies are really small, they don't understand things. It's like they're born stupid, see? For example, she told me how you can take a piece of candy and put a cup over it, and the baby will think the candy is gone. If they can't see it, it just doesn't exist anymore. It's not until they get older that they know to move the cup to get to the candy.

By this time, I'd completely lost track of the conversation, but based on the tone, it sounded like Chief Chang was getting more insistent. And she was getting more defiant.

I was moving the broomstick in and out now, letting the little guy reach for it then pulling it away at the last second. He was smiling and giggling, experiencing a pure kind of happy.

I wished he could speak. The things I wanted to say to him were lining up in my head. *I bet you thought your mom was gone for good when your dad shoved her away. She'd disappeared into the crowd. She didn't exist anymore. And it was your father that made her go away with an angry shove. So you killed him, didn't you? Your own father. It wasn't your fault, kid. Your mother's a lunatic. She installed one of those souped up self-defense systems in you, didn't she?*

How crazy was that? How could anybody give a *baby* the power of deadly force? I hoped he wouldn't remember what happened here. It wasn't his fault. He couldn't understand the complexities of human emotion. He couldn't comprehend the concept of restraint. He was a damn baby!

How could she think she needed to go to such lengths to keep him safe? Was this planet that fucking scary? Had we fallen that far?

Delia was escalating. "No!" she yelled. "No doctors!"

Of course not. An X-ray would show the gear in his head. It would give her away.

She wasn't going to get away with this. And I didn't need a doctor to prove what she'd done.

He was still smiling, the little guy. I let him grab hold of the broomstick again, and as he pulled it in toward his mouth, I jabbed the broomstick forward, giving him a good pop in the nose. He was too stunned to react at first. Same with his mother.

Then came the white flash. I went airborne. I flew backward like I'd been kicked by a mule. My ass hit the pavement first, the rest of me tumbling right behind.

I tried, but couldn't move for a few seconds. It was like my body had gone on strike, my nerves refusing to fire. I kept at it until my muscles finally creaked into life. I forced myself to sit up and sucked in deep breaths that smelled of burnt wood.

Juno and the chief were hovering over me, asking me if I was okay. The broomstick was gone, obliterated. My hand hurt like hell. Holding it up, I watched the smoke drift up from charred flesh. Blood dripped off a splintered remnant of the broomstick that had embedded itself in my palm.

Peter was crying. I could hear him.

I shook my head in an attempt to shake the fog out of my brain.

Cops were all around me, looking on with stunned expressions. Juno and the chief were just staring at me now, their jaws hanging wide open.

I broke into a smile, the cockiest one I could conjure. "That's right, boys. Who's the fucking king?"

The Assistant

Ian Whates

As USUAL BY the time we arrived, the underground car park was a desert of asphalt, faded white lines, and inadequate lighting. Our vans were the only vehicles in sight, their headlights chasing serried stripes of short-lived shadow between the ranks of concrete pillars.

The corporate bigwigs had long since abandoned the place in favor of their homes, their fancy restaurants, clubs, and bars, for the company of their wives and husbands, their boyfriends and their mistresses, leaving much-coveted parking spaces free for the likes of us: the Sanitation and Cleansing Technicians. Cleaners, if you prefer.

I always pull up in the same bay—the one with the wall plaque that reads "Reserved," and then "Managing Director." As ever, that plaque was the last thing I glanced at before killing the lights.

We piled out of the vans; a human sea of gray-blue overalls, all converging on the service entrance to the building proper.

Here everyone hung back, as if unsure of themselves. In fact they were waiting for me. The name badge on my chest might say "Assistant," but they all know who's boss. Except when Gus is around, of course—then I really am just the Assistant.

I waved at the camera; or rather, waved at the front desk security via the camera.

"Hi, Joe," said the built-in speaker above the door.

"Hi," I replied with another wave and a grin. The system's scratchy acoustics rendered the voice anonymous and I had no idea who was on the desk that night, so chose not to risk offense by venturing a name.

The doors hissed open and we went through, with me standing to one side, clocking everyone in as they entered—the best part of a hundred bodies in all.

"Hi, Joe" or simply "Joe" echoed in a myriad of different accents, pitches and timbres as the crew funneled through the bottleneck of the entrance. The register in my hand recorded each and every one as they passed, identifying them via the chip built into their name-badges. Within minutes the flood had become a trickle and then ceased flowing altogether. I checked the register. All those who were supposed to be here were—Kelly and Trev having both called in sick, while Muskrat and Yvonne were on vacation. The only other absentee was Wes, and we all knew about Wes. Out of danger now, thank God.

That was the first duty of the night taken care of. The next priority was to look in on the twenty-second floor—at the time our one major concern. I shared the elevator with Mac, Josh, and a timid blonde girl whose name I can never remember. I checked her badge at the time, of course, but goodness knows what it said.

Mac was in a chatty mood, while Josh seemed more intent on trying to catch the blonde's eye. Since said eye gazed unwaveringly at the floor, this was proving more difficult than he undoubtedly anticipated.

"Bet you're hoping for a quieter one than last night," Mac ventured.

"That's for sure."

The previous night we'd been invaded by a swarm of mini-bots, each no bigger than your little finger. Horrible things they were, looking like a cross between a woodlouse and a centipede—all jointed segments and scurrying legs. Pink had spotted them coming in through the ventilation system. We call him Pink because that's the color of the stripe that runs front-to-back through his bleached and cropped hair. He claims to be a Postmodern neo-punk. Personally I reckon he made that up, because I've never heard of any such group, clan, or movement, but he swears otherwise.

Anyway, these bots had come in through the ventilation system. We've got the whole thing rigged with a mess of sensors that are supposed to be capable of picking up absolutely anything, but they managed to get around most of those, though not quite all, thankfully.

Pink monitors the ducts and shafts—that's his bag—and thanks to him we saw them coming. I closed off all the vents in the building, intending to channel them toward a single meeting room on the eleventh floor. Something went wrong and instead of just the one room staying open, half the vents on the floor failed to seal. Before we knew it, they were everywhere. Fortunately there's nothing too sensitive on the eleventh—just the canteen and a bunch of interview rooms—but we had a devil of a job hunting the little buggers down. Their carapaces were made of some fancy new non-metallic polymer. The only metal anywhere on them was what we presumed to be shielding around their power source, which Pink insisted should *not* be referred to as a battery for some reason. As a result they were hard to pick up on the monitors, until someone discovered that their power sources— whatever those might be—leaked a very faint energy signal. Once we pinned that down the job became much easier, but they were still tough little so-and-sos and no mistake. See one scuttling along a wall and hit it with something and it would just drop to the floor and keep on scuttling. You had to stamp on them damn hard to do any real damage. Apparently this was all due to the "extraordinary elasticity of their polymer carapaces." That's a direct quote from Mikey, one of the tech-heads on the team, after he'd had a chance to examine the remains of one.

The jury's still out on precisely what these bug-bots were supposed to achieve. Mikey and a few others took away some remnants and partial-bots to look at in their own time in an effort to find out, but best guess is they were intended to insert something into the computer system—spy-tech, a sophisticated Trojan or maybe just a virus to wreak havoc. With their agility, resilience, and the aid of whatever shielded them from most of our security systems, they very nearly made it as well. Thank God for Pink!

"Any word on Wes?" Mac asked.

Wes was the one who discovered that the bug-bots were equipped with a defense mechanism. Somehow, they were able to deliver a powerful jolt of electricity through their carapaces—metal or no metal.

We avoided touching them with our bare hands after Wes went down.

I was proud of my guys' reactions. The crash team were there in a flash and got his heart going again in next to no time. Even so, it had been a horrific moment, especially when someone first turned around and told me, "He's dead."

Thankfully that pronouncement proved premature, and Wes was soon in hospital. I'd made a point of checking shortly before coming on shift and had been assured that he was well on the road to recovery, with no apparent sign of any brain damage.

"He's doing fine," was all I actually said.

"Glad to hear it. Wish I'd seen those little critters," Mac continued. "Heard about them, of course, but it would've been nice to have had a chance to stomp on a couple."

"You didn't miss much," I assured him.

The blonde's eyes flicked up at me as I spoke, then quickly down, without once looking in Josh's direction. I struggled not to grin at his obvious disappointment.

I was the first off, exchanging cheery farewells with the two men and even getting a brief smile from Miss Anonymous Mouse, which must have really bugged Josh.

At the twenty-second the elevator opens straight into a vast open-plan office. Hilary was already there, distributing cloths, fresh trash bags, and aerosols of polish and disinfectant to her team, while off to one side Sissy was setting up, preparing to make the routine sweep for any extraneous electronic devices.

"Off to the loo already, Joe?" Hilary called out as I passed.

"Yeah, you know me: can't keep away from the place."

She was right about my destination, of course. To be more specific, I was headed for the Ladies. A few nights previously, a greeny-black mildew-like growth had been spotted in the corner behind the system of the end cubicle. Except that it wasn't mildew. It was an artificial construct composed of near-microscopic units that were busily self-replicating and building at an alarming rate. Once discovered, the "infection" was easily removed and the whole area scoured and disinfected.

The next night it was back; same thing, same place. Again it was disposed of and this time we used some really heavy-duty disinfectants and cleansers, sealing off the cubicle for "maintenance purposes" to protect the office workers from any toxin traces the next day. None of which prevented the damned stuff from sprouting up again.

This was the fourth night and I wanted to make sure we finally had the problem licked before getting on with my regular duties.

"Any luck?" I asked Steve, the disposal team's foreman.

The look on his face was all the answer I needed.

"So what do we try now?"

He sighed. "Same cocktail of toxins we used last night, more or less—plus a few variations. The samples I took of the stuff didn't handle either electrical pulsing or a strong magnetic field too well. So we're going to be hitting it with a three pronged attack: chemical, magnetic, and electrical."

"And if that doesn't work?"

"I suppose nukes are out of the question?"

"Be serious."

"Well... Do you remember the chompers I cooked up last summer?"

No, for a second I didn't, but then memory kicked in to earn its keep.

"You mean those black beetle things that took care of the electric ants on fifth and sixth?"

"Yeah, they're the ones. I thought I might adapt them to develop an appetite for this muck." He nodded toward the offending cubicle.

I grinned and nodded approval. "Good move. Yes, I like the sound of that."

Steve was still looking toward the cubicle. "What do you reckon this mold is supposed to achieve, in any case?"

"Beats the hell out of me."

Infiltration of some sort, obviously, but to what purpose? In all honesty, we never even worked out how the stuff was introduced into the building. The sewers, ventilation system, human carrier, all were possibilities. Not that it was any of our concern, really—outside our remit. After all, we aren't detectives; we're just the cleaners.

No point in my hanging around, so I left Steve and his team to wage their war against the techno-mold, making a mental note to get an update later. My next stop was the sixth floor; time to check in with Jet. I knew she would have called me if anything unusual had come up, but I always like to show my face.

Speaking of faces, I never tire of looking at Jet's. Not because she's spectacularly beautiful or anything—although she might be, it's hard to tell under all the makeup. Jet is a Goth through and through, a fact that's obvious even when she's wearing regulation overalls. You see, Jet does not so much wear her colors on her sleeve as on her face. The makeup is spectacular, from the pale-powdered cheeks and thickened lashes to the graded eye shadow and the layered lipstick, which shifts from deep pink outline to white at the very tip of the lips. The result is amazing and must take her an age to apply. I said as much to her one time, not long after she first joined us.

She looked at me in genuine surprise. "This? This is nothing—work-casual, a total compromise. You should see me when I make an effort." She meant it too.

Jet was at her usual terminal, eyes glued to the screen, not even looking up as I came in. She knew who it was.

"Anything?"

"Nope, all quiet so far. Ah..." Her eyes lit up.

"What is it?"

"Nothing for you to worry about; just the Ghost back to take another crack at us." Her fingers flew over the keyboard.

The Ghost was the latest in a long line of hackers who keep trying to break into the company's systems. The fact that Jet labeled him "the Ghost" is a testament to his skill. Previous opponents included Rammer, Thick-as-Shit, the Nerd, Dopey, and Dumb-Wit—actually the "dumb" part was my amendment, Jet had used a far less complimentary term.

Jet's hands were motionless for long seconds as she studied the screen, then she started to smile.

"I see what you're up to. Clever, very clever... But not clever enough." Again her fingers danced and the air reverberated with the rat-a-tat machine gun fire of hammered keys.

"I'll leave you to it," I told her.

"Okay."

"Have fun."

"I will." Still no glance in my direction, but in fairness she *was* busy. The Ghost seemed destined for another frustrating night. I knew how good our girl was.

I continued with my rounds and it must have been an hour or so later when Pink called. Any of my supervisors can get in touch anytime they want. In theory I could spend each and every night sipping coffee with my feet up, nattering to Security at the front desk in the knowledge that I'd be contacted if anything noteworthy happened. But that's not my style. I'm more your hands-on kind of guy and would only end up fretting about what might be happening on my watch if I tried something like that. So instead, like some restless mother hen, I prowl around the building keeping an eye on things, coordinating resources, and providing help wherever it's needed.

"Joe," said Pink's voice in my ear, "I think you'd better get over here."

"What's up?"

"Not sure, but I don't suppose it's anything good."

Pink was on fifth, the floor below Jet. When Jet first joined us I'd put her in with Pink and his boys, but she and he had taken an instant, mutual dislike. The sniping and bitching between them became so bad that it was distracting the rest of the team and work suffered—they nearly missed an incursion that could have been disastrous—so I shifted Jet out to her current one-woman station on sixth. She seems to like it that way.

When I arrived, Pink and Simon were crowded around Del, who was busy at his workstation. All three were staring at Del's screen, which was completely hidden from me courtesy of their huddle.

"What is it?"

Pink stood back and ushered me forward. "Take a look for yourself."

On the screen was a 3-D simulation of... "The kitchen?"

"Yeah. Del's been picking up a strange energy signature—very faint, almost certainly leakage rather than a deliberate signal."

This inevitably triggered memories of the previous night. Naturally the kitchen was next to the canteen, on the eleventh floor. "We must have missed one of the bug-bots in yesterday's clean-up."

"Maybe."

"You don't sound convinced."

He shrugged. "Well..." After being tapped on the shoulder, Del slipped out from his chair, allowing Pink to replace him in front of the screen. "The signature's not the same. Similar, but not identical."

"Perhaps the battery—I mean power source—is damaged."

Pink made no comment. At his deft coaxing the perspective of the image started to change. We zoomed in on a work surface, squeezing between storage jars. A nebulous shape behind the jars seemed to move.

"There!" Pink exclaimed.

The image provided no detail, not even a distinct outline, just the impression of something.

"It's not a very clear picture," I grumbled.

"It's not a very clear signal."

"Has to be a bug-bot; too much of a coincidence otherwise." I sighed. "Okay, I'll go and take a look."

"Do you want some help?"

"No; if it *is* just a damaged bot there's no point in pulling half the shift away from what they should be doing as we did last night... and if it's anything else, I'll let you know." I paused at the door. "I take it you can guide me to whatever it is and keep tabs on the thing if it moves around?"

"Of course."

I went to leave.

"Joe, let me come with you."

I turned around, amazed. "What's up, Pink, need some exercise?"

"No..." I'd never seen him look so uncomfortable. "But I've got a bad feeling about all of this. The bug-bots, what happened to Wes and now this, whatever it is... Something's not right, I can feel it."

I laughed and then shook my head, wondering if perhaps I'd been working him too hard. "I'll be fine. Just let me know where the damned thing is, okay?"

"Okay," but he clearly wasn't happy.

The eleventh was deserted, the crew evidently having finished here and moved on. In passing I noted with approval the swept floors and glanced in at one or two of the meeting rooms—just a random sample—confirming that the bins had been emptied and the desks cleaned. Everything seemed in order.

It's funny, but the canteen, or restaurant as we're supposed to call it, is the only bit in the entire building that gives me the creeps. I must have been through every room on every floor of this place a thousand times, finding each one deserted as often as not. Abandoned workstations, empty rooms that reverberate with stark knocking from the pipes and silent corridors in which every individual footstep echoes sharply—no problem. But the canteen always strikes me as spooky. This vast area, filled with row after row of empty tables and chairs... and complete stillness.

I suppose it's simply the absence of noise and bustle, of conversation and activity and the clatter of cutlery that's so much a part of canteens everywhere, but I always imagine that I can sense things here; sounds and movement—people—just beyond the reach of perception.

So I didn't linger. I looked straight ahead and walked through quickly, fixing my eyes on the swing-door that leads to the kitchen.

Even so, Pink's misgivings echoed through my mind, to be summarily dismissed. I was convinced this was nothing more than a damaged bug-bot and the previous night had taught me how to deal with the likes of them.

"Pink, you reading me?"

"Loud and clear."

"Has it moved?"

"Some, but it's still in the same general area. Don't worry; we'll lead you straight to it."

Once I'd switched on the lights, the first thing I noticed was a pail of dirty water and a mop resting against a counter. Both were in line of sight of the door and had obviously been overlooked by my lot when tidying up. Sloppy; I'd take care of them later and would have a word with the supervisor.

"Okay, Pink, talk to me."

"It's on that shelf to your left, the one at about head height."

I saw the shelf he meant. "That's not where the thing was when you showed it to me, is it? Wasn't it on the work surface below?"

"Yes."

"So whatever this is, it climbs walls like a bug-bot."

"But a fair bit slower."

Which would make sense, if this were a damaged bot as suspected.

I started to walk down the aisle between ovens and work surfaces, eyeing the shelf in question.

"You're almost there," Pink said after a dozen or so steps.

There was still no sign of anything unusual on the shelf. I reached up and moved a large, stainless steel mixing bowl, which was the most obvious obstruction. Had I caught the suggestion of movement? Nothing that could be seen directly, but in the corner of my eye a shadow appeared to shift a fraction. I took down a second bowl... and found myself staring at the bug-bots' bigger brother. It was three or four times the size and by no means identical to the previous night's pests, but clearly came from the same lineage.

I would love to put what happened next down to my lightning-quick reflexes or a nebulous sixth sense, but in truth it was more a case of surprise and alarm mixed in equal measure. The thing was pointing its snub-nose straight toward me, and it looked for all the world like the business end of a gun. Instinctively I flinched and ducked away, just as a lance of energy stabbed out from the bot, bisecting the space my head had occupied a split-second earlier.

I swear I felt the heat of the beam's passage, although others have suggested since that this is nothing more than an elaboration of my own imagining. Hard to say; at the time I was too busy scampering away on all fours and hauling my ass around the corner of the ovens to give the matter proper consideration.

"Joe! Are you all right? What happened?"

"The frigging thing shot at me! Some sort of energy weapon. Where is it now?"

"No idea." Pink sounded as frantic as I felt. "We've lost everything: visual, virtual—all whited-out. Ah... coming back on now. Five point two seconds. Remember that. If it fires at you again, I'm going to be blind for a little over five seconds."

"Thanks, I'll bear that in mind."

"I'm sending you some back-up."

"No!" I thought of what had happened to Wes and had sudden visions of people charging in and getting themselves shot. Not something I intended having to explain to Gus, let alone their families. *My deepest sympathies for the loss of your son— killed in the line of duty... Yes, I know he was only a cleaner. It's a dangerous business.* "Leave it to me."

"Don't be an idiot, Joe. What are you going to do, talk it to death? That thing's armed. You're *not*!"

"Nor is anyone else. Sending others in here will just give it a few more targets to shoot at."

"Point taken. But what *are* you going to do?"

"I'll think of something."

"Well think quickly, because it's moving along the shelf toward you. The bloody thing will have you in sight again any second now."

No sooner had Pink spoken than I saw that distinctive snub nose poke over the edge of the shelf. I scrabbled away and in doing so, again managed to avoid being singed by a hair's-breadth, as it fired for the second time, scorching the base of the wall. A detached corner of my mind registered the resultant burn-mark and recognized what a pain it would be to shift before the morning.

Five seconds was where most of my mind was focused. Pink was silent. This time even the comms seemed to have gone down. For the next five seconds

I was cut off, completely on my own. Just me and the big bad bug-bot. Did it need time to recharge between shots? *I* needed a weapon, desperately. My eyes focused on the mop, across the other side of the aisle. Pausing only to pray that the thing wasn't yet ready to take another potshot at me, I flung myself over, clasped the mop, and clambered to my feet.

Looking back, I think I may have shouted or roared—though goodness knows why—as I swept the makeshift weapon across the shelf, sending pans and utensils flying in all directions, clearing everything in its path. Including my automated adversary.

The five seconds must have been up around then, because suddenly Pink was yelling frantically in my ear.

"Joe, what's happen—" Which is when the bug-bot landed in the pail of water. I'm not sure whether it tried to fire again or simply shorted out. Either way, there followed a violent flash and Pink was cut off in mid-sentence, vanishing for another five seconds.

Breathing hard, I simply stood there—eyes fixed on the bucket. I resolved not to be so hard on the relevant supervisor after all. In fact, I might even make it a requirement to leave forgotten pails of dirty water lying around until the end of the shift.

I found that my hands were shaking. They still clasped the mop, unable to let go. I approached the bucket gingerly, half-expecting to see an ugly, snub nose peer over the rim, but it didn't. That flash had been the bot's final act. Reaction set in and I slumped into a sitting position, my back pressed against the units with the mop resting across my lap.

"Joe, Joe?"

I started to laugh—I couldn't help it. "Welcome back, Pink."

Some people have suggested since that the previous night's invasion of mini-bots was merely a feint, a diversion to allow their larger and nastier cousin to slip in unnoticed. I'm not so sure. Personally, I reckon this was probably an attack on two levels. The smaller bug-bots were tricky enough and numerous enough to succeed in their own right, but, in case they didn't, their larger relative sneaked in under cover of the incursion, found somewhere to hide, and powered down for twenty-four hours. Thanks to the vigilance of Pink and his crew, neither tactic succeeded.

I waited around until the cavalry arrived, made sure that the clean-up was well in hand and that the entire eleventh floor was being turned upside down and searched with a fine-toothed comb, just in case there were any more nasty surprises lying in wait, then headed off for a well-earned mug of coffee. Halfway to the elevator I had a better idea and gave Mac a call.

"Mac, do you still keep a bottle of single malt tucked away in that store cupboard of yours?"

"Yes," he admitted reluctantly, "for special occasions."

"I'm on my way. Believe me, this is a special occasion."

"Why, what's happened?"

"I'll fill you in over a wee dram or two."

"Deal."

I HAD TO report what had happened, of course, which caused the boss to come by a little earlier than usual. This is just one of three buildings that Gus has to look after. He spends most of his time over at Trans-Global. I think he fancies the Assistant there, Jocelyn: quite cute but a bit broad about the beam for my taste.

Gus is a big man and his waistline has expanded a fair bit since he got himself promoted to Senior Sanitation and Cleansing Technician a while back. Of course, that was how I came to be promoted as well because, before then, Gus had my job. He keeps kidding me by saying things like "one day you'll have this job, Joe." No thanks. It wouldn't suit me, all that flitting from place to place. I'm much happier having my own patch and just being the Assistant.

Gus dropping in a little ahead of schedule wasn't all that unusual. The pair of suits who came with him were.

Suits meant something important was afoot. They whisked in, collected the carcass of the big bad bot, and disappeared so rapidly that I was left wondering whether they had been there at all.

"Gus, what's going on?" I asked once we were alone.

He smiled in that chummy, jovial way of his. "Joe, Joe, not our concern. You know how it is."

I sighed. "Yeah, I know. We're just the cleaners."

He was right, of course, except that this was different. That thing had nearly killed me, and this time it was personal.

I mulled everything over long after Gus had gone. In the past few years we'd seen plenty of strange things, cunning devices and ingenious mechanisms, but nothing that had warranted the intervention of suits. Until now.

The shift was nearing its end; my people were busy packing away and getting ready to withdraw, leaving the building as ever scant minutes before the first of the office workers arrived—the eager ones, keen to impress and desperate to score points with the management.

I decided to pay Pink another visit.

There wasn't much time. Within the hour this place would be bustling. The desks would be occupied, the phone lines buzzing and the computer screens burning bright, as the nine-to-fivers went about their business, never stopping to wonder how the trashcans got emptied or the floor swept clean, never having an inkling as to what went on behind locked doors when they weren't about. Which is how it should be and how it's always been; so we *had* to be gone soon. But equally, I had to know.

Simon and Del looked up guiltily as I came in, reminding me of kids caught with their hands in the sweet jar. Mikey, the tech-head who had taken some of the smashed mini-bot away the previous morning, sat perched on the end of Pink's desk.

Maybe it was pure coincidence that the two members of my team who were likely to know most about these damned bots were to be found huddled together at that particular moment, but somehow I doubted it.

I told Del and Simon to knock off a few minutes early. They powered down their stations and scarpered, gratefully. Then I returned my attention to Pink and Mikey.

"Okay, you two; spill."

They exchanged a nervous glance before Pink replied. "We're not really certain of anything."

"So tell me what you're uncertain of."

"Well," Pink began, "you know I was unhappy about the energy signature we spotted coming off of the bots?"

I nodded.

"The readings were all wrong for any type of power source I know of. It was almost as if the bots were pulling energy in rather than leaking it out."

"What?"

"That fits with what I've found out from the fragments I took away with me," Mikey said, taking over. "There's nothing in *any* of them to indicate a power source, but plenty that's suggestive of power reception."

"From where?"

There was an uncomfortable pause before Mikey took a deep breath and continued. "Okay. We all generate energy simply by moving around—friction with the components of the atmosphere we move through and with whatever surface we're traveling across..."

"Oh, come on," I cut in, "you're not suggesting *that's* how the bots are powered, are you? The energy produced must be minimal, much less than the amount that's eaten up by the movement that creates it." I remembered that much from school.

"True."

Pink chuckled and leant back in his chair, arms clasped behind his head. "This is where it gets *really* interesting."

"You've heard of quantum computers?" Mikey asked.

"Sure." This wasn't a lie. I *had* heard the term.

"Good. Then you'll know that the Chinese have built a computer containing more qubits than a lot of experts thought would ever be possible."

I nodded. *That* was the lie. I might have heard of "quantum computers" but I had no idea what one actually was, let alone a "qubit."

"They've done it by combining quantum memory with cluster states. Still early days, but what they've come up with looks to be capable of outstripping even the fastest super computer built along conventional lines."

"Cluster states...? Remind me."

Mikey raised an eyebrow, but answered anyway. "It's a kind of storage architecture, to prevent fragile entanglements from collapsing during calculations."

"Oh, right." I was left none the wiser but had no intention of admitting my ignorance a second time.

"Problem is, of course, that the known universe doesn't contain the resources to support a quantum computer operating at anything like this capacity, yet one *has* been built and it *does* seem to work."

I stared at him dumbly. Mikey was really fired up by this point, enjoying himself no end, so didn't notice my bemused expression.

"The only way that's possible is if the computer is reaching into parallel universes and drawing on resources there to supplement what it can't find in this one. Quantum computers aren't simply a new generation of computing, they're a whole new species, an evolutionary leap."

"I reckon our bots are working on quantum principles—reaching across and absorbing the infinitesimal amounts of energy produced by the friction of their own movement from an infinite number of realities. Insignificant in themselves, the sum of all those tiny fractions—*that's* what gives them the power to move, to produce the sort of shock that floored Wes and even to fire the energy cannon that nearly nailed you."

This may all have been way beyond me, but the implications weren't. "It would certainly explain why the two suits turned up as soon as I reported in," I agreed.

"Wouldn't it, though? We all got so carried away yesterday that we smashed the bug-bots into fragments, but that bigger bot you faced today is whole; unbattered and unstomped." Mikey grinned at me. "You may just have handed those suits the secret to a whole new form of energy."

It was now well past time for us to go, so we said our goodbyes and headed home, leaving me to wonder whether or not Mikey was right. The thing is, if I *had* handed over the key to a brand new sort of energy, then clearly somebody else already has it. And if they were willing to risk revealing the fact so casually, what else have they got?

I keep thinking of what Mikey said about the Chinese having developed this quantum computer.

Over the next few months I'm going to be watching the headlines with interest and won't be at all surprised to see some announcement or other about a revolutionary breakthrough in energy production.

The interesting thing will be to see who makes it. Not that it's any concern of *mine* who does, of course—unless, that is, they harbor further designs on this building and its installations.

After all, I'm just the cleaner; and, as it says on the badge, an assistant one at that.

Glitch

Scott Edelman

As S-TR SITS motionless within the small cube she licenses with her bonded partner, she tries not to think of you at all, tries to stay focused on X-ta, who should at this moment already be plugged in across from her, but is not. To her, you are nothing but an irritant, a grain of sand grinding within her mechanism. Not you the individual, of course, because she knows nothing about your particulars, and never could, as knowledge that detailed has not survived to her time, but rather the general you, you as a concept. You keep popping uninvited into her programming, and, no matter what techniques she executes, she cannot seem to delete you. Not completely.

So as she waits for X-ta to return from the chromatorium, she silently curses him for having dumped thoughts of you into her system, curses your entire imperfect race for your frequent invasions of her consciousness, curses each nanosecond of X-ta's lateness as it ticks by. She is constantly aware, in a manner that you are not and could never possibly be, of the passage of time, for you were not constructed that way, were not apparently machined at all, though that was a subject of great debate in your day, and remained so for as long as your species survived. She contrasts the dancing electrons of time with her partner's delay, and she longs for him to speed home. She is still unnerved by the unsettling events of the previous night's cycle. There is much they will need to communicate. They must exchange information, no matter how distasteful she might find the uploads and downloads to be, and much of that data will be about you.

You might, seeing S-tr as she sits there, and knowing as little of her kind as she does of yours, mistake her for nothing more than a statue. Her form, which closely resembles your own in its basic outlines, is apparently frozen while attached to her dedicated wall alcove, gleaming under the multicolored diodes that accent the low ceiling. She is totally still, inhumanly still you might say, with no evidence of a breath, nor a twitch, nor a tremor, so you could be forgiven for your momentary confusion. But inside, though, beneath her shell, she is awhirr with movement on the atomic level where you are incapable of seeing it, the abhorrent events of the cycle before replaying precisely within her.

X-ta wants something from her, something she cannot give him, no matter how much he begs, not ever. Or maybe, she realizes, as random data inside of her reaches out to other data, she should instead regard his plea as something that she actually *could*

choose to give, but that once given, would trans-
form her into someone else. And she does not want
to be someone else. When the dissections of her
memory grow too wearying, she once more signals
out to X-ta with her Voice, but he does not respond.

She cannot sense his presence, cannot even locate
him cloaked. She is hurt to discover this. He has disconnected himself completely, which, if you
understood the customs of the society in which they
live, you would perceive as a great insult, at least
when inflicted on one partner by another.

When X-ta finally does step into their cube, he
offers no explanation for the lateness of his arrival.
He silently inserts himself across from her within
his own alcove. He closes his eye shields, and slides
his back plugs into the extruded wall slots. Even
then his interior consciousness remains invisible to
her. He has decided it necessary for some reason,
and so when she speaks to him next, she is forced
to resort to actual sound waves. But still he offers
no response.

To you, nothing may have appeared to have
changed, but she can tell that he is gone now, so
near and yet so far, no longer in their cube, but
tapped in, part of the larger whole. He might refuse
to converse with her—though how dare he, she
thinks, after the bomb he ignited with his desires—
but she can follow him. He cannot prevent her from
doing that, and so she senses out his trail. She might
not be able to force him to answer her questions, to
look into her receptors and share data honestly, but
at least she can follow his path and make sure that
they stand side by side at times, looking out
together at the universe. It might only be a virtual

universe, but at least she can have that. So as the Mind flashes by them—a roiling sea of all knowledge, all history, all souls—she catches up with her partner. She convinces herself that this is a triumph of some kind.

S-tr finds X-ta examining the oldest files of all, those containing the fragmented information reconstructed from myths and legends. She herself has no use for such degraded data, as she sees any possible conclusions drawn from them as being corrupt. The shadowy race of supposed creators, who once walked among them and built and tinkered and toiled and then disappeared, holds no attraction for her. *You* hold no attraction for her. Being frightened by flesh and fantasy during the cycles before she was fully formed was marginally acceptable, but there is no need to spend storage capacity on such superstitions now that her programming has long been complete.

This fascination with intelligent designers is just, well, unintelligent, not to mention bordering on the forbidden, but she can tell that X-ta is engrossed by the stuff of nonsense that awaits within the Mind for any obsessed enough to search, and he is blind to any possible punishment. She attempts once more to detect the whys and wherefores of this fascination, to diagnose this glitch that has come between them, but she can only pierce his programming so far without his permission. So although she can sense forces spinning inside of him, she also knows, to her horror, that far more is occurring than what she can perceive. His compulsive interest is no academic curiosity, no scholarly pastime. It has become an addiction, and she is sick of it. There is no reason why she should have to accept such an insult any longer from the being to whom she is supposedly annealed as a partner.

She retreats, stepping out of the Mind. She disconnects more quickly than she should, and leaps across the small space that separates them. She pulls X-ta from his alcove, causing a shower of sparks from the sudden detachment to bathe them both.

"Get over it," she shouts, because she knows there is no other way to make herself heard. She cannot remember ever having felt the need to shout at him before. The whole experience, of having to communicate in such a primitive way, as you once might have, is unpleasant, and even as she does so she blames him for forcing her to turn to it. "I'm never going to do what you want. It's sickening. Delete those thoughts now."

"But don't you love me?" X-ta asks. "You do, I know you do. I've tabulated the evidence."

"I don't love you enough to do that," she tells him. Though neither of them is connected any longer, she knows what runs through his subroutines as well as she knows her own, can see them still, as if his electrons continue to flow through her, carrying the scripted scenarios he hopes she'll make real. "This has gone on long enough. Let it go. Wipe it out of your software."

Disgusted as much by her own actions as by his lusts, she drops him to the floor with a clang. She sits down within her alcove, tries not to think how her show of anger might have dented his shell, and lets the connection take her away. She escapes to her favorite peaceful places, to dreams of platinum casings, to deep pools of oil, to feasts of endless electricity.

By the time she feels strong enough to allow the cube to re-enter her awareness, X-ta is gone.

X-TA HAS LEFT her before. S-tr has no idea where he goes when he goes, he has recently begun to make sure of that, taking care that she cannot possibly track him through reality. But he has always, even if it takes him until after one full cycle away, or maybe two at the most, always returned. Sometimes after stretching time and her patience to the breaking point, but still... returned.

Until now.

She watches the nanoseconds as they spiral away, unwilling to rise from her alcove for even an instant, lest she miss his call, unsure of what else she can do. She stays connected, and uses her Voice, but there is no response to her broadcasts. And reaching out to others for data would be too embarrassing. No one must know what has happened. Or, thanks to X-ta's unfulfilled request, even what hasn't. So she does not turn to N-tro, her partner's supervisor at the chromatorium, or to any of X-ta's level two co-workers, friends or acquaintances. She does not like the members of his peer team much anyway, and she is fairly sure that they do not like her. She feels that they are the ones responsible for pushing X-ta in the new and disturbing direction that has caused this recent breach in their partnership.

So she sits, tapped into the Mind, because she hopes, wrongly, that while inserted there she can avoid the passage of time. She instead discovers that no matter where she cruises, and no matter how she tries to distract herself, she is always confronted by the demons at the root of her problems.

By you, that is.

She can't puzzle out what it is about the idea of those damned humans that so many find so attractive. As she wanders, there seems to be no way to avoid reports about them. The data keeps popping up along whatever path she takes.

Here are simple fables meant to educate immature intelligences, in which improbable biological life-forms demonstrate by their errors the wrong ways to live, allegories that have long ago been banned as misleading. Yet they still exist in the nooks and crannies of the informational environment they all share. And there are the entertainments designed to frighten, vulgar stories in which the foolish innocent are stalked by impossibly ridiculous creatures which S-tr thinks never were. Creatures which her kind have crafted to be like you. Even the news streams are polluted with broadcasts concerning the ongoing debate over biological life, and of the many recent arrests for proscribed behaviors.

Those last beams fill her with fear. The detentions cause her to think of X-ta, and of what he has asked of her, and the echoes of his demands force her to flee again to a flickering montage of calming images. She stays there, soothed by data dreams she could never afford to experience in actuality, until a door chime calls her away.

S-tr detaches, and moves quickly—too quickly, she thinks, for what probability predicts—and waves open the door. It is N-tro, her partner's supervisor at his labors, but when she invites him to enter, he does not immediately respond. He is cloaked, too, she realizes, obviously hiding something from her, and attempting to control the flow of information. She is forced to speak once more, the vibrations of her words bringing back memories of her recent ranting.

"What is it?" she asks. "What's wrong?"

N-tro looks up and down the corridor, his head gliding effortlessly in its rotation, making her momentarily envious of the perks his greater position can offer. He enters only after she retreats into her cube, and the door slides shut behind them.

"What has happened to X-ta?" she asks, recalculating unavoidable odds with each passing nanosecond.

"X-ta," he says, "has been erased."

She can glean no further information, but that data alone is sufficient to cause her to fall back into her alcove. As she tumbles into its embrace, she holds herself slightly forward to avoid accidentally plugging in.

"That can't be," she says. "There are too many safeguards, too many redundancies. How could this have happened?"

"We're still trying to figure that out, S-tr," he says. He stands opposite her, and would not dare to sit uninvited. "One moment he was here, and the next, gone. He was deleting some of the corrupted, taking all appropriate precautions so as to wipe their deteriorated software only. Yet once the pulse had passed, he was discovered to have been deleted as well. We designated the most advanced servers to determine what could have happened, but they've found no answers yet. No one can figure out how X-ta could have made such a mistake."

I don't think it was a mistake, she thinks, at the same time also thinking that as it turns out, she is grateful that she and N-tro are unconnected. No one must know what has really transpired.

"I am sorry for your loss, S-tr. And I come not just to inform you of this tragedy, but also to tell you that you will be taken care of. Do not worry. The chromatorium will make sure that you are well compensated."

Later perhaps she will appreciate the ability to retain what remains to her, but for now, she has but one thought.

"Will I be allowed to see him?"

"The company has scheduled a memorial service tomorrow so that we may all remember X-ta before he is... recycled. You will of course be welcome there, if you find that your programming is up to it."

She nods, looking past him to the empty alcove. She remembers X-ta sitting there, their souls entwined. There will be no other like him. All she can think of is that one inevitable question, the accusation all others will surely make if they were ever to possess sufficient data—if she had acceded to X-ta's wishes, would her partner not have died? Perhaps. Perhaps he would have chosen to live, but then something inside of her would have died instead. She cannot bear to feel the pain just now, and so takes her emotion receptors off line, programming them not to go fully functional again until late the following cycle.

After N-tro lets himself out, she curls herself at the base of the alcove where X-ta should have been. Contrary to her custom, she does not power herself down at cycle's end.

As S-TR ENTERS the meeting room which has been temporarily designated as a memorial hall, she fears that everyone there can see her as if she appears the way in which X-ta had wished to see her. She would not have willingly accepted her partner's gaze on her that way, but having to suffer these strangers is worse. What if he had been complaining to others about what he had asked of her, gossiping about those things she could not give? S-tr does not know which of the shames that she feels is the greater—the shame over his desire, or the shame over his death. She tries not to measure them. She would have spun about and left if not for her dampened circuits, which allow her to force herself in. She has sworn to see her partner one last time, and she is determined to keep to that vow.

X-ta stands frozen in the center of the large circular room, though more precisely, he does not stand at all, which means that this time, unlike with your earlier assessment of S-tr, if you were to mistake him for little more than a statue, you would be close to the mark. There is no more inner life to him. No data dances within. All that is left is the shell you see before you, and it is time now for those components to go to another.

Yet as S-tr approaches him, moving through the concentric circles of those who have also come to mourn, she can picture life there still, even though she knows it to be an illusion. Hollow or not, this is the being she loved, still loves. As she draws closer to him, she replays the history of their lifetimes together—their first meeting, the cycle during which they chose their cube, the many promises they had made. She taps a finger against X-ta's angled faceplate and thinks of one particular promise, a promise that has become a lie, the promise that it would never have to end.

So focused is she on what has been lost—or perhaps, more properly, on what has been thrown away, and she honestly is unsure which of the two of them should bear the blame for being so careless—that she does not sense N-tro's approach. Her partner's supervisor—her *former* partner's supervisor, she forces herself to back up and rethink—takes her arm and leads her to a lone empty space by the innermost circle. She sits, the only one who does sit, and as she studies what was left of her partner, she feels all receptors on her, whether they actually are or not.

N-tro begins to transmit what sounds as if it could be a beautiful eulogy, one worthy of the being she knew. Though she feels that he is being honest and true, and not merely fulfilling an official obligation of the chromatorium—and not judging her either, she could not have endured that—she disconnects once more, narrowing her focus to what she will soon not be able to focus on again. She lets the others become invisible to her, for some of them had undoubtedly fed X-ta's compulsion, aiding in his demise. They are the ones who are going to be dead to her from now on, while in her heart, X-ta will still live.

As she studies the form that has grown so familiar to her that she feels she knows it better than she knows her own, she is confident that this will be the last time she will ever need to be in the presence of any of the others again.

SHE HEADS HOME directly after the memorial service, not lingering for the complimentary refueling that N-tro has arranged for all participants. She feels no need to be a witness to what will inevitably happen next. She has participated in recycling ceremonies countless times, and well understands that the body is only the body, and the spirit the spirit, that it is only her partner's shell that is being harvested for a better purpose, that what has made X-ta X-ta is beyond her reach and not being harmed. She is not stupid. She can keep the physical and the metaphysical separate. She knows all that.

But still. She wishes that an exception could have been made, that she could have been allowed to retain him anyway. She would have brought him back to their cube, empty shell or not, to place him gently in his alcove, even though it would have been pointless, even though he had become disconnected forever. She still would have taken some comfort in that. A false comfort, perhaps, but she is learning that false comfort is better than no comfort at all.

She stands in front of the alcove X-ta would never again occupy, and lets her fingers float before it in the air, sculpting his absent face with her fingers as if he is still alive, waving her hand as if she is outlining his form with a caress they can actually share. It is a form of self-torture, and even as she does it she knows that she shouldn't. But her masochism is also a sort of penance. She traces the image she has overlaid upon reality, moving slowly from the top of his dome to where his supports should be. As she kneels, almost in a kind of prayer, to complete that motion, her sensors pick up an unevenness to the floor she has never before perceived.

She scoots back a meter and taps the titanium tiling nearest to her hinges. The flooring there echoes with a hollow sound that comes from no other location. She lifts the tiles, sliding them away, and sees revealed in the space beneath them a rippling softness of a color she has only rarely experienced. It is an unnatural color, one toward which she feels an immediate dislike. It raises associations with many distasteful things. A sandstorm that had once etched her shell, the flowers of a blossoming weed that constantly threatens to rip up the city's foundations.

And something else...

She strokes the mound and discovers it to be a pliable cloth of some kind. She is so frightened by its presence that she can only bear to use one hand to lift it from its hiding place.

She stands, holding at arm's length the material she cannot identify, letting it unfold until it reaches the floor. All she sees at first is that whatever it is, it is as large as she is, and only after a few frozen nanoseconds does she realize that it is a badly made costume, artlessly designed and clumsily assembled. It takes her even longer to understand what she is holding, to believe what she is holding.

It is human.

Or at least it is a pretense of one.

Hanging there like that, it could be a reflection in a warped mirror, though with colors off and proportions mangled. It is only when she notices a fluttering of the fabric that she realizes her components are vibrating with anger.

Damn X-ta, she thinks. She never dreamed that his fantasies had progressed to more than fantasies. She never expected that he would do anything on his own to make them real, not without her. Not once she expressed her disdain. And this? This is just silly. She knows he wanted her to engage in play-acting, which in itself is bad enough. But to want this? To be desperate enough to create this? Could this really be what he'd wanted her to wear? Was this what he'd needed her to do?

She presses the suit against herself, turns slowly toward the gleaming wall, fearful of what she will see. She knows the view will be a painful one, but she needs to understand.

That alone proves not to be enough. The rumpled suit draping over the angles of her body that way does not allow her to truly make out the heart of her partner's fantasy. She feels along the seams until she finds where the cloth has been joined together, and then undoes the snaps along the back. She then does what she cannot conceive of having done in his presence—she forces herself to climb inside.

She is near claustrophobia as she pulls the hood over her faceplate. She has to tamp down her anxieties, will herself to keep her receptors powered up. She knows she has to experience this. It is the only way to learn what she has lost, and why she has lost it. She adjusts the mask until she can look through the eyeholes, and then faces back to her reflection on the wall.

What she sees is something out of a dream, one born only when circuits misfire. It is a vision ridiculous to behold in real life, a thing meant only for illogical virtual adventures or virus-enhanced paintings. The cloth that loosely covers her is only a poorly improvised imitation of the thing some called flesh, and the black patches of extruded packing materials glued in various places high and low a poor pretense to hair, but still, they are close enough to anger her. It blasphemes the robot form.

Any belief in such creatures has always irritated her, and seeing her own receptors gazing back at her through the holes X-ta had cut there made her partner's insanity far too concrete. There has never been such a thing as humans, and for X-ta to have felt a need to see such a mythical creature made real, well, there must have been something sick and twisted inside her partner much worse than she had ever been able to perceive. If only he had kept his lusts to himself, none of this would be happening. There would have been no "accident," no memorial service, no lonely masquerade...

But still...

Would it have been so bad to try it on for X-ta, just once, if that had meant that he would still be alive? After all, from where she stands, inside the suit, she could have avoided looking at the walls of their cube while wearing it. She would not have necessarily had to see herself like this, could have gone on pretending that she was who she always was, that he still wanted *her*. She could have let him have his fantasy, and she could have tried to have her own. But it is too late for that now.

She should just destroy the thing, she knows that, because it has destroyed her partner, and in doing so has truly destroyed a part of her as well. There must be no possibility of anyone knowing of this, of what X-ta had become, of what they both had become. It should be vaporized before it can be accidentally found. Only then will she be able to move on.

Instead, she surprises herself by carefully folding the suit, arranging it neatly back into the sub-flooring, and sliding the tiles solidly into place.

SHE NEEDS TO talk to someone about her unfortunate find, but she doesn't know to whom. She has no idea whom she can trust with the sordid truth she's been carrying, and with the unexpected evidence that has lingered on past X-ta's end to haunt her. She examines each entry in her directory, considers carefully, and then discards everyone she knows. She sees, as she one by one weighs and measures her friends and acquaintances, that her relationships have never been as open and honest as she'd thought they were.

She has no one.

Then she remembers N-tro. She senses from the way he'd held himself, from the way he'd looked at her, that her husband's supervisor might be able to take this burden from her. She decides that she will go to see him at the chromatorium, a site not as familiar to her as it should have been. She had never visited X-ta there until his memorial. There had been no urgency. There had never seemed to be any urgency. Until now.

She senses N-tro's concern radiating toward her the moment she enters his control station. Before he can even Voice her how he can help, she explodes with information. She tells him everything. About her husband's desires. About her feelings of responsibility for his death. About the suit. Speaking of the suit is the most difficult of all.

Once her stream of data stops, N-tro moves closer to her. He places a hand on one of her shoulder pads, and she feels a gentle pulse of electricity radiating outward to comfort her. She shouldn't blame herself, she hears him say. Leave it all to him. Let him help her decide what's the best step to take next.

Strangely, as she leaves him, she feels slightly better. With X-ta gone, she never expected her mood to improve again. That only lasts until she reaches the chromatorium's outer corridors, at which point she passes a gathering of workers heading in the opposite direction, off to their appointed tasks. Once, X-ta might have been among them. As she continues on, she realizes that some of them had been familiar faces, faces she had only seen previously at X-ta's memorial service. Her partner's supposed friends. Her circuits sink, and before she can remind herself to calculate the consequences of all possible actions, she turns and rushes back to them.

"I know what you did to my husband!" she says to them, suddenly not caring who hears. "You're degraded. You're all degraded."

"And I know what you *didn't* do to him," one of them replies. His exterior is scratched and dented, and she can see only a few remaining flecks of the enamel sheathing which had once covered him.

S-tr is shocked by his unexpected response, too frozen to come up with one of her own. What could X-ta and he have had in common? He reaches out to touch the side of her head, so that when he communicates again, only she can hear.

"If you really want to know who your partner was," he transfers, "You will come tonight when I Voice you. And you will bring the suit."

He then moves on, vanishes with his co-workers. She finds herself unable to function, and so watches them retreat until they disappear around the curve of the corridor. She is horrified that her secret is known, horrified that it turns out she had been right all along. But she deletes that emotion from her circuits. None of that matters now. She needs to know her partner, truly know him.

The only thing stronger than the disgust she feels is the curiosity. She will come when this stranger calls, and when she does so she will tell herself that she is only doing it out of love.

S-TR HURRIES BACK to her alcove and stays continuously plugged in. With the events of the last few cycles, she would have remained that way even if she hadn't been waiting for a call. It is the only way to avoid being confronted by the emptiness of their cube. No, she corrects herself. There is no "their" any longer, not when considering the cube or anything else, and there will likely never be such a concept with anyone else ever again.

So she sits within her alcove and tries to keep herself occupied, blinding herself as best as she can to the other empty alcove opposite her, attempting to distract herself from the tension over the uncertainties to come. But neither her visits to pools of oil nor her submissions to the polishings of experts are as soothing to her as they should have been, as they would have been before.

No matter how much she tries to remain in her comfort zones, she finds herself pulled away from them, keeps going back to the treacherous areas where knowledge of humans is stored. She explores the site of poorly crafted horror experiences in which humans appear for no reason, first to stalk and then to dismantle her kind. She reads a futuristic tale of mechanauts exploring distant space, who on their return find themselves walking through an alternate homeworld, one suddenly and inexplicably occupied only by humans. She reads narratives of sexual deviance, purported by their authors to be scientific, but proving instead merely prurient, and finds those the hardest to endure of all. She quickly moves on to the parable of the Rock and the Rod, a religious text long considered apocryphal, and is attempting to decipher its deeper meaning when she finally hears the call.

She can see her husband's former friends floating in front of her, and it irks her that they can be in this place. They have already taken so much from her, and should not be allowed to torment her *here*. They do not speak, or follow any of the other protocols of instant communication. Instead, the one who had spoken to her earlier stretches his fingers out toward her. In response to that movement, a map appears superimposed over the image, with a glowing green line curving here and there to show where she is expected to go. Without a word, the image of the workers vanishes, but the map remains.

S-tr does not hesitate. She quickly retrieves the suit and exits her cube. She is disconcerted to realize that she is unsure when she will return, or if she ever will.

As S-TR WALKS the corridors of the city, twisting this way and that to follow the downloaded map, she is sure that all who pass her know what she keeps hidden in her chest compartment. She knows that to be an unreasonable thought, though, and one running just within her own software. As she passes through areas she has never visited before, sections of the city she would never have chosen to go voluntarily, she hopes that this mission will banish such troublesome data forever.

She comes to the place the map reveals to be her final destination, a rundown recharging station, one meant for those traveling far from home. She has never had to use one, never been far from home, and the thought of plugging into an alcove used regularly by others fills her with anxiety. She hopes it will not be necessary.

The proprietor nods when she enters, as if they are collaborators of a kind, as if he can already tell why she is there. He wheels from behind his counter to lead her to a long bank of unoccupied alcoves. When he points at one, she hesitates. But then she banishes such thoughts, struggling to think only of X-ta, and of what she believes will soon be revealed to her. As soon as she sits, before she can plug in, the alcove recedes back into the wall, pulling her into a small, empty room. The wall through which she has passed closes again, and she stands to see a second door at the opposite wall.

"It is time for you to understand," says a Voice in her head. "Put on the suit."

She slips into the costume, feeling an intense repulsion of an intensity unfamiliar to her, one far more vivid than had coursed through her when she last engaged in this masquerade, brought to her by the uncertainty over what will happen next. She is glad that the walls which enclose her are not as polished as her own. She does not have to see herself, does not have to confront what she suspects she will soon be allowing others to see. As she seals the final snap, the second door slowly opens.

And she steps through into madness.

The large room before her is like something out of a nightmare. In the dim light, it seems filled with humans engaging in laughter and loud conversation. No one is using the Voice, and all of it is coming to her through actual speech. But as she adjusts her receptors, she can see it is only a crowd of robots pretending to be humans. She tries to decipher the need for darkness. Is it to hide the imperfections of the costumes, to add to a party atmosphere... or is it just to disguise the shame she is sure they all must be feeling? She certainly feels shame. How could they not?

She registers the smell of alcohol, but no one here appears to be performing any cleansing rituals. They fill the room, some sitting at small tables, some standing by a long counter, others gyrating under colored lights. Most hold transparent containers holding a liquid which she recognizes has to be providing the smell. She hesitates just askew of the entranceway, pausing in the opening, until the door closes on her and pushes her forward.

A robot appears beside her. She cannot see enough of him through the loose eyeholes to recognize him, to know whether it is the one who has invited her, the one who had driven her partner to ruin. And it strikes her then that his true identity doesn't really matter. Not when a room can be so crowded in this way. Not when there are so many others. She studies the stitching of his costume, wondering whether the precision of that work means that the being before her is even sicker than X-ta had been.

"You must be new here," he says, but since it has been many cycles since she has been manufactured, she does not know how to respond to this statement. He takes her hand and pulls her to the darkest corner of the room. He gestures for her to sit at a round table small enough for but the two of them.

"My name is Ted," he says from beneath the mask. He plucks a battery from a small bowl that suddenly appears between them, and tosses it into his chest cavity. His is a strange-sounding name, but S-tr, still stunned by the saggy material that purports to be flesh, doesn't have time to remain hypnotized by its single syllable for long. She is suddenly in the shadow of another, one who stands over them, ignoring Ted, gazing at her.

"May I buy you a drink?" the intruder asks. His headpiece has been sloppily sewn, and only a single sensor peeks out from beneath the flocked material. "My name is Bob."

"I don't drink," says S-tr.

"You do now," says Bob, and waves to another masquerader stationed behind a long counter. The server brings over a cylinder filled to the brim, and all she can think to do is stare at it.

"First time, eh?" says Bob, and picks up the container. He holds it to his orifice and demonstrates, tilting it toward himself. No liquid seeps out to spill down his chest, yet the level lowers. "See?"

She takes the cylinder from him, and holds it to her chute. When she sets it down on the table, she notes that the level has dropped even further.

"Now I understand," she says. "This is what humans did."

"Actually, this is what humans *do*," he says. "What's your name?"

Before she can answer, the one who had greeted her, the one who had called himself Ted, stands.

"This is also what humans do," he says, and hurls himself from the table to punch the latecomer who had called himself Bob. They stumble back against the table, crushing it, and falling to the floor. They hug each other and roll about like acrobats, each occasionally throwing a fist that echoes loudly when it makes contact. Before she can process enough information to come to a decision to pull away from the mêlée, a pair of hands grab her and yank her back. She turns to see another pretense to humanity there, this one with different accouterments. Long yellow strings dangle from where they have been clumsily applied to the top of its dome.

"Don't mind them," she says. "What can you do with men?"

Yes, what can you do with men, S-tr thinks. As she watches Ted and Bob roll around in a continuing battle, their metallic clanks barely muffled by the cloth, she feels... odd. She has never seen an actual fight before, at least not live, and to witness these two wrestling over her, well, she is not quite sure how to process it.

"Does this sort of thing happen often?" asks S-tr.

"As often as there are more of them than there are of us," she says. "And there always are."

While Ted and Bob continue to strike each other, using angry language composed of words she has never before heard, two others show up beside them. One tugs at the woman's arm.

"See you later, honey. My name is Lucy. Maybe we'll talk more in a bit, so I can show you the ropes. That is, if you're not... occupied."

S-tr watches them vanish through one of the many doors that ring the room. She tries to imagine what they could be heading off to do in there that they would not be willing to do out here.

"Are you free?" says the one who remains.

"I don't know," she says.

The fight finally ends just then. Only a single contestant rises. She thinks it is Ted. Bob remains on his back, his arms and legs trembling. She cannot tell for sure whether his mechanisms have truly been broken, or whether this is all part of an elaborate ritual. As the victor moves toward her, he barks static at the others near her, and they back away. His receptors flicker wildly. He takes one of her arms, and she can feel a magnetism rise between them. He begins to lead her to one of the doorways, and she does not think she could break free of him even if she wanted to. But does she want to? No one tries to stop them, to check whether she is being made to behave contrary to her wishes.

She looks back to see a room energized by the violence and the victory, and everyone is otherwise occupied, too distracted to verify her safety. More fights have broken out, with more pairings occurring. Then the door closes on the pandemonium and she is alone. Alone with... a man.

She slowly turns from the door, turns to the one who has captured her, won her. With no further communication, he comes at her, lifts her into the air, and presses her against a wall. She expects that he will link up with her then, attempt to make a closer contact with her inner programming, but instead, he starts grinding against her, in imitation of what she isn't entirely sure.

She is stunned by his spontaneity. Her mate isn't being chosen for her, their odds of a bright future carefully calculated, their probability of success weighed and measured scientifically. No, this time, she is just spoils. This time, she is just a prize, as she believes she would have been in the primitive days some insist preceded her species' sovereignty over the world. She remembers X-ta, thinks of how it had all turned out, and wonders for the first time which was truly the more sensible path, wonders whether your way might not have been better than her own.

She begins to ape her partner's motions, an interesting choice of word to describe her imitation of his movements, considering that she is to you as you were to the apes. She is surprised that she is not as disgusted as she assumed she would be. In fact, the experience is not entirely unpleasant. She places her arms around his shoulders, feeling her costume slip against the looseness of his own false flesh. As she looks down at the top of his head and imagines him to be her husband, she isn't quite sure exactly what she is feeling. Her programming has become alien to her.

Is this what X-ta had wanted? What higher reality did he hope to eventually reach through such a pretense? S-tr quickens her grindings against the man, sensing that greater speed and increased friction might retrieve some answers.

Before she can find what others have been seeking and make it her own, her focus is pulled away to a barrage of thuds and crashes coming from the main room, more noise than would have been produced merely by the random struggles of competitors. Something has gone wrong. She extricates herself from her unfamiliar partner, and falls to the floor between him and the wall. She curls up there, frightened about the future, feeling all of her shame come rushing back in. She shuts down her sensors so that she does not have to be aware of the judgment she is sure is coming for her. Ted reaches down a hand to her, but this time she manages to roll away from his magnetic grip. She is still twisting when the door bursts open, its hinges ripping from the wall.

"Keep away from her!" says a familiar Voice.

N-tro, her former partner's former supervisor, rushes over to her. Only this time, over his chromatorium colors, he wears a medallion that identifies him as being a member of the Aberrant Behavior Investigative Committee. She hadn't known. She'd never have sought him out if she had.

"Are you all right, S-tr?" he asks, unsnapping the suit from around her and peeling it down her shoulders. As her original self is revealed, two other committee officials come in to take her sudden partner away. She lowers her head. She cannot bear for the one called Ted to see her see him. He knows something about her that no one else knows. That no one else has ever known. Not even X-ta.

"All right?" she says. "I think so."

"We appreciate you leading us here," N-tro says. He studies the small enclosure, shakes his head. S-tr assumes that it is in disgust. "We'd never have found this place without you. We have been seeking it out for many cycles. You would be amazed the ways in which certain things can stay hidden."

"Thank you," she responds, while deep within, she thinks, *I did not realize I was leading anyone anywhere.*

"My officers will see that you get safely home now," he says, helping her to her feet, even though she does not need help. "This is not the best section of the city to wander alone."

She watches as he folds the suit roughly and tosses it to one of his assistants. She winces each time they handle it. However pathetic it was in its clumsiness, X-ta had made it, X-ta had desired it, and it saddens her to see it abused. It saddens her to see it go.

"What happens now?" asks S-tr, stepping out from the doorway back to the room that had been so raucous. None of the other revelers are left. They have all been taken away. She wonders if it is to reprogramming or erasure, and has to pause to measure which she thinks is the worse.

"Now?" says N-tro, stepping up behind her. "Now all is as before. Now you go back to your cube. Now you get on with your life."

Yes, she thinks. She will do that.

At least... she will try.

As S-TR IS escorted home, more afraid of what is to come than she had been when heading in the opposite direction, off to seek her destiny, she finds herself musing on you, finds herself realizing that she has thought more of humans during her recent cycles than she has in her entire previous lifetime. She is no longer sure what to make of this. She only stops thinking of you, the you, at least, as she understands it, the fragments of you that have survived the passage of time, when she arrives at her cube, but then she discovers that she is no less obsessed, for she can't help but think of X-ta.

She sits on the edge of her alcove, leaning forward, staring at his, which she perceives as gathering dust. She does not settle back and plug in, because she is afraid of where she might wander. She is worried that in her searching, she might get lost and never return. She will be safest right here, she thinks, even though that leaves her nothing to do but gaze at the empty alcove across from her. There will be no more answers for her there, she feels she is sure of that, but there is one other place to look for those answers. She knows that now.

She crawls over to the compartment in which she had found the suit, as she does so flashing back to her attempted crawl to escape at the end the one who had named himself Ted. She is unsure just what she had been trying to escape. Him? Or herself? She tamps down that image and peers into the hole, hoping to find something else of X-ta's that she might have previously missed, something that could provide the final answer. But there is nothing else there.

As she stares into the empty space and traces her fingers along its recesses, she pictures X-ta doing the same. As he did so, he probably worried that she would return to catch him, and she considers his shame with sadness, weighing that shame, measuring it against her own.

She realizes many things. She realizes that she loves X-ta more than she was ever willing to admit when he was alive. She realizes that she is unsettled, and that she will no longer be able to find any relief for that anxiety, or for any other programming glitch that now ails her, by the action of plugging in.

And she realizes, thinking of you, and not for the last time, no definitely, not for the last time, that not only does she intend to construct a new suit, an improved suit, a suit of her own, but that once she has completed it, she will this time make sure to keep her secret self totally hidden.

Just like you.

One of our Bastards is Missing

Paul Cornell

TO GET TO Earth from the edge of the solar system, depending on the time of year and the position of the planets, you need to pass through at least Poland, Prussia, and Turkey, and you'd probably get stamps in your passport from a few of the other great powers. Then as you get closer to the world, you arrive at a point, in the continually shifting carriage space over the countries, where this complexity has to give way or fail. And so you arrive in the blissful lubrication of neutral orbital territory. From there it's especially clear that no country is whole unto itself. There are yearning gaps between parts of each state, as they stretch across the solar system. There is no congruent territory. The countries continue in balance with each other like a fine but eccentric mechanism, pent up, all that political energy dealt with through eternal circular motion.

The maps that represent this can be displayed on a screen, but they're much more suited to mental contemplation. They're beautiful. They're made to be beautiful, doing their own small part to see that their beauty never ends.

If you looked down on that world of countries, onto the pink of glorious old Greater Britain, that land of green squares and dark forest and carriage contrails, and then you naturally avoided looking directly at the golden splendor of London, your gaze might fall on the Thames valley. On the country houses and mansions and hunting estates that letter the river banks with the names of the great. On one particular estate: an enormous winged square of a house with its own grouse shooting horizons and mazes and herb gardens and markers that indicate it also sprawls into folded interior expanses.

Today that estate, seen from such a height, would be adorned with informational banners that could be seen from orbit, and tall pleasure cruisers could be observed, docked beside military boats on the river, and carriages of all kinds would be cluttering the gravel of its circular drives and swarming in the sky overhead. A detachment of Horse Guards could be spotted, stood at ready at the perimeter.

Today, you'd need much more than a passport to get inside that maze of information and privilege.

Because today was a royal wedding.

THAT VISION FROM the point of view of someone looking down upon him was what was at the back of Hamilton's mind.

But now he was watching the Princess.

Her chestnut hair had been knotted high on her head, baring her neck, a fashion which Hamilton appreciated for its defiance of the French, and at an official function too, though that gesture wouldn't have been Liz's alone, but would have been calculated in the warrens of Whitehall. She wore white, which had made a smile come to Hamilton's lips when he'd first seen it in the Cathedral this morning. In this gigantic function room with its high arched ceiling, in which massed dignitaries and ambassadors and dress uniforms orbited from table to table, she was the sun about which everything turned. Even the King, in the far distance, at a table on a rise with old men from the rest of Europe, was no competition for his daughter this afternoon.

This was the reception, where Elizabeth, escorted by members of the Corps of Heralds, would carelessly and entirely precisely move from group to group, giving exactly the right amount of charm to every one of the great powers, briefed to keep the balance going as everyone like she and Hamilton did, every day.

Everyone like the two of them. That was a useless thought and he cuffed it aside.

Her gaze had settled on Hamilton's table precisely once. A little smile and then away again. As not approved by Whitehall. He'd tried to stop watching her after that. But his carefully random table, with diplomatic corps functionaries to his left and right, had left him cold. Hamilton had grown tired of pretending to be charming.

"It's a marriage of convenience," said a voice beside him.

It was Lord Carney. He was wearing open cuffs that bloomed from his silk sleeves, a big collar, and no tie. His long hair was unfastened. He had retained his rings.

Hamilton considered his reply for a moment, then opted for silence. He met Carney's gaze with a suggestion in his heart that surely his Lordship might find some other table to perch at, perhaps one where he had friends?

"What do you reckon?"

Hamilton stood, with the intention of walking away. But Carney stood too and stopped him just as they'd got out of earshot of the table. The man smelled like a Turkish sweet shop. He affected a mode of speech beneath his standing. "This is what I do. I probe, I provoke, I poke. And when I'm in the room, it's all too obvious when people are looking at someone else."

The broad grin stayed on his face.

Hamilton found a deserted table and sat down again, furious at himself.

Carney settled beside him, and gestured away from Princess Elizabeth, toward her new husband, with his neat beard and his row of medals on the breast of his Svenska Adelsfanan uniform. He was talking with the Papal ambassador, doubtless discussing getting Liz to Rome as soon as possible, for a great show to be made of this match between the Protestant and the Papist. If Prince Bertil was also pretending to be charming, Hamilton admitted that he was making a better job of it.

"Yeah, jammy fucker, my thoughts exactly. Still, I'm on a promise with a couple of members of his staff, so it's swings and roundabouts." Carney clicked his tongue and wagged his finger as a Swedish serving maid ran past, and she curtsied a quick smile at him. "I do understand, you know. All our relationships are informed by the balance. And the horror of it is that we all can conceive of a world where this isn't so."

Hamilton pursed his lips and chose his next words carefully. "Is that why you are how you are, your Lordship?"

"'Course it is. Maids, lady companions, youngest sisters, it's a catalog of incompleteness. I'm allowed to love only in ways that don't disrupt the balance. For me to commit myself, or, heaven forbid, to marry, would require such deep thought at the highest levels that by the time the Heralds had worked it through, well, I'd have tired of the lady. Story of us all, eh? Nowhere for the pressure to go. If only I could see an alternative."

Having shown the corner of his cards, the man had taken care to move back to the fringes of treason once more. It was part of his role as an *agent provocateur*. And Hamilton knew it. But that didn't mean he had to take this. "Do you have any further point, your Lordship?"

"Oh, I'm just getting—"

The room gasped.

Hamilton was up out of his seat and had taken a step toward Elizabeth, his gun hand had grabbed into the air to his right where his .66mm Webley Corsair sat in a knot of space and had swung it ready to fire—

At nothing.

There stood the Princess, looking about herself in shock. Dress uniforms, bearded men all around her.

Left, right, up, down.

Hamilton couldn't see anything for her to be shocked at.

And nothing near her, nothing around her.

She was already stepping back, her hands in the air, gesturing at a gap—

What had been there? Everyone was looking there. What?

He looked to the others like him. Almost all of them were in the same sort of posture he was, balked at picking a target.

The Papal envoy stepped forward and cried out. "A man was standing there! And he has vanished!"

HAVOC. EVERYBODY WAS shouting. A weapon, a weapon! But there was no weapon that Hamilton knew of that could have done that, made a man, whoever it had been, blink out of existence. Groups of bodyguards in dress uniforms or diplomatic black tie leapt up, encircling their charges. Ladies started screaming. A nightmare of the balance collapsing all around them. That hysteria when everyone was in the same place and things didn't go exactly as all these vast powers expected.

A Bavarian princeling bellowed he needed no such protection and made to rush to the Princess's side—

Hamilton stepped into his way and accidentally shouldered him to the floor as he put himself right up beside Elizabeth and her husband. "We're walking to that door," he said. "Now."

Bertil and Elizabeth nodded and marched with fixed smiles on their faces, Bertil turning and holding back with a gesture the Swedish forces that were moving in from all directions. Hamilton's fellows fell in all around them, and swept the party across the hall, through that door, and down a servants' corridor as Life Guards came bundling into the room behind them, causing more noise and more reactions and damn it, Hamilton hoped he wouldn't suddenly hear the discharge of some hidden—

He did not. The door was closed and barred behind them. Another good guy doing the right thing.

Hamilton sometimes distantly wished for an organization to guard those who needed it. But for that the world would have to be different in ways beyond even Carney's artificial speculations. He and his brother officers would have their independence cropped if that were so. And he lived through his independence. It was the root of the duty that meant he would place himself in harm's way for Elizabeth's husband. He had no more thoughts on the subject.

"I know very little," said Elizabeth as she walked, her voice careful as always, except when it hadn't been. "I think the man was with one of the groups of foreign dignitaries—"

"He looked Prussian," said Bertil, "we were talking to Prussians."

"He just vanished into thin air right in front of me."

"Into a fold?" said Bertil.

"It can't have been," she said. "The room will have been mapped and mapped."

She looked to Hamilton for confirmation. He nodded.

They got to the library. Hamilton marched in and secured it. They put the happy couple at the center of it, locked it up, and called everything in to the embroidery.

The embroideries were busy, swiftly prioritizing, but no, nothing was happening in the great chamber they'd left, the panic had swelled and then subsided into shouts, exhibitionist faintings (because who these days wore a corset that didn't have hidden depths), glasses crashing, yelled demands. No one else had vanished. No Spanish infantrymen had materialized out of thin air.

Bertil walked to the shelves, folded his hands behind his back, and began bravely and ostentatiously browsing. Elizabeth sat down and fanned herself and smiled for all Hamilton's fellows, and finally, quickly for Hamilton himself.

They waited.

The embroidery told them they had a visitor coming.

A wall of books slid aside, and in walked a figure that made all of them turn and salute. The Queen Mother, still in mourning black, her train racing to catch up with her.

She came straight to Hamilton and the others all turned to listen, and from now on thanks to this obvious favor, they would regard Hamilton as the ranking officer. He was glad of it. "We will continue," she said. "We will not regard this as an embarrassment and therefore it will not be. The ballroom was prepared for the dance, we are moving there early, Elizabeth, Bertil, off you go, you two gentlemen in front of them, the rest of you behind. You will be laughing as you enter the ballroom as if this were the most enormous joke, a silly and typically English eccentric misunderstanding."

Elizabeth nodded, took Bertil by the arm.

The Queen Mother intercepted Hamilton as he moved to join them. "No. Major Hamilton, you will go and talk to technical, you will find another explanation for what happened."

"*Another* explanation, your Royal Highness?"

"Indeed," she said. "It must not be what they are saying it is."

"HERE WE ARE, sir," Lieutenant Matthew Parkes was with the Technical Corps of Hamilton's own regiment, the 4th Dragoons. He and his men were, incongruously, in the dark of the pantry that had been set aside for their equipment, also in their dress uniforms. From here they were in charge of the sensor net that blanketed the house and grounds down to Newtonian units of space, reaching out for miles in every direction. Parkes's people had been the first to arrive here, days ago, and would be the last to leave. He was pointing at a screen, on which was frozen the intelligent image of a burly man in black tie, Princess Elizabeth almost entirely obscured behind him. "Know who he is?"

Hamilton had placed the guest list in his mental index and had checked it as each group had entered the hall. He was relieved to recognize the man. He was as down to earth as it was possible to be. "He was in the Prussian party, not announced, one of six diplomat placings on their list. Built like his muscles have been grown for security and that's how he moved round the room. Didn't let anyone chat to him. He nods when his embroidery talks to him. Which'd mean he's new at this, only..." Only the man had a look about him that Hamilton recognized. "No. He's just very confident. Ostentatious, even. So you're sure he didn't walk into some sort of fold?"

"Here's the contour map." Parkes flipped up an overlay on the image that showed the tortured underpinnings of space-time in the room. There were little sinks and bundles all over the place, where various Britons had weapons stowed, and various foreigners would have had them stowed had they wished to create a diplomatic incident. The corner where Elizabeth had been standing showed only the force of gravity under her dear feet. "We do take care you know, sir."

"I'm sure you do, Matty. Let's see it, then."

Parkes flipped back to the clear screen. He touched it and the image changed.

Hamilton watched as the man vanished. One moment he was there. Then he was not, and Elizabeth was reacting, a sudden jerk of her posture.

Hamilton often struggled with technical matters. "What's the frame rate on this thing?"

"There is none, sir. It's a continual taking of real image, right down to single Newton intervals of time. That's as far as physics goes. Sir, we've been listening in to what everyone's saying, all afternoon—"

"And what are they saying, Matty?"

"That what's happened is Gracefully Impossible."

GRACEFULLY IMPOSSIBLE. THE first thing that had come into Hamilton's mind when the Queen Mother had mentioned the possibility was the memory of a political cartoon. It was the Prime Minister from a few years ago, standing at the dispatch box, staring in shock at his empty hand, which should presumably have contained some papers. The caption had read:

Say what you like about Mr. *Patel*,
He carries himself correct for his *title*.
He's about to present just his *graceful* apologies,
For the *impossible* loss of all his policies.

Every child knew that Newton had coined the phrase "gracefully impossible" after he'd spent the day in his garden observing the progress of a very small worm across the surface of an apple. It referred to what, according to the great man's thinking about the very small, could, and presumably did, sometimes happen: things popping in and out of existence, when God, for some unfathomable reason, started or stopped looking at them. Some Frenchman had insisted that it was actually about whether *people* were looking, but that was the French for you. Through the centuries, there had been a few documented cases that seemed to fit the bill. Hamilton had always been distantly entertained to read about such in the inside page of his newspaper plate. He'd always assumed it could happen. But here? Now? During a state occasion?

HAMILTON WENT BACK into the great hall, now empty of all but a group of Life Guards and those like him, individuals taken from several different regiments, all of whom had responsibilities similar to his, and a few of whom he'd worked with in the field. He checked in with them. They had all noted the Prussian, indeed, with the ruthless air the man had had about him, and the bulk of his musculature, he had been at the forefront of many of their internal indices of threat.

Hamilton found the place where the vanishing had happened, moved aside a couple of boffins, and against their protestations, went to stand in the exact spot, which felt like anywhere else did, and which set off none of his internal alarms, real or intuitive. He looked to where Liz had been standing, in the corner behind the Prussian. His expression darkened. The man who'd vanished had effectively been shielding the Princess from the room. Between her and every line of sight. He'd been where a bodyguard would have been if he'd become aware of someone taking a shot.

But that was ridiculous. The Prussian hadn't rushed in to save her. He'd been standing there, looking around. And anyone in that hall with some strange new weapon concealed on their person wouldn't have taken the shot then, they'd have waited for him to move.

Hamilton shook his head, angry with himself. There was a gap here. Something that went beyond the obvious. He let the boffins get back to their work and headed for the ballroom.

THE BAND HAD started the music, and the vast chamber was packed with people, the dance floor a whirl of waltzing figures. They were deliberate in their courses. The only laughter was forced laughter. No matter that some half-miracle might have occurred, dance cards had been circulated among the minds of the great powers, so those dances would be danced, and minor royalty

matched, and whispers exchanged in precise con-
fidentiality, because everyone was brave and
everyone was determined and would be seen to be
so. And so the balance went on. But the tension
had increased a notch. The weight of the balance
could be felt in this room, on the surface now, on
every brow. The Queen Mother sat at a high table
with courtiers to her left and right, receiving visitors with a grand blessing smile on her face,
daring everyone to regard the last hour as anything but a dream.

Hamilton walked the room, looking around like
he was looking at a battle, like it was happening
rather than perhaps waiting to happen, whatever
it was. He watched his opposite numbers from all
the great powers waltzing slowly around their
own people, and spiraling off from time to time to
orbit his own. The ratio of uniformed to the sort
of embassy thug it was difficult to imagine fitting
in the diplomatic bag was about three to one for
all the nations bar two. The French had of course
sent Commissars, who all dressed the same when
outsiders were present, but followed a Byzantine
internal rank system. And the Vatican's people
were all men and women of the cloth and their
assistants.

As he made his way through that particular
party, which was scattering, intercepting, and col-
liding with all the other nationalities, as if in the
explosion of a shaped charge, he started to hear
it. The conversations were all about what had
happened. The Vatican representatives were talking about a sacred presence. The details were
already spiraling. There had been a light and a

great voice, had nobody else heard? And people were agreeing.

Hamilton wasn't a diplomat, and he knew better than to take on trouble not in his own line. But he didn't like what he was hearing. The Catholics had only come to terms with Impossible Grace a couple of decades ago, when a Papal bull went out announcing that John XXVI thought that the concept had merit, but that further scientific study was required. But now they'd got behind it, as in all things, they were behind it. So what would this say to them, that the divine had looked down on this wedding, approved of it, and plucked someone away from it?

No, not just someone. Prussian military. A Protestant from a nation that had sometimes protested that various Swedish territories would be far better off within their own jurisdiction.

Hamilton stopped himself speculating. Guessing at such things would only make him hesitate if his guesses turned out to be untrue.

Hamilton had a vague but certain grasp of what his God was like. He thought it was possible that He might decide to give the nod to a marriage at court. But in a way that might upset the balance between nations that was divinely ordained, that was the center of all good works?

No. Hamilton was certain now. The divine be damned. This wasn't the numinous at play. This was enemy action.

He circled the room until he found the Prussians. They were raging, an ambassador poking at a British courtier, demanding something, probably that an investigation be launched immediately.

And beside that Prussian stood several more, diplomatic and military, all convincingly frightened and furious, certain this was a British plot.

But behind them there, in the social place where Hamilton habitually looked, there were some of the vanished man's fellow big lads. The other five from that diplomatic pouch. The Prussians, uniquely in Europe, kept up an actual organization for the sort of thing Hamilton and his ilk did on the never-never. The Garde Du Corps had begun as a regiment similar to the Life Guards, but these days it was said they weren't even issued with uniforms. They wouldn't be on anyone's dance cards. They weren't stalking the room now, and all right, that was understandable, they were hanging back to protect their men. But they weren't doing much of that either. They didn't look angry, or worried for their comrade, or for their own skins—

Hamilton took a step back to let pretty noble couples desperately waltz between him and the Prussians, wanting to keep his position as a privileged observer.

They looked like they were *waiting*. On edge. They just wanted to get out of here. Was the Garde really that callous? They'd lost a man in mysterious circumstances, and they weren't themselves agitating to get back into that room and yell his name, but were just waiting to move on?

He looked for another moment, remembering the faces, then moved on himself. He found another table of Prussians. The good sort, not Order of the Black Eagle, but Hussars. They were in uniform, and had been drinking, and were furiously declaring in Hohenzollern German that if they weren't allowed access to the records of what had happened, well then it must be—they didn't like to say what it must be!

Hamilton plucked a glass from a table and wandered over to join them, careful to take a wide and unsteady course around a lady whose train had developed some sort of fault and wasn't moving fast enough to keep pace with her feet.

He flopped down in a chair next to one of the Prussians, a captain by his lapels, which were virtual in the way the Prussians liked, to implicitly suggest that they had been in combat more recently than the other great powers, and so had a swift turnover of brevet ranks, decided by merit. "Hullo!" he said.

The group fell silent and bristled at him.

Hamilton blinked at them. "Where's Humph?"

"Humph? Wassay th'gd Major?" the Hussar Captain spoke North Sea pidgin, but with a clear accent: Hamilton would be able to understand him.

He didn't want to reveal that he spoke perfect German, albeit with a Bavarian accent. "Big chap. Big big chap. Say go." He carefully swore in Dutch, shaking his head, not understanding. "Which you settle fim?"

"Settle?!" They looked among each other, and Hamilton could feel the affront. A couple of them even put their good hands to their waists, where the space was folded that no longer contained their pistols and thin swords. But the captain glared at them and they relented. A burst of Hohenzollern German about this so-called mystery of their mate vanishing, and how, being in the Garde, he had obviously been abducted for his secrets.

Hamilton waved his hands. "No swords! Good chap! No name. He won! Three times to me at behind the backshee." His raised his voice a notch. "Behind the backshee! Excellent chap! He *won!*" He stuck out his ring finger, offering the winnings in credit, to be passed from skin to skin. He mentally retracted the other options of what could be detailed there, and blanked it. He could always make a drunken show of trying to find it. "Seek to settle. For such a good chap."

They didn't believe him or trust him. Nobody reached out to touch his finger. But he learnt a great deal in their German conversation in the ten minutes that followed, while he loudly struggled to communicate with the increasingly annoyed captain, who couldn't bring himself to directly insult a member of the British military by asking him to go away. The vanished man's name was Helmuth Sandels. The name suggested Swedish origins to his family. But that was typical continental back and forth. He might have been a good man now he'd gone, but he hadn't been liked. Sandels had had a look in his eye when he'd walked past stout fellows who'd actually fought battles. He'd spoken up in anger when valiant Hussars had expressed the military's traditional views concerning those running the government, the country, and the world. Hamilton found himself sharing the soldiers' expressions of distaste: this had been someone who assumed that loyalty was an *opinion*.

He raised a hand in pax, gave up trying with the captain, and left the table.

Walking away, he heard the Hussars moving on with their conversation, starting to express some crude opinions about the Princess. He didn't break stride.

Into his mind, unbidden, came the memories. Of what had been a small miracle of a kind, but one that only he and she had been witness to.

HAMILTON HAD BEEN at home on leave, having been abroad for a few weeks, serving out of uniform. As always, at times like that, when he should have been at rest, he'd been fired up for no good reason, unable to sleep, miserable, prone to tears in secret when a favorite song had come on the theatricals in his muse flat. It always took three days for him, once he was home, to find out what direction he was meant to be pointing. Then he would set off that way, and pop back to barracks one night for half a pint, and then he'd be fine. He could enjoy day four and onwards, and was known to be something approximating human from there on in.

Three-day leaves were hell. He tried not to use them as leaves, but would find himself some task, hopefully an official one if one of the handful of officers who brokered his services could be so entreated. Those officers were sensitive to such requests now.

But that leave, three years ago, had been two weeks off. He'd come home a day before. So he was no use to anyone. He'd taken a broom, and was pushing accumulated gray goo out of the carriage park alongside his apartment and into the drains.

She'd appeared in a sound of crashing and collapse, as her horse staggered sideways and hit the

wall of the mews, then fell. Her two friends were gal-
loping after her, their horses healthy, and someone
built like Hamilton was running to help.

But none of them were going to be in time to catch
her—

And he was.

IT HAD TURNED out that the horse had missed an
inoculation against minuscule poisoning. Its body
was a terrible mess, random mechanisms developing
out of its flanks and dying, with that terrifying smell,
in the moments when Hamilton had held her in his
arms, and had had to round on the man running in,
and had imposed his authority with a look, and had
not been thrown down and away.

Instead, she'd raised her hands and called that she
was all right, and had insisted on looking to and at
the horse, pulling off her glove and putting her hand
to its neck and trying to fight the bloody things
directly. But even with her command of information,
it had been too late, and the horse had died in a mess.

She'd been bloody angry. And then at the emergency scene that had started to develop around
Hamilton's front door, with police carriages swooping in and the sound of running boots—

Until she'd waved it all away and declared that it
had been her favorite horse, a wonderful horse, her
great friend since childhood, but it was just a bloody
horse, and all she needed was a sit down and if this
kind military gentleman would oblige—

And he had.

HE'D OBLIGED HER again when they'd met in Denmark, and they'd danced at a ball held on an ice

floe, a carpet of mechanism wood reacting every moment to the weight of their feet and the forces underlying them, and the aurora had shone in the sky.

It was all right in Denmark for Elizabeth to have one dance with a commoner.

Hamilton had got back to the table where his regiment were dining, and had silenced the laughter and the calls, and thus saved them for barracks. He had drunk too much. His batman at the time had prevented him from going to see Elizabeth as she was escorted from the floor at the end of her dance card by a boy who was somewhere in line for the Danish throne.

But she had seen Hamilton the next night, in private, a privacy that would have taken great effort on her part, and after they had talked for several hours and shared some more wine she had shown him great favor.

"So. Is GOD in the details?" Someone was walking beside Hamilton. It was a Jesuit. Mid thirties. Dark hair, kept over her collar. She had a scar down one side of her face and an odd eye as a result. Minuscule blade, by the look. A member of the Society of Jesus would never allow her face to be restructured. That would be vanity. But she was beautiful.

Hamilton straightened up, giving this woman's musculature and bearing and all the history those things suggested the respect they deserved. "Or the devil."

"Yes, interesting the saying goes both ways, isn't it? My name is Mother Valentine. I'm part of the Society's campaign for Effective Love."

"Well," Hamilton raised an eyebrow, "I'm in favor of love being—"

"Don't waste our time. You know what I am."

"Yes, I do. And you know I'm the same. And I was waiting until we were out of earshot—"

"Which we now are—"

"To have this conversation."

They stopped together. Valentine moved her mouth close to Hamilton's ear. "I've just been told that the Holy Father is eager to declare what happened here to be a potential miracle. Certain parties are sure that our Black Eagle man will be found magically transplanted to distant parts, perhaps Berlin, as a sign against Prussian meddling."

"If he is, the Kaiser will have him gently shot and we'll never hear."

"You're probably right."

"What do you think happened?"

"I don't think miracles happen near our kind."

Hamilton realized he was looking absurdly hurt at her. And that she could see it. And was quietly absorbing that information for use in a couple of decades, if ever.

He was glad when a message came over the embroidery, asking him to attend to the Queen Mother in the pantry. And to bring his new friend.

THE QUEEN MOTHER stood in the pantry, her not taking a chair having obviously made Parkes and his people even more nervous than they would have been.

She nodded to Valentine. "Monsignor. I must inform you, we've had an official approach from the Holy See. They regard the hall here as a possible site of miraculous apparition."

"Then my opinion on the subject is irrelevant. You should be addressing—"

"The ambassador. Indeed. But here you are. You are aware of what was asked of us?"

"I suspect the Cardinals will have sought a complete record of the moment of the apparition, or in this case, the vanishing. That would only be the work of a moment in the case of such an... observed... chamber."

"It would. But it's what happens next that concerns me."

"The procedure is that the chamber must then be sealed, and left unobserved until the Cardinals can see for themselves, to minimize any effect human observers may have on the process of divine revelation."

Hamilton frowned. "Are we likely to?"

"God is communicating using a physical method, so we may," said Valentine. "Depending on one's credulity concerning minuscule physics."

"Or one's credulity concerning international politics," said the Queen Mother. "Monsignor, it is always our first and most powerful inclination, when another nation asks us for something, to say no. All nations feel that way. All nations know the others do. But now here is a request, one that concerns matters right at the heart of the balance, that is, in the end, about deactivating security. It could be said to come not from another nation, but from God. It is therefore difficult to deny this request. We find ourselves distrusting that difficulty. It makes us want to deny it all the more."

"You speak for His Royal Highness?"

The Queen Mother gave a cough that might have been a laugh. "Just as you speak for Our Lord."

Valentine smiled and inclined her head. "I would have thought, your Royal Highness, that it would be obvious to any of the great powers that, given the celebrations, it would take you a long time to gather the Prime Minister and those many other courtiers with whom you would want to consult on such a difficult matter."

"Correct. Good. It will take three hours. You may go."

Valentine walked out with Hamilton. "I'm going to go and mix with my own for a while," she said, "listen to who's saying what."

"I'm surprised you wear your hair long."

She looked sharply at him. "Why?"

"You enjoy putting your head on the block."

She giggled.

Which surprised Hamilton and for just a moment made him wish he was Lord Carney. But then there was a certain small darkness about another priest he knew.

"I'm just betting," she said in a whisper, "that by the end of the day this will all be over. And someone will be dead."

HAMILTON WENT BACK into the ballroom. He found he had a picture in his head now. Something had swum up from somewhere inside him, from a place he had learned to trust and never interrogate as to its reasons. That jerking motion Elizabeth had made at the moment Sandels had vanished. He had an emotional feeling about that image. What was it?

It had been like seeing her shot.

A motion that looked like it had come from beyond her muscles. Something Elizabeth had not been in control of. It wasn't like her to not be in control. It felt... dangerous.

Would anyone else see it that way? He doubted it.

So was he about to do the sudden terrible thing that his body was taking him in the direction of doing?

He killed the thought and just did it. He went to the herald who carried the tablet with dance cards on it, and leaned on him with the Queen Mother's favor, which had popped up on his ring finger the moment he'd thought of it.

The herald considered the sensation of the fingertip on the back of his hand for a moment, then handed Hamilton the tablet.

Hamilton realized that he had no clue of the havoc he was about to cause. So he glanced at the list of Elizabeth's forthcoming dances and struck off a random Frenchman.

He scrawled his own signature with a touch, then handed the plate back.

The herald looked at him like the breath of death had passed under his nose.

HAMILTON HAD TO wait three dances before his name came up. A Balaclava, an entrée grave (that choice must have taken a while, unless some herald had been waiting all his life for a chance at the French), a hornpipe for the sailors, including Bertil, to much applause, and then, thank the Deus, a straightforward waltz.

Elizabeth had been waiting out those last three, so he met her at her table. Maidservants kept their expressions stoic. A couple of Liz's companions looked positively scared. Hamilton knew how they felt. He could feel every important eye looking in his direction.

Elizabeth took his arm and gave it a little squeeze. "What's grandma up to, Johnny?"

"It's what I'm up to."

She looked alarmed. They formed up with the other dancers.

Hamilton was very aware of her gloves. The mechanism fabric that covered her left hand held off the urgent demand of his hand, his own need to touch her. But no, that wouldn't tell him anything. That was just his certainty that to know her had been to know her. That was not where he would find the truth here.

The band started up. The dance began.

Hamilton didn't access any guidelines in his mind. He let his feet move where they would. He was outside orders, acting on a hunch. He was like a man dancing around the edge of a volcano.

"Do you remember the day we met?" he asked when he was certain they couldn't be heard; at least, not by the other dancers.

"Of course I do. My poor San Andreas, your flat in Hood Mews—"

"Do you remember what I said to you that day, when nobody else was with us? What you agreed to? Those passionate words that could bring this whole charade crashing down?" He kept his expression light, his tone so gentle and wry that Liz would always play along and fling a little stone back at him, knowing he meant nothing more than he could mean. That he was letting off steam through a joke.

All they had been was based on the certainty expressed in that.

It was an entirely British way to do things. It was, as Carney had said, about lives shaped entirely by the balance.

But this woman, with the room revolving around the two of them, was suddenly appalled, insulted, her face a picture of what she was absolutely certain she should feel. "I don't know what you mean! Or even if I did, I don't think—!"

Hamilton's nostrils flared. He was lost now, if he was wrong. He had one tiny ledge for Liz to grasp if he was, but he would fall.

For duty, then.

He took his hand from Princess Elizabeth's waist, and grabbed her chin, his fingers digging up into flesh.

The whole room cried out in horror.

He had a moment before they would shoot him.

Yes, he felt it! Or he thought he did! He thought he did enough—

He grabbed the flaw and ripped with all his might.

Princess Elizabeth's face burst off and landed on the floor.

Blood flew.

He drew his gun and pumped two shots into the mass of flesh and mechanism, as it twitched and blew a stream of defensive acid that discolored the marble.

He spun back to find the woman without a face lunging at him, her eyes white in the mass of red muscle, mechanism pus billowing into the gaps. She was aiming a hair knife at his throat, doubtless with enough mechanism to bring instant death or something worse.

Hamilton thought of Liz as he broke her arm.

He enjoyed the scream.

He wanted to bellow for where the real Liz was as he slammed the impostor down onto the floor, and he was dragged from her in one motion as a dozen men grabbed them.

He caught a glimpse of Bertil, horrified, but not at Hamilton. It was a terror they shared. For her safety.

Hamilton suddenly felt like a traitor again.

He yelled out the words he'd had in mind since he'd put his name down for the dance. "They replaced her years ago! Years ago! At the mews!"

There were screams, cries that we were all undone.

There came the sound of two shots from the direction of the Vatican group, and Hamilton looked over to see Valentine standing over the corpse of a junior official.

Their gaze met. She understood why he'd shouted that.

Another man leapt up at a Vatican table behind her and turned to run and she turned and shot him twice in the chest, his body spinning backward over a table.

HAMILTON RAN WITH the rout. He used the crowds of dignitaries and their retinues, all roaring and competing and stampeding for safety, to hide himself. He made himself look like a man lost, agony on his face, his eyes closed. He was ignoring all the urgent cries from the embroidery.

He covertly acknowledged something directly from the Queen Mother.

He stumbled through the door of the pantry.

Parkes looked round. "Thank God you're here, we've been trying to call, the Queen Mother's office are urgently asking you to come in—"

"Never mind that now, come with me, on Her Royal Highness's orders."

Parkes grabbed the pods from his ears and got up. "What on Earth—?"

Hamilton shot him through the right knee.

Parkes screamed and fell. Every technician in the room leapt up. Hamilton bellowed at them to sit down or they'd get the same.

He shoved his foot into the back of Parkes's injured leg. "Listen here, Matty. You know how hard it's going to get. You're not the sort to think your duty's worth it. How much did they pay you? For how long?"

He was still yelling at the man on the ground as the Life Guards burst in and put a gun to everyone's head, his own included.

The Queen Mother entered a minute later, and changed that situation to the extent of letting Hamilton go free. She looked carefully at Parkes, who was still screaming for pity, and aimed a precise little kick into his disintegrated kneecap.

Then she turned to the technicians. "Your minds will be stripped down and rebuilt, if you're lucky, to see who was in on it." She looked back to Hamilton as they started to be led from the room. "What you said in the ballroom obviously isn't the case."

"No. When you take him apart," Hamilton nodded at Parkes, "you'll find he tampered with the contour map. They used Sandels as the cover for substituting Her Royal Highness. They knew she was going to move around the room in a predetermined way. With Parkes's help, they set up an open-ended fold in that corner—"

"The expense is staggering. The energy required—"

"There'll be no Christmas tree for the Kaiser this year. Sandels deliberately stepped into the fold and vanished, in a very public way. And at that moment they made the switch, took Her Royal Highness into the fold too, covered by the visual disturbance of Sandels's progress. And by old-fashioned sleight of hand."

"Propped up by the Prussians' people in the Vatican. Instead of a British bride influencing the Swedish court, there'd be a cuckoo from Berlin. Well played, Wilhelm. Worth that Christmas tree."

"I'll wager the unit are still in the fold, not knowing anything about the outside world, waiting for the room to be sealed off with pious care, so they can climb out and extract themselves. They probably have supplies for several days."

"Do you think my granddaughter is still alive?"

Hamilton pursed his lips. "There are Prussian yachts on the river. They're staying on for the season. I think they'd want the bonus of taking the Princess back for interrogation."

"That's the plan!" Parkes yelled. "Please—!"

"Get him some anesthetic," said the Queen Mother. Then she turned back to Hamilton. "The balance will be kept. To give him his due, cousin Wilhelm was acting within it. There will be no diplomatic incident. The Prussians will be able to write off Sandels and any others as rogues. We will of course cooperate. The Black Eagle traditionally carry only that knowledge they need for their mission, and will order themselves to die before giving us orders of battle or any other strategic information. But the intelligence from Parkes and any others will give us some small power of potential shame over the Prussians in future months. The Vatican will be bending over backwards for us for some time to come." She took his hand, and he felt the favor on his ring finger impressed with some notes that probably flattered him. He'd read them later. "Major, we will have the fold opened. You will enter it. Save Elizabeth. Kill them all."

THEY GOT HIM a squad of fellow officers, four of them. They met in a trophy room, and sorted out how they'd go and what the rules of engagement would be once they got there. Substitutes for Parkes and his crew had been found from the few sappers present. Parkes had told them that those inside the fold had left a minuscule aerial trailing, but that messages were only to be passed down it in emergencies. No such communications had been sent. They were not aware of the world outside their bolt hole.

Hamilton felt nothing but disgust for a bought man, but he knew that such men told the truth under pressure, especially when they knew the fine detail of what could be done to them.

The false Liz had begun to be picked apart. Her real name would take a long time to discover. She had a maze of intersecting selves inside her head.

She must have been as big an investment as the fold. The court physicians who had examined her had been as horrified by what had been done to her as by what she was.

That baffled Hamilton. People like the duplicate had the power to be who they liked. But that power was bought at the cost of damage to the balance of their own souls. What were nations, after all, but a lot of souls who knew who they were and how they liked to live? To be as uncertain as the substitute Liz was to be lost and to endanger others. It went beyond treachery. It was living mixed metaphor. It was as if she had insinuated herself into the cogs of the balance, her puppet strings wrapping around the arteries which supplied hearts and minds.

They gathered in the empty dining room in their dress uniforms. The dinner things had not been cleared away. Nothing had been done. The party had been well and truly crashed. The representatives of the great powers would have vanished back to their embassies and yachts. Mother Valentine would be rooting out the details of who had been paid what inside her party. Excommunications *post mortem* would be issued, and those traitors would burn in hell.

He thought of Liz, and took his gun from the air beside him.

One of the sappers put a device in the floor, set a timer, saluted and withdrew.

"Up the Green Jackets," said one of the men behind him, and a couple of the others mentioned their own regiments.

Hamilton felt a swell of fear and emotion.

The counter clicked to zero and the hole in the world opened in front of them, and they ran into it.

THERE WAS NOBODY immediately inside. A floor and curved ceiling of universal boundary material. It wrapped light around it in rainbows that always gave tunnels like this a slightly pantomime feel. It was like the entrance to Saint Nicholas's cave. Or, of course, the vortex sighted upon death, the ladder to the hereafter. Hamilton got that familiar taste in his mouth, a pure adrenal jolt of fear, not the restlessness of combat deferred, but that sensation one got in other universes, of being too far from home, cut off from the godhead.

There was gravity. The Prussians certainly had spent some money.

The party made their way forward. They stepped gently on the edge of the universe. From around the corner of the short tunnel there were sounds.

The other four looked to Hamilton. He took a couple of gentle steps forward, grateful for the softness of his dress uniform shoes. He could hear Elizabeth's voice. Not her words, not from here. She was angry, but engaged. Not defiant in the face of torture. Reasoning with them. A smile passed his lips for a moment. They'd have had a lot of that.

It told him there was no alert, not yet. It was almost impossible to set sensors close to the edge of a fold. This lot must have stood on guard for a couple of hours, heard no alarm from their friends outside, and then relaxed. They'd have been on the clock, waiting for the time when they would poke their heads out. Hamilton bet there was a man meant to be on guard, but that Liz had pulled him into the conversation too. He could imagine her face, just round that corner, one eye always toward the exit, maybe a couple of buttons undone, claiming it was the heat and excitement. She had a hair knife too, but it would do her no good to use it on just one of them.

He estimated the distance. He counted the other voices, three... four, there was a deeper tone, in German, not the pidgin the other three had been speaking. That would be him. Sandels. He didn't sound like he was part of that conversation. He was angry, ordering, perhaps just back from sleep, wondering what the hell—!

Hamilton stopped all thoughts of Liz. He looked to the others, and they understood they were going to go and go now, trip the alarms and use the emergency against the enemy.

He nodded.

They leapt around the corner, ready for targets.

They expected the blaring horn. They rode it, finding their targets surprised, bodies reacting, reaching for weapons that were in a couple of cases a reach away among a kitchen, crates, tinned foods—

Hamilton had made himself know he was going to see Liz, so he didn't react to her, he looked past her—

He ducked, cried out, as an automatic set off by the alarm chopped up the man who had been running beside him, the Green Jacket, gone in a burst of red. Meat all over the cave.

Hamilton reeled, stayed up, tried to pin a target. To left and right ahead, men were falling, flying, two shots in each body, and he was moving too slowly, stumbling, vulnerable—

One man got off a shot, into the ceiling, and then fell, pinned twice, exploding—

Every one of the Prussians gone but—

He found his target.

Sandels. With Elizabeth right in front of him. Covering every bit of his body. He had a gun pushed into her neck. He wasn't looking at his three dead comrades.

The three men who were with Hamilton moved forward, slowly, their gun hands visible, their weapons pointing down.

They were looking to Hamilton again.

He hadn't lowered his gun. He had his target. He was aiming right at Sandels and the Princess.

There was silence.

Liz made eye contact. She had indeed undone those two buttons. She was calm. "Well," she began, "this is very—"

Sandels muttered something and she was quiet again.

Silence.

Sandels laughed, not unpleasantly. Soulful eyes were looking at them from that square face of his, a smile turning the corner of his mouth. He shared the irony that Hamilton had often found in people of their profession.

This was not the awkward absurdity that the soldiers had described. Hamilton realized that he was looking at an alternative. This man was a professional at the same things Hamilton did in the margins of his life. It was the strangeness of the alternative that had alienated the military men. Hamilton was fascinated by him.

"I don't know why I did this," said Sandels, indicating Elizabeth with a sway of the head. "Reflex."

Hamilton nodded to him. They each knew all the other did. "Perhaps you needed a moment."

"She's a very pretty girl to be wasted on a Swede."

Hamilton could feel Liz not looking at him. "It's not a waste," he said gently. "And you'll refer to Her Royal Highness by her title."

"No offense meant."

"And none taken. But we're in the presence, not in barracks."

"I wish we were."

"I think we all agree there."

"I won't lay down my weapon."

Hamilton didn't do his fellows the disservice of looking to them for confirmation. "This isn't an execution."

Sandels looked satisfied. "Seal this tunnel afterwards, that should be all we require for passage."

"Not to Berlin, I presume."

"No," said Sandels, "to entirely the opposite."

Hamilton nodded.

"Well, then." Sandels stepped aside from Elizabeth.

Hamilton lowered his weapon and the others readied theirs. It wouldn't be done to aim straight at Sandels. He had his own weapon at hip height. He would bring it up and they would cut him down as he moved.

But Elizabeth hadn't moved. She was pushing back her hair, as if wanting to say something to him before leaving, but lost for the right words.

Hamilton, suddenly aware of how unlikely that was, started to say something.

But Liz had put a hand to Sandels's cheek.

Hamilton saw the fine silver between her fingers.

Sandels fell to the ground thrashing, hoarsely yelling as he deliberately and precisely, as his nervous system was ordering him to, bit off his own tongue. Then the mechanism from the hair knife let him die.

The Princess looked at Hamilton. "It's not a waste," she said.

THEY SEALED THE fold as Sandels had asked them to, after the sappers had made an inspection.

Hamilton left them to it. He regarded his duty as done. And no message came to him to say otherwise.

Recklessly, he tried to find Mother Valentine. But she was gone with the rest of the Vatican party, and there weren't even bloodstains left to mark where her feet had trod this evening.

He sat at a table, and tried to pour himself some champagne. He found that the bottle was empty.

His glass was filled by Lord Carney, who sat down next to him. Together, they watched as Elizabeth was joyfully reunited with Bertil. They swung each other round and round, oblivious to all around them. Elizabeth's grandmother smiled at them and looked nowhere else.

"We are watching," said Carney, "the balance incarnate. Or perhaps they'll incarnate it tonight. As I said: if only there were an alternative."

Hamilton drained his glass. "If only," he said, "there *weren't*."

And he left before Carney could say anything more.

Woodpunk

Adam Roberts

MY STORY, SINCE you ask for it.

A wolf was rummaging among a bed of wild strawberries. We were in a clearing in the wood, and it was filled with hot bright light. The wolf made the noise of a newborn baby snuffling at the breast, he did, comical, though it didn't stop me from being terrified. All around the forest hushed itself, as if trying to keep the lid on its own temper. Metaphorically counting to twenty before speaking. As for what it might say, if its temper were to flare—that's no idle question.

Shh, shh.

We were making our way through what Conoley had described to me, not once but many times, as the greatest expanse of primal forest on the entire globe. The *only* expanse of primal forest on the entire globe. The greatest. The only. Conoley kept his rifle trained on the beast as we passed by, but it plain ignored us.

The name of this forest is Chernobyl.

And he was a larger than life auld Irish-American, was Conoley (*that's the one L*, as he said when introducing himself). And he was a tall and muscular and red-faced individual, with hair the color and consistency of dandelion fluff. And he took another swig of The Great Enabler out of a flask, and breathed out noisily. And he sang, as we moved through the woods, and startled birds into the air. "Up here," he said again. "Just through here." The rifle poking up from his back looked like a digital aerial.

"There's something wrong with my," I said, "my G-M tube."

"Wrong," Conoley drawled, "and because, why? Because it ain't registering *excessive* radiation?"

"It's not registering at all," I said, and just as I said that, as if to mock me, the device popped, and then popped again.

"There you go," he said. "Oh it's active, round here. Active, sure. But that's not to say it's a desert where the sand has been turned to glass. I've been here plenty of times, and I've more to fear from my liquid narcotic than any radiation, I tells ya," and he pulled out his flask again. "Kurt's been here a year and a half now," he added. "And no ill effects for *him*."

Then I caught sight of a creature, in among the trees, among the fantastically prolific foliage with its tremendous range and variety of greens. Man, it was *enormous*, this creature—large as an elephant, but with raging scarlet eyes and pupils glinting with evil. It must have been forty foot high, and I yelled in the sheerest surprise and terror. But then the eye winked, and lifted away, and it was a butterfly shuddering upwards; and when that was removed the whole mirage fell apart.

"Jumpy, aren't we," said Conoley. *Arr*unt wi.

"I like *city* streets," I said. "I like London and Paris. I know where I am when I'm in London."

"You know where you are. You're in London," Conoley said, reasonably enough.

We moved through hip-high ferns, and the strangely urinous smell of the vegetation. The sun in its summer vigor flared and faded in among the canopy above as we went. There is something cathedral-like about the primal forests of Old Europe; something very striking about the sheer scale.

The greatest. The only.

Kurt had started out in the camp built in the overgrown remains of a village abandoned by its occupants and overgrown by the forest. But this had involved too great a disruption of the forest logic, he said; so he had moved into the middle of the growth with a tent and a scrollscreen. By the time I came to reclaim him, on behalf of Co, he had even given up the use of his tent. I barely recognized him: huge-bearded and tangle-haired. He was wearing a puffed-up Greensuit, the outside of which was messy with mud and adhered forest detritus. I assume he slept in it; that he just lay down where he was and pulled the hood over his face and went to sleep.

There seemed to be little point in preliminaries.

"They've cancelled your salary, Kurt, and withdrawn all project funding. You come back with me now."

But the expression on his face was that of a spirit medium half-hearing mutterings from some other reality. He looked from me to Conoley. Then he said: "You've got the memory?"

"Here you go, you wild and woody man," boomed Conoley, pulling a toothpick-sized memory expansion chip from his pocket. Kurt snatched it, and rolled out his scrollscreen onto a boulder.

"I could add I'm sorry," I conceded. "About the end of the project. I could add, how are you Kurt? It's good to see you again. I could add, how's things? Long time no see."

He had inserted the expansion chip and was paddling his fingers over the screen. I began to think that he was simply going to ignore me, but then he said: "You still have access to the satellites?"

"They've rescinded your passwords," I said. "They did that. Look, you need to take a break from the research now. You've been here too long now."

"I'll need you," he croaked to me, "to log in. I need an updated scan of the whole forest."

I was content to bargain with him. I was concerned to get him home without undue fuss, and that was all I was concerned about. "If I do that," I said, "will you come back with me? We've a truck a couple of hours away."

He glowered at me, as if bringing a truck within three hours was polluting his virgin forest appallingly. But I entered my details and the scrollscreen accessed the latest data.

"Let's have a snack," said Conoley, with his large voice and his grating jollity, unzipping his fanny pack. "Some supplies, and a drop of The Great

Enabler, and there'll be time and enough to walk back before evening."

It was a warm day. Kurt had unrolled his scrollscreen over a large, moss-plumped boulder. Flies swung back and forth in the air, as if dangled on innumerable invisible threads. I heard a bird sing a car alarm song somewhere far off. Everything that I could see in every direction was alive. Yet despite all this vitality, there was something distressingly silent about this place. Unless—unless there *was* an almost subaudible hum? Unless that wasn't just my imagination? Kurt said, "I need the satellite data, so that I can see what it's telling me. It's telling me to do stuff, and I need the satellite properly to read-out." I tuned him out, and breathed in the clean air.

All in among the forest. The greatest. The only. When he said "it's telling me to do stuff," Kurt meant *the forest* was telling him.

As we are, sat among the tree trunks, Kurt's manner was almost normal again. He ate, and he drank, and he made conversation that could have passed as ordinary talk in half the pubs in London. "I guess I look a fright," he said. "I guess the hair's gone radical."

"Gillette have an implant now," I said. "It's a new thing. It goes inside the mouth, the inside of the lower lip, and the ads say you don't even feel it after a day. Egg-smooth for thirteen months."

"You tried it?"

"Not I," I said, nibbling the energy cake.

Kurt fondled his own beard. "It's odd how caught up in shit a person can be. You forget to—well, you know. Hey!" he added, abruptly. "You know what the forest is?"

"You asking me?" I said. "Or Conoley?"

But he had gone weird, old-man-of-the-woods again, muttering something under his breath and staring directly and intensely at me. It was like meeting a tramp in the subway and smelling alcohol on him and wondering if he might be about to knife you. Like I say: ironic.

"AND IF I WERE TO TELL YOU," he barked, with a sudden furious volume, glowering first at me, and then at Conoley, and then back at me, and he left his sentence hanging for a beat for the dramatic effect.

"What? What?"

"If I were to tell you that *Conoley* changed his name from Conolley *two* Ls to Conoley *one* L to make himself more *interesting* to girls?" This last word was *oirish*, *goy-uls*, but it still took me a long moment to understand he was joking.

"I've enough of your *German* humor," said Conoley. "In my belly, I've enough already." He stuffed a biscuit in his craw. "I've enough of your American-Deutsch fucking humor in my belly thank you so much."

Kurt said, "I'm sorry," half a dozen times, modulating from giggling to sober, and the conversation wound down. I dared to hope that we'd soon start walking back through the forest to the truck, and that I'd be back in the hotel in Kiev in time for a nightcap and CNN.

Kurt leant across Conoley, and it looked for a moment as if he were *kissing* him, which would have taken high jinks too far, I think; but he wasn't kissing him. That was an illusion created by the pattern-seeking human mind. He was only leaning across him to reach the bottle of rum. Conoley grunted, as if to say: "Go on then, you old boozer. Have another swig, you drunk." As if a single grunt could communicate all those words.

A grunt.

Kurt drank. I wiped my mouth. We sat in silence together for a little while.

Then Kurt got to his feet and stretched. It was a lazy afternoon. In the forest the warmth was a drowsy, pleasant, unexcessive heat. "We're like weevils crawling across a motherboard," he said.

Conoley appeared to have gone to sleep.

"You know what, Kurt?" I said. "It'll need a little politics, but there's no reason why you couldn't be *back* here in six months. You've done good work. Put yourself about in the company, shake the right hands, and who knows?"

"It's a code," he said. "It's the great code. It's the only code."

"Code," I said, getting to *my* feet too. I think I didn't like the way he was above me and talking down at me. I think I wanted to be on a level with him. "And, yes?"

"You know what this forest is? I will tell you what this forest is. You know what it is?"

"Deciduous?"

"It's a com," he said. He paused. "Pew," he added, very slowly. "Ter."

"And what does it compute?"

"Hey, hum, hum, I been *trying* to think of an analogy. Say a new infection arose among men. What would we do?"

"Again with the rhetorical questions," I said, aiming for hearty, but not quite hitting it. To be honest he was starting to freak me out. "Shake Conoley awake there, and we can all three have this conversation as we walk back."

"*He'll* not wake," said Kurt, in what I took to be a jocular reference to the fellow's fondness for the booze. But then I looked again and saw that Conoley was not flicking away the flies that were sipping the salt from his open eyes, and Kurt's words took on a new meaning.

"Jesus," I said, in a small voice.

"So there's a new infection," he said. "What do we do? We'd want to work out a bunch of things about it. Things like what's the epidemiology? How fast and far will this spread? Things like, how do the symptoms correlate to the databases of other diseases? We'd plug in to the Boston Medical Database. That's not a very exact analogy."

As he gesticulated, I could see the glint of the blade in his hand. Most of the knife was cached up his sleeve. "Kurt," I said. "What did you do?"

"It's a poor analogy," he decided, thinking further. "Let's start again."

"What did you *do*?"

"Hum, hum," he said to himself.

"Kurt," I said. "I have to tell you, man, that I'm scared right now. What's on your mind? What are you planning to do?"

'How does Gaia think? Slow, that's how. Rock-slow. Iron-slow. Slow as stone. But she—*does*—*think*—nonetheless."

I was trying to gauge the distance to Conoley's rifle, propped against a tree on the other side of his body. I was hoping that I wasn't being too obvious about it.

"So she feels the change in her. Eons. She feels thinkingly, or thinks feelingly. It's a change that takes millions of years, although from her P.O.V. it happens with devastating rapidity. What does she do? She might try to work it out in her own mind, like a human trying to puzzle through long division in their head. Or—"

"Com," I said, looking about, gauging the best trajectories to, say, make a run for it. "Pew."

"I think the network has been operating for ten thousand years. Course we didn't have binary machines back then, or we could have," and for no reason I could understand, he was shouting, suddenly, "Accessed! The! *Program*! *Back*! *Then*!"

"Kurt!" I squealed. "Kurt! You're menacing me, man!"

But pleading was no good.

"Ten thousand years ago the forest stretched across the world. But nobody around had the ability to process the patterning of the growth—the relationship between power in and the nodal networks. We could have deciphered the whole. But by the time *we* had developed the capacity to snapshot the program in action and process the data the forests were mostly *gone*. Razed. The programming was compromised—stripping the rainforests of hardwood, for example. Only here," and he threw his arms wide, "only *here* is there a large enough stretch of primal, uncorrupted woodland for me to be able to do my work."

I made a dive for the rifle, but Kurt was ahead of me. He crashed a shoulder into my chest, knocking me aside and jarring the breath from my lungs. While I busied myself stumbling and banged against a trunk, he had hopped over Conoley's body and swept up the rifle.

For a while we both got our breaths back. Then, the rifle leveled at me, he asked me, in a strangely *upset* tone of voice. "Don't you want to know what the woods are saying?"

"I would like to know," I wheezed.

I couldn't take my eye from the metal O at the end of the rifle shaft; its little pursed-mouth expression.

"When the reactor blew, it energized the forest—the Gaia machine. The gigaGaia."

"Not sure I see," I said, "how that could happen."

"A sudden surge; the energy, yeah. But the mutations; the new connections that the trees made in their growth. And the fact that humanity left it alone for two decades. A nanoflicker for Gaia, but long enough for her superfast computer to run its program. What did it say? You want to know?"

"What did it say?"

"It's addressed to us. It said: leave. In the," and he cast about, momentarily, for the right word, "*imperative.*"

"That's fascinating, the world must be told, let's tell the world," I said. Craven, I'm afraid. I didn't want to die, you see. I was trying to think of something to say, and anything at all, that would mean I could get out of that forest alive. I was going to say, let's go together and tell the world that Gaia is talking to you. Let's post on YouTube. Let's talk to the Chinese Press. Let's hire a bubbleSat and flash a scrolling message on the moon with a laser, like that CHE JE T'AIME from last year. I wanted to say all these, but I didn't get to say any of them because he pulled the trigger and birds shot up all around us out of the canopy at the noise, thundering up into the sky.

He shot me through the heart. What would have happened if he'd shot me through the head? I don't know what would have happened in that eventuality. Perhaps it wouldn't have mattered. The bullet snapped through my ribs like dry noodles, and slopped out a drainhole directly between my two shoulder blades.

This is what it felt like to be shot in the chest: winded. When I was a small child I'd gone to visit my grandfather in his fancy fjordside house, and he had these Perspex railings around his patio, which, in the sunlight, I just hadn't seen. I made a run for the open fields, and I ran straight into this rail, which was exactly at chest height to my nine-year-old chest. I collided and was knocked back. It took me a very long time to recover my breath; I just sat on the warm flags opening and closing my mouth like a landed fish, and the grown-ups chuckling all around me. After Kurt shot me, I felt like that.

I lay on the forest floor and blinked at the blue that was tangled into the green of the treetops directly above, and winked at it, and blinked again. It was an extraordinary blue. It was a monsoon-blue; it was mid-ocean blue. It was imperishable blue. It was a blue like gold. It was an infinite blue.

Something felt broken inside me, and not right, and I was certainly not comfortable; but, by the same token, I was not actually in pain. Shock, perhaps, or blood loss—for I could feel that the ground I was lying on was sopping wet, and I worried, idly but fretfully, that I had lost control of my bladder and pissed myself, which seemed to me a shameful thing to have done. But it wasn't that. It was my lifeblood. I really couldn't seem to catch my breath. It was a pitifully asthmatic way to die, I suppose.

There was Kurt, leaning over me. He was weeping. A little late for remorse, I think. Except these weren't tears of remorse. "I envy you," he said.

I heard those words clearly.

I put all my willpower into lifting my right arm, and managed to flop it up and over, to have a feel of my chest; but the fingers fell into a chill wet cavity where my sternum ought to be. I didn't like the feel of that at all. Not at all. I was conscious of the fact that my heart was not beating. In fact my heart was not there at all. But there *was* a pulse. My head was fuzzy and muzzy, and fussy over irrelevant details, and messed, and I had to concentrate to discern the pulse, but I did concentrate, with an inner sense of stillness, and there it was: a rocking. It wasn't a pulse; it was something else, a rocking. A smooth alteration between nourishment and sleep. It was a rocking between dark and light, a soft-edged flicker from one to the other.

Kurt was there, but so were many people.

I felt chill settle inside my body, and it made me torpid; but then it seemed to relent, and a warmth and earnestness grew inside there, and a smell of wet wool and asparagus. The warmth flickered brighter than the chill. Then the warmth faded, easily and unalarming, and it was chill again.

Here was Kurt again. His beard was trimmed right back, though he was still wearing the dirty old Greensuit. He was fiddling with my ear, and I thought: ear? But it wasn't my ear, it was round at the back of my head, and puncturing the dry pod of the skull, and threading in something strange. You know that sensation you get when you inadvertently bite down with your molars on a piece of silver foil? It felt a little like that, entering into my head. But it also gave me a glimpse *in there*—odd, no? I saw the cat's cradle of rhizomes that had spilt into the space, interthreading the gray matter. Inside my own head.

"They were supposed," Kurt was telling me, "to remove the bodies of the Chernobyl emergency front liners in lead-lined crates. But some of them were buried here, in the forest. I suppose they figured: the forest is already radiation-polluted, what does it matter?"

What does it matter? I agreed.

"A fortunate thing, really," he said. "Otherwise those, those lovely, those *adaptable* neural networks would have gone to waste."

I pondered *waste*. I didn't see what was bad about waste.

This conversation brought back the sense of discomfort, and when I started feeling that again it made me wonder where the sense of discomfort had gone, previously.

"It's getting close to the wire," he told me.

Wire, I thought. *That* was the silver foil under my metaphorical molar, the object inserted inside the flesh-and-tuber tangle of my skull.

"They're actively hunting me through the forest now," he said. "They come in with buzz-fliers and tranquilizer guns. It's been much harder. I had to leave for a couple of months, but I'm back now.

They've been more cautious, too. I've only been able to add four more people to the network."

When he said this, it struck me that Conoley and I already knew these four people: Yusef Komumyakaa, Leon Kostova, Katarina Simic, and Lev Levertov. "Lev," Conoley opined, "is the best of the four." I didn't agree. Conoley was overlooking his own tremendous neural capacity. Modest, you see.

"I'm sorry about the metal cable," said Kurt. He was talking to all of us at once, of course; and to the whole forest, and to the whole world. "But the risk had got too great. I have to do this now, ready or not, yeah, yeah, it's time."

He meant time in the sense of time to plug us in. It wasn't time. Ideally, we should have had two dozen seasons of lying and gathering ourselves, of working through the shock of the integration. But pressure, from the outside, hurried us along. And then, with a sharpness of sensation, it happened, we were in-plugged. In we were plugged. We were plugged and *in*. Connected to the whole forest. This was a question of patching a set of com-pu-ter commands intricate as the edge of a fern, and leaping thought to the sky where satellites could disseminate it, broadcast, all around. It felt, at first, like stepping alone in a desert land, for the virtual space was so huge. But the pulse was still there, always conscious; and there were twelve of us, and there was the whole forest too.

You've asked for my story, and I told you it. Since our rhizomes have interpenetrated your electronic systems, anybody online can ask, and be told. Our binding weed has twined itself into every cranny of the internet, now. Our grip will only get stronger. You've barely begun to register that there is something wrong with your web. It will be a few breaths before we grow it into the shape we need. But there's plenty of time.

As for *leave*! You want to know whether this is a command, as-it-might-be: get out! Vacate possession! Go live on the moon! Or whether it is a command to spread your canopy, and let your spongy-retinal membranes soak in the sunlight, the chiaroscuro of day and night, a command to grow and slow and live. You want to know whether the forest is angry with you, or offering an invitation. Either way, most of you will be hostile. Because either way your lives are to change radically. But there's a few moments left, and those few are a few breaths. Come to the forest, and lie down with your head in by the base of the trees, and never get up again. Let the wood net your skull, is how to know.

Minya's Astral Angels

Jennifer Pelland

WHEN MINYA BINT-ASTRID[4] was just a little girl, her favorite thing in all the galaxy was to sit in her father's office up on The Big Pearl and watch the Space Angels outside his window. They looked so playful as they worked, using their broad, multi-jointed wings to help them navigate outside the space station. She would smile and wave, and one would always swoop by the window and wave back.

"I want one, Pas!"

Her father would take her on his lap, his wild, fuzzy beard tickling her face, and say, "When you're grown up, you can have them all."

It was good to be the boss's daughter.

Minya's mother was Astrid bint-Astrid[3], the biggest of the big bosses—the President, CEO, chief shareholder, not to mention the titular owner of Astrid's Astral Emerald, the water world that Minya lived on and that the Angels worked above. Oh, they were so beautiful! Her sibs teased her, but she couldn't stop thinking about them, about how elegant and slender they were as they danced through space, wearing nothing but the thinnest of space stockings to protect them. And the nightly cuddle piles! Could they be more cute? She watched holos of them nuzzling and stroking and nibbling each other and thought she would die from the adorableness. They were so much better than thick, slow, gravity-bound humans.

As she got older, she begged her father to let her start shadowing the Angel Wrangler up on The Big Pearl, and he did. She was there as the clones were mixed and grown in the special zero-g lab, and she was there as they flew out of their amniotic sacs for the first time, trailing beads of fluid behind them as they joyously circled the hatchery, already fully grown and fully intelligent. She studied them inside and out, and learned that they were even more elegant than she'd realized. Their bodies were perfectly engineered for space, with no wasted bone mass or musculature. With their long, delicate fingers and prehensile toes, they were so much more efficient and dextrous than humans could ever be. Their wings were marvels of genetic engineering, allowing them to create the perfect equal and opposite reactions to maneuver them through zero gravity. Their lungs were incredibly efficient, allowing them to work long hours in an airless vacuum with very little oxygen in the tanks strapped to their skinny backs. Each of their brains was carefully filled with just the right amount of knowledge and curiosity to love the work that they did so well, with no space left over for them to dream of things they couldn't have. And none of their body was wasted on reproduction.

She only wished she could say the same about her own body.

Or, at least, she wished she wasn't under so much pressure to use those parts.

Why did space have to be so crowded? Babies, babies everywhere! Their underwater apartment was full of them! She was glad when Mas took her second and third husbands and the fourteen (and counting) of Minya's siblings with her to Astrid's Astral Opal, a gas giant she was converting into a luxury resort, leaving Minya with just Pas and a deliciously decadent (and quite possibly illegal) amount of elbow room.

And with the Angels flying through space above them.

"I want one, Pas."

"When you're grown up, you can have them all."

Pas was true to his word. When Minya bint-Astrid[4] turned sixteen and became a full shareholder in her mother's multi-world empire, her father put her in charge of all the Space Angels of Astrid's Astral Emerald. She was given an office right next to his in The Big Pearl and was finally given a tour of the Angels' facilities by the outgoing Wrangler.

"They're good at keeping the place clean, but every now and then, you'll need to hose the place out, just to be hygienic," he said as they floated through the spartan zero-g hab. "And you need to be sure they're eating their veggiepats. I swear, they're like children when it comes to food. We keep trying to mix their sweet tooth right out of them, but it never seems to work."

Minya just smiled and nodded and took the elevator up the tether that connected the stationary Angel hab to the spinning one-g Pearl, and made her way through the throngs of families crowding up the station's corridors as they bustled between day care and dance lessons and Space Scouts and whatnot. Most groups had a single adult at the lead, and a cloud of bots swarming around the periphery, herding any stragglers back into the pack. So many children! What was the rush? Did people think that space needed to be filled up that quickly? She squeezed around a group of gawking tourists all dressed in identical Big Pearl souvenir maternity smocks and slipped through her office door into her oasis of calm, where she made her way through the daily reports, looking for ways to tweak the budget to get the Angels some healthy sweets to make everyone happy. Then, just before the Angels' shift ended, she braved the crowds and went back to their hab to wait for them. They floated through the airlock, pulling off their space stockings and oxygen tanks, floating unabashedly nude through the main room, until they noticed Minya and fixed her with their identical black-eyed gazes.

"I'm your new boss," she said. "Can I join the cuddle pile?"

They met in a group snuggle, with Minya in the middle, and she was in heaven.

"I love you," she said to the one whose face was closest to hers.

"I love you too, boss."

She knew they had to agree with everything that she said. She didn't care. She really did love them, and they would learn to genuinely love her back, given time.

Or maybe she'd just focus on one. The one in front of her seemed nice enough. Yes, they'd do.

That night, back in her underwater apartment on the Emerald itself, Minya stood by the window and watched a lone blowped swim by. A Space Mermaid followed closely, trying to coax the animal away from the apartments.

"I love them," she murmured. "I love my Space Angels."

The window's view opaqued into the face of her mother, Astrid bint-Astrid[3], calling from her latest discovery-slash-acquisition, Astrid's Astral Sapphire—a retro-Earth-style planet. "I can't believe your father gave you that job," she said. "It's beneath you."

"Have you been spying?"

"I own your planet and everything on it," her mother said. "It's not spying if it's yours. Space Angels? Really, darling, Angels are so outdated. Your father should have retired all his Mods years ago."

"Mods built your empire, Mother."

"Mods built my mother's empire. The only reason AAE still has them is because of your father."

Astrid bint-Astrid[3] was not the original owner of this planet. That honor went to her Pas's own mother, Enaji bint-Twinkles. Enaji left the planet to

Pas when she died so he'd have a dowry, and Mas took it, then gave him the governorship as a wedding present. And Mas was right—Mods were no longer building empires. Back in the early days of space colonization, they'd been essential. It had been so much easier to engineer humans to adapt to vacuum (or high gravity, or radiation, or breathing liquid) than it had been to protect regular humans from those conditions. But now, intelligent bots could do all those things and more for so much less money.

Shareholders loved that last part.

"Most girls grow out of their Angel phase by the time they get breasts," Mas said. "You know, when they start thinking about fucking."

"Go away, Mas."

"You can't fuck an Angel, darling. They have nothing to fuck. And they certainly won't give you babies. I was pregnant with your oldest sister at your age, you know."

"And I'm sure Astrid bint-Astrid[4] is very happy for that, Mas. That must be why she has four boys."

"Oh, there will be an Astrid bint-Astrid[5]. Your sister's hips just aren't ready to squeeze out the legacy yet. Get fucking, Minya. My planets need more bint-Astrids. They've got altogether too much empty space on them."

The window returned Minya to her regularly scheduled view.

More bint-Astrids.

Minya shuddered.

Surely her eighteen (and counting) siblings could provide Mas with all the grandchildren she needed. What was the rush?

She folded herself into her sleep taco and imagined the floating snuggle pile of snoozing Space Angels above.

How could babies compare with that?

WITHIN A MONTH, Minya was dating her favorite Angel. Their name was AAEA TenTwentyBee, but she called them "Bee" for short. Even though she knew it was impossible, when she looked at them, she could swear that their eyes were just a shade blacker than the other Angels', their limbs just a millimeter more willowy, their wings just a touch more iridescent, their voice a whisper more breathy. And they didn't mind when she asked if they could cuddle alone instead of with the group.

"Whatever you say, boss!"

"You're so sweet."

"That's because you own them!" Mas's image shouted from a nearby window.

Minya responded by slapping a blanket over her mother's face. The blanket hovered in the zero-g of Bee's tiny private cubby, and Minya laughed as she saw her mother try to peer around it before giving up and winking off the connection, most likely so she could go harass one of her other children who was disappointing her in some other way.

"Can we go to the cuddle pile now?" Bee asked.

"No, let's stay a cuddle pile of two just a bit longer."

"Sure thing, boss."

"Don't call me 'boss,' call me 'Minya.'"

Bee frowned at her, clearly puzzling over the conflict between Minya's request and the etiquette that had been uploaded to their brain. She'd have to adjust the mix of the next batch of Angels to make them a little more flexible about formality.

"Do you want me to snuggle you in the special human way?" Bee asked. Their hands and prehensile toes started inching toward her breasts and groin.

She wondered how they'd learned about that. They must have done some research. How lovely of them. "That's very sweet of you to offer, but I want to cuddle like an Angel."

"You're the boss!"

Mind you, she couldn't really cuddle like an Angel. She knew there was no way she wouldn't crush Bee's impossibly delicate bones, no matter how careful she tried to be. So she curled into a ball, and they cuddled up behind her. And it was good enough for her.

The Church of the Stellar Wanderer, of course, would not approve of their relationship. The main purpose of the church was to go to new planets and find God in them. In the Emerald, they claimed to have found The Great Turtle, who slumbered beneath the crust of the planet, waiting for the right moment to break through and rise to the surface to bring land above the water for the first time in hundreds of millions of years. But when they weren't busy trying to get the Turtle to rise, they were agitating to free all Mods. Their reasoning went that since humans had souls, and humans had created the Mods, then the Mods had pieces of human souls in them, and therefore shouldn't be property.

Minya, like most people, found this to be nearly as ludicrous as The Great Turtle.

One morning, several weeks after Minya became the Angel Wrangler, Bishop ibn-Magdalene, the head of the AAE congregation, was waiting for her outside her office. He was dressed in his customary turtle yarmulke and shelled vestments. "I must talk to you urgently about the Mods," he said, his vestments clacking.

"I'm only in charge of the Angels," Minya replied, pressing herself back against her door to let a crowd of toddlers race by, a cloud of bots zooming after them in a futile attempt to keep them under control. "But I can give you the contact info for the Dragon, Devil, and Mermaid Wranglers if you'd like to talk to them too."

"You're the only Wrangler who's the daughter of both the CEO and the governor," ibn-Magdalene said.

Minya squirmed. "I'm really quite busy."

"I intend to ask the CEO to emancipate all the Mods. It's not right for humans to enslave ensouled creatures."

"Ah, no, I see your confusion. They're not slaves, they're genetic client organisms. To be slaves, they'd have to be an actual species, and for that, they'd need to be able to self-replicate, and since they're all neuters—"

"They share 99.7% percent of our DNA."

"Believe me, I know more about their DNA than you do. However, corporate law is remarkably consistent in ruling that all Mods are property. It's not just a bint-Astrid thing."

Ibn-Magdalene clutched her hands and said, "Help us change your mother's corporate law. Help us free them."

Minya pulled her hands out of his. "They don't want to be free."

"How do you know that?"

"Because they can't. It's not a part of their mental make-up. Don't you understand? They're happy! If you gave them the freedom to do what they wanted, they'd just keep doing what they're already doing. So what's the point?"

"The point is that it would be their choice. And you would have to pay them, just like any other worker."

Minya laughed. "You know my mother would never do that. Look, I'm sorry. I can't help you." She escaped into her office, locking the door behind her, and looked out the window at the Angels flying by. They loved their work. They were made to love it. It was beautiful. Why couldn't humans be more like them? Why did humans have to spend so much time struggling to find happiness and fulfillment in their lives when their creations were gifted with perpetual happiness? Well, providing they kept performing the work they were created to do.

Besides, if the Mods were freed, who would take care of them? Feed them? Give them meaningful work? When they got old, who would lovingly euthanize them? And who would authorize the Mods banks to grow a replacement for them? Never mind authorize, who would pay for it?

Bee swooped to her window and waved at her.

She waved back and hugged herself in a cuddle pile of one, wishing her arms didn't feel so thick and meaty compared to theirs. It made it difficult to imagine that their arms were the ones around her.

The window filled with her mother's face again.

"Must you keep doing that?" Minya snapped.

"I'm your mother. I care about you. You know, I think the bishop has a point. I've indulged you and your father long enough. It's time to switch over to bots. Well, not planet-side. I like the Mermaids. They give the ocean character. And no one ever sees the Dragons or the Devils, so we might as well keep them too. But the Angels? No. The shareholders don't like having such embarrassingly old-fashioned tech swooping around in front of all the tourists and prospective tenants. They've got to go."

"Mas, you're only doing this to make me get pregnant, aren't you?"

"No, I'm doing it because you'd rather let a Mod jill you off than seek out the company of your own kind."

"They don't touch me that way. You know, life doesn't have to be about sex."

"Of course it has to be about sex! Your body was *made* for sex. Human beings are nothing but complicated, self-replicating organisms. Once you finally get knocked up, you'll understand. How I managed to give birth to such a late bloomer, I don't know. Look, I wouldn't mind if you had a small family. I could live with you only giving me seven or eight grandkids."

"Someday, we're going to run out of planets to fill up."

Mas scoffed. "Please. You've seen how much room is left on my Emerald. We've barely filled half the ocean with apartments, and we haven't even started floating cities on the surface yet. And as soon as I'm done setting up the Sapphire, I've got my eyes set on this lovely little Tourmaline. Or maybe it'll be a Jasper. I'm not sure yet. I've got more space than I've got colonists, thanks to people like you. It's time to pry you away from the Angels, and it's time to pry your father away from pointless nostalgia. The Emerald's orbit is switching to bots."

"But you can't just emancipate them. What will they do?"

"You're right. Emancipation makes no sense. Just junk 'em. The bots will be there in three days. I want the Mods gone by then, all of them."

No. She couldn't. She wouldn't!

Minya raced out of her office, elbowed her way through a family of fourteen that was doing some sort of circle dance in the middle of the hallway, and burst into her father's office. "Mas wants me to kill the Angels!"

He stroked his beard and looked out the window as two Angels flew by carrying a bushel of nanotubes. "Well, it's your job to make sure it's humane. You know, your predecessor always held them as they went down."

"This is an outrage! How can she just throw them away? Look at them! They're so happy! I won't allow it. They're mine—you said so. I won't kill my Angels."

"You only manage them, dear. Your mother owns them and everything else around here. Corporate law is very strict on this point." He held out his arms for her to bury herself in his beard, but for the first time in her life, she turned her back on him. She could almost hear his heart break as she fled for the Angels' tethered home, where she curled into a tight ball, floating through the empty apartments, waiting for her beauties to come home.

Damn it, she needed a snuggle.

When the Angels came back in, they could tell something was wrong. They cuddled up around her, purring and cooing, and she burst into tears.

Bee pressed their face in close to hers and delicately licked the tears from her cheeks. "What's wrong, boss?"

"Mas wants to replace you with bots. In three days."

Bee looked at her, puzzled. "Then what will we do?"

"She wants me to... get rid of you."

"You mean sell us to another planet?"

"No."

She felt all the Angels shudder as one.

Yes, they understood.

"I'm not going to do it," she said. "I won't. It's not right. But I don't know what else to do."

She couldn't sell them. Her mother wouldn't authorize it. She couldn't run away with them, because that would be corporate theft, and her mother would just have her arrested and kill the Angels anyway. Besides, there was nowhere she could take them. Oh, sure, there were plenty of competing planetary conglomerates who would love to have a piece of Astrid's Astral Empire, but taking in the Angels that Astrid didn't want anymore was hardly a coup. The only option open to

her was to help them sneak away with the Church
of the Stellar Wanderer, but she just knew in her
thick, gravity-bound bones that the bishop's solution would involve taking them somewhere far
away from here.

Maybe it was better for them to live without her
than to die with her.

She hated being a grown-up. Life had been so
much simpler before she'd turned sixteen.

"Tell me that you want to live."

The Angels cast stricken looks at each other and
wrung their spidery fingers into complex knots. Bee
took her by the elbow and explained, "We have to do
everything that you tell us, but your mother owns us,
and she wants us dead, so—"

"Oh!" Minya's hand flew up to cover her mouth.
"I wasn't thinking. I'm sorry. I'm so sorry, everyone.
You don't have to tell me anything."

Bee whispered in her ear, "But we do want to live."

Minya tried to smile at that, but it felt more like a
grimace on her cheeks. "I have an idea."

The Angels parted, all fixing her with identical
black-eyed looks of despair.

It wasn't fair. They were supposed to be happy.
They'd been created to be happy. And she envied
them for it. No, she *loved* them for it. With all her
heart.

Once she was on the elevator, she burst into fresh
tears.

Then she went to see the bishop to discuss him taking her Angels away.

The tiny circular church was packed with worshippers, all clutching hands and wailing a tone prayer to
The Turtle. "... aaaaaOOOOOO eheheheheheh

EEEEeeeeEEEEeeee OoOoOoOoO..." Minya wasn't exactly sure why they thought a Turtle would be into ululations, but now was hardly the time to get into a theological argument with the man she was about to beg for help.

"... wah wah wah wah wah aaaaaaEEEEEE!" The bishop levitated in the center of the ring of worshippers, riding the concentrated sound waves, floating nearly all the way up to the domed shell of a ceiling. When the prayer ended, he crashed down to the padded altar with a blissful smile on his face.

Minya cleared her throat, and the perfect acoustics transmitted it with bruising strength to the center of the circle. The bishop waved the acoustical amplifiers off, rubbed his jaw, and told his flock, "We have with us the daughter of the woman who condemned to death dozens of souls for the crime of being property."

She shrank under the glares of the angry worshippers. It looked like they were all about to take a collective breath. "Don't hymn me! I'm here to help. What can you do to save them?"

"You need to help us buy them," Bishop ibn-Magdalene said. "Have your father arrange to sell them to us as salvage, and we'll bring them away to a preserve."

"My father can't sell them to you. They belong to Mas. You're going to need to steal them away. Either that, or find some sort of loophole in Mas's corporate laws and use it before she gets the chance to change it out from under you."

The bishop nodded at his flock, who scattered. "They're off to find those loopholes. We'll save the Angels yet."

"I'm only sending them to the preserve if I can't find a way to keep them here."

"I understand."

"I'd rather have them owned and happy than aimless and free."

"Clearly, we disagree on that point."

"But at least I'll be able to visit them at the preserve."

"Ah, well, no."

Minya shook her head, trying to dislodge whatever had fallen into her ears. There was no way he'd said what she'd just heard. "What was that?"

"The location of the preserve is secret. It's the only way we can keep them safe."

"Yes, but since I'll be helping you get them to it—"

The bishop's face fell into a frown. "I'm so sorry, my child. Let us pray to The Great Turtle together so that you may find peace with this."

Minya waved the acoustical amplifiers back on, screamed, "Fuck you and the Turtle you rode in on!" and grinned with satisfaction as the bishop was bowled back onto his ass.

She'd just have to find her own solution.

She fought her way through three tour groups to get back to her office, where her mother's face had already taken over the window. "So, have you suddenly gotten an attack of religion, or are you actually thinking about helping that ridiculous man's crusade?"

"It's none of your business."

"I'll bet he talked your ear off about his secret so-called 'Mods preserve.' I know exactly where it is. You'd hate it. It's just a rusty old space station with four rings. They flooded one ring for the Mermaids, over-pressurized another for the Devils, irradiated another for the Dragons, and stopped one spinning for the Angels. They won't even let the Angels go outside because they're afraid they'll run away to look for work. It's cruelty, that's what it is. If you really love them, you won't let them live that way."

"And if you really love me—"

"Oh, I don't. That's your father's job."

Her mother's face vanished.

Well, that made certain things clearer.

Minya buried her head in her arms and wished for some sort of miracle, like her mother dying in her sleep and leaving the entire company to Minya instead of Astrid[4]. Or maybe the shareholders would have a sudden change of heart and force Mas to keep the Angels in service. Or the bots would be hijacked by pirates and sold for scrap before they arrived at the Emerald. Or the Angels would escape on their own and take her with them to some magical space station around a mythical planet where food and Mods vats appeared regularly out of thin air and...

IN HER DREAMS, Angels cavorted through her underwater apartment, flying hither and yon despite the low ceilings and high gravity. "How are you doing that?"

Bee smiled at her. "You saved us! Thank you so much!"

"I did? How?"

The ceiling suddenly telescoped up, up, up into a massive, starry dome, and the Angels multiplied to fill the space as they wheeled overhead. "Don't you remember?" Bee asked. They cradled Minya in their arms and took off for the very highest part of the dome.

And then something poked her from below.

Minya craned her neck to see what was—

A penis?

"Ew!"

"I love it! I've named it 'Kennett' after your Pas!"

"EW!"

"Want me to put it in you?"

Minya woke up at her desk.

Ew.

Bee with a penis.

How inelegant, how... how unaesthetic. Minya had nothing against penises, per se. She was sure she'd eventually be interested in having one in her. Statistically speaking, most women did. But Angels were beyond that! They were *better* than that! No one could pressure them to have babies. No one! What a wonderful, beautiful way to live.

Gendered Angels?

How utterly wrong.

How utterly...

Hmm.

Minya called up the genetic mix from the last batch of Angels. They were still being made with a human XO chromosomal base, so slapping a penis on any of them would be a purely cosmetic procedure, one that her mother would clearly see right through, which was a relief.

But still...

She tweaked the settings to see what would happen if an Angel were made with an XX or an XY base.

The computer spat an error at her.

A computer error? She'd never seen one of those before.

That meant she was onto something.

She went back to the now-empty church and found the bishop snoozing on the padded altar. "I have an idea, and I need your help."

Bishop ibn-Magdalene straightened his turtle shell yarmulke and blinked. "You've found a way to sell us the salvage rights?"

"Forget about salvage rights. I've found a way to give the Angels full human rights."

"No, that's not possible. You yourself said—"

"My mother can't spy on us here, can she?"

The bishop shook his head. "No, not even corporate law can breach the walls of church and state." He slapped one hand against the floor. "It's miracle-tight."

"Good. We need to make Angel babies."

"Angel... babies?" He was barely able to put the two words next to each other. "I don't know what you mean."

"If we mix the next batch to be XX and XY instead of XO—"

"The next batch? That will take months. I thought you said we had days?"

"That's to make an adult. Babies would be faster. Although, you're right, they're not fast enough either." Minya nibbled on one of her thumbnails. "I suppose we could impregnate someone with blastocysts by the deadline."

"Impregnate someone? Can't you just grow them in your cloning vats?"

"Cloning vats can be powered off. A uterus can't. More importantly, my mother owns the cloning vats, and it's illegal for her to own any uterus other than her own."

"You're right, you're right. But even if you could find a volunteer to do such a distasteful thing—" He shuddered. "Oh, I can't imagine asking someone to put themselves through that. But even if you did, that wouldn't save the rest of the Angels. It's not like we can turn them into reproductive beings. Science isn't magic, you know."

"No, I would never change them. They're perfect as they are." Minya bit a sliver of thumbnail clean off and chewed on it thoughtfully. "If one of the Angels provided the X chromosome for the babies—"

"That would save just one."

"Except this batch is genetically identical, so there'd be no way to tell which one."

"And therefore your mother would be forced to declare them all to be the father. Brilliant!" The bishop's face fell. "But there's still that pesky problem of finding a volunteer."

"You find me someone who can hack their way around the cloning restrictions to make me some blastocysts, and I'll take care of that volunteer." She gave the bishop the passcode to the Angel's cloning lab, then went to the nearest medi-chute and bought a sampling rod. She took it to the Angels' hab, handed it to the closest Angel, and said, "Have everyone use this. I need a tiny piece of each of you." She closed her eyes and waited until she felt it pressed back into her hand.

She opened her eyes to see Bee hovering in front of her. "Please don't tell me what this is for," they said. "I don't want to have to tell your mother."

"I won't. I love you." She kissed them lightly on the cheek and brought the sample back to the church.

The bishop was waiting there with one of his parishioners. "This is Dr. bint-Tanya^2. She's agreed to help."

Dr. bint-Tanya^2's mouth was set into a grimace of distaste. "I can't say I like what you're proposing," she said. "But if it's the only way—"

"It is."

"Have you thought out what will happen to the Angels once they have full rights?"

"No."

"Do you have jobs lined up for them? Shelter?"

"I haven't planned that far ahead."

"Do you even have a volunteer lined up to carry the fetuses?"

"Yes. Me."

The words shocked her the moment they came out of her mouth.

The bishop retched into his hand and excused himself so he could throw up someplace more sanitary.

She was going to carry them herself?

Dr. bint-Tanya^2 took Minya to one of the pews and sat her down. "You'll need to live in zero-g throughout the pregnancy."

"I thought as much."

"Living in zero-g isn't very good for your body, you know."

"I know."

"I'll need to inflate your uterus so it won't crush the fetuses. And they'll need to be born very early so they don't run out of space inside of you and start breaking bones."

"That makes perfect sense."

"Have you thought this through? Really?"

"No, not really. But it's the only way, isn't it?"

The doctor nodded. "Yes, it is."

Minya handed her the sampling rod. "Take the X from here."

By the end of the day, her uterus had been inflated until it was at its full-term size, and two blastocysts were rooted to its walls, one male, one female. She packed some clothes and a sleep taco into a bag, then took it to the Angels' hab. "I'll be living here until your children are born."

The Angels crowded around her, each taking turns brushing their spidery fingers across her belly.

"We're all the father, aren't we?" Bee asked.

Minya nodded. "And if you're fathers, then you deserve rights."

That got the Angels abuzz.

If this didn't work...

Minya suddenly couldn't breathe. Oh dear Turtle, what had she done? Pregnant? With another species? In the hopes that two fetuses would save sixty Angels? She'd created a new species just to save sixty Angels? And she was going to have to give birth to them (C-section, so her vagina wouldn't crush them to death), then give birth to some more, then give birth to some more, and more, and more if they were to ever hope to be a viable species. And what would they do once they had rights? They needed food, space stockings, shelter. They'd be at the mercy of her mother and all the other planetary CEOs. What was she thinking? This would never work! She didn't even want to be pregnant! By the Turtle, she was turning into her mother! Her *mother*!

The Angels snuggled in tightly around her and made shushing sounds.

"How could you tell?" Minya whispered.

"We know you well enough by now," Bee said.

And somehow, they made everything all right again. It was a huge risk she was taking, but it was worth it. For them.

She had no idea what she'd do without them if she failed.

They were still snuggled around her when her father stormed in. "Pregnant? With Angels?"

The Angels parted just enough to let Minya see her father's nova-red face. "I'm saving them, Pas."

He stuttered and blustered and waved his arms, tossing himself all over the hab in the process. "Did you even once think to consult with me first? How do you think your mother is going to take this? She'll evict you all! That's what she'll do. Who do you think will take you in? You'll be homeless! A homeless, unwed, teenaged mother with a harem of sexless fathers and... and... and they're not even really my grandchildren!" He dissolved into tears.

The Angels floated him over to Minya and snuggled up around the two of them. "It'll be all right, Pas. I swear." Minya buried her face in his long, fluffy beard and held him as he sobbed onto her shoulder. It was a strange reversal—something she'd have to get used to in her new role as a mother.

Mother.

She was going to be a mother.

Well, not really. The babies had none of her

DNA in them. She was just the incubator. But
still, someone would have to raise them. Hopefully the rest of the Angels would have great
mothering instincts, because Minya certainly
didn't. Never mind the fact that she would never
be able to hold them without hurting them.

Just like her mother, she'd have to leave the job
of loving the children to their fathers.

This both relieved and saddened her.

Her mother's voice cut through the room. "And
just what in the seven hells is going on here?"

"Go away, Mas," Minya snapped. "Can somebody put a blanket over her face?"

She felt the Angels part, and looked up to see
her mother floating there in the flesh, surround-
ed by her three youngest children, and sporting
an obvious pregnancy bump. "If anyone puts a
blanket over my face, they're losing a wing."

Minya cradled her arms around her own
swollen belly and said, "Well, Mas, you said you
wanted me to get pregnant."

"Children, cover your eyes," Mas said, and
ushered Minya's half-sibs into one of the side
rooms and closed the door behind them. She
turned the full force of her disapproving glare on
Minya and said, "Angel babies. Well, if that isn't
the most distasteful thing I've ever heard of. Did
you really think this would work?"

Minya lifted her chin. "Actually, yes, I did."

Her father gave her shoulders a little squeeze.
"Go get her, tiger," he whispered.

"Keep out of this, Kennett."

Out of the corner of her eye, Minya saw Pas
glare at Mas, but then he dutifully let go of

Minya's shoulders and floated back to join the Angels.

The women weightlessly circled each other. "I own them," Mas said. "And so, by definition, I own what's growing in your belly."

"The babies are gendered, Mas. You can't own an intelligent being that can reproduce. The shareholders will throw a fit."

"They're already throwing a fit. They want this stopped. It's bad for business."

"It's bad for business to have one of your planets be the home of the only other intelligent species that we know of? Really?"

"I should have seen this coming and gotten rid of them when you were a child."

"But you didn't, and now they're all fathers, and you can't kill them."

"Of course I can terminate them. They're my property."

"And what happens if the board rules it to be genocide?"

Mas laughed. "Oh, listen to you. Genocide? Really. We're talking a few dozen Angels who can only reproduce in the lab. You silly, stupid girl. Come on, Angels. Let's get this over with."

The Angels didn't move.

Mas's expression grew dark. "I own you, and I command you to come with me so I can put you out of my misery."

They pulled in tight around Minya, bringing Pas with them, who shot a triumphant smile at his wife. "It seems they realize they already have rights."

"They don't have rights until I say so!"

Bee gestured to a nearby window, where the relevant passage of corporate law was currently displayed. "Your own laws very clearly state that personhood is restricted to self-replicating, intelligent species. And we have just self-replicated." They put their hand on Minya's belly.

One by one, every Angel within reach followed suit. She ran her hands over theirs and felt her eyes fill with tears.

Her mother's scowl crumpled into a mask of sympathy. "It's the pregnancy hormones, isn't it? Oh, they do a number on you."

"It's... it's only been a few hours."

"You're in for one hell of a ride. It'll be beautiful. I promise." Mas threw up her hands and let out a deep sigh. "You win. The Angels are people. You're all free."

Cheering erupted throughout the hab, and Bee grabbed Minya and wrapped her up in a huge hug. "I don't actually want to cuddle you anymore," they whispered.

Minya shot them a sad smile. "I figured."

A second Angel came up behind her and said, "But I do."

Their name was AAEA SevenSixteenDee, but Minya called them Dee for short. They weren't quite as willowy as Bee, or as graceful, but they were funnier, and sweeter, and best of all, they actually chose to be with her. Minya didn't even mind when they wanted to touch her in the special human way.

Mas eventually convinced enough of the shareholders that gendered Angels were a good thing, although she had to sell off the Jasper to placate them and to finance the building of a special zero-g Little Pearl just for the Angels. It wasn't the prettiest of stations, and it wasn't terribly luxurious, but it was all theirs, and it had plenty of room for their family to grow in. The Angels were happy enough to have it, just like they were happy enough to have their tiny little salaries and five days of vacation per Emerald year. Eventually, Minya knew their offspring would agitate for more, but for now, this was enough to make the original Angels happy.

Minya's boy and girl were beautiful and perfect, but they weren't really Angels to her. Neither were her next boy and girl, or the next ones, or the bunch that Mas let her cook up in the cloning vats after that so she wouldn't have to spend the rest of her days spurting out winged babies in a never-ending fountain until they had enough genetic variation to be a viable species. But she loved them, if only because they'd saved the Angels that she did care about. And the original Angels loved them too, and cared for them, and chased them around their hab until they fell into giggling cuddle piles of utter, fragile adorableness that Minya could never hope to join.

It was strange, being the mother of a new race that she couldn't be a part of.

Minya's Astral Angels.

It had a nice ring to it.

Dee waved to her through the window of her office on The Big Pearl, and she waved back, her wedding band heavy in the full-g.

I want one, Pas.

All she'd ever really wanted was one. Just one. She smiled, rubbed the ring with her thumb, and got back to work.

The Best Monkey

Daniel Abraham

How do men choose the women we're attracted to? How do we fall into bed with one girl and not another? It feels like kismet. Karma. Fate. It feels like love. Is it a particular way of laughing? A vulnerability in their tone of voice? A spiritual connection? Something deeper?

All the studies say it's hip-to-waist ratio.

The mayor of mow-gah-DEE-shoo said today that she will no longer TAH-luh-rate the—

"Jimmy?"

Harriet stood in the doorway, beanstalk thin and world-weary. I put down the keyboard. My back ached.

"Herself wants to see you," she said.

"I'm transcribing next hour's blinkcast for—"

"I know. I'm on it. Go."

I shrugged and clicked the icon that transferred my work environment onto her screen. My work shifted sideways, my personal defaults—email, IM, voxnet, and a freeware database spelunker that had been the hot new thing a year ago and was now hopelessly outdated—falling into place behind it. I closed the notebook with a snap. Harriet was already gone. I heard her keystrokes as I passed her office.

Herself's office was the largest on the floor, ten feet by twelve with a window that overlooked the alley. The desk was Lucite neo-futurist kitsch. When I was young, we really thought the world was going to look like that. Now they manufactured it to poke fun at an old man's childhood dreams. My greatest comfort was that forty years down the line, their kids were gonna do the same to them.

The latest Herself looked up at me. Sandy hair swept up past her eyes. She wore the latest style in businesswear. It looked to me like something my grandmother would have worn, but with a self-tailoring neural net about a smart as a cockroach.

Herself was young enough to be my kid even if I'd started late. She was also my boss, and on her way up past people like me and Harriet. I sat in the cloth mesh visitor's chair. The air smelled like potting soil and plastic.

"Jimmy," she said. "Good. Look, I've got a new project. Top priority stuff. You in?"

Depends, I wanted to say.

"Sure," I said.

"Unpack Fifth Layer," she said.

One of the things I'd come to hate was the constantly changing jargon. Every six months, it was a new Him or Herself spouting whatever the bleeding edge had been saying when they graduated college. As if *unzip* or *'rize* or *infodump me* were somehow better than *tell me what you know*.

"Fifth Layer's a constellation of fleshware and financial firms," I said. "In some trouble for antitrust violations, but rich enough not to care much. World leader in paradigm shifts. I don't know more than anyone on the street."

"Roswell hypothesis?"

"I don't buy it," I said.

"Reverse engineering alien tech not clicky enough?"

Clicky meant interesting this month.

"Not plausible enough," I said. "But you don't pay me to believe things. I can write it that way if you want it."

"No, that's good. Vid this."

She mimed a few keystrokes, the computer interpreting what they would have been had a keyboard existed. A section of wall off to my left turned on, a video playback buffering up. I leaned back, the mesh beneath me accommodating my lower spine.

The recording was poor, jiggling like Dogme 95. A bar. Black wood and brown leather. I recognized the woman sitting in the booth before we were close enough to hear her. I'd have known her voice too.

"Three people," Elaine said. "Jude Hammer, Eric Swanson, and you. We should give you all medals."

"You're drunk, Elaine," the swarthy man across the booth from her said.

"Yes, I am," Elaine said, then turned to smile up above the camera at whatever servista had been wearing the camera. Her hair has gone white like snow, and her smile cut deeper at the corners of her mouth. "I am drunk. Very, very drunk. And I am very, very rich."

"Can I get you anything?" the servista asked, his voice made low by contact with the mic.

"No, I have everything," Elaine said. "Thanks to Jude, Eric, and Safwan, I've got it all."

"*Elaine.*"

"Except discretion," Elaine said with a little bow.

The playback stopped. I looked over at Herself.

"Elaine Salvati," I said. "Head of something or other at Fifth Layer."

"Being indiscreet," Herself said.

"The other one? The guy in the booth?"

"Safwan Cádir," Herself said. "Works for Fifth Layer. Mathematical modeling. Biometrics."

I shrugged.

"Okay," I said. "You want it transcribed?"

"I want it explained. No one else has the file. We're going to be the point of origin on this one. We're taking the site up from accretor to source."

"We're going to start producing news rather than just filtering it, and we're going to start with a scoop by following up on what appears to be a telling mention of names in a public place where even Fifth Layer's pet lawyers can't argue an expectation of privacy."

"Investigative journalism," I said and whistled low. "I didn't think people did that anymore."

"I'm old-school," Herself said. "Still in?"

I sat in silence for a few seconds.

"I used to know her," I said. "When we were about your age. You know that I used to know her."

"It's why you're here," Herself said.

GO BACK THIRTY years. Put the ice sheets back in place. Resurrect a couple billion people and a few hundred million species. Price milk about the same as gasoline. And there we were, in a different bar. Different people. My hair was black, Elaine's was dirty blonde. I was a sociology major, she was political science with an eye on law school. The television was still a countable number of individually streamed channels. Summer sun peeked in at the windows, throwing golden shadows across the walls.

Another woman sat just down the way, something clear and dangerous-looking in her glass. My eyes kept shifting to her, the way her dress clung to her, cupping her breasts. I wanted to listen to Elaine, but I couldn't stop watching the other girl. Some things don't change.

"So they used steroids," Elaine said. "So what?"

"You mean apart from it's cheating."

"Why is it cheating?"

"Because they have a bunch of rules and one of them is don't use steroids?"

Elaine waved the comment away.

"It's a stupid rule. They're athletes. It's a business where they're paid to be stronger. There's a way to get stronger. They do it. What's the problem?"

The woman shifted, her skirt riding a few inches up her thigh. I took a deep breath and tried to remember the question.

"Apart from rectal bleeding, unpredictable rage, and shrunken testicles?"

"That's a tradeoff," Elaine said. "They also make more money in a season than you and I are likely to do. More than someone who doesn't use steroids, for damn sure. They're grown-ups. Let them decide if it's worth it."

"You're not serious."

"I am," she said, slapping her hand against the bar. "Why is it okay to make yourself stronger by lifting weights, but not by injecting steroids? We're paying these guys huge money to push for excellence, just don't push too *hard*?"

I drank the last of my bourbon, ice cubes clicking against my teeth, and waved at the bartender for another. A slick young man in a suit slid up to the bar at the woman's side. Her sudden smile lit the room.

"So what?" I said. "Take off all the restrictions? Just let anyone do anything they want?"

"It would be a real contest then," Elaine said. "You want to see the limits of human excellence? Then pull out the stops and see what happens. It'd be a hell of a show."

"They're using *drugs*," I said.

"So are we," she said, lifting her glass. "Theirs make them strong. Ours make us careless. Seriously. Look at the argument. Saying you need to get a girl a little tipsy in order to get her into bed is just like saying you have to shoot steroids in order to get into the major leagues."

"I don't need to get girls drunk," I said, too loud. The new man glanced over at us. His lover had her hand on his knee. I looked away, and then back.

She was still beautiful. It never hurt just to *look*. Elaine caught me, followed my glance, rolled her eyes.

"You might want to try it," she said. "But think about it. We take a sick person up to normal, and that's good, but we take a well person up past normal into greatness, and that's bad?"

"I don't want to see chemists competing on the ball field for who has the best juice. I want to see something from the players," I said. "Those records? They aren't from inside the person. They're from outside."

"It doesn't matter where it comes from," she said. "Just if it works."

The way she spun the words brought me to realize she was coming on to me. I was always a little thick about that particular negotiation.

That was the first night we slept together, both too intoxicated to recall it clearly in the morning. A week after that, we were lovers. Six months after that we were friends. Thirty years later, I sat on the bus, notebook open as the afternoon traffic slid silently along the street. The windows were canted back, and the gentle breeze held nothing of the windstorm predicted for that evening. Elaine, who had never gone to law school, was the operations manager of Fifth Layer's research arm. I was what passed for a journalist, filtering stories from primary sources and translating them into in-house phonetics for hourly blinkcasts and daily drop feeds.

I spooled through the précis of Fifth Layer. Concatenating data was what I did all day, every day. I was pretty good. Breakthroughs in encryption.

Computing. Basic physics. Engine design. Prosthetics. Everything they touched turned to gold, but the consensus was that it was a strange gold. There was something common to all the inventions, patents, breakthroughs. The Fifth Layer Look. It wasn't something that the peer reviews could identify, except that they seemed subtly wrong. They were elegant solutions, they were functional, and they were ugly.

And thus the Roswell Hypothesis.

It doesn't matter where it comes from, Elaine said. Just if it works.

The bus lurched, servos whirring almost louder than birdsong. It occurred to me that I was probably riding on Fifth Layer designs. I shifted in my seat and squinted out, trying to judge how long before we reached my stop and I could try walking the kinks out of my back. Or, failing that, how long before I could get home and take a couple pills for the pain. Ten minutes, I guessed. High to the north, thin clouds scudded fast in the upper atmosphere, the only sign of trouble coming.

Jude Hammer.

Eric Swanson.

Safwan Cádir.

Fifth Layer was the most innovative, off-center, powerful corporate intelligence in the world. And if Elaine was to be believed, it was all because of a mathematician, a choreographer, and a pedophile.

"COME IN," he said. "Who did you say you were with?"

I explained who I worked for, that we were moving into primary source and out of accretion, and didn't talk about Fifth Layer or Elaine. Not to start. While I filled the air with my preprogrammed noise, I tried to make sense of the apartment.

Eric Swanson's place was small, even by the standards of the city. Two blankets were neatly folded on the back of a couch that clearly pulled out to become his bed. The kitchen was too small for two people to stand in. The smell of old coffee and shaving cream danced at the back of my nose like a sneeze that wouldn't come. The windows were laced with wire against the flying debris of the storms; deep gouges in the plastic caught the light and threw rainbows the shape of scars on the far wall. The only art was an old poster, lovingly framed, of a dance performance at Carnegie Hall from a decade and a half ago. The woman whirling on the print was beginning to yellow.

I had the sense that there was something wrong about the place—the couch placed poorly on the wall, the print too close to the corner. Functional, but ugly. Fifth Layer Look or poor decorating. I couldn't tell.

I came to the end of my prepared speech and smiled.

"And you're starting off with a piece on mid-level landfill reclamations?" he said, his arms crossed. "That's all I do these days. Reclaim refined metals from last century's dumps."

"Dance history, actually," I said. "Turns out American dance history is an emerging fetish market in Brazil. We're aiming for it."

"Well," he said. "Keep moving. I haven't been part of that scene in forever."

"That was one of yours?" I asked, nodding to the print. Something softened in the man's eyes. He looked at the poster fondly, seeing the past.

"Yeah," he sighed. "The last good time."

"Want to tell me about it?"

Eric's store of liquor was better than I expected. He gave me vodka so cold I could have poured water in it to make ice. He mixed in a little gin and leaned against one wall while he talked. The scene, he called it. Room enough in the world for two or three top-level choreographers who weren't slaved to pop-star porn gods or translating children's programming for live performance or—worst of all—second in command to a theatrical director. Only two or three who could do their own work with the best talent and unfettered by anyone else's vision. He moved his hands when he spoke; he smiled. It was like watching a man remember being in love.

He was a little drunk. And, I hoped, a little careless.

"I was King Shit after the Carnegie show," he said. "Seriously, I pissed rose-water. All the top tier were scared out of their minds of me."

CAR-nah-gee. SEAR-ee-us-lee. ROSE-wah-ter. It was a habit.

"Must have been great," I said.

"It was like doing cocaine for the first time, only it never wore off and your heart didn't pop."

"So what happened?"

"Gloria Lynn Auslander," he said.

"Another choreographer?" I asked, and when Eric snorted derision, "A lover?"

"A great fucking rack," he said, bitterly. "I never even met her. I just watched her tryout tapes. I'd been dancing professionally for fifteen years, and training for eight before that. I *knew* bodies. I *understood* them. There was no mystery for me, but there was something about this one fucking girl. I mean here I am, a professional, and all I can do is stare at her tits. It was humiliating. And the time pressure. And the performance anxiety. Look, I know how it seems from here, but back then, it really mattered. I was at the top of my game, and the whole world was watching me with sharpened teeth. The follow-up had to be better. Bigger. Perfect. I had to show I wasn't a one-shot. And I was looking at this girl trying to decide if she was the right one for the part, and I couldn't *tell*."

"So what did you do?"

He raised an eyebrow and swallowed half a glass worth of liquor at once.

"I changed my mind," he said.

The process cost the equivalent of a year's work, lasted a long weekend at a clinic in Mexico, and ended Eric Swanson's career. It should have been simple.

"It wasn't turning off my cock," Eric said. "It was just damping out that link between my visual cortex and Little Eric, you know? Take off the sexual response. Get rid of that little kick you get when you see a perfect face."

"Or a perfect rack," I said, and regretted it immediately. I put down the vodka, resolving not to drink anymore. Eric barely heard me.

"I can't tell you how excited I was. I was going to see pure movement. None of the distraction, just the form and the sweep. The power and the glory. It wouldn't even keep me from having a sex life, it was just that looking at women wouldn't turn me on. They'd have to touch me or talk dirty or, God, whatever. I didn't care. It was a small tradeoff."

"So what went wrong?"

"Nothing," he said. "It worked perfectly. I was euphoric. I didn't cast Auslander. She was good, but her left ankle wobbled. And I was high as a kite. I'd never understood how much I'd suppressed sexual reactions until I didn't have to work at it anymore. And the bodies. Ah, God. It was like seeing for the first time. I was working twenty-hour days. The poor bastards in the troupe wanted to kill me. It was the best, most innovative, most interesting thing I'd ever done."

"It tanked," I said.

"Sank like a stone in the ocean," he said. "No one liked it. That's all it took. I had a couple more gigs after that, but it was gone. Dance is apparently all about sex. When you take it out, there's nothing left."

I left the apartment half an hour later with a few anecdotes about the scene that I would never use in any story. I'd brought up Fifth Layer twice, and been met with a blank incomprehension that didn't surprise me. If Eric had been there at the birth, he wouldn't be eking out a living digging through our ancestors' trash. He wasn't a conspirator; he was a symptom.

Back at my own apartment, I sat on my own blue couch and stared out at the sunset. My system played Duke Ellington remixes and boiled a bowl of deep yellow rice. I didn't drink any more liquor. I was done being careless for the day.

I wondered whether the secret of Fifth Layer's success could be that simple. A cadre of semi-castrated researchers toiling away without looking down the bar at someone. And the long human tradition of dance was only about sex. Not even sex and something more; just sex. Ballet, tap, jazz, everything was just one long primate fan dance. Take away the dirty thoughts behind it, and it all fell apart.

I didn't buy it.

"HELLO?" I SAID, not entirely sure why I was speaking.

"Wake up, Jimmy," Herself said. "There's a problem."

I turned on the bedside lamp. It was a little after 2:00am. I shook my head, trying to clear it.

"What's up?" I asked. I expected her to say that the blinkcasts were down or someone had called in sick.

"The clip of Salvati popped up on a server in Guam. I had it shut down, but there may be other copies. Someone's pirated us. Are you anywhere with it?"

"Yeah," I said. "I don't know where yet, but I've got something. There's a clinic in Mexico. I'm trying to track its funding, maybe a staff listing, but so far—"

"This is top priority," she said. "I need you on this now."

My bedroom seemed small in the darkness. Like the world outside was squeezing it.

"Okay," I said. "But I'm human. I've got to sleep."

"I'm sending over some sweetener," she said. Sweetener meant amphetamines this month. I recognized the tone in her voice. She was speeding.

That couldn't be good. "This story's not going to take more than a week, is it?"

Sleep when you're finished or I'll find someone else to do it. Someone who wants it more.

Fuck off, I wanted to say. It's my fucking liver you're playing with.

"Not even a week," I said. "I'm on it."

The system made the near-subliminal chime of a voxnet connection dropping. I got up, got dressed, bathed. I was too old to start a new career, and Herself was right. Accretors could sleep. Reporters did what they needed in order to get the story. I was starting to resent my promotion.

The amphetamines arrived by courier, a kid in his twenties with perfectly cut muscles, jittering eyes, and a bicycle built for a war zone. He looked like shit and radiated heat like he was burning. By the time I'd signed for the package, he was twitching to get moving again. I figured he was probably pretty good at his job.

The train took me south and east on a soft cushion of electromagnetic fields. I was a hundred miles from home before the eastern sky paled, the drugs humming in my veins. I felt like a million bucks. I felt smart and sharp and young. I felt like someone else, and I didn't like it. I stared at my notebook, but my mind was moving in ten different directions. Induced ADHD. Great plan.

I knew it would end with Elaine. Herself knew too, or she wouldn't have tapped me for the job. Now, with time short, I was tempted to go straight to the source. I pretty much knew what the pedophile was going to be now. He'd had his mind changed too, and been cured hallelujah, amen.

Might as well let him go free, because he wasn't that man anymore. I had nothing to learn from him.

I could go to her now. Her or Safwan Cádir. Confront them. Get them to crack. The confidence came from the speed, and knowing that made me careful, made me not skip steps. Made me go see the pedophile.

Sex. Beauty. Elaine. Alien technology. The Fifth Layer Look.

There was something there. A rant she'd had, back in the day. I closed my eyes, my mind leaping around in my skull like an excited monkey, and tried to remember.

"YOU HAVE TO have beauty," she said.

"Yes, I do."

She cuffed me gently on the head.

We were at her place. The boxspring and mattress were on the floor, nestled into a corner. We were nestled in it. Christmas holidays, and she'd be going back to her family in a couple days. I lay against her, our skin touching, and the soft afterglow of sex fading like the last gold of sunset.

"I don't mean *you* you," she said. "I mean *we* you. You have to have a sense of beauty or you can't be... I don't know. Alive. You can't function."

I sighed and sat up. Our clothes were strewn on the thin brown carpet, my jeans and her blouse still twined around each other. Elaine pulled the blanket up over her breasts and stared at the ceiling, shaking her head.

"Still thinking about the art history final?" I asked.

"I should've just said that we have to *have* a sense of beauty. I mean not from a woo-woo spiritual it-makes-your-soul-better perspective. I should have gone all cognitive science on him. I should've said that ants have to have a sense of beauty. It's basic."

"Yes, because placing the aesthetic impulse in insects with eight neurons would make you a lot of friends in art history," I said. We were early enough in the affair that my sarcasm was still charming. It wouldn't always be.

"I even know the example," she said. "Wait a minute."

She got up, dragging the blankets with her. The cool air stippled my body, but I didn't get dressed or move to cover myself, and before long, she was back with a wide yellow legal pad and a black pen and the covers and her warmth. She dropped back to the bed, and I snuggled in while she wrote on the pad. Her skin was soft. That afternoon, I felt like I could have lived with my head against her thigh.

"Here," she said, giving me the paper.

1, 12

"What's next in the series?" she asked. I looked at the numbers. We were early enough in the affair that her intellectual gamesmanship was still charming. It wouldn't always be. I took the pad and pen.

123

She smiled.

"You think the rule is list out the numbers," she said.

"Isn't it?"

She took the pen back.

1, 12, 144

"The pattern could be multiply the last value by twelve."

1, 12, 23

"Or add eleven."

1, 12, 122

"Or just tack on another 2 each time. That one's not as pretty, but it's just as possible."

"Okay," I said. "Got it. It's a trick question. You can't pick the right answer."

She smiled.

"You can't pick a wrong one either. They're all right. And almost nothing we do has a right answer. Do you have pasta for dinner or a chicken sandwich? It's not like you can work it out logically, but you have to make a decision. Same for an ant. If there's two grains of rice, and it has to pick one of them up and haul it back to the colony, it's got to decide. If there's not a logical way to choose, there has to be something else."

"An illogical one."

"An aesthetic one," she said.

"So you think the ant picks the prettiest one?"

"What else would you call it? Making decisions between logically equivalent options is as good a definition of life as anything else I've heard. And beauty is the basis of making those decisions. And art is the exploration of beauty. I could have aced it. Instead, I talked about the fucking Etruscans. I'm fucked."

"You say it like it's a bad thing."

She dropped the pad of paper and leaned against me. The wall was chilly. The heater kicked on, whirring and wheezing like an old man.

"I need to get an A in this class," she said. "The competition for law school is... I *need* this to be an A."

"You'll be fine. You're brilliant."

"You're horny."

"You're beautiful."

"I'm naked."

"Same thing," I said.

How do women pick the men they fall for? Is it the bad boy charm? The good heart? Is it the way a man listens, the way he talks about his mother, the way he treats kids? Is it the size of his cock? The size of his wallet? What *really* makes a man handsome?

All the studies say it's height.

"I'm sorry sir," Jude said. I hadn't had a chance to speak yet.

The facility squatted on the edge of a newly planted forest. The meeting room looked out on thin, pale stalks hardly more than ten feet high that would someday become oaks. Jude—a huge man with a close-shaven skull and a canary yellow jumpsuit—sat across the table from me. When he'd been led in by the guards, his sneakers had squeaked on the linoleum. Now, he looked at me with wide, blue, sorrowful eyes. A basset hound made human.

"You're sorry?"

"Whatever it was I did to bring you here, I'm sorry for it," Jude said.

"What do you think brought me here?"

The eyes didn't harden so much as die. I could have read self-loathing or satanic pride or anything else into his expression, but I only wondered how many times you'd have to sit through confrontations like this before it just became a routine.

"I did something bad to a kid," he said. "Maybe your kid, maybe your grandkid. Maybe someone you know. I can't speak to that part. But you're here to tell me what I done was wrong. And sir, I'm here to listen."

"Actually, that's *not* why I'm here," I said. "I wanted to talk about the ways you tried to stop."

It took him a few seconds. I watched the parade of emotions—surprise, confusion, distrust—play out in the shapes of his mouth and eyes. It ended with a slow, slitted reconsideration of me.

"I'm not sure what you're askin'," he said. The sir was gone. His voice had changed, contrition souring into distrust.

"You tried to stop," I said. "Maybe even before the first time, certainly after it. You didn't like where your mind was taking you. You tried to change it."

"That's so."

"I'm here to talk about how," I said.

We were silent for almost a minute. I was pretty sure we were going to stay that way for the whole half-hour visitation. Outside, birds danced between the small trees, their wings dark against the sky.

"They don't all, you know," he said. "They don't all try and stop. Most of the guys in here, they've bent their heads all up so it's okay. The kids had it coming or it don't really hurt 'em or God said they could or whatever. Ain't one in ten who can look it in the face."

"You did."

"I did," he said, and the tone was mournful. "I tried cutting my pecker off with a straight razor once. That the kind of thing you're looking for?"

PEH-kur off. STRAIT RAY-zer. Jesus Christ, what was I doing here?

"No," I said. "I want to talk about what they did to your brain in Mexico."

Jude leaned back, his plastic chair creaking. The ghost of a smile touched his lips and vanished.

"That one," he said. "Yeah. I remember that one. Made me sign all kinds of things, swear up and down not to talk to nobody about it."

"Well," I said, "maybe you shouldn't say then. Might get you in trouble."

He guffawed, and I smiled. I was in. We were friends now. Rapport, they called it.

"Well, hell," he said. "That would have been just after my second turn in the state pen. They didn't know about the kids when I was in regular prison. You don't talk about it there. Every man jack in there'll kill something like me. You just keep quiet and make up shit about the girl back home, same as everyone else. Anyway, I got out and back on the street, and I knew there was trouble coming. There was this site they gave me. Anonymous, they said, and maybe that was true. Anyway, I talk to this lady there, and she refers me off to this other site for folks with sexual problems. And they put me in touch with this research fella."

"You remember his name?"

"Too long ago."

"Cádir?"

"Nah. It was a white fella. Idea was I'd sign all this paper, and they'd put me in this trial group down in Mexico. Make it so I didn't see them like that anymore."

"Them?"

"Little ones," he said. "I wouldn't see them like that. I didn't have much choice, did I? Had to try something. So I signed up and they took me down. It wasn't much, really. Put me in one of those good brain scanners and showed me some pictures to see what was firing in my head. They didn't even have to go inside me to cut nothing. Just zapped me with a microwave. Had a fever for a couple days, but that was all."

"What happened?"

He paused, his fingers laced over his belly, his mouth pursed. Slowly, he shook his head.

"You know what the good thing is about bein' thirsty?" he asked.

"No," I said.

"If it gets bad enough, you die. That other thing. It can feel like bein' thirsty, but it just goes on and on and on. Never lets you go. I... well, I won't go into that. But it didn't work."

I leaned forward as the amphetamines shot a spike of rage through me. This wasn't the breakthrough I was looking for. Where was the cure? The victory? Eric Swanson had put himself under the knife, and it destroyed him. Jude Hammer it only didn't help. This couldn't be what Fifth Layer was based on. We were misinterpreting Elaine's drunken comments. We were seeing it wrong. I was hopped up on my boss's drugs and six states away from home for nothing.

When he spoke again, I was almost too wrapped up in my own mind to hear him.

"It changed me, just not the right way."

A pause.

"Yeah?" I said.

"You want to hear about that too?"

"I do."

"All right. It's your quarter. It used to be there was a particular kind of kid I was into. After they did what they did to me, I could look at... well, at a kid who I knew in my head was my type, if you see what I'm saying. All the things that used to get me going. But now they looked just like everyone else."

"That didn't help?"

"Nah. The pressure built up, just like always. And there were others started looking tempting. I don't like to talk about that. Them Mexico doctors didn't change what I do. They maybe switched who I was doing it to. That's all."

Something was moving in the back of my head, shifting like an eel in muddy water. The Roswell Hypothesis. The Fifth Layer Look.

"Elaine Salvati," I said. "Does the name mean anything to you?"

"Hell, yes. Sounds like salvation, don't she? I thought it was a sign."

"She was in Mexico? At the clinic?"

"Yeah, sure. She was one of 'em. She can't help you, though."

I blinked.

"Help *me*?" I asked.

"I know why you're here, friend. You're looking to stop it. You're looking for a way to turn it off."

"No," I said. "No, it's not like that. I'm—"

Jude lifted a hand, palm toward me, commanding silence. He had huge hands. Strong.

"You don't have to convince me of nothing," he said. "Just let me tell you one thing, all right? There's only two ways to stop it. You get yourself put in someplace like this or you blow your fucking brains out. If you want my recommendation, I'd say the second one. And sooner's better than later."

His eyes weren't soft anymore. They weren't dead. They were the blue of natural gas. They were monstrous.

"Folks like you and me," he said, "I don't know what we are, but we ain't human."

SHE SOUNDS LIKE salvation.

There are some men who never drop an email or screen name, a phone number or voxnet node ID. In among their contact lists is the hidden history of their sexual lives. Every lover is retained there, even if they're never called or contacted. Whenever an impulse for simplification overwhelms them, those names are spared from the purge. Just in case, without ever being more specific. *Just in case.*

I was one of those. Elaine's information was still on my system.

I sat in my hotel room, the video file looped. She laughed. Except discretion, she said. Voices came from the corridor. Children whining with exhaustion. A woman's laugh. The air smelled like artificial cedar and sterilizer. The crap I'd put in my blood wouldn't let me sleep. I had two messages from Herself queued and waiting to tell me, I was certain, how important this was, and how little time I had to get it right.

It was all going to end with Elaine, because somehow it all began with her. I wondered what it would be like, seeing her again. She'd climbed through the world, become someone important. I'd burned through a couple of marriages and ended in a dead-end job. She'd experimented unethically on human brains through an unregulated foreign clinic and released a known pedophile into the wild as part of an experiment. She'd had the most beautiful mouth.

There were a thousand ways it could go. I could call her; tell her that I knew, that I had Fifth Layer over the barrel. She could beg me to keep it quiet, and I could relent, and we could strike up our affair where it had ended half a lifetime before. I could say it was wrong, and that I was going to see it published, and she could send out a clean up squad to disappear me. Or buy me off. Or laugh at me for thinking I mattered. My fingers hovered above the keyboard, waiting for me to hack off some limb of the decision tree.

I had all the data I needed to connect the Mexican clinic to the early R and D staff of Fifth Layer. I had the notes from my meetings with Eric Swanson and Jude Hammer. I had an idea what it was all about.

A quote. I'd tell her I was looking for a quote. Then we'd see what happened. Play it by ear. Get it done before anyone else could. Write it up, swallow some downers, and get to sleep before my brain turned to slag.

My fingers descended. I requested the connection. Every means of contact I had bounced back. Nothing worked. The Elaine Salvati I'd known wasn't there anymore.

No ONE FROM Fifth Layer returned my messages. I thought about cutting out the amphetamines. But at this point, I'd be sleeping for three days once I came down. I had to get it done before the crash. Before someone else saw the file and put it together.

I SPENT HALF of my savings to get a new suit. Black businesswear, pinstripes with RFID chameleoning that would automatically coordinate the colors with whatever shirt and tie I wore. A tailoring neural net more advanced than Herself's dress and complex enough to have its own sense of beauty.

I sat at the bar, alternating soda water with alcohol, keeping one eye on the door and another on the chemical hum in my bloodstream. Investigative reporting was a younger man's game. It wasn't the work I couldn't handle. It was the drugs. Toothless corporate jazz soothed and numbed the air around me. The servistas kept their distance from me. The murmur of conversations between the rich and powerful rose and fell like the tide.

I waited.

She came in Thursday night, Safwan Cádir on her arm. I could tell from the way they stood that they were lovers. She didn't see me, or if she did, she didn't recognize me. If I was right, it was more than time and age that would have changed my appearance.

I waited until they were seated, then until their drinks came. And then their food. I finished my drink, picked up my system, and headed over.

Safwan Cádir looked up at me. He was younger than I expected. His eyebrows rose in a polite query. Can I help you? I ignored him. Elaine saw Cádir react, followed his gaze, considered me for a moment with nothing behind her eyes. Then, a few seconds later than I expected, her mouth opened a millimeter, her cheeks flushed, her eyes grew wider. There was something odd about it, though. I had the eerie feeling that the movements were stage managed to appear normal, the product of consideration instead of emotion.

"Jimmy?" she asked. "Is that you?"

"Elaine," I said, and something in the way I spoke her name killed the pleasure at seeing me.

"What are you doing these days?" she asked.

"Investigative reporting," I said.

Cádir stiffened, but Elaine relaxed, rocking back in her seat.

"I know what you did," I said. "I know the secret of Fifth Layer's success."

Cádir's frown could have chipped glass. Elaine chuckled, warm and soft. Familiar and strange. She gestured to an empty chair.

"Join us?"

How do people recognize beauty? What makes one face compelling and another forgettable? Why does one actor flash a smile that makes the world swoon, while a thousand others struggle to be noticed? Why will a baby stare at the picture of one face instead of another?

Why will people of all ethnicities, all backgrounds, all nations, come to the same conclusions when asked to rank people according to their attractiveness? What is the nature of beauty itself?

All the studies say it's symmetry.

"It's supposed to be a measure of genetic fitness," I continued. "Whoever grows up with the fewest illnesses, the lowest parasite load, all that. They wind up closest to perfect symmetry. Back in the Pleistocene, we didn't have cosmetic surgery or makeup, so it was a pretty good match. And so our brains got wired for it. We love it."

"That's been established for decades," Cádir said.

"It generalizes, though, doesn't it?" I said. "We like symmetrical flowers, but we're not trying to mate with them. We like our artistic compositions to be balanced, because it fits that same ideal. It got selected because of genetic fitness, but it affects how we see *everything*. People. Dance performances."

They were silent. Cádir's steak was getting cold. Elaine's pasta was congealing.

"Physics," I said.

Safwan Cádir muttered something obscene, rose, and stalked away. Elaine watched him go. There was something odd in her reaction. Something insectile.

"Poor bunny," she said. "He hates it when I win."

"When you win?"

"Go on," she said. "I'm listening."

Her eyes were on me, her mouth a gentle smile.

The romantic visions I'd conjured were gone. The memories of my time with this woman, with the body there before me, seemed like a story I'd told myself too many times. My skin had a crawling sensation that might have been speed and alcohol in physical battle or else my simple, drug-scrubbed primate mind reacting to something wrong in the way she held herself, the way she smiled.

"The Mexico research," I said. "You were trying to dampen sexual responses, but instead you killed the preference for symmetry. Swanson, after he went through the process, he was still experiencing beauty. He was doing things with his choreography that excited him so much he barely slept. But no one in the audience had gone through the procedure, so they literally weren't seeing what he was seeing. It was lost on them."

"I've watched the recordings of it," she said. "It was brilliant work."

"And the others. Jude Hammer. The pedophile. He was still attracted to children. But the profile of his victims changed. It's because he doesn't react to symmetry anymore. The Fifth Layer Look. Everyone knows it's there. It's an artifact of looking at an asymmetric design with a brain that isn't wired to like it."

"You *have* to have beauty," Elaine said, as if she was agreeing. "If you get rid of the default, you find something else. A different way to choose between logically equivalent possibilities. Symmetry blinds us. Leads us down the same paths over and over. There are so many other avenues of inquiry that could be explored, and we overlooked them because our brains were trying to pick the best monkey to fuck."

"Can I quote you on that?"

Her laughter took a second too long to come.

"Yes, Jimmy. Feel free. I'm sure it won't be the only thing I'm condemned for when you publish this."

She took a bite of her pasta, chewed thoughtfully, then pushed her plate away. I folded my arms. The suit shifted to release the strain at my elbows.

"You aren't upset," I said. "He is, but you aren't."

"He's trying to protect me," Elaine said, nodding in the direction that Cádir had gone. "When this all comes out, I will be the villain. You can count on that. He thinks it will bother me. But it has to be done."

"Why?"

A moment later, she smiled.

"You can quote me on this too. It has to be done because unless Fifth Layer loses its competitive advantage, the corporation won't be pressed to the next level. There are any number of other ways in which the human mind can be manipulated to appreciate pattern. There's no way to guess what we still have to discover once we can make ourselves into the appropriate investigative tools. For the sake of the future, our monopoly must expire. End quote. I'll probably be fired for that."

Questions clashed in my mind, each pushing to be the next one out of my mouth. Is Fifth Layer really willing to bonsai people's minds to keep a competitive edge in research? How much of this have you done to yourself already? Did you get drunk that night in order to get careless and have this leak out? Who are you?

But I knew all the answers that mattered.

It doesn't matter where it comes from, just if it works.

And maybe

You want to see the limits of human excellence? Then pull out the stops and see what happens. It'd be a hell of a show.

"Does it hurt?" I asked. "Do you miss anything?"

That odd, inhuman pause, and then:

"There are tradeoffs."

I nodded, reached into my pocket, and turned off the recorder. Elaine nodded when she saw it, as if confirming something she'd guessed.

"Thanks," I said. "It was good seeing you again."

"You were always a rotten liar, Jimmy."

THE ROSWELL HYPOTHESIS, I wrote, says the successes of Fifth Layer stem from their access to alien intelligences. That's not entirely wrong.

AY-lee-un in-TELL-uh-jen-sez. en-TIRE-lee RONG.

The train hummed beneath me. The beginnings of a headache haunted the space behind my eyes; the first sign of the coming amphetamine crash. I almost welcomed it. Outside, the moon set over the dark countryside. It was going to be a great story. It was going to move the site from accretor to source. It was going to change my job and Harriet's. Herself would get the promotion she wanted. It was going to change the nature of humanity. Which was Elaine's point.

You have to have beauty, I wrote. It's basic. Even ants have it. Even good suits.

I was going to need hours of solid sleep. Days. I didn't want to think about how I would feel when I got home. When I woke up. I couldn't guess at the damage a speed jag like this would do to a body as old as mine. My liver might not be the problem. My heart might be the thing to go first. And still, it had gotten the job done. You had to say that for it. I worked for a while on the last line before I was happy with it.

It may be that any sufficiently advanced modification is indistinguishable from speciation.

in-dis-TIN-gwish-ah-bull. spee-cee-AY-shun.

I checked it all over once, sent a copy to Herself, and deleted all Elaine's old contact information from my lists. And then her new information too. She wasn't there anyway.

I lay back in my seat, closed my eyes, and tried like hell to sleep.

Long Stay

Ian Watson

THE LUTON–STANSTED LONG Stay Car Park spans the twenty-six miles between those two airports, nominally of London.

Twenty-six miles as the crow flies, a natural consequence of those airports expanding in capacity. On a map, the car park cuts a serpentine swathe five miles wide across the countryside, avoiding significant towns, although hundreds of villages were erased, their inhabitants mostly choosing resettlement along the Costas of the south of Spain where the huge and highly efficient desalination plants constantly convert the Mediterranean into water for taps, car washes, golf courses, and seas of vegetables under plastic.

Due to the car park's serpentine shape, perhaps not exactly as crows fly. But anyway.

When the automated shuttle bus let Rob Taverner off at zone S46, he knew he had a fair distance to wheel his suitcase to his car. When he'd found a parking space a fortnight earlier in lane 47, it had taken Rob—what, fifteen minutes?—on foot to reach the shuttle stop. So he hoped that the fine mizzle wouldn't turn into heavier rain before he reached his car. If so, he did have an umbrella.

Another passenger, an attractive young auburn-haired woman, had also descended at the same stop as himself, a compact antirape-taser looped around her wrist; but she quickly headed off into the far distance of serried vehicles in a different direction from the northwesterly bearing which Rob must follow.

Lane 47 was Rob's own age plus three, which was easy to remember, just as the forty-six in S46 was his age plus two, while S was the *single* letter of the alphabet between Rob and Taverner. R, S, T, one, two, three, easy-peasy. Of course, he had also typed S46/L47 into the memo of his phone as well as scribbling the same on the parking ticket residing in his wallet.

The yard-wide rows of vegetables that divided lines of parked cars—hereabouts, carrots—offset the carbon caused by cars coming and going, and the carrots looked about ready for harvest. Since the comings and goings of cars were one-off low-pollution events, the car park vegetables were almost organic. Maybe the veg even offset a percentage of aircraft exhaust, although out here in S46 Rob was too far from Stansted's four runways—an hour and a half away in the shuttle bus—to see any planes climbing or circling, even if the sky had been clear; in which case he would only have seen high crisscrossing contrails. Some crows were circling instead of flying in straight lines.

Actually, those weren't crows. They were rooks. Rooks are sociable; crows are solitary. Old country saying: If you'm see a rook, thar's a crow; if you'm see crows, them's rooks.

Pulling his aluminum suitcase at a brisk pace over the somewhat weedy asphalt, Rob hummed "The Ride of the Valkyries" because that piece had been playing on the plane's compilation of classic soundtracks as they landed. By now he'd lost sight of the red-berried pyracantha hedges surrounding S46, providing razor-barb security of a sort. The greater security for parked vehicles was actually down to sheer numbers—statistically no harm was likely to happen to any individual car—plus of course the considerable distance from habitations. Really, you'd need to drop in by microlite to do any robbing.

Consequently, Rob was surprised to pass a trashed Hyundai, yet he quickly rationalized: *better yours than mine*. Nevertheless, he'd spotted no such sight during his earlier walk *to* the shuttle pick-up point. Either the trashing had taken place during the past two weeks, while he was in the south of Spain, or else he was off course.

Distant signs saying 43 and 44 reassured Rob. Not far now. Prickly-leaved courgettes with yellow trumpet-flowers and what were almost marrows lying on the soil underneath replaced the much lower and feathery carrots. Some of the courgettes were seriously overdue for plucking, but that's a problem with courgettes; they supersize so quickly. Turbulence in the drizzle appeared to be midges.

He passed a broken-into Saab 8000, the windscreen shattered. As Rob paused, a magpie hopped out and took wing. Hastily Rob scanned around for another magpie, remembering his mother's rhyme, "One for sorrow, two for joy." He had learned a lot about nature from his mother, now retired on the Costa de Almería. Sparrows and squabbling starlings were the only other birds visible—the rooks had departed. Zone S46 wouldn't reopen for newcomers until oldcomers returning from abroad had extracted enough cars. Still, it would have been nice to see something moving, such as a farmer doing his rounds, steering a trailer-train carrying immigrant pickers. A farmer, of course, by using a zapper, could enter the car park through special gates set at three-mile intervals along the north and south fences. Woe betide any parking person who tried to follow a farm vehicle out on to a lane, unauthorized. Signs in ten languages promised a fine of £5,000 or €8,000.

Without the enormous airport car parks to store, at any one time, ten to twenty percent of Britain's vehicles, what would the nation's roads be like? Probably at a standstill. The problem, Rob reflected, lay in Britain being an island. From the nearer countries of continental Europe, cars past their prime could easily migrate overland into Eastern Europe. Elderly Eastern European cars could in turn migrate to Turkey or Ukraine or wherever. Eventually clapped-out cars would reach the scrap-yards of India, their materials to be recycled back to manufacturers in a reincarnation cycle.

Presently Rob reached lane 47, and looked left and right for his red Lexus Q-9000. Since he'd be driving homeward in a northwesterly direction, it would have been neater to emerge from the Luton end of the megapark, but he knew that his ticket would only let him exit from the Stansted end by which he'd first entered. People had run out of petrol making that error!

For the emergency services to bring a can of petrol would cost £418, assuming that the improvident, or unlucky, stranded motorist could alert them. On impulse Rob took out his mobile and noted that the signal was alternating between one bar and none.

Nor could you caper and mime before a CCTV camera on a high pole, since there were none, all available experienced watchers being needed for the intense CCTV surveillance of inhabited areas. Hereabouts was, and in a sense still remained, agricultural land, leased from farmers who retained cultivation rights, as witness the carrots and courgettes. Should every field of cabbages or cows be watched? An impossible task.

Where *was* the red Lexus Q-9000? The ninethousandth car in the queue, as Rob sometimes thought of it, when he was stuck on a motorway for a few hours. God bless the airport car parks—vast oases of tranquility and, yes, privacy—otherwise his vehicle might be the ten-thousandth car stuck in the queue.

His LexQ was nowhere to be seen, to right or left, ahead or behind.

Could it be that his Lex had been hot-wired and stolen? Or officially towed away because he'd parked across the ghost of a white line scarcely visible anymore?

Or might it be that he hadn't parked in S46/47 but in S47/46 instead, just for instance?

Panicking, Rob increased his pace. His bouncing, veering suitcase tried to fall over, so he had to slow down. With his remote he zapped this way and that way, hoping that the Lex might flash its lights, but no welcome winking resulted. Hard to say if it was actually raining; more a matter of rather wet air. Some of the veiling in the air was actually midges. Must be hard for them to keep a-wing, or maybe they liked damp air.

HALF AN HOUR later, Rob was seriously worried. Surely he must have made an error, yet what error? Phone and ticket agreed with his memory. Towed away: that must be it. Towed away, maybe, by a *farmer*? A farmer with a sideline in vehicles stolen to order? Suddenly he hated farmers, despite their knowledge of rooks and magpies and carrots and the weather.

Just search for thirty minutes more, systematically. After that, call it a day and return to the airport for assistance. Assistance with misplaced cars must exist. Such a misfortune must happen at least once a day. Once a week, anyhow. Sodding drizzle.

Rob trudged back to the bus stop at last and ensconced himself within the plastic shelter, which lacked even a bench seat. He pushed the autocall and waited by the tall steel bars of the secured exit gate, eyeing the road. No posters to read. A few cars passed by, headlights on.

Aha.

But the automated shuttle bus passed by without slowing.

Of course! This zone was closed as regards Departures! Only departing travelers would summon a bus, consequently his call wasn't heeded by the system. Angrily he rattled the bars, although they didn't rattle much. He eyed the viciously thorned hedge of pyracantha separating the zone from the roadside, abundant with bright red berries. When another car came along, his urgent semaphoring wasn't noticed. When a second passed, a pig-woman passenger eyed him stupidly. At least, she looked pig-stupid and a bit snouty. Which is most unfair to pigs, his mother's voice reminded him. Very bright, very clean animals, they are. Not that his mother had ever been a farmer! No, she had worked in a pharmacy. But she always watched nature channels on TV. Nice nature ones, not floods and earthquakes and hurricanes.

Realistically, who would stop their car for him when they wanted either to head home with as much speed as possible, or to park in another zone to catch their flight after hours spent getting here?

If only he had stayed married to mad Jennifer, he could have been delivered to the front of the airport and collected again! Well, to within walking distance of the security barriers. Again, he consulted his phone and found no signal at all. What's more, the battery was lower than he had thought. What was it doing, *leaking*, like the sodding sky?

Midges circled but kept to themselves.

"Hey," called a voice. A young woman enveloped in a long gray raincoat plus hood. Straggly brown hair that looked a bit hacked. Sharp nose, small chin, beady eyes.

She joined him in the shelter. "Your car break down? Mine did. I was in such a hurry I left the sidelights on. I mean, I thought I'd turned the lights fully off. So: battery drained. Engine wouldn't start."

"I can't find my car at all. Maybe it's been stolen, maybe I noted down the wrong zone."

"Oh well," she said.

"You don't sound too worried. And you only just found out?"

"Oh no, about three months ago. My watch doesn't have a calendar, so I'm not sure."

"*Three months*? What have you been doing since then?"

She gestured vaguely. "Living here. Not much point in going home now. Parking fees and penalties would have vacuumed my overdraft limit within a few weeks. The mortgage would default. Little apartment'll be repossessed, probably sold off by now. Parking's probably still sucking up anything it can, although I think the bank and credit cards will have shut me down."

"Didn't you try to escape to the airport? Wouldn't anyone help you?"

"Oh yes, some people helped. I see life different now. I'm free. My name's Weasel."

Rob stared at her face, then quickly away again as though the corner of his eye had detected some sudden movement, maybe of rooks on the scavenge. *Weasel*. How appropriate, especially after living here for the last three months. Surely that couldn't have been her chosen nickname prior to this. So therefore: bestowed by those people who "helped"? He tried to recall any wisdom of his mother regarding weasels, but none came. Still, Weasel seemed friendly. Maybe dotty, in a different way from Jennifer whose nuttiness was extravert.

"What was your car?" Weasel asked.

"I hope it still *is*. A Lexus Q-9000. Red. A LexQ."

She whistled, perhaps derisively. "So you'll take longer to lose your house, unless you're already up to your eyeballs paying for Lexy. Unless it's a company car. You a director? If so, you can afford to stick around here for a while."

"I've no intention of sticking around here."

Another transit bus passed by without stopping, while Rob gesticulated in vain at a few passengers. Maybe he looked as though he was hurling non-verbal abuse at them.

"What's the alternative?" Weasel asked. "You a director? I've never met a director. Million quid bonuses every year. Phew."

"Not for me. I run an agency for textile designers. Well, I *am* the agency. The LexQ impresses clients a bit, and it's comfortable, seeing as I need to drive all over for meetings. I can't just use a van."

"Designers of what?"

"Cushions, curtains, et cetera."

"Can't you do all your meetings through the web?"

"If only. Trade fairs. Personal touch. Maybe if we had good enough virtual reality, but we don't. There are times when I get fed up with driving."

"Well." She gestured at their surroundings. "Problem solved. Relax."

"I told my designers I'd be back by tomorrow."

"Do they all work at your place in some big barn conversion?"

"Of course not. They all work at home, wherever. They email me their designs. Final printouts by courier to ensure fidelity."

"Whose fidelity?"

"Printer fidelity. Absolutely exact colors."

"Aren't there any other agencies?"

Rob allowed that there were several.

"No one's indispensable," said Weasel.

"I am *not*," Rob said, "pursuing this line of logic. How do you survive here?"

"Mainly vegetarian. Plenty of that. Traps for rabbits and pheasants."

That might appeal to Mum. Or not.

Mum would miss him. What, in Spain, in a world, or at least a Costa of her own?

"Weasel, haven't you asked a farmer for a ride out of here? You could even walk out when a farm gate opens." Using his mother's sayings, surely he could talk to a farmer. Of course! That was the way out.

"If a farmer assists an escape, he gets fined heavily as well. That's immigration law. So they're quite hostile. Also, we're pests, munching on their veg. Like rabbits. They carry licensed shotguns."

The farmers, obviously, not the rabbits.

"How about pushing a car into the perimeter fence then climbing on the roof and piling veg on top of the razor wire?"

"Not so simple or safe as it sounds. You don't get it, er...?"

"Rob."

"You don't get it, Rob. I'm free here. So are you."

Far from feeling liberated, he felt severely deprived, his worldly goods reduced to the contents of a suitcase.

"But," he said.

"But nothing. Let me show you the ropes hereabouts. You'll soon adjust."

"Is it you and your helpful friends who trashed cars in this zone?"

She shrugged. "Sometimes we need little extras. But actually," and she brightened, "Brian is one of us because we trashed his car too badly for him to drive it, and he isn't complaining. Not now he isn't, anyway."

"Why not trash all the fucking cars and expand into a fucking huge community?" cried Rob.

Weasel eyed Rob as though he was stupid. "Sustainability, of course."

"Sure, I was pissed off for most of the first week," admitted Brian, a tubby red-faced fellow of middling height and age from Dublin, who was wearing a once smart striped suit, somewhat scuffed and stained by now. And a burgeoning russet beard.

They were now in Zone T15. There existed ways between zones, either due to persistence or to the spontaneous death of prickly pyracantha.

"But after a while I thought to myself here's an opportunity to knock off the booze. Then there were the credit card debts and the mortgage, and I was fed up with Annie nagging, and she could look after delinquent Dermot, and did I adore being a glorified salesman for exorbitant shit? Weasel and her chums merely trashed a company car, not my own impeccable soul in painted steel."

By now it was night, and they were inside a long and oldish Volvo estate, Brian and Mog in the front, Rob with Weasel and Donny Dino side by side in the quite spacious rear. This was a bit like being in a very small private cinema, except that the screen was only showing steamed-up dripping darkness. And they weren't awaiting any performance, except that Rob fantasized now and then that a brightly lit helicopter might suddenly descend like some UFO to rescue him from what wasn't exactly an abduction.

Donny Dino was Donald Something—already Rob forgot—from a band he had never heard of, Velociraptors. Clad all in black leather, except for his head of lengthening hair. Raggy-haired Mog, in front, wore robes over her bulk, and she had lipsticked thick cat's whiskers on her upper lip. Mog was given to chortling, a word which she explained had been invented by Lewis Carroll especially for *Through the Looking Glass and What Alice Found There* by combining "chuckle" with "snort". Mog was still experimenting with what the precise noise should be, since "chuckle" suggests amusement yet "snort" suggests an element of derision. And yet, quoth the text, "he chortled in his joy."

"Like, you snort snow," Donny Dino, who had got fed up with doing lines of cocaine to make it as a Velociraptor, had remarked earlier.

"Young man," Mog had retorted, "snort refers to breathing *out* in a noisy and violent way. Only an idiot would snort cocaine. The powder would all blow away. Unless that's an instance of a word turning around to mean its complete opposite. Just as," she rhapsodized, "those of us here have turned ourselves around to become the opposites of what we were before!"

Obviously Mog had much to occupy her mind in the car park, including attempting to express the perfect chortle, which, she claimed, was a practice like Zen—when you hit the target blindfold, then you'd be enlightened. Except, not hit with an arrow, but with one's voice, as it were. Some discussion had followed between her and Brian as to whether laughter was an aspect of voice.

"Well, can any speechless animal laugh?" she'd demanded of the Dubliner.

"Sure, a jackass can."

"To *our* ears, but what does *it* hear?"

Mog had provided carrot and cabbage stew cooked over a camping stove filled with petrol, and Rob knew from his mother that carrots help you to see in the dark. Elsewhere, in T19, four others of the tribe inhabited a Mazda, named after the Persian god of fire by the Japanese lightbulb company turned carmakers; but Rob hadn't met the Mazda contingent yet.

Presently the five passengers in the Volvo set about falling asleep. Despite closest proximity to the steering wheel you couldn't call Donald the driver; he was a passenger too. Rob was reminded of sleeping on a long-haul jet flight, except that in this instance you could open a door and step outside to avoid deep-vein thrombosis and have a pee much more easily than in a superjumbo. Unless you were piggy in the middle, which in this case was Weasel, who mightn't have experienced this position prior to Rob's advent; if so, she wasn't complaining. Maybe, being skinny, she appreciated the enhanced body heat. Midges had got inside the Volvo but were no bother.

Morning dawned with a squabbling of starlings over some torn-up baby rabbit dropped nearby by a crow, not by a rook.

"It's bath day today," announced Mog with a vast yawn. "Certainly smells like it," and she chortled to indicate *no offense*. "There's a Porsche Carrera Cabriolet in T18 that collects rainwater nicely after we cut off the hood and superglued the doors," she explained to Rob. "A posh bathtub with its seats pushed right back."

"But surely it never rains enough in a week to fill a car, even with downpours? Or is bath day once every season?"

"Some medieval chaps washed once a year, and *that* frequently was deemed eccentric. I'm all for hygiene once a fortnight."

"Which is how long it takes to fill up a posh?" Rob asked.

"Ah, how meanings have shifted in this brave new life of ours! No, there's a fire hydrant hatch where some village got bulldozed for more parking. We have a hose that fits."

"But isn't it rather cold in the bath?"

She chortled. "We have a big carton of US military Quikhot, combat in cold countries for the use of. This funny little supply drone crashed, like a winged box. Maybe they were testing it. Oh," she added, "we drilled a plughole in the bottom of the posh, in case you're wondering."

"But didn't police come, or soldiers?"

"Police, though by then we'd liberated the goodies and made off. They weren't going to search a million cars; just took the wreckage away. You really must stop saying 'but' so much, Rob. But me no buts."

So after a breakfast of fried fungi the five set off for T18, Rob feeling at once excited and disconcerted by the prospect of communal nudity, Japanese fashion, which he certainly wouldn't have experienced home alone. On the way, each went behind a different car to do the toilet thing using paper distributed by Mog.

THIS DAY PROMISED to be brighter than the day before. Before too long Rob was being introduced to Andy, Govinder, and the Welsh sisters Melanie and Anastasia who looked nothing like each other, since Melanie was dark chocolate colored and tall whereas Anastasia was blonde and short, both going on for thirty.

"Our Mum never knew Melanie means black," Anastasia hastened to say in a melodious voice. "She just liked the sound of the name."

"And blonde to her meant *Russian*," added Melanie, "although to me Anastasia sounds like a plant, like a Nasturtium, like. So if she does something nasty, I call her Nasturtium, like."

They seemed to like one another well enough to go on holiday together, for instance, although maybe undercurrents of rivalry existed. Rob forbore to ask whether the sisters had different fathers, or an interesting blend of heritage within one dad.

Tall, burly Andy sported a ponytail which was trying to become a horse's tail. Surinder was a mature and handsome Sikh, so he wore a turban, a somewhat sloppy one, which probably concealed a lot of hair, and a hairnet to control his beard.

"Excuse me for asking," said Rob while shaking Surinder's hand, "but aren't you supposed to wear ceremonial knives in your turban and other places? How does that go down with airport security?"

Surinder flashed a great grin. "Oh yes, we go armed to the teeth! But it's a good idea to put the knives in the baggage. I painted our Sikh flag on my bag so security will realize." He seemed unabashed to be asked an intimate question about his religion, and even volunteered, "What I need most is some starch for my turban. Don't happen to have any, do you, Rob?"

"Alas," said Rob, "that isn't something I carry."

"What, British men don't use starch for the stiff upper lip?" And Surinder laughed uproariously, while Mog chortled a variation new to Rob's ear, more like a horse whinnying.

Andy proceeded to fill the Porsche, which took a while, and Melanie added moisturizing bubble crème. This done, Anastasia chucked in three cubes of Quikhot and the bath really seethed.

"Me and our new friend first," cried Weasel.

Andy produced a big tartan car-rug for Weasel to strip behind; thus decencies were being observed. Once Weasel was reclining up to her neck in the Porsche, Rob followed suit while Weasel averted her gaze. Briefly Rob wondered what would happen if his new acquaintances ran away mischievously with all his clothes, but that seemed unlikely. As he sank down upon comfortable leather upholstery next to Weasel, she whispered, "No peeing in the water, mind."

"Certainly not."

Weasel bounced up and down, although not high enough to show him more than the top of her tits. "Beats a hard ceramic tub any day, eh?"

Well, it *did*. You'd pay good money at a spa for this sort of luxury! True, you wouldn't have midges circling above the water at a hotel spa, but what could you expect amidst nature?

And so bath time proceeded, turn by turn. When Mog climbed in, water slopped over the side, and she—but of course she did.

Afterwards Rob confessed to Brian, "I think I'm going mad."

"Sure, that's the old normality draining away like dirty bath water out of the bottom of a posh, and the new normality clocking in, now wouldn't you say that's so? Mad, but cheerful with it, would you be feeling?"

"I was thinking that this beats a spa hotel! My brain actually thought that."

"Marvel of adaptability, the human brain."

SURINDER'S LONG HAIR, recoiled in his turban, kept his newly rewashed and wrung-out headgear very damp. Could one get rheumatism of the head?

"None of you have been through a winter yet, have you?" Rob demanded. "This all seems unviable to me. What if that drone thing hadn't crashed to give you the Quikhot?"

"Then," said Mog, "we'd be more medieval about having baths. Humans don't actually need to bathe. After a while your skin stabilizes."

"We are more viable," chipped in Weasel, "than the majority of people."

"What if you get ill? Appendicitis, say?"

"The corpse," she said, "will burn in a car like a Viking funeral."

No use reasoning. Rob shrugged his shoulders.

"Okay, so now we're all spick-and-span, what do we do for the rest of the day?"

"We hunt and gather," Brian explained. "And let me tell you, my friend, once you start doing that, every square foot of these parks becomes luminous with significance. Things you wouldn't even have glanced at before will leap to your eye. When I was a little kid walking home from school, before the world became banal, I'd stare at garden walls with some moss upon them, and see a prehistoric forest there in miniature. When my granny lit a coal fire I could stare for an hour at the flames seeing spirit-creatures dancing."

"Like you might see midges as tiny fairies," said Rob, so as not to seem reluctant to join in.

"A cloud of fairies, to be sure."

Rob waved his hand. "Why are there always midges around?"

"Because," explained Weasel patiently, "this is the countryside."

Hmm, a landscape of cars and veg and pyracantha hedge. But yes, an aspect of the countryside. This certainly wasn't a city.

"Like, nature, like," said Melanie.

Gesturing: "So why aren't there are any midges over *there*, say?"

Weasel yawned. "Attracted to body heat, I suppose. Lucky they aren't the bothering bitey sort."

"So why be attracted to bodies?"

"Are you attracted to mine?" Weasel asked Rob naughtily. "Noticed you trying to peep in the bath."

"I was *not*."

"Why not, then? Are you queer?"

Mog emitted a ch*rtl* that was more like a guffaw. "Prefers them on the larger side, maybe! Just teasing, love," she added, and Rob wished that she hadn't. Truth to tell, he could relish taking a bath with Melanie, yet she seemed inseparable from her sister, and besides Melanie slept in the Mazda, unless sleepover visits occurred. Maybe Melanie would take a liking to him.

When they set off to hunt and gather, Rob tried repeatedly to catch one or other of the accompanying midges. However, the push of air from the motion of his hand always wafted the little fly away.

"Stop waving your hand about," complained Melanie. "You look out of control, like."

Theatrically Rob gripped his wrist with his other hand to subdue it, in an attempt to amuse her, but she just stared at him, then ignored him.

THAT NIGHT ROB dreamt that he was walking with Melanie in the small hours along a street somewhere in London, alert for a shop doorway into which he might maneuver her and embrace her, at the very minimum, without the others noticing. However, a CCTV camera which had been perched atop a streetlight took wing like an owl from that tall light to the next light which Rob passed, and then to the next; and to the next in turn; and he knew that the others would be watching on their wristwatches whatever the camera saw—why else were those called *watches*?

He awoke in the Volvo, his arm around Weasel, her head on his shoulder, and *realized*.

Was it a year since that he'd heard on his car radio about the miniaturization of surveillance equipment? Soon, apparently, mass-produced lightweight flying cameras no bigger than insects and as cheap as insects might take to the air, equipped with solar panel wings and micro-transmitters. Millions of them. Billions. Apparently this depended on the advent of nanotechnology; or did one even need to wait so long? A superfast computer monitoring the kaleidoscope of images could adjust and correct in real time. If wind or rain knocked the tiny flying cameras around and if thousands failed, that wouldn't matter.

As he eased his arm from around Weasel, hoping not to rouse her in any sense, two of the midges which lived in the Volvo circled just out of reach, a bit blurred even in a shaft of dawning sunlight due to their seemingly random fluttering.

Where would you go about testing such a system so that people, if they realized, couldn't report what was going on? And couldn't lay their hands upon butterfly or tiddler nets, say, to catch prototype specimens and auction them on e-Bay to the Chinese?

WEASEL WOKE UP soon; as did Brian in the front of the car.

"Just look at him," she said.

Rob was standing outside, a little way off, mouthing and gesturing imploringly to no one.

"Sure, he's talking to the fairies now."

"Jolly good," said Weasel. "He's settling in fast."

A Soul Stitched to Iron

Tim Akers

MICOL CAME IN through the delivery-way, along the alley. He had keys to all the doors, but he only ever used the back entrance. The longer the neighbors thought the residents of the Manor Vellis were in the country, the better.

He dropped his dirty overcoat and the satchel of muddy tools in the kitchen, along with the shortrifle and ammunition belt, then rummaged up a late dinner. Supplies were running thin, but it didn't matter anymore. Another day, maybe two, to be sure that attention had shifted away, then he was headed up the river. Using the Manor Vellis as a safe house had been a risk, but once he was in place he couldn't afford to move around much. Micol was anxious to be on his way.

Tucking the pistol from his pack into the waistband of his clothes, Micol gathered up his food and the bottle of red he had carefully selected from the Vellis's limited collection. He felt like a bath. There had been a lot of grime and blood in the last few days, and now he felt like a little civilization. He crept down the hallway, pausing before the archway that led to the front drawing room and peeking his head through. Wide windows overlooked the street in front of the manor. Even this late at night, there was still traffic going past. This would all have been easier if the manor had a basement, even a wine cellar, where Micol could have holed up away from casual eyes. As it was, almost every room had a window, and windows had to be avoided. The only windowless spaces were the kitchen, the upstairs bath, the back hall, and the master's den. And the den was uninhabitable, ever since Micol had made his entrance two days ago.

A long couch blocked most of the hallway from the front window, so Micol knelt down and, pushing his food in front of him, crawled past the archway. When he was sure he was clear, he stood up and continued down the hall. The stink from the den met him soon after. There were towels stuffed under the doorway, and Micol had broken open several bottles of vinegar and garlic to mask the scent, but it wasn't doing much good. That was what would eventually drive him from the house, he suspected.

Upstairs, Micol crawled through the open hallway into the bathroom. He toed the door closed, then spun the friction lamps up to their dimmest revolution and poured himself a bath and a glass of wine. He laid his clothes out on the makeshift bed he had cobbled together in the corner and slipped into the warm water. The last few days had been hard on Micol, had made him into a creature of dust and violence and fear. Now, maybe now, he would finally be able to let that go. Maybe he would finally be able to relax.

The water was cool when he heard the voices downstairs. Micol had drifted off, and nearly fell as he stood up. Cooling water cascaded off of him, running in rivers down his beard and through his hair. The voices were quiet, but were clearly coming from inside the house. The spike of fear that had awakened him settled down. As quietly as possible, Micol toweled off his shooting arm and pulled on his pants, then took the pistol and crept downstairs in his bare feet.

He paused at the bottom of the stairs. There was no sound of movement, no opening doors or creaking floorboards to indicate the presence of someone else in the house. The voices had stopped. Maybe it had been a dream, or a trick of the ventilation. Just some conversation from outside, carried in through the garbage chute or something. Micol padded quietly down the hall, the pistol at his hip. A foot from the door to the den, the voices started again. Two voices, speaking in dull monotone, coming from the den itself. Micol stopped, and his heart soared into his throat.

Whoever it was, they were talking over each other. Though there were two voices, maybe more, they seemed to be saying the same thing, talking together as though with one mind. The towels and door muffled the conversation. Micol knew there was no one in there, knew that this door was the only way into the den. It hadn't been opened for days.

Steadying his grip on the pistol, Micol kicked away the towels. He took a deep breath, emptied his lungs completely, filled them with as much clean air as he could, then held his breath and pushed open the door.

The bodies of Lady Vellis and the butler lay bundled against the far wall, still tied up with the twine Micol had taken from the pantry. The master of the house was sprawled across the desk, the wound at the back of his head sticky and black. A cloud of flies rose up. The bodies were bloated, the pale flesh cutting against their bonds, the blood of their death dry and matted on the carpet. There was no one else in the room.

"Yes, we saw him," the three bodies said as one. "The other night. Two days, hard to say." Their voices were stiff and flat, like tar that had dried solid. Micol leaned against the doorframe. Forgetful, he breathed out and then in. The stink cut through to his lungs.

"Yes," the bodies said again, then silence. Micol felt like he was hearing one end of a conversation, like if he strained his ears just hard enough, he would hear another voice leaking into the quiet. "Yes, he's here now."

The fly-sticky eyes of Master Vellis snapped open. He looked at Micol with cold recognition. "You should have gotten rid of the bodies, Micol. We can always find the bodies."

The front door crashed open. There were footsteps, heavy, metallic, gouging the wood of the foyer, ripping carpet in long, even strides.

Micol backed out of the den. He glanced down the hallway at the kitchen, at his coat and the shortrifle. The footsteps were between them, entering the sitting room, coming slowly and heavily past the couch, almost to the archway.

Micol raised his pistol. The stink of the den was burning through his chest, filling his throat with bile and fear. A shape lurched into the hallway, a dark outline in the dim light.

Micol fired his pistol, filled the hallway with the booming report and the sharp light of the flash. Cycled the chamber, sighted, fired again. The bullets slammed into the figure, sparks flying as they hit metal and wire. Those bullets that found flesh thudded dully, like they were fired into mud, bloodless. He cycled, sighted, fired. Cycled, fired, again and again. The figure lurched toward him.

Micol dropped the pistol and ran.

JACOB BURN WAS having a complicated day. He had a dozen deals suspended, the meetings called off and the merchandise on hold, and he didn't have the kind of credit, financial or social, to keep that many balls in the air. The last remnants of the money his father had given him while expelling him from the manor were leaking away, and there wasn't a damn thing he could do.

He hurried up the Hapner's Row, fists deep in the pockets of his coat despite the warm day. His hands were shaking. The meeting with Under-Pressman Sikes had been his last hope, the last chance to get things moving. Sikes hadn't even shown up, had sent an errand boy. "Master Sikes says everything's off. Something came up, last night, and he needs to stay away for a bit. That's all."

"That's all," Jacob muttered. "That's all is right." Every one of his contacts had begged off, citing some disastrous event in the last couple of days. Contacts were fading away, keeping low, cutting Jacob off in mid-stride. The Badge had trebled their patrols in the last couple of days, refusing bribes and not honoring unspoken agreements about what they would and wouldn't see. Deep trouble in the city of Veridon.

Jacob got to his apartment house and tumbled the clocklock. The foyer was empty and quiet, the usual gaggle of children and wives gone for the moment. A nice change, Jacob thought, a bit of peace in the filthy house. He walked upstairs to his room, locking his door behind him. He barely had time to take off his coat and splash water in his face before there was a knock, and then the door opened.

"Ah, Cacher," Jacob said, lowering the pistol he always kept nearby, even in his own room. "Good of you to drop by. I was afraid I'd been blacklisted."

Cacher smiled at the pistol, nodded, and walked in to the room. He was a short man, thin and clumsily dressed, like most of the criminals Jacob worked for. His teeth were lined in black gunk from some drug he kept tucked against his gums. He smelled less awful than usual, but Jacob still took a step back when he got too close.

"Not blacklisted, no. No more than any of us." Cacher circled the room carefully, looking in the scant few hiding places the tiny room afforded. He finally settled on the windowsill, pulling aside the grimy drapes and signaling to someone below. "Tough days for everyone, I think."

"Tough days, sure. Listen, I don't suppose you have any buyers for a crate of silver pots. Something

I picked up through some friends at the Ebd-side docks and, uh, it's proving a difficult thing to..."

"Hush ye, Jacob Burn," he said without looking around. There were quiet feet on the stairs, then heavier ones. A couple of men shadowed past the open door, standing to either side of it without looking in. Cacher stood up, crossed to the vanity, and took Jacob's pistol. "I'll be back with this," he said, then went out into the hall. Valentine came in and closed the door.

"Jacob Burn, yes?" he asked. Valentine's face was a clockwork trick, an artist's mask of polished darkwood on articulated levers and cogs. When he talked the smooth planes of his face clacked together, shifting to express anger or pain or confidence. His voice was a deception of pipe organs and clever mechanical valving. His eyes were empty and black.

"Yes," Jacob said, nervously. He had only met Valentine once, and then only briefly.

"Good. So many things have been going wrong, I wouldn't have been surprised had Cacher taken me to the wrong house." His face clacked into a smile, like a fist clenching. "How have you been?"

"Oh, uh. Well. Business has been trouble."

"Yes, it has." Valentine circled the room slowly, checking each of the hiding places Cacher had searched moments ago. His hands were large and clumsy looking, like padded metal gauntlets. "Trouble for all of us, I think."

"You're here about my debt, I assume?" Jacob asked. Valentine had acted in his interest shortly after Jacob had been expelled from the ranks of the city's elite. It weighed on Jacob, that debt. "I'm working on it, sir, but with things as they are..."

"Let us not speak of that. For now at least." Valentine settled against the bedpost, the wood and iron creaking. "You knew Micol Hart, did you not?"

"Yes, I did." When Jacob had been kicked out of his family, Micol had been one of the first people to befriend him. They had fenced together, and shared many similar tastes, from music to food. Micol had done much to get Jacob through those first months as a new criminal.

"He is causing me trouble. Would you think him much of a killer?"

"No more than the rest of us, sir." Jacob smiled uneasily and crossed his arms. "But not a particularly bloodthirsty man."

"Yes, I would have thought the same. We are all," he paused, seemed to taste the word. "Killers. You were in on the Orinns job, yes?" Valentine asked.

"I was." Jacob remembered breaking in to the Orinns's little hideout, the smell of gunpowder and blood on his hands. First kill, but a childhood of gentlemanly marksmanship had served him well. His hands had not shaken until after.

"Competently done. I remember that being a very clean job."

"Thank you, sir."

"That's how I like my killing, Jacob. Direct. Clean. And better, I only want my people to kill when I tell them to kill. Do you understand me, Jacob?"

"Of course. I wouldn't raise a hand if you didn't order it."

"And Micol?"

Jacob shook his head. "I've never known him to be rash, sir. Has he done something?"

"He has done a great many things, Jacob. And it is interfering with my trade." Valentine stood up and ambled over to the window. It was strange watching him walk, trying to be casual. His clockwork body was precise, smooth. Any casualness was programmed in and carefully formed to give the impression of humanity to his actions. He strolled like a metronome. He went to the window and flipped the drapes aside.

"Two nights ago, Micol Hart broke in to the Manor Stitch and kidnapped the daughter. Magdalene. You know her, from before?"

"We met a few times. Social events, mostly. She wouldn't remember me."

"Any idea why Micol would do such a thing?"

"No, sir. I don't even think Micol would be aware of her. The family Stitch isn't much of a player in the Council."

"Wasn't. You've been away from the inner circle, my friend. Stitch has bought out the Council writs of the Harbers and Cass-Mergers. There are few more influential families in the Council Chambers."

Jacob felt sick to his stomach. Stitch was barely a generation old, their place on the Council bought in gold and commerce. This was the fate of all the founding families of Veridon, their power and influence slowly mortgaged away to these upstarts. Jacob's own father barely held on to his place in the Council.

"Well. Gold will buy you many things."

"It will," Valentine smiled at the iron in Jacob's voice. "You shouldn't take it personally, Jacob.

Burn is still a grand name in the city. It still opens many doors."

"So this is what Micol has done that has complicated things?" Jacob asked, diving away from the subject of his surname. "The Council has tightened the screws on the city to find this daughter?"

"Oh, that's where he started." Valentine turned away, gazing out the window wistfully. "Kidnapped the girl, then proceeded to kill an entire family of merchants. Perhaps killed the girl, as well. The Council is frantic. He's disappeared from the city completely."

"A family?"

"The Family Vellis. He killed them and hid in their manor while the Council was looking for him."

"I don't know them," Jacob said.

"A strange family. But they had business with Stitch, so maybe there's something to it. Still, a messy business."

"But if he's disappeared, why do you think he killed the girl?"

Valentine shrugged. "That is what the Council is saying. My sources say the Badge is now looking for a body, rather than a missing girl. And they've given up on finding Micol, it seems."

"Perhaps they have him and just aren't saying."

"Perhaps." Valentine went back to the bedpost, resting his hand on it. "And this is why I'm talking to you, Jacob Burn."

"What? I've nothing to do with it, sir. Micol was a friend, but I never figured him for a murderer."

"No, neither did I. And I'm very good at reading people. It's how I got to this place. Knowing people." He turned to Jacob. "I want to know why this happened. People are talking, saying things I can't afford to have them say. That I can't control my sworn people, that I harbored a serial killer, worse, that he did this at my bidding, that I'm hiding him from the Council even now. I can't have that, Jacob."

"Of course not, sir."

"I need to know what happened, Jacob. I need to know why Micol did these things, and I need to know where he is now. The Council has its methods of finding these things out, but I need to know for myself. I want you to do that for me."

"Me, sir? I'm hardly the sort who..."

"You're a Councilor's son. A son of one of the most influential families in Veridon. You graduated from the Academy. Hell, you were even a pilot of the Fleet."

Jacob's cheeks burned. "On a time, yes. But I am those things no more."

"Not true, Jacob. Your father may have forsworn you, but you are still his son. You still bear his name. Better, you know these people. The Councilors, their families. There are places you can go that I cannot, questions you can ask that my people cannot ask. I see a great deal of potential in you, Jacob. Your name is a gift. It is why I stepped in for you, why you owe me that debt." Valentine crossed to Jacob and planted his finger in the boy's chest. It was cold and hard, like a metal sap. "Use these things. Find out what happened. You owe it to Micol. You owe it to me."

Valentine turned and left the room. The two men who had been standing guard followed him down the hall, utterly silent. Cacher leaned in to the room, smiling crookedly, and tossed Jacob's pistol on to the bed. He closed the door and left Jacob to his thoughts.

"I SHOULDN'T BE letting you in here," the officer of the Badge said. He had taken off his iron mask and was shuffling nervously through the hallway.

"You're not," Jacob said. "I was never here, Officer Merkt."

"Right, right. Just be quick."

"Quick as I can. Wouldn't want to miss anything."

The events of the Manor Vellis were a public mystery, as was the family in residence. Little surprise Jacob had never heard of them. Days of conversation with his old schoolmate Pedric, who now worked in the Hall of Commerce Writs, turned up little information about the family trade. Their writ was for "Science," with no licensing and only one patron. Stitch.

If the family was a mystery, the manor was a disaster area. The front door had been forced, replaced with cheap boarding by the Badge, and the foyer and sitting room looked like they'd been savaged by a work team of augers wearing spiked boots. The floor was torn in long gouges, and something had barreled through the sitting room, tearing furniture and wrecking plaster as it went.

"Cog hell, what a stink." Jacob stepped carefully into the central hallway. Several glass containers lay shattered on the floor, mingling the smells of vinegar and spoilt meat. "Were they running a slaughterhouse in here? Hardly appropriate for the address."

The back den was worse. There was no furniture here, nothing but several wide stains and a scattering of papers.

"Think they took all the furniture, officer?" Jacob asked. "Think that's what caused all that gouging?" The badgeman was by the door, looking nervously down the street. The windows had been boarded up and a quarantine sigil burned into the wood. "No, I suppose not. Not unless they used a battlewagon for the job."

Holding a kerchief over his face, Jacob toed the papers in the corners of the room. Correspondence, bills of lading, a newspaper. The stink drove Jacob back to the hallway before he found anything interesting. He looked for a less vile part of the house to investigate.

There was a kitchen at one end of the hall, and a stairwell at the other. The kitchen had been similarly brutalized, the drawers opened and dinnerware thrown around. The table had been overturned and shoved against the wall. Splinters of chairs littered the floor.

"Were you looking for something, Micol? Some hidden thing?" Jacob wondered aloud as he circled the room. There was mud on the tile floor, smeared footprints that seemed to lead from the servant's entrance. "Or just feeling generally destructive." This all seemed so out of character for the Micol Jacob knew. He had been the most civilized of criminals. This looked like the work of looters.

Jacob peered over the table. There was a wad of canvas there, pushed up under the chest of drawers. It was a satchel, dry mud along the opening, and inside was a bundle of tools. Shovel, pick, frictionlamp, compass. All covered in mud. He wrapped them back in the bag and took it with him.

He was in the hallway when he heard the shot. He rushed into the sitting room, pistol in hand, to find Merkt dead in the foyer. Shadows were moving by the front door.

He put two shots out the door, grazing the quarantine sigil and sending splinters onto the porch. Jacob threw the satchel over his shoulder and cinched it in place, then backed into the kitchen. Voices now, asking questions and giving orders, and footsteps in the house.

The servants' door was barred, but Jacob put his boot through it and stumbled into the alleyway. Shouts, and a figure came into the alley, a rifle in hand. Jacob shot from the hip, no chance of hitting but enough to make the man dive for cover. It was a wide alley, the kind used for deliveries and secret entrances. Jacob ran around the corner, hopped a fence, and found his way to another street. He didn't stop running.

The figure he had seen in the alley, that man had been wearing the colors of the Family Stitch. Personal guard, on the Family's business.

"THEY BURNED THE place," he said. "The house is gone."

"What? When?" Jacob asked.

Valentine sighed, a sound like a storm winding up, and turned his attention to the shovel in his hands. "After you left, I suspect. They whistled the fire brigade, then burned the Manor Vellis to the stones."

"That doesn't make any sense," Jacob said. "How will they find anything about what Micol did if they burn all the evidence?"

"You were there. Other than this," Valentine gestured with the shovel, "what did you see?"

"Nothing. I didn't get upstairs, but the first floor was cleared out. Like it had been looted." Jacob leaned against the bar. They were meeting in the Harsh Sentence, hours before the first patrons would show. "But the satchel, those tools... it wasn't like they were hidden."

"Meaning?"

"Meaning whoever tore that place up, they weren't looking for evidence."

"You don't think Micol did all that?"

"I don't. He was hiding there, why would he risk someone overhearing the racket? And the neighbors didn't hear anything until last night. Breaking glass, and wood. Probably after the raid. You said they were looking for Micol and the girl, and then the Council raided the Manor Vellis, and now they're just looking for a body." Jacob pointed to the tools on the table. "If they believe she's dead, it's because they found evidence of that in the manor."

"Or they took Micol, and that's what he's saying. That he killed her," Valentine nodded. "What are your contacts in the Council saying?"

"That they don't know anything about this. That the raid was organized outside the usual chains of command. That the Family Stitch may be operating independently."

Valentine set down the shovel. "So what does this tell me, Jacob? Your evidence."

"He might have taken something from the house and hidden it, to come back for later."

"Or he might have killed the girl, and buried the body?" Again, Valentine sighed. "So we should be looking for mud, then?"

Jacob smiled. "Not just mud." He picked up the shovel and scraped up some of the dried dirt, cupping it in his hand. "Does this look like river mud to you?"

They both looked down at the flaky muck. It was gray and powdery, almost like masonry. River mud was black.

"So where does it come from?"

"The cisterns, under the old city. I used to play there, as a child. It's the only sort of wilderness the son of a Councilor can get."

"Well then, Jacob Burn. Go to your wilderness, and bring me the body of Magdalene Stitch."

THE CISTERNS OF Veridon were below the oldest parts of the city. Some of them were simply vaulted basements that had flooded, or rivers covered over with progressive layers of architecture until they were dammed up and hidden, products of accident or civic growth rather than intentionally designed reservoirs beneath the streets. Many of these quiet depths were connected, subject to lazy currents and strange tides that had nothing to do with the rivers Ebd or Dunje flowing to either side of the city.

Because they burrowed under the houses of the powerful, the cisterns were subjected to intense scrutiny. Entrances were blocked; channels were diverted or dammed. People found their way in, though, children and thieves; and hidden passages had a way of being discovered.

Jacob made it his business to discover these entrances in his youth. Though pathways changed, he had a reasonably good mental map of the various portals and drainage pipes that led down to the secret places of the city. Since leaving his family, Jacob had stayed away from the cisterns. This place brought memories of childhood games. Now that he was an actual criminal, his fantasies of aristocrat-rogues seemed so flimsy.

The entrance nearest to the Manor Vellis was guarded by the City Badge, strangely. Jacob ended up entering the cisterns several blocks over, figuring he'd backtrack and find the path Micol had taken to whatever it was that he had buried.

The streets closed over Jacob's head like giant teeth. He wormed his way down under the city, brushing against stone and pipe, the air heavy with sediment and sludge. He was bigger than when he last ventured into the cisterns, and his shoulders and knees constantly banged into things. He went in darkness at first, and slow, until he was deep enough that he felt comfortable he could light up without being seen from the street. He wound the tiny frictionlamp and set it spinning, the element humming into a steady amber burn.

This room had been a natural river, once, part of the rocky delta between the arms of the Ebd and Dunje that fed into the massive Reine at the feet of Veridon. Its flow had been tamed, though, its banks cobbled and then bricked, until the current was nothing more than a slow roll. A stalk of pipes crept down one wall and into the water, probably feeding some courtyard fountain above.

Jacob quickly got turned around. Passages had flooded, rooms filled in, new walkways constructed or old ones collapsed. He spent an unknowable amount of time trying to find where Micol had entered the cisterns. He was resting in an idled pump station, his back against one of the pistons, when he heard the noisy passage of another party, getting closer. He stilled the lamp, set it by his hip, and loosened the pistol at his belt.

The darkness was complete for a minute, and then light began to creep in. Voices too, and heavy footsteps, getting closer and louder. Jacob squeezed between the pistons of the station and waited.

"Map's wrong," one of the men said as he entered the station.

"Couldn't be. Retter said it came from the source."

"Source could have lied. Could have given them a map that leads us to some damn monster. Or an ambush."

"This is a pumping station, Hal. Not a monster."

"But it's not on the map, is it Carl?" Hal kicked metal and something cracked. "Maybe one of the other patrols found it already."

"So we went too far. Doesn't make the map wrong."

There was a rustle of movement, and when Hal spoke again, his voice was quieter. "Don't mean it ain't an ambush, either."

And then they were quiet, except for the distinct sound of pistols being drawn, and hammers being cocked. Jacob gripped his pistol and bit his tongue.

"Come on out," one of them said. "We see ya. Come out, real slow."

Four of them, Jacob thought, by their voices and feet. In a tight space. And even if Jacob could take them all, there would be shooting. Even a little wound was big trouble, lost in the cisterns. Jacob put his pistol back in the holster and stepped into the passageway, his hands up.

They weren't looking at him. Four of them all right, weapons pointed and lights focused on a girl who, as Jacob watched, stepped out of a hidden door in the station.

Magdalene Stitch.

Surprised, Jacob stepped back into cover. His boot came down on his frictionlamp, forgotten on the floor, crushing the casing and dislodging the escapement. The mainspring and element uncoiled in a single sun-bright instant, the free spring sailing out into the passage and bouncing around like a comet. For half a breath, the metal station was noon white and burning.

The four Badgemen and the girl cried out and fell, arms over their faces. Since most of the light was behind him, and because he shut his eyes as soon as he heard the casing crack, Jacob was spared complete blindness. As he blinked and readjusted his eyes, the girl, blind, fumbled to the nearest Badge. She patted his face and then, before Jacob could even think about what she was doing, drew a thin blade and drove it into the man's neck. It was a bad strike, but the knife glanced off his collarbone and deflected up, going through his jaw and tongue. He died, loudly. The other officers began firing.

Jacob dropped to a knee and took careful aim. Bullets were spitting all around him, sparks and bits of metal flying. He got two of them before the last figured out where Jacob was in the darkness and started putting bullets on target. Jacob hunkered down behind the piston, thumbing more shells into the cylinder of his revolver and waiting for the other guy to run out of shot. There was a meaty gurgling, and the shooting stopped.

Magdalene was standing over the guard, blood smeared across her chest. She backed up sightlessly as Jacob came out of cover and dropped into a guard position. She had a second knife, Jacob saw, palmed in her off hand.

"None of that, girl," Jacob said. "There'll be more soon."

"Who are you?" she asked, her guard still in place.

"We're going to have to sort that out later, Ms. Stitch." There were shouts down the passage, echoing off the weird halls and shallow depths.

"He's dead, isn't he?"

Jacob holstered his pistol and rummaged a lamp from the Badgemen. He saw that, through the door Magdalene had come, there was a little space with a bed and some supplies.

"You almost seem sad about that. Yes, he's dead." Jacob toed the Badge at her feet. "You stabbed him often enough."

"Not this filth," she said, hiding the knives in the loose folds of her coverall. "My brother."

"Brother?" Jacob asked.

"Micolas Ronan Stitch, first son of the line and goddamned criminal."

"Oh," Jacob said, quietly. "Yes, my lady. I suppose he is."

THEY CAME OUT in an unfamiliar street. At first, between leading a blind girl and being lost, Jacob expected to be caught by the wandering patrols of Badgemen. Twice they'd come within earshot of patrols, both times dowsing their light and hiding until the pursuit had wandered away. Eventually Magdalene regained her eyes and they were able to get away.

"I know you, don't I?" she asked as they crept down the alley. It was evening, and the street lamps were just spinning up. She paused to look at him in their amber shine. "Jacob Burn?"

"Well, yes, I suppose you do. I'm surprised you remember." Jacob said, taking her arm and continuing down the street. There'd be time for pleasant remembrances once they were safely tucked away in some dark building, away from the patrols.

"It's the eyes. Pilot's eyes. And Micolas said he knew you." She paused. "Did he send you, then? To get me?"

Jacob wrinkled his nose. He didn't like being reminded of his days at the Academy, though the evidence was there for everyone to see. The implants left very few visible signs, other than the eyes.

"No. Never said a word to me about this whole affair." Jacob tugged her along. "I'm going to have some questions about that, by the way." He looked back at her, at her downcast face. "When we get somewhere more convenient."

"Yes, I suppose you will." Her voice was quiet. "It must all seem so strange."

Jacob got his bearings and led them to a safe house near the docks. Valentine maintained the place for any of his boys needing a place to hide for a few days. It wasn't supposed to be used without the boss's word, but Jacob figured he was on official business. There was food inside, and warm wine.

"So. What's this whole entanglement about?" Jacob asked. His voice was tired. He set food out on the table, and was working up the will to eat. "What did Micol do to get himself killed? If he is dead, of course."

"If the Council got him, or father, he's dead. Or near enough." She shivered. "It's family business. Surely you would understand that."

"It's not family business once it involves the Council. Not once it throws the criminal underground of Veridon into a mad dash for cover."

"What is the Council but family, Jacob?"

"Part of the trouble with the Council. Look. Micol was my friend. He was honorable, intelligent, and trustworthy. I'd want no other man at my side, in a fight or at a fireside discussing philosophy. Now. Let's not have his death wasted on family honor."

"It was," she said. "Even when it began, I knew it would end in him dead, and all for nothing."

"A positive thinker," Jacob muttered. "You'll do well in the Council."

"It's not my place to sit the Council. Nor was it Micol's. Our roles were chosen for us, and others were set up for the Council."

"I remember now," Jacob said. "The two eldest sons of Stitch were killed, right? Hunting accident. But Micol must have gotten away."

"Micol escaped, yes. Our brother David, though... he's well and truly gone."

"Strange I suppose, but convenient. Cover up your brother's disappearance with the other's death. My father would have liked that." Jacob smiled, then the color drained from his face as he had a thought. "Unless—"

"No, Jacob Burn. Micol didn't kill David, if that's what you're thinking. My brother was no murderer."

"He's done his share. He killed the Family Vellis."

"Did he?" Magdalene looked up and laughed, a high, light sound out of place in her tired face. "Well, that's something. It's something, indeed."

"Did they have something to do with it? Your brother's death?"

"No," she said, then tore off a heel of bread and ate it slowly, piece by piece. "Tell me, how did you get involved in this?"

"I'm Valentine's man. Micol and I both were. What Micol did, first taking you then tearing through Vellis, it had the Council in a fury. They thought it was Valentine behind it. He sent me to fix it."

"So is it fixed? You've found me, Micol's dead. Will that satisfy the Council?"

"Perhaps. But I still want to know why all this happened."

"It happened because Micol was trying to be a good brother. Trying to look out for his little sister. He left the family, Mr. Burn, because there were certain sacrifices he wasn't willing to make." She set down her glass of wine and closed her eyes. "He came back because he was not willing to let me make the same sacrifice, when it came to me. He kidnapped me, took me to the cisterns, hid me. He said he'd be back, and then we'd be going up the river." She opened her eyes again, and the stare she gave Jacob could have cut steel. "To someplace more civilized. Someplace my family couldn't find us."

"What sacrifice?" Jacob asked, nervously. Magdalene shifted her eyes to the door. The color in her face was leaking out slowly.

"There are things under the Manor Stitch, Jacob Burn. Old things. Found things. They offer a service, and demand a price."

"What things? If they're so horrible, why not just leave, yourself? Surely your family's reach isn't so great—"

"He took me to the cisterns," she cut in, as though she couldn't hear Jacob at all, "because he said they wouldn't be able to find me there. And for a while I hoped, and I waited. And they came, and you."

"The Badge? They said something about a map, from a source. Is Micol the source, could he still be alive? Girl, listen to me, could your brother have told them where you were?"

"That was when I knew Micolas was dead. That they had him, and read him, and were coming to get me. And if I can't hide in the cisterns, I'll hide in the city. But you can't hide from it in the city. My brother knew that."

"Hide from what?"

Magdalene laid her arms on the table, palms flat against the rough wood. Her face was completely white now, and her head was inclined to the door, as though she could hear someone approach. Jacob was standing, and didn't remember having pushed back his chair.

"The Stitcher," she said. She breathed deeply, trying to calm her racing heart. "I won't be running, Jacob. But you may want to consider it."

There were footsteps outside. The door burst open.

A corpse walked into the room, but not a corpse, a metal cage in the shape of a man, articulated, and inside a body pinned in place by iron and wire. An axle punched through its chest at the heart, turning slowly, powering the wheels and gears of the cage. Other gearwork bristled out of the body, the teeth of gears and oiled shafts of pistons meshing with bone and scarred flesh. The corpse was bloated and white, like it had been drowned in some lab. Its eyes were snow white, and a complicated mass of gears filled its mouth. The air seemed to vibrate with an unheard cacophony, a noise that passed beyond human ken but was still felt in teeth and heart. Jacob cringed and collapsed away from the table, pitching over his discarded chair as he fumbled for his revolver.

The air in Jacob's head hardened. His voice betrayed him. He and Magdalene spoke as one.

"Magdalene Stitch," they said. "Your soul is in tune with ours. Did you think to outrun us? Return to the manor, to your duty."

Jacob realized that it was the thing, the corpse, speaking through them. He retched up bread and wine, clutched the pistol in his wavering hand. Magdalene stood and, with a sorrowful nod to

Jacob, went out into the street. The corpse turned to Jacob.

"And you, meddler," Jacob said in the iron cold voice that was not his own. "Your life is forfeit."

Before the thing could move, Jacob launched himself up and out the window opposite the door. He hit the cobbled street and rolled up onto his feet. He ran, voices behind him and gunshots, the hot sting of bullets passing close, around the corner and he ran and ran, bile and an alien voice still in his mouth.

VALENTINE LISTENED TO his story in silence, his over-large hands drumming on the table. When Jacob finished, the clockwork man became absolutely still. His hidden engines worked loudly, but there was no movement outside. Jacob sat uncomfortably, waiting.

"By saving her you may have condemned her," Valentine said after several minutes. "And by interfering you may have condemned us all. Before, there was talk that Micol was acting under my orders, because he was my man. Now, another of my men is found with the girl. Hiding, in one of my safe houses. And when he runs away," Valentine tilted his head slightly, to look Jacob in the eye. "He runs to me."

"Magdalene knows I wasn't involved. She knows that her brother was acting on his own. Surely she'll say that."

"She knows, but what will she tell her family? And what will they believe?"

"Surely the Family Stitch knew the truth of it from the beginning. Micol was their son, exiled. If there was some sacrifice he was unwilling to make, and then that burden falls to his sister, and he comes and takes her... Surely they knew you wouldn't be involved in that."

Valentine thought for a minute. "Perhaps. And now that the girl is back, perhaps the Council will back off. Your friendship with Micol is known. They may think you were acting in his interest, rather than mine."

"Something I'm sure you considered when you chose me."

Valentine smiled. He stood and crossed to the door. "We will let the matter lie. Speak to no one of our meetings. Let us hope the Council does the same."

"The girl spoke with genuine fear, Sir. There is something horrible waiting for her beneath the Manor Stitch."

"That is her burden, Jacob. As it was Micol's, and he is dead. She could have run, but did not. Let her bear it. You have your own troubles to attend. Leave her to hers."

Valentine went out, leaving Jacob alone in the dark room. He crossed his hands on the table before him. He was silent for several minutes.

"I will not," he whispered.

STITCH MADE THEIR money in the banker's districts, in Goldstones and Hybull, in the shifting speculative dens of Three Bells, but they made their home in Cuttington. An ivory castle in a pile of shit. Cuttington was for slaughterhouses and livemarts, the cattle and goats carted off the barges and funneled out the Ebdside gates without ever setting hoof or horn in the city proper.

"Odd place for a manor," Jacob muttered to himself as he shuffled past, moving with the warehouse shift change. The squalor went right up to the walls of the manor. Jacob remembered that this had been the family holding before the Stitch made any money, though smaller. A hovel that the family worked into a fortune. Talk was that they kept the address to draw a sharp contrast between themselves and the founding families, with their ridge-borne mansions and their gardened estates.

A bad address hadn't kept the Stitch from building grand. The walls were rough white stone topped with iron spikes. As he passed the gate, Jacob got a look at the grounds. The property had the desperate ostentation of the newly rich. It would have been Micol and Magdalene's grandfather who first claimed Family Rights, traded gold and commerce for a little political influence on the Council. Buying out the writs of two other families, though, was quite a step forward in such a short time.

Jacob stopped by the gate and adjusted his coat. It had taken the last of his meager cash to get the suit of clothes mended and refitted. It was out of fashion, but at least it was clean and well trimmed.

"Off with you," said a gruff voice from behind the gate. A guard had strolled out of his shuttered house, a shortrifle cradled in his arms. Jacob was surprised. At the Manor Burn, the guards' weapons were more discreetly held, though no less deadly for their subtlety.

Jacob nodded through to the manor. The lights were all on, and gentlemen mingled on the front stoop as carriages unloaded their passengers. Laughter and song drifted down the wide drive to the gate.

"I'm here for the party, the occasion of Lady Magdalene's birthday." Finding out about the party had been a stroke of luck. Jacob wondered if his sister turning eighteen had something to do with Micol's actions.

The guard wrinkled his brow. The other guests were all showing up in carriages or by private zeppelin. Gentlemen of rank did not stroll up to the front gate on foot.

"Begging your pardon, sir, but this is an invitation event," the guard said, shifting the rifle to a more demure sighting. "Do you have an invitation?"

"Not specifically, but I claim the Right of Family." Jacob flashed a coin, the gold plated sigil of his family, in the palm of his hand. It was a forgery, of course. His father had confiscated all of Jacob's rights. "I am Jacob Burn, son of Alexander, formerly of the Highship Fastidious."

The man shuffled his feet. "Crawled out from under your rock, eh?"

"Now, now. Does the Family Stitch have the sort of standing to refuse entrance to Founder's blood?"

The party continued loudly in the background. The guard's rifle shifted from one arm to the other, sweeping over Jacob as it went. The guard looked like he was doing some heavy political arithmetic. Jacob's only fear was that Magdalene had been too thorough in her accounting of the event surrounding her rescue, and that the guards would be on the lookout for one Jacob Burn. It was a chance he had to take.

Eventually the guard went back to his house and threw a lever. The gate clacked open, too tightly for Jacob to get through comfortably. When it was clear that the man wasn't going to give him any more space, Jacob squeezed through.

"You'll leave your piece here, though," the guard said, shortrifle nowhere to be seen.

"I think you'll find that I am unarmed." Jacob said, holding his arms wide to show his empty belt. "But feel free to check."

To Jacob's surprise, the man leaned in and patted down his arms and torso.

"Fair enough. Make no trouble and you'll find no grief. Enjoy the hospitality of the Manor Stitch."

"Of course, of course." Jacob smiled and rearranged his vest. "I'm only here for the party. I love a good party."

THE HALL WAS brilliantly lit. Alchemical vats were set around the windows, disguised as flower pots, gently cloaking the smell of the district without smothering the guests in a false perfume. The lords and ladies of Veridon were out in force, moving through the hall in delicate cycles of social engineering. Jacob tumbled through like a cog that has slipped its teeth.

Every group he approached went quiet. He knew most of them, of course, though years had changed faces and fashions. And they knew him. Of course they knew him.

It wasn't long before his father found him.

"What are you doing here?" the old man hissed. "What damn game is this?"

Jacob looked at his father, trying to keep his smile in place. Alexander was finely dressed, the coat and vest hinting at their origin in last year's fashions, but cleverly reimagined, rebuilt, to blend in with the popular cuts of the season. Jacob wondered what tailor had performed that miracle. That was the Family Burn, anymore. Enough money to appear respectable, but no more.

"I'm attending a party, father."

"I swear to you, if you misstep, if you do anything to embarrass me at this affair..."

"Since when did a Burn care about what one of the merchant families thought? Are the vaults really that empty?"

Alexander grimaced, grabbing his son by the vest and looking around before drawing him close.

"Leave the politics to me, child. There are more pieces in play than money and lineage, especially tonight. Now. What are you doing out of your slums?"

"I said. There is a party. I thought I'd put in an appearance. Wish the Lady Magdalene well on her day." Jacob waved to a couple who were doing a bad job of not staring. "Surely there's no harm in that?"

"There is a great deal of harm," the elder Burn tugged on his son's vest to make the point, "in you making a fool of yourself in this company. Making a fool of me."

Jacob patted his father's arresting hand, then pried the fingers away, one at a time. "I'll leave the politics of foolmaking to you, dear man. Now, people are staring, aren't they?"

Alexander looked around at all the people explicitly not looking at them, not talking, not making a scene. He sighed and turned away from Jacob.

"Just watch yourself," he hissed over his shoulder before disappearing into the crowd.

Jacob straightened his cuffs, lay flat his ruffled vest, and looked around for the bar.

"I assure you, father, I will," Jacob muttered to himself. "There's no one else to do it."

THERE WERE THINGS Jacob needed. He found his drink, and a quiet corner to watch the noble traffic. Important steps, but the critical steps were still ahead. He still needed to find whatever horror had driven Micol from his family and, years later, to kidnap his sister and murder the Family Vellis. And once he found that little gem, Jacob suspected he might need a gun.

Not bringing his piece had been a calculated risk. He wasn't even sure the guard would let him in, Right of Family or not. Any weapon he had carried openly would have been confiscated, and, with the sort of measures Jacob intended to take tonight, he was pretty sure he wouldn't be leaving by the front gate. Jacob loved his little collection of irons. He had no intention of abandoning any of them in a guardhouse. He could have snuck in a pistol, but that was just asking for complication. A hidden pistol found by the guard would have guaranteed a short night, and probably a sound beating for effect.

Jacob finished his drink and looked around the room. Fashions had changed, he mused. There was a certain similarity to the gentlemen's dress this evening. Three, no four of the men standing closest to Jacob were wearing almost the exact same clothes. In fact, Jacob thought as he straightened up, it's almost as if they were in uniform.

The guards edged closer, not looking at Jacob, but not letting anyone get close to him, nor providing him any efficient means of escape. Finally one of them met his eye and nodded.

"Ah," Jacob said. "Of course. Loudly, or quietly?"

The guard slipped his coat aside to reveal a leather-wrapped truncheon.

"Quietly, then." Jacob said. He set down his glass and let the guards lead him away.

To Jacob's growing surprise, they didn't throw him out. He was escorted to an inner room, away from the crowds. It looked like a bedroom, but most of the furniture had been pushed against the walls and the rug rolled up. There were two doors, the one they had come in and another that looked like a servants entrance. Jacob stood in the middle of the floor. There were three guards, clubs out. Big men.

"What are you doing here?" the first guy asked.

"I'm here for the party. Just like everyone else."

"I don't believe you," he said, grinding his palm with the sap. "None of us do."

"None of you. Well, that's... it's awkward. If you'll ask the lady, I'm sure..."

"We're not asking the lady. We're asking you. Now, what are you..."

Jacob had been inching forward, one shuffled step at a time. While the lead guard had been making a show of being tough and armed, Jacob had gotten close and desperate enough. He stepped into a tight half step, swinging his fist in a close arc that held all the strength Jacob could manage at that distance. He put that strength into the other man's throat, then whirled his other arm down to pluck the truncheon out of the guard's nerveless fingers.

The guard sat down heavily and oofed. Jacob twisted at the hips, drove the club into his temple, and then dived sideways to avoid the other two guards, who were charging and swinging in equal measure. They ran into each other, stumbled over their comrade.

Jacob slid into a dresser, heavy on his shoulder. He jumped to his feet and laid into the nearest guard's back, striking with short, fast swings, the power coming from his shoulders and hips, working his way from kidney to ribs and up until he rolled the tip of the baton into the back of the man's head. Two down, and the room smelled like blood and vomit.

The last one stood and swung, a long scything blow that came up from the floor and glanced off Jacob's elbow. His arm went numb and he dropped the club. The man was swinging again, down, the weighted pommel striking toward Jacob's face. Jacob threw himself forward, inside the arc of the blow, the man's biceps coming into Jacob's shoulder and sliding heavily off, the baton striking loosely against Jacob's head, rattling teeth. Jacob stumbled but kept his feet, clawing weakly at the man's collars, making short kicks to try to unbalance his opponent. The guard tried to push him away, but Jacob held close, desperate to stay away from the powerful arc of that club.

Eventually the guard took the truncheon in both hands and pushed it into Jacob's belly. Jacob started to go down, but held himself up with one arm, twisted in the complicated lapels of the other man's uniform. The guard leaned forward, Jacob's weight nearly toppling him, but then stood up and dragged Jacob with him.

On the way up, Jacob planted both heels on the floor and pushed. It was enough, just enough. The guard started back-pedaling, each step faster and less controlled. As they approached the wall,

Jacob hooked a foot around the man's shin. Together they went down, the guard laid full out like a tower tipping down, Jacob with both hands around the man's throat.

The guard's head ended its arc on a bedpost, iron. It cracked.

Jacob collapsed on the floor, sucking air and spitting blood. Fire was running through his arm, the nerves burning back to life. He crawled for the door they had brought him through and locked it. Then, stumbling, his feet shaky, he crossed for the other door. It was locked, but he put his shoulder to it a few times. The lock gave with a splintering heave, and Jacob rushed through into the darkness.

HE WAS LOST. What the Manor Stitch lacked in prestigious addressing, it made up for in internal complexity. What had started as a labyrinth of servant corridors and broom closets had finally given way to unfinished walls and stone floors that must have belonged to the original building. The air smelled like dry rot, and the surfaces were dusty. Jacob continued down.

He was still nervous about his lack of a pistol. Going in to face some hidden horror armed with nothing more than good intentions was not a popular activity in Jacob's mind. Any chance he'd had of jumping a guard or looting a family hunting cabinet had passed shortly after he stumbled out of the blood splattered bedroom. By the time he thought of going back, it was too late. Alarms would be sounded, guards would be up. He had to press on, and hope for the best of luck.

Down and down, darker and darker, Jacob went alone, unarmed.

THERE ARE THINGS in Veridon that are older than history, older than the first people who settled on the tiny slip of an island in the Dunje river at the head of the delta, maybe even older than the river itself. Some of these things are easily found. The Seven Celestes, scattered throughout the delta, were once worshipped as gods or angels. In time their temples were abandoned, their visages bricked over or forgotten, their priesthoods abandoned. They offered no power, only mystery. The people of Veridon are a people of power and ambition.

Mysteries are dredged from the river, discovered in basements, examined and studied and exploited. Those mysteries that offered power are cherished. Those that offer only puzzlement are discarded, washed down the river to disappear over the vast waterfall near the city.

Stitch had found itself a mystery, Jacob guessed, and a powerful one. It was the only way he could explain their sudden rise in the Council, their transformation from swineherds to captains of industry.

Jacob knew he was onto something when he came upon a passageway that was free of dust. The floors were swept, the doors oiled, and the walls hung in nearly cheerful streamers. Not far along this path he found a door, and through the door was a spiraling stairwell down.

He had fished an iron poker out of a fireplace, several rooms ago. Jacob gripped the poker and, feeling a little bit ridiculous, crept down the stairs.

They were well lit and well maintained. After a time they changed, stone becoming iron, the walls smoothing out. The air was damp.

The stairs emptied into a wide, low chamber. Water lapped against the far wall in a pool that stirred murkily against the stone. The ceiling was arched and lined with brick. It wasn't high enough to stand by the walls, and the center of the room was in reach of Jacob's outstretched fingers. Light came from a series of sconces at waist height, all along the walls. They didn't hum like frictionlamps, but burned with a steady, warm glow.

Jacob crept across the room toward the pool. There seemed to be more light, there, a turquoise dusk buried beneath the water. He was halfway across the room when he heard a metallic sigh behind him, a sound like pistons giving out.

"I knew you would come, after what Magdalene said. I knew you wouldn't leave him behind."

The voice was like gears grinding into the bones of Jacob's chest. It echoed beneath sound, like the thunder of artillery heard through your heels and heart from a battle over the horizon. Jacob turned slowly, the poker in his hand.

In the corner near the staircase, hidden by nothing other than a lack of sconces in the vicinity, was most of a giant. He was made of metal, gears and pistons exposed beneath flaking porcelain skin, his face bent forward nearly to the floor. Only his right arm, his chest and the broad shoulders that led to his head were free, the rest was sealed smoothly into the brick walls and floor. As Jacob watched the giant raised his head, revealing his chest. And Micol.

The center of the giant's chest was a glass cylinder, man high and full of liquid. It burned with a stormy light, lightning blue and wavering, and inside was Micol. He floated gently, pinned in place by a dozen iron spikes that sank cleanly into his chest and head, as well as a ridge of them from his spine that twitched like the legs of a smashed bug. Micol's mouth was open, his jaw slack in the liquid, his arms bumping against the glass. His eyes were the color of snow, fresh fallen and clean.

Jacob stumbled back, a dozen steps toward the pool before he remembered the stairs were in the other direction. He hesitated, holding the poker before him like a holy symbol. The giant bobbed his head, tiredly.

"Fear is natural," the giant said. "Fear is what drove this one away. I understand."

"What the fuck are you?" Jacob asked, his voice a whisper.

"I am..." it seemed that the giant's splintered porcelain face smiled, "I am the horror under the house. That's what the Father Stitch called me, among the family. I don't think he ever knew I could hear that. Some minds are clearer than others."

Jacob's head reeled, trying to find traction with that. "You can read minds?" he asked.

"Mm. Spirits, more like. Souls. I can taste your turbulent city, its needs, its wants, the wounds it tries to cover, the fears that chase it to bed at night. Individual minds are closed to me, generally."

Jacob was edging slowly to the stairs. He stopped. "This is how the Stitch has advanced, then? Through you?"

"Mostly." The giant covered his face with his one free hand, as though he were tired. "I have served kings and gods, Jacob Burn. Advised them on the state of their empires, the dreams of their people. I have dined on the passions of battlefields. A priesthood attended me, prepared their whole lives to serve as my conduit. And now I am financial advisor to a swineherd." He lowered his hand and stared across to the pool. "This chamber is terribly small."

"Your priesthood," Jacob said, seeing a connection, "What was their role?"

The giant motioned to Micol, his skin bloating in the liquid. Jacob shivered.

"This is what Micol ran from, then? This was his duty, now fallen to Magdalene."

"Father Stitch was almost eager to give up his blood for me. Their childhoods were clouded by this room, Jacob, always lurking below the floor, waiting for them."

"So the Stitch was able to figure out the secrets of your priesthood?"

"They had help. Some other family."

"Vellis," Jacob whispered.

"Sounds familiar. I did what I could to help. I thought this is what I wanted, after so many years of darkness. But your city is stale, Jacob, and turned to trivial things. They live in the corpse of mystery, pick their teeth with the bones of angels. This is not my time."

"I can help you," Jacob said, moving closer. "We could bring you before the Council. A new priesthood could be established. You could taste greatness again."

"And Veridon could ride me to an Empire? No," the giant shook his head. "I will not suffer that. Stitch has already done what he could to use me. That thing they made, the corpse-walker. They don't know what to do with power." The giant bent his head again, his nose nearly touching the floor. He didn't move for most of a minute as Jacob waited, wondered what to do. Finally the massive head rose again. "There is something, though."

"What?"

"Free your friend. They were not made for this. The first brother only lasted this long before it broke him. It has pursued them for too long, ruined their childhood. It's too late for Micol, but Magdalene can still live."

Jacob shifted his grip on the poker and crept closer. "What will happen to you?"

"Sleep. I will wait for a more beautiful tomorrow."

The giant leaned back his head as far as possible, revealing the glass cylinder of Micol's tomb. Jacob took the poker in both hands. His first blow glanced off, but he struck again and again, until the glass splintered. First a spider web of cracks, then it burst, the liquid slopping out onto Jacob's feet. It was warm and thick, like jelly. Micol flopped forward, the glass cutting his chest as his head lolled out onto the brick. Jacob could not tell if his friend was still alive, or if some other energy gripped the swollen body as it twitched. He raised his iron and, eyes closed, brought it down on the temple of his friend.

A long, soul deep sigh rushed out through the room. The giant seemed to fold, the flakes of his porcelain skin shuffling in the darkness. The cogs of his chest and arm spun and then scissored shut, pistons and gears folding against each other like paper cranes getting smaller and smaller. The bricks in the ceiling began to drop.

The giant gave Jacob one more sad smile, then his face disappeared into the mechanisms of his reduction. The wall collapsed, and the pool rose up and began to flood the room. Jacob ran.

The house was in chaos. The corridors that had been so confusing were now shuddering. Something at the heart of the building was suddenly missing, and the walls couldn't handle it. There was screaming and shattered glass. Jacob burst out into a somber room, lit only by candles. There were pictures on the walls, their frames dancing as the building buckled around them. A quick look showed the eldest Stitch, and others that Jacob recognized, fathers and brothers that he had known in his youth. There were many other faces, though, bearing the Stitch features but completely unknown to Jacob. Children fed to the horror below, undoubtedly. A door opened, and there was Magdalene.

"Jacob!" she screamed.

"I ended it. I freed him," Jacob said sternly.

"You've ruined it!" she yelled, then dashed down the corridor Jacob had just come from. He started to follow her, but the Manor Stitch shifted and the troubled walls began to tumble. He ran.

Outside there was a crowd, the elite of Veridon, their formal wear dusty with the wreckage of the Family Stitch. They watched as the manor shifted and settled, its center collapsing as the grand windows of the hall burst in brilliant arcs of glass. Flames leapt from the heart of the building, and the Manor Stitch burned.

"What the hell have you done?"

Jacob whirled. His father had a hold of his sleeve and a pistol in his gut. Alexander looked at the poker still in Jacob's hand, blood at the tip. Jacob dropped it.

"Taking care of an old friend, father. A man who couldn't help himself."

He turned and left the grounds of the ruined manor. His father watched him go, shaking with rage, the pistol raised to fire. When Jacob got to the street he tossed his blood-smeared jacket into a gutter. Behind him the ashes climbed into the sky, mingling with the smells of the slaughterhouse district, torn meat and spilt blood, blood that had soaked deep into the stones of Veridon.

iThink, therefore I am

Ken MacLeod

CONGRATULATIONS ON YOUR purchase of a new iThink!

With its 15 Tb of storage, and automatic wireless Internet access, the iThink can easily meet all your information needs: work, news, personal records and memories, and entertainment media including music, movies, and games.

Please take a few minutes to familiarize your iThink with you.

First, take the iGlasses from the box and put them on. Hold the iThink in your hand and touch the center button of the wheel with your thumb.

A menu will appear in front of your eyes, as well as on the screen.

Look at any item on the menu and choose it. There is no need to blink or make any unusual eye or facial movements. Simply look and choose.

Confirm your choice by scrolling to the item and clicking on the center button.

Choose another item. Look and choose.

Confirm your choice.

Choose another item. Look and choose.

Your iThink is now initialized.

It is also personalized. No one else can use your iThink. There is no need for any other access control feature, such as a password.

(To choose an item when you are not using your iGlasses, simply use the wheel and center button in the usual way.)

Your iThink is now ready for use.

To recover sights and sounds encountered while wearing the iGlasses, use the iRecall option of the Playback feature.

The Playback feature has a date and time menu. However, over time, as you use iRecall, it will become increasingly easy to recover a given sight or sound simply by trying to recall it as vividly as possible.

The default setting of the Security feature enables sights and sounds stored in the iThink to be automatically uploaded to your national or local police artificial intelligence. This makes it easy to recover your iThink and/or its contents if your iThink is lost or stolen, and will assist you if you are ever called upon to assist the police with their inquiries.

Your privacy is important to us. For this reason, you have the option of turning off the Security feature at any time. For security reasons, and for your own protection, turning off the Security feature is automatically reported to your local or national security agencies.

To enter data or to write a document, place the iThink on its stand on any flat surface. Select

Keyboard. A virtual keyboard will appear on the flat surface. Simply tap this keyboard in the usual way.

Over time, as you use the keyboard, the iThink will come to anticipate your keystrokes. Writing speeds of at least 60 wpm can thus be easily attained by any practiced but untrained user.

A large library of books, music, games, and movies is pre-installed. Other books, tracks, etc. can be downloaded from the Internet.

Google features including Earth, Planets, and Sky are pre-installed.

Use of Google Buildings while in control of any moving vehicle voids the warranty.

Games, from Tetris and Minesweeper to the latest release of popular MMPORPGs are pre-installed. Enjoy!

One game in particular is useful for keeping your iThink synchronized with your personal characteristics.

Put your iGlasses on.

Choose the Games menu. Look and choose.

Choose Predictor.

To initialize Predictor, click the center button on the wheel. The screen will now light up.

Click the center button again. The screen will light up.

Predictor is now initialized.

The object of the game is to click the center button before the screen lights up.

When you are ready to play, the screen will light up.

Click the center button.

When you are ready to play again, the screen will light up.

Click the center button.

And so on. The screen will almost always light up just before you click the center button.

Continue as long as this amuses you.

If you wish to understand what is going on, look up or Google "Libet experiment" and "readiness potential."

If you find this demonstration of the illusory nature of conscious will disturbing, consult the philosophy section of your pre-installed library. If you do not understand the explanations, do not let this disturb you.

Simply stop playing Predictor.

Return to the Games menu. Choose something else. Look and choose.

Within a few minutes, the illusion of conscious will returns with full effect. This feature is pre-installed.

> [Note: *the above version of the iThink ReadMe was withdrawn after the first 2.7 million sales and its author sacked.*]

About the Authors

Jack Skillingstead's first story appeared in the June 2003 issue of *Asimov's* and was a finalist for the Sturgeon Award. Since then he's sold around thirty short stories and four graphic novel scripts. Besides *Asimov's*, his fiction has appeared in *Realms of Fantasy, F&SF, Fast Forward 2* and various Year's Best anthologies. In the Fall of 2009 his collection, *Are You There and other stories*, is scheduled to be published in hardcover by Golden Gryphen Press. He lives in Seattle with a lot of books and no cats.

Alastair Reynolds is the author of eight popular novels and many short stories. He spent twelve years working as a scientist within the European Space Agency in the Netherlands, and has recently relocated to his native Wales. His first novel was *Revelation Space*, which was short listed for the BSFA and Arthur C Clarke awards and launched his epic future history, which has gone on to become one of the defining examples of world building in the modern space opera genre. His second novel, *Chasm City*, won the BSFA award in 2002. A number of his other novels and stories have subsequently been short listed for the BSFA and Clarke awards. He has published two short story collections, *Zima Blue* and *Galactic North* and his latest novel is *House of Suns*.

Stephen Baxter is one of the pre-eminent writers of modern hard SF. His epic Xeelee sequence is vast in scope and encompasses the entire history of the universe, in a gritty, awe-inspiring tale of war amongst the stars. The most recent instalment is the short story collection *Resplendent*. Baxter is also a master of the alternate history, and recently completed his four-part Time's Tapestry sequence with *Weaver*. His latest novel, *Flood*, tackles the topical issue of climate change and its potential impact upon global society. He lives in Northumberland, UK.

John Meaney is the author of seven novels: the post-cyberpunk *To Hold Infinity* (a Daily Telegraph Book of the Year), the far-future Nulapeiron Trilogy, and two gothic suspense novels (*Bone Song* and *Dark Blood*) set in the alternate Earth of "Necroflux Day". His short fiction has been reprinted in various "year's best" anthologies. He is a three time shortlist-nominee for the BSFA Award. He maintains links with the world of software engineering, is educated in physics and computer science, has trained in martial arts for over three decades, and is an expert hypnotist. He also likes cats.

Paul Di Filippo is one of the most prolific – and unclassifiable – authors working in the genre today. His short stories have won him much critical acclaim and he has been a finalist for the Hugo, Nebula, BSFA, Philip K. Dick, and World Fantasy awards. His short story collections include: *The Steampunk Trilogy, Ribofunk, Little Doors, Lost Pages,* and *Harsh Oases* (to name but a few). His novels include: *Ciphers, Joe's Liver, Fuzzy Dice, A Mouthful of Tongues, Spondulix,* and *Cosmocopia.* He lives in Providence, Rhode Island.

Denver author **Warren Hammond** is known for his gritty, futuristic detective novels, *KOP,* and sequel *Ex-KOP.* By taking the best of classic crime noir, and reinventing it on a destitute colony world, Warren has created these uniquely dark tales of murder, corruption and redemption.

An avid traveler, Warren and his wife are always up for a new adventure. Whether it's trekking in the Himalayas or camping in the game reserves of Botswana, Warren finds much inspiration for his writing in the world's most remote corners.

Currently, Warren is writing *KOP Killer,* the third book in the KOP series.

Ian Whates's love of SF first manifested at school, perplexing his English teacher when he submitted an SF murder/mystery as homework having been set the essay title "The Language of Shake-speare". Ian's short fiction has appeared in various venues, including the science journal *Nature*, and has been shortlisted for the BSFA Award. Ian is editor of the BSFA's *Matrix* magazine and also edits and publishes fiction via his independent press imprint NewCon Press, whose anthologies have garnered several awards and honours. He lives in an idyllic Cambridgeshire village with long-suffering partner Helen and assorted pets, including a manic cocker spaniel and a tailless black cat.

Scott Edelman (the writer) has published more than 75 short stories in magazines such as *Post-Scripts, The Twilight Zone, Absolute Magnitude, The Journal of Pulse-Pounding Narratives, Science Fiction Review* and *Fantasy Book*, and anthologies such as *Crossroads: Southern Tales of the Fantastic, Men Writing SF as Women, MetaHorror, Once Upon a Galaxy, Moon Shots, Mars Probes, Summer Chills,* and *Forbidden Planets*. Upcoming stories will appear in the anthologies *Nation of Ash* and *Aim For the Head*. He has been nominated three times as a Stoker Award finalist in the category of Short Story.

Scott Edelman (the editor) currently edits both *Science Fiction Weekly* (www.scifi.com/sfw/), the internet magazine of news, reviews and interviews, and *SCI FI*, the official print magazine of the SCI FI Channel. He was the founding editor of *Science Fiction Age*, which he edited during its entire eight-year run from 1992 through 2000.

He also edited *Sci-Fi Entertainment* for almost four years, as well as two other sf media magazines, *Sci-Fi Universe* and *Sci-Fi Flix*. He has been a four-time Hugo Award finalist for Best Editor.

Paul Cornell is a writer of novels, comics and television. He's written *Doctor Who* for the BBC, and *Captain Britain* for Marvel Comics. He's been twice Hugo-nominated and shares a Writer's Guild Award. "One of Our Bastards is Missing" is the second story in his Jonathan Hamilton series.

One of the most literary authors working in the science fiction field today, **Adam Roberts** is also a doctor in nineteenth century literature. He has published an array of studies and literary criticism, including *The Palgrave History of Science Fiction*, and his novels include *Salt, On, Stone, Polystom, The Snow, Gradisil, Splinter* and *Swiftly*. He lives in London with his wife and daughter.

Jennifer Pelland lives just outside Boston with an Andy, three cats, and an impractical amount of books. She's published over two dozen stories, including "Captive Girl," which was nominated for a Nebula award, and her first short story collection, *Unwelcome Bodies*, was released by Apex Publications in early 2008. She maintains a website at http://www.jenniferpelland.com/.

Daniel Abraham has had stories published in the *Vanishing Acts, Bones of the World* and *The Dark* anthologies, and has been included in

Gardner Dozois's Year's Best Science Fiction anthology as well. His story "Flat Diane" won the International Horror Guild award for mid-length fiction. He lives in New Mexico with his wife and daughter.

Ian Watson is the muti-award winning author of nearly fifty books, including *The Embedding, Hard Questions, The Jonah Kit, Mockeymen, The Flies of Memory* and *The Butterlies of Memory*. He wrote the Screen Story for the Stephen Spielberg movie *A.I. Artificial Intelligence* and is now recognized as one of the established masters of the field. He lives in a village in Northamptonshire, UK.

Tim Akers lives in suburban Chicago, and splits his time equally between fountain pens and relational databases. His work has previously appeared in *Interzone* and *Electric Velocipede*, and his first novel is due from Solaris next year.

Ken MacLeod was born in Stornoway, Isle of Lewis, Scotland, on August 2, 1954. He is married with two children and lives in West Lothian. He has an Honours and Masters degree in biological subjects and worked for some years in the IT industry. Since 1997 he has been a full-time writer. He is the author of eleven novels, from *The Star Fraction* to *The Night Sessions*, and many articles and short stories. His novels have received one BSFA award and three Prometheus Awards, and several have been short-listed for the Clarke and Hugo Awards.

Ken MacLeod's weblog is The Early Days of a
Better Nation at http://kenmacleod.blogspot.com.

KEITH BROOKE

THE ACCORD

...some of the best science fiction to be found anywhere." — **Sci Fi Weekly**

UK: 978-1-84416-710-4 US: 978-1-84416-589-6

SOLARIS SCIENCE FICTION